O PIONEERS!
and OTHER TALES
OF THE PRAIRIE

Willa Cather

THE NEW YORK PUBLIC LIBRARY

*Collector's
Edition*

O PIONEERS!
and OTHER TALES
OF THE PRAIRIE

———

WILLA CATHER

DOUBLEDAY

New York London Toronto

Sydney Auckland

FRONTISPIECE: Portrait of Willa Cather, ca. 1917,
photographer unknown.

PUBLISHED BY DOUBLEDAY
a division of Random House, Inc.
1540 Broadway, New York, New York 10036

DOUBLEDAY and the portrayal of an anchor with a dolphin
are trademarks of Doubleday, a division of Random House, Inc.

Book design by Marysarah Quinn

Photograph of Willa Cather by Carl Van Vechten used by permission
of the Carl Van Vechten Trust.

Excerpt from *On Native Grounds: An Interpretation of Modern American Prose
and Literature*, copyright 1942 and renewed 1970 by Alfred Kazin, reprinted by
permission of Harcourt, Inc.

Library of Congress Cataloging-in-Publication Data
Cather, Willa, 1873–1947.
O pioneers! and other tales of the prairie / Willa Cather.
p.   cm. — (The New York Public Library collector's edition)
Contents: The Bohemian girl — O Pioneers! — A lost lady.
1. Nebraska—Social life and customs—Fiction. 2. Frontier and
pioneer life—Nebraska—Fiction. 3. Historical fiction, American.
I. Title.   II. Series.
PS3505.A87A6   1999b
813'.54—dc21   98-56013
                                                                    CIP

ISBN 0-385-48720-7
About Willa Cather, About This Edition, Suggestions for
Further Reading, captions, and illustrations copyright © 1999 by
The New York Public Library, Astor, Lenox and Tilden Foundations.
The Bohemian Girl first published 1912. *O Pioneers!*
first published 1913. *A Lost Lady* first published 1923.

ACKNOWLEDGMENTS

This volume was created with the participation of many people at The New York Public Library. For their help in developing this edition of *O Pioneers! and Other Tales of the Prairie,* we are grateful for the contributions of the curators and staffs of the Miriam and Ira D. Wallach Division of Art, Prints and Photographs, the Henry W. and Albert A. Berg Collection of English and American Literature, the Manuscripts and Archives Division, and the General Research Division. Special recognition and thanks go to researcher and writer Kenneth Benson; Anne Skillion, Series Editor; and Karen Van Westering, Manager of Publications.

The New York Public Library wishes to extend thanks to its trustees Catherine Marron and Marshall Rose, as well as to Morton Janklow, for their early support and help in initiating this project.

Paul LeClerc, President

Michael Zavelle, Senior Vice President

CONTENTS

ABOUT WILLA CATHER

W[HEN ALEXANDRA BERGSON], the radiant heroine of Willa Cather's second novel, *O Pioneers!* (1913), strode resolutely into American literature, a new chord was struck. It was as if a sharp, invigorating wind had blown open the parlor windows. Cather began her career as a disciple of Henry James, but with *O Pioneers!*, she turned her back on the drawing room and faced the wild Nebraska prairie land, the "iron country" that had nurtured her. "Life began for me," Cather said, "when I ceased to admire and began to remember."

Like Alexandra—a spirited Swedish immigrant who tames the "vast hardness" of the Nebraska plain, wresting from it a splendidly thriving farm—Cather created something bracing and new with *O Pioneers!* Alexandra is strong, direct, enterprising, and boldly imaginative when it comes to the land and its potential. She gazes at the long swells of the Divide—the high, dry prairie country that lies between the Little Blue and the Republican rivers in southeastern Nebraska—and, we are told, "For the first time, perhaps, since that land emerged from the waters of geologic time, a human face was set toward it with love and yearning." It was of course Cather whose compassionate vision swept over the open country of the

Portrait photograph of Willa Cather, taken by Hollinger in 1915, the year she published The Song of the Lark.

Divide, a difficult land that seemed "to overwhelm the little beginnings of human society that struggled in its sombre wastes." But, again like Alexandra, Cather sensed the life pulsing beneath the forbidding land—and she struck for the passionate centers of her characters.

Cather created several unforgettable heroines, of whom Alexandra Bergson is one of the most beloved. In this Collector's Edition, she is joined by two other remarkable—and very different—women: the vivacious, restive Clara Vavrika Ericson of Cather's story "The Bohemian Girl" (1912) and the enchanting but curiously baffling Marian Forrester of *A Lost Lady* (1923), a luminous novella that for many critics and readers stands as the most exquisite example of Cather's art.

Willa Cather was born on December 7, 1873, in the home of her maternal grandmother, Rachel Seibert Boak, at Back Creek, in Virginia's Shenandoah Valley. She was the first child of Charles Fectigue and Mary Virginia Boak Cather; six more children would follow. Cather was especially close to her father, a kindhearted man who raised sheep, and to the two eldest of her brothers, Roscoe (b. 1877) and Douglass (b. 1880). Cather's relationship with her mother was difficult. Virginia Cather was a strong-willed woman, and writers on the exceptional daughter frequently describe the mother as "imperious." Willa Cather was baptized Wilella, in memory of one of her father's sisters, who had died as a child, and called Willie by her family, but she renamed herself Willa at an early age. Later, she gave herself a middle name. With a nod to her much-loved grandmother and an uncle who had died in the Civil War, she became Willa Sibert Cather (dropping the "e" from Seibert), the name under which she published her first six books.

In 1877, Cather's paternal grandparents emigrated from Virginia to Webster County, Nebraska, following a son and daughter-in-law who had moved to that sparsely populated prairie country four

In the decades following the Civil War, advertisements like this one drew millions westward. In 1883, Charles Cather and his family, including his oldest child, Willa, pulled up stakes in Virginia and headed west.

years earlier. Charles Cather and his family stayed on at the family's Virginia farm, which he continued to manage for his father until 1883, when the huge sheep barn burned to the ground. That spring, Charles and Virginia Cather and their (now four) children joined the great tidal wave of westward migration that was transforming America's immense central plains, leaving the lush hills and meadows of the long-settled Shenandoah Valley for the wild and bleak land of the Divide. For Willa, the transition was a shock. After Virginia, the landscape of Nebraska seemed to stretch monotonously, endlessly, in all directions, "as bare as a piece of sheet iron." As she recalled in a 1913 interview, Cather never forgot her first ride out to her grandparents' homestead, eighteen miles outside the little town of Red Cloud, Nebraska: "I was sitting on the hay in the bottom of a Studebaker wagon, holding on to the side of the wagon to steady myself—the roads were mostly faint trails over the bunch grass in those days. The land was open range and there was almost no fencing. As we drove further and further out into the country, I felt a good deal as if we had come to the end of everything—it was a kind of erasure of personality."

Cather quickly overcame her homesickness for Virginia, however; the first thing in the new land that piqued her interest was the heavy steel-tipped cane with which her grandmother killed rattlesnakes when out in the garden. "She had killed a good many snakes with it," Cather said, "and that seemed to argue that life might not be so flat as it looked there." The great majority of immigrants on the Divide were foreign-born: Danes, Swedes, Bohemians, French, Germans, were Cather's neighbors now, and in particular she relished the companionship of the old women—even though many spoke but little English—whom she would ride all over the county to visit on her pony. Her admiration for these women, the "real pioneers," resonates through her novels and stories. In the beautiful barn-raising scene in "The Bohemian Girl," Nils Ericson gazes at a "fine company of old women" who have repaired to a corner, "behind the pile of watermelons":

"Crossing the Prairies," an illustration from a Union Pacific Railroad guidebook of 1870. The anonymous author wrote, "A solitude which no words can paint, and

the boundless prairie swell, convey an idea of the vastness which is the overpowering feature of the plains." Cather would find the words.

In reality he fell into amazement when he thought of the Herculean labors those fifteen pairs of hands had performed: of the cows they had milked, the butter they had made, the gardens they had planted, the children and grandchildren they had tended, the brooms they had worn out, the mountains of food they had cooked. It made him dizzy.

For Cather, as for her surrogate, Nils, these women were artists. She said that she never found "any intellectual excitement more intense" than when she spent mornings with these women, her neighbors, at their baking and butter making. It was in those rough-hewn but comfortable kitchens that the novelist was born; for it was there that a young girl—just by listening attentively and sympathet-ically—first came to feel she had "actually got inside another per-son's skin." An old friend would explain many years later that, as a child, Cather was "a flesh and blood dictograph—eyes in every pore."

Charles Cather told his daughter that "you had to show grit in a new country." Promotional pamphlets extolling the wonders of Ne-braska, which was desperate for labor, flooded the Eastern states (and Europe) from the 1860s on. One, from 1870, urged the home-less and landless of the world to "COME WEST: If you have ordinary health, determination, self-reliance, energy and ambition, come West in fall or spring, and bring all your friends with you. . . . We want true men, true women—men and women of generous impulse and noble aspirations—for all such we extend a cordial welcome." But in the event, Charles Cather came to realize that he himself was not at all cut out for the arduous life of a homesteader, the difficulties of which (isolation, harsh weather, un-predictable reversals) the state's boosters invariably glossed over. So in the fall of 1884, he sold out and the Cather family moved into a small rented house in Red Cloud, the county seat. Charles Cather set up a small business (real estate and farm loans); his daughter,

The cover of Lawrence D. Burch's Nebraska As It Is: A Comprehensive
Summary *(1878)*, a generally rapturous account of the state and all that it had to
offer. Reports of *"drouth," "hot winds," "Indians,"* and *"grasshoppers"* are
dismissed as the wild exaggerations of Eastern newspapers.

with her characteristic pluck, made herself at home in the dusty little village (population 2,500) that had been staked out less than fifteen years before.

Red Cloud may not have looked like much, but for a genius, it was enough. When asked, in a 1921 interview, if Nebraska was "a storehouse of literary material," Cather responded brusquely, "If a true artist was born in a pigpen and raised in a sty, he would still find plenty of inspiration for his work. The only need is the eye to see." Fortunately for Cather, Red Cloud, as unprepossessing as it may have appeared, did indeed have a great deal to offer to a young girl whose intellectual curiosity and strong sense of independence may have been outstripped only by her energy. She made many lifelong friends, including the four Miner sisters, with whom she staged plays and tramped about the undulating countryside outside Red Cloud. (The Miner clan is immortalized as the Harlings in *My Ántonia*.) Cather also had a gift for striking up friendships with adults, and this had a profound effect on her intellectual development. As improbable as it sounds, there was a classics-loving Englishman in town, William Ducker, who clerked in a store; he taught Cather Latin and Greek, and soon she was reading Virgil, Ovid, and Homer. Mrs. Miner exposed Cather to classical music; opera, in particular, was to become a lasting passion for her. And there were the Wieners, a cultivated German-French couple, neighbors whose love for literature inspired Cather to learn French. She of course read widely on her own—Shakespeare, Carlyle, Dickens, Byron, Poe, George Eliot, Emerson—and she began to assemble a private library, which ranged from Bunyan's *Pilgrim's Progress* to Louisa May Alcott's *Jo's Boys*, some volumes inscribed with her signature, "Wm Cather Jr."

When she was thirteen, Cather cut off her hair, began to dress like a boy, and decided that she wanted to be a surgeon. In addition to "Wm Cather Jr.," she now signed herself "William Cather, M.D." She became a fervidly dedicated proponent of vivisection, which she practiced on frogs and cats; and she accompanied the town's doctors on their calls, even assisting one of them during an amputation. During the last twenty years, feminist literary critics and biographers have carefully scrutinized that young woman with the Civil War cap and cropped hair, whose idea of perfect happiness was "amputating limbs" and whose closest emotional attachments, throughout the course of her life, and aside from those with her father and her two eldest brothers, were formed with women. What they discovered, to the disappointment of some, was a writer whose gods were all male—Virgil, Tolstoy, Turgenev, Flaubert, and James—and who may or may not have been a lesbian. Nothing much more definitive can be said. Cather believed that anything a reader needed to know about her was to be found in the pages of her books, and she did all she could to frustrate the curious-minded. She instructed her correspondents to destroy her letters; she burned most of her own personal papers; and she expressly decreed (in her will) that, should any of her letters have somehow escaped the bonfire, these were never to be published, or even quoted.

Whatever Cather was, she was an unusual fifteen-year-old, as witness a friend's album, which recorded the "Opinions, Tastes and Fancies" of some young Red Cloudians, among them, "Wm Cather M.D." Some of Cather's "favorites" are unsurprising, if rather austere, even for someone twice her age: "Poet or Poetess: TENNYSON"; "Prose Writer: EMERSON"; "Composer: BEETHOVEN"; "Flower: CAULI-FLOWER"; "Animal: CAT." Her replies to some of the other queries are more intriguing:

Occupation during a Summer's Vacation: "SLICING TOADS"
My Pet Hobby: SNAKES & SHEAKSPEAR
The trait I most admire in women: FLIRTING
The trait I most admire in men: AN ORIGINAL MIND
The fault for which I have the most toleration in another person: PASSION
The greatest wonder of the world, according to my estimation, is: A GOOD LOOKING WOMAN

The greatest folly of the Nineteenth Century, in my opinion is:
DRESSES & SKIRTS
My motto: ENJOY, LET OTHERS WEEP

As Carrie Miner Sherwood, nearing a hundred, reminisced about her dear friend, the vivisecting Latinist who would one day make Red Cloud known round the world: "[W]e knew she would be *something* unusual, *something* special."

Cather graduated from Red Cloud High School in June 1890. After a year of preparatory work at the Latin School in Lincoln, Cather entered the University of Nebraska, which had only recently been founded in that booming prairie town. Incredibly, this matriculating freshman was already a published author; one of Cather's professors was so taken with an essay she had written on Thomas Carlyle that he submitted it, without her knowledge, to the *Nebraska State Journal,* the major Lincoln newspaper, which published it on March 1, 1891. The effect of this unexpected coup on Cather was electrifying. She of course had planned to study medicine. "But what youthful vanity," she later joked, "can be unaffected by the sight of itself in print!" Within a couple of years, Cather was an astonishingly prolific (and not rarely, vitriolic) contributor to the *Journal,* as well as to various university publications. This apprenticeship was of enormous importance to Cather's development as a writer, to the gradual evolution of her magisterial, inimitable style, because, she said, "it enabled me to riot in fine writing until I got to hate it, and began slowly to recover."

For Cather, Lincoln must have seemed quite the cosmopolitan metropolis after Red Cloud; there was a rich smorgasbord of theatrical and concert performances to savor, mounted by touring troupes and various luminaries who in great numbers passed through the state. By 1893, Cather was both a regular columnist and drama critic for the *State Journal,* which gave her free rein to practice and polish her skills. The *Journal*'s readership was no doubt occasionally flabbergasted by Cather's "high-stepping rhetoric" (as

she later humorously dismissed these early journalistic outpour-
ings). Will Owen Jones, the *Journal*'s managing editor at the time,
recalled that Cather wrote reviews "of such biting frankness that
she became famous among actors from coast to coast . . . as that
meatax young girl."

In June 1895, Cather graduated from the university, having gar-
nered a reputation for the many stories, poems, sketches, essays, and
reviews she had somehow managed to find time to write while
pursuing her studies (everything from ancient Greek and Anglo-
Saxon to chemistry); acting in university theatricals; editing the
school's newspaper and literary annual; and forging a number of
passionate, and sometimes lasting, friendships with some very accomplished women, including Dorothy Canfield Fisher, later a well-
known novelist and critic, and Louise Pound, who would become
the first woman to be elected president of the Modern Language
Association. During her sophomore year at Lincoln, Cather had
enjoyed the pleasure of seeing her first short story, the grim "Peter," published in a Boston literary magazine. But by her senior
year, she had begun to admire "writing for writing's sake," and so
quite naturally fell under the spell of "The Master," Henry James.
Cather would later characterize her early stories as "bald, clumsy,
and emotional." Many are also fatally suffused with what can only
be called Jamesian preciosity and artificiality (which, of course, in
his hands was art). It would be years before Cather could say, with
confidence, that she had finally "walked off on her own feet." James
looms rather insistently over a number of the stories in her first
collection, *The Troll Garden*, which Cather did not publish until ten
years after she had taken her A.B.; but during that long stretch, she
was anything but idle.

After a dissatisfying postgraduate year spent partly in Lincoln,
but mostly in Red Cloud, Cather was offered a position as managing editor of the *Home Monthly*, a new magazine, put out in Pittsburgh, that was intended to give the *Ladies' Home Journal* a run for
its money. Cather was more than ready to get out of "Siberia" (Red

The old volcanic mountains
That slope up from the sea—
They dream and dream a thousand years
And watch what-is-to-be.

What gladness shines upon them
When, white as white sea-foam,
To the old, old ports of Beauty
A new soul comes home!

Willa Cather

May first
1924

Cather

Cather's first book, April Twilights, *a collection of poems, appeared in 1903. In a copy of the revised edition that was published by Alfred A. Knopf in 1923, she inscribed on the front flyleaf her "Recognition," one of the new poems added to the collection.*

Cloud), and so she accepted the job with alacrity, though she soon found herself chafing at an editorial policy that emphasized mass appeal (i.e., "trashiness"). But she worked very hard, all but filling several numbers, under assorted pen names, with her own copy; and she was noticed. She subsequently worked for the *Pittsburgh Leader,* writing theater and book reviews, and continued to send articles, reviews, and a tough-minded column, "The Passing Show," to the Lincoln papers. She frequented Pittsburgh's artistic and theatrical circles, making many friends, through one of whom Cather was to meet what some have called the great love of her life, Isabelle McClung.

Cather was introduced to McClung, the daughter of a wealthy and patrician Pittsburgh judge, in the actress Lizzie Collier's dressing room in 1899. That night marked the beginning of an enduring and extremely close bond that survived even the disaster (for Cather) of McClung's 1916 marriage to the violinist Jan Hambourg. For Cather, the beautiful and cultivated McClung was a galvanizing muse. In 1901, Cather was invited to live in the very grand McClung mansion on Murray Hill Avenue. She was given a studio of her own, and in that same year, she bade farewell to the dubious joys of the life of an underpaid and overworked journalist, and began a five-year stint as a teacher of English and Latin in Pittsburgh-area schools. Such a transition may strike some as an unaccountable retreat, but Cather knew that she would be able to write what she wanted to write in the summers.

In 1903, Cather sent off some of her stories to the New York publishing dynamo S. S. McClure, who was so impressed that he asked her to come East for a meeting. Two years later, he published *The Troll Garden,* reprinting several of the stories (including Cather's most famous tale, "Paul's Case") in his magazine, the eponymous *McClure's Magazine,* then one of America's most prominent venues for quality fiction and muckraking journalism. After many of the most important writers at *McClure's* left, McClure informed Cather that he wanted her for his editorial staff. In the

A photograph of Cather, second from right, at the dinner given in celebration of Mark Twain's seventieth birthday at Delmonico's in New York City, on the evening of December 5, 1905. Years later, she would say, "A book is made with one's own flesh and blood of years. It is cremated youth. It is all yours—no one gave it to you."

spring of 1906, she moved to New York City, which would be her home for the remainder of her life.

For Cather, the six years spent at *McClure's*, first as an editor, then as managing editor, were enormously stimulating and enormously draining. She plowed through hundreds of manuscripts, ninety-five percent of which, she came to realize, "were written for the sake of the writer—never for the sake of the material." These stories, she felt, were meant to dazzle the reader with the author's cleverness and wit; but where was the life, the passion of the writer who had a tale that he simply *had* to tell? Through this crucible of editorial analysis, Cather began to clarify her ideas about her own fiction, and she gradually came into her own country. "I had been trying," she said, "to sing a song that did not lie in my voice."

Cather spent much of 1907–08 in Boston, doing research for a biography of Mary Baker Eddy that she was editing for *McClure's*. It was there that she met the New England writer Sarah Orne Jewett, whose stories and especially whose collection of Maine sketches, *The Country of the Pointed Firs,* could be counted among the very few works written by a woman that Cather admired unreservedly. Cather developed a deep affection for Jewett; and although their friendship was short-lived (Jewett died in 1909), it had a tranforming impact on the younger writer's life. Late in 1908, Jewett wrote Cather an extraordinary letter. Considering the Cather masterpieces for which, in a way, this letter served as the catalyst, it is well worth quoting at length. "I cannot help saying," wrote Jewett

. . . what I think about your writing and its being hindered by such incessant, important, responsible work as you have in your hands now. I do think that it is impossible for you to work so hard and yet have your gifts mature as they should—when one's first working power has spent itself nothing ever brings it back just the same. . . . If you don't keep and guard and mature your force and, above all, have time and quiet to perfect your work, you will be writing things not much better than you did five years ago. . . . you must find your own quiet centre of life and write from that to the world. . . . To work in silence and with all one's heart, that is the writer's lot; he is the only artist who must be solitary, and yet needs the widest outlook upon the world.

Four more years would pass before Cather was financially—and perhaps psychologically—secure enough to follow Jewett's advice. In the spring of 1912, she did publish her first novel, *Alexander's Bridge*, a none-too-compelling tale of Boston sophisticates à la Henry James. But the previous fall, Cather had taken a leave of absence from *McClure's*. She rented a house in Cherry Valley, New York, with Isabelle McClung; there, for three months, she worked on "The Bohemian Girl" and an early draft of what would become *O Pioneers!* When the latter was published in June 1913, it was clear that Cather had found her voice; and for the most part, the critics were warmly enthusiastic. In a loving essay published many years later, Katherine Anne Porter looked back "to the big lonely slow-moving girl who happened to be an artist coming back from reading Latin and Greek with an old storekeeper to talk down an assertive brood of brothers and sisters, practicing her art on them, refusing to be lost among them—the longest-winged one who would fly free at last." With *O Pioneers!*, Cather took wing.

In a 1921 interview, Cather declared, "Tremendous output, tremendous reserve, that's the secret of success in any vocation." That formula pretty much tells how she proceeded with her life after the success of *O Pioneers!* In January 1913, Cather moved into an apartment at 5 Bank Street in Greenwich Village with Edith Lewis, a copy-editor and -writer and fellow Nebraskan whom she had first met on a trip back to Lincoln in 1903. For the next thirty-four years, until Cather's death in 1947, Lewis devoted herself to Cather with singular and self-effacing competence. Elizabeth Ser-

geant summed up the essence of the Cather/Lewis relationship alle-
gorically. "A captain," she observed, "must have a first officer, who
does a lot the captain never knows about to steer the boat through
rocks and reefs."

Cather and Lewis lived in their spacious and quiet Bank Street
home until 1927, when the building was demolished to make way
for a larger apartment house. The years at Bank Street were
Cather's most productive, rich in both achievement and acclaim.
The apartment was comfortable but almost spartan (although they
employed a superb French cook, who "made life a joy"). In her
touching memoir, *Willa Cather Living,* Lewis wrote, "What money
we had we preferred to spend on flowers, music, and entertaining
friends." And needless to say, there was work, work, work. In 1915
came *The Song of the Lark,* in which the secret of the heroine's
sovereign artistry is explained by her music teacher. "It is every
artist's secret—passion. That is all. It is an open secret, and perfectly safe. Like heroism, it is inimitable in cheap materials." This,
of course, was Cather's secret, too. Three years later, she published
her intensely moving portrait of a pioneer woman's life, *My Ántonia,* the favorite, for many readers, among her works. *One of Ours*
(1922), Cather's story of a young Midwesterner who dies on the
field of battle in France during World War I, was panned by the
high-brow critics, but it sold very well, made its author a lot of
money, and won the Pulitzer Prize. As Alfred A. Knopf, Cather's
much-trusted publisher, said of this time, "Her chariot was indeed
beginning to roll."

In 1925, Cather published *The Professor's House,* a very dark
story of a historian's midlife crisis. On either side of this rather
unlikely bestseller stand two masterful novellas, *A Lost Lady* (1923)
and *My Mortal Enemy* (1926). The latter is Cather's most relent-
lessly pared down and harrowing work; the story of another lost
lady, the flamboyant and strangely alluring Myra Henshawe, *My
Mortal Enemy* is bitter, perfectly controlled, and shocking. James
Woodress has suggested that it "drained the last bit of gall from

~~Allxmx~~ My mother and sisters were asked to dinner at my aunt's
on the day of Mrs. Henshaw's arrival, but she had whispered to
me, "I want you to come in early, an hour or so before the others
and get acquainted with Myra."

That evening I slipped quietly in at my aunt's front door, and
while I was taking off my wraps in the hall I could see, at the
far end of the parlor, a short, plump woman in a black velvet
dress, seated up on the sofa and softly playing on cousin Bert's
guitar, ~~Her head xxx tipped forward over the instrument~~. She must
have heard me, and glancing up she saw my reflection in a mirror;
she ~~xxxx~~ put down the guitar, rose and stood to await my approach.
She stood markedly and pointedly still, with her shoulders back
and her head lifted, as if to remind me that it was my business
to get to her as quickly as possible and present myself as best
I could. I was not accustomed to formality of any sort, but by
her attitude she succeeded in conveying this idea to me.

I hastened across the room, with so much bewilderment and
concern in my face that she gave a short, commiserating laugh as
she ~~very formally, I thought,~~ held out to ~~gave~~ me her plump, charming little hand.

" Certainly this must be Lydia's dear Nellie, of whom I have
heard so much. And you must be fifteen now, by my mournful arith-
metic,- am I right?"

~~Her voice had a beautiful quality; it was~~ what a humming voice; so bright and gay and
carelessly kind,- but she continued to hold her head up haughtily.
She always did this on first meeting people,- partly, I think, because
she was beginning to have a double chin and was very sensitive
about it. ~~(which was a great annoyance to her)~~

Cather's revisions on the typescript of her 1926 masterpiece, My Mortal Enemy.
*Here the novel's narrator, Nellie Birdseye, first meets the glamorous and terrifying
Myra Henshawe. In* My Mortal Enemy, *Cather applied with the greatest severity
her celebrated theory of the novel "démeublé," in which suggestion, rather than
elaboration of detail, reveals character and tells the story.*

Cather's system," clearing "the way for the serene historical novels of the next decade and a half." Foremost among these is *Death Comes for the Archbishop* (1927), which was inspired by the lives of the first Bishop of New Mexico, Jean Baptiste Lamy, and his Vicar General, Joseph Machebeuf. In this novel, Cather attempted to do "something in the style of legend, which is absolutely the reverse of dramatic treatment." The result was a tour de force of unusual beauty, even for Cather, who claimed that it "wrote itself." *Death Comes for the Archbishop* was a popular success, and it remains one of her most-read works.

In the 1930s and '40s, Cather saw both her fame and her public grow steadily. She was heaped with awards, medals, and many honorary degrees, including one from Princeton University (its first to a woman) in 1931, in recognition of a body of work distinguished by "an inexorable sense of truth"; and that same year, Cather was named one of "America's Twelve Greatest Women" by *Good Housekeeping* magazine. In 1944, she was awarded the Gold Medal for Fiction from the National Institute of Arts and Letters. While Cather adamantly refused to allow any of her novels or stories to be adapted for radio or film, and was vigilant about keeping them out of the clutches of book clubs, textbook editors, and anthologizers, her books sold briskly, and they were translated into many languages. She did break down once, selling *A Lost Lady* to Hollywood in 1925; the result so horrified her that she ordered Knopf to turn down further offers out of hand, and she wrote a ban on any further adaptations into her will. (As copyrights have expired, television adaptations of Cather's works have begun to appear, including a 1992 version of *O Pioneers!* starring Jessica Lange and a 1995 version of *My Ántonia*.) According to the sympathetic Knopf, Cather despised book clubs because she "felt most strongly that she wanted only people who really *wanted* to read her books to have them."

As Cather's celebrity (and sales) increased throughout the 1930s, her critical fortunes declined precipitously. Many of the more socially engaged writers of the period attacked Cather as a nostalgist whose marked disinterest in factories, labor conditions, the plight of the urban poor, and class conflict—in short, in her own times— disqualified her work from serious consideration. Cather's last novels, *Shadows on the Rock* (1931), *Lucy Gayheart* (1935), and *Sapphira and the Slave Girl* (1940), met with very mixed reviews, but again, they flew off the shelf. *Obscure Destinies,* the last collection of short stories to appear in her lifetime, including perhaps her greatest, "Old Mrs. Harris," came out in 1932. In "Old Mrs. Harris," Cather returned home, evoking the "accords and antipathies" that bonded three generations of women in a family together, creating unforgettable portraits of her Grandmother Boak, her mother, and her own restless, ambitious, and "heartless" self at fifteen.

Robert Frost said, memorably, but with some exaggeration, "With Carl Sandburg, it was 'the people, yes.' With Willa Cather, it was 'the people, no.' " As a matter of fact, Cather had many dear friends, and even into her fifties and sixties, she welcomed new people into her life, including the dazzling violin prodigy Yehudi Menuhin and his two sisters, whom she met through the Hambourgs, and with whom she loved to walk in Central Park. But when she ventured out of the fortress-like, very proper Park Avenue apartment house she and Lewis had moved into in 1932, Cather hated to be approached by strangers. "She never had," said Elizabeth Sergeant, "the least little bit of small talk, not an iota of ease or light friendliness with a stranger who seemed intrusive." Read my books, Cather's demeanor would implicitly signal on such occasions; you do not need to shake my hand. Cather's last years were marked by a significant decline in her productivity (an irksome succession of health problems, especially an injury to her right hand, often prevented her from working), as well as by the inevitable, but still crushing, losses of those she loved.

Cather died at home on April 24, 1947. When Sinclair Lewis won the Nobel Prize for Literature in 1930, he said that it should have gone to Cather. By the time of her death, there were few critics around who would have seconded Lewis's opinion; but her legions of readers would have quietly concurred. Cather was buried at her cherished Jaffrey, New Hampshire, a lovely spot where she and Edna Lewis had often vacationed over the years. On the tombstone were carved a handful of words from *My Ántonia:* "That is happiness; to be dissolved into something complete and great."

"I had searched," said Cather in 1921, "for books telling about the beauty of the country I loved, its romance, and heroism and strength and courage of its people that had been plowed into the very furrows of its soil, and I did not find them. And so I wrote Pioneers!*"*

◆ ◆ ◆ ◆ ◆ ◆ ◆ ◆ ◆ ◆ ◆ ◆ ◆ ◆ ◆ ◆ ◆ ◆ ◆

ABOUT THIS EDITION

ILLUSTRATED WITH TREASURES drawn from The New York Public Library, this collection of three stories pays tribute to the writer whom Rebecca West described as the "most sensuous of artists," one who "builds her imagined world almost as solidly as our five senses build the universe around us." Rare prints and photographs from the Library's collections document pioneer life in Nebraska, part of the massive westward expansion that remade America's heartland after the Civil War and that formed the setting for Cather's heroic tales. And an interesting selection of portraits of Cather, ranging from 1905 to 1936, offers glimpses of the very private woman.

THE STORIES

Though Cather lived most of her adult life in New York City, she never forgot and never stopped loving the "sea of grass," the open, untamed country of her youth. Consider the way the land beckons to Clara Vavrika Ericson at the climax of "The Bohemian Girl"; "The great, silent country seemed to lay a spell on her. The ground seemed to hold her as if by roots." Gathered together in this unique collection are three of the finest of Cather's works, tales that are part of the rich harvest of a passion Cather was never able to shake.

"The Bohemian Girl" was first published in the August 1912 number of *McClure's*. Cather was offered the then rather mindboggling sum of $750 for the story, but she refused to accept more than $500 (the top rate for a short story at *McClure's*, as she knew better than anyone). Cather of course had written about Nebraska before; but in early stories like "A Wagner Matinee" and "The Sculptor's Funeral," she was unsparing in her depiction of the cultural impoverishment, coarseness, and crushing small-mindedness (as she then saw it) of life in a small town on the frontier. The louts, like Clara's dull, clumsy, unimaginative, and avaricious husband, Olaf Ericson, are not spared in "The Bohemian Girl"; but for Clara, there is a chance of escape when the prodigal son of the wealthy Ericson clan returns home. Nils Ericson has come to steal Clara away, and she is—perhaps—ready to fly. She explodes to Nils about her in-laws, his family: "There never was such a family for having nothing ever happen to them but dinner and threshing. I'd almost be willing to die, just to have a funeral. *You* wouldn't stand it for three weeks."

Clara is right about Nils, who tells her that remembering what she used to be like, before she married his boorish brother, was "like hearing a wild tune you can't resist." The vivid, discontented Clara is "not an altogether pleasing" personality, but when she flashes her eyes at the dashing Nils, they seem to say, "Yes, I admire you, but I am your equal." That is what was so remarkable about "The Bohemian Girl," which the *Nebraska State Journal* reviewer uneasily allowed was "beautiful but disturbing." For here was a fiery woman throwing away her wit on the impregnable rectitude of the Ericsons, her "capacity for delight," as Nils warns, beginning to wither. She may well despise the "housewifely arts," but Clara makes a choice, and it is hers.

For the title of her second book, Cather turned to Walt Whitman. She was stirred by the poet's ringing tribute to the great

The front cover of the August 1912 issue of McClure's Magazine, *illustrated by Charles Dana Gibson, which gave pride of place to Cather's romantic story, "The Bohemian Girl."*

Western movement of his day, "Pioneers! O Pioneers!" (1865), which calls out:

> *O you daughters of the West!*
> *O you young and elder daughters! O you mothers and you wives!*
> *Never must you be divided, in our ranks you move united,*
> *Pioneers! O pioneers!*

In *O Pioneers!*, Cather gives voices to two of those "daughters of the West": the steady and true Alexandra Bergson and her younger Bohemian friend, the charming, unhappily married Marie Shabata; and with none of the raucous heartiness of the cosmos-bedazzled Whitman, she tells a story that has its own special kind of epic grandeur. *O Pioneers!* is often spoken of as the fulfillment of the promise Cather had shown in "The Bohemian Girl," but it is a much less melodramatic work (although there is terrible, shattering violence), and it has a quality of classically restrained, meditative poignancy about it that gives the story an almost mystical dimension, which is entirely lacking in the earlier work. *O Pioneers!* is really a double elegy: to the land and the pioneer spirit; and to the "insupportable sweetness," "fierce necessity," and "sharp desire" of youth, which, as Cather shows, has been given to Marie and to Alexandra's youngest brother, Emil, in too full measure.

Not all devotees of the exquisite subtleties spun by Henry James and Edith Wharton, the literary lions of the day, were impressed with Cather's immigrants and farmers. "I simply don't care a damn what happens in Nebraska," said one New York critic, adding, "no matter who writes about it." But many more were moved by a work that is now recognized as a classic tale of human endurance. Cather knew she had done something special in *O Pioneers!*: "It was the country that was the hero, or the heroine," she wrote to a friend. The copy of *O Pioneers!* that Cather presented to Carrie Miner Sherwood in 1928 is inscribed on the flyleaf: "This was the first time I walked off on my own feet—everything before was half real and

"No. 54. Front Street, North Platte Station," by A. J. Russell, ca. 1868–73. The future looked very bright for scraggly little Nebraska prairie towns like North Platte and Red Cloud (the Hanover of O Pioneers!), once they were opened up to the world by the transcontinental railroad in the 1860s and '70s.

half an imitation of writers whom I admired. In this one I hit the home pasture and found that I was Yance Sorgenson and not Henry James."*

The final work included in this collection, *A Lost Lady,* was first

---

* In *The World of Willa Cather,* Mildred R. Bennett has helpfully explained that Yance Sorgenson was a farmer at the Norwegian settlement in Webster County whom Cather knew when she was young. He prospered beyond his wildest dreams, but refused to install bathrooms or heat in his house. When Charles Cather remonstrated with him that it was shameful that he did not modernize his home, Yance replied, "I'm so much more comfortable than I ever expected to be."

serialized in *The Century Magazine*, in April, May, and June 1923. In an interview two years later, Cather talked about the kind of writer she admired, one with a "brain like Limbo, full of ghosts." In that 1925 interview, Cather explained that the captivating, "lost" Marian Forrester was drawn directly from a "beautiful ghost" from her past:

> *A Lost Lady* was a woman I loved very much in my child-hood. . . . I didn't try to make a character study, but just a portrait like a thin miniature painted on ivory. A character study of Mrs. Forrester would have been very, very differ-ent. I wasn't interested in her character when I was little, but in her lovely hair and her laugh which made me happy clear down to my toes.

A sort of Madame Bovary of the Plains, Mrs. Forrester is the much younger wife of Captain Daniel Forrester, a pioneering railroad man. The most prominent citizen of Sweet Water (Red Cloud), Captain Forrester is part of a dying breed, those "great-hearted adventurers who were unpractical to the point of magnificence," whose passing from the scene Cather deplored. Captain Forrester, his repose "like that of a mountain," is succeeded by the likes of the odiously materialistic and up-to-date Ivy Peters; and for Cather, that signaled that a dream had come to an end, that the heroic age of the "road-making West" was done.

The Forresters were modeled on the undisputed aristocrats of Red Cloud society when Cather was a child: Silas Garber, banker and ex-governor of Nebraska, and his glittering wife, Lyra Caroline Garber. Red Cloud was founded (and named) by Silas Garber in 1870; three years later, he went to California to visit a brother, and returned to his homestead with his beautiful wife, who, with her sister, had been known as "the toast of the coast." Cather's portrait of the couple in *A Lost Lady* is wonderfully shaped. She catches a kind of afterglow, but indirectly; just as Niel Herbert, through

Engraved portrait of Silas Garber, the model for Captain Forrester in A Lost Lady, *from the* Portrait and Biographical Album of Johnson and Pawnee Counties, Nebraska *(1889). The biographical sketch says of this distinguished Nebraska citizen, "He was indeed a pioneer of the Great West, for when he located in Webster County there were but two settlers in the county."*

whose eyes, for the most part, we observe the beguiling Mrs. Forrester, at one point marvels, "And never elsewhere had he heard anything like her inviting, unforgettable laugh, that was like the distant measures of dance music, heard through opening and shutting doors." Much ink has been spilled over exactly how Marian

Forrester—or even Niel—is "lost." To the gossips of Sweet Water, she fatally compromises her already rather dubious reputation by consorting with Ivy Peters after her husband's death; and Niel's final judgment of the woman whom he had long worshipped is harsh, even contemptuous, for he cannot forgive her for preferring life "on any terms," damn the consequences. But of course Niel is very young, and many years later she does return to him as a "bright, impersonal memory," and he can think of her without chagrin or bitterness. In her essay, "The House of Willa Cather," Eudora Welty wrote: "[Cather] lacked self-righteousness, and she just as wholly lacked bitterness; what a lesson *A Lost Lady* gives us in doing without bitterness. It is impossible to think of diminishment in anything she thought or wrote." Of Lyra Garber, Cather was fond of saying in her later years, "Wasn't she a flash of brightness in a grey background, that lady?"

COME WEST!—IMAGINING NEBRASKA

Cather said that she was "jerked away" from Virginia as a child; her shock at what she saw next is spoken by Jim Burden in *My Ántonia:* "There was nothing but land: not a country at all, but the material out of which countries are made." In this Collector's Edition, stereographic views and vintage engravings provide a resonant counterpoint to Cather's matchless stories of the men and women "who had put plains and mountains under the iron harness," who had made their countries. Cather was unswerving in her allegiance to the hearty, resolute souls who had subdued the wild prairie and built the railroads and towns; the pioneers who first sowed and harvested the grain, and raised the herds that would one day feed millions. "The old-fashioned farmer's wife," she maintained with hauteur, "is nearer to the type of the true artist and the prima donna than is the culture enthusiast." (She hated women's clubs, which she thought middle-brow and a complete waste of time; better to *make* something, like a comforter, a bookcase, a novel, rather than just sit around chatting about Botticelli.)

When Cather and her family landed in Nebraska in 1883, the state had been part of the Union for less than twenty years. But it was not shy about proclaiming its many advantages and limitless potential. Cather herself succeeded in "imagining Nebraska" so vividly, and with so much art as to astound some "eastern" critics, including John Chapin Mosher of *The Writer,* who in 1926 blithely stated, "Certainly no environment would seem less promising to the literary career than Red Cloud, Nebraska, except that it was the scene of Willa Cather's early days there, blessedly untouched by the blight of suburban 'culture.' " But then Mosher had the wit to suggest that Cather's peerless excellence just might manage to instill "a cruel dubiety as to the value of the Manhattan program."

> It is perhaps fortunate that the New York habit has so strong a hold on its victims. Otherwise we might have the picture of a caravan of covered wagons filled with literary and artistic people, critics and columnists, with maids and managers, trouping out to the great prairies. Fortunate, that is, for Nebraska.

The completion of the transcontinental Union Pacific Railroad, with the famed driving of the "Golden Spike" at Promontory Point, Utah, on May 10, 1869, was one of the great technological achievements of the nineteenth century. Stereoscopic views, many commissioned by the railroad companies to publicize their projects and celebrate the feats of engineering they had brought off, carried images of this colossal, virtually unexplored "continent in itself" into the homes of armchair travelers around the world. Stereo views by three of the most important photographers who documented both the great railroad building program and the new land and its settlers, A. J. Russell, W. H. Jackson, and John Carbutt, are included in the present volume. These provide an often startlingly

"On Elm Creek, Near Red Cloud, Webster County," an engraving from Lawrence D. Burch's Nebraska As It Is *(Chicago, 1878).*

poetic visual record of the grand age of westward empire-building that brought the pioneer to the central plains (and beyond), an area that had seemed as boundless as the sea.

Cather had little interest in the implacable, often destructive power of the will toward expansion—the essence of raw, nonchalant force expressed, for example, in a 1870 pamphlet published by the Nebraska State Board of Commissioners of Immigration, in a description of the great Republican River Valley:

> The Indian held this beautiful valley as his hunting ground. The Indian title has long been extinguished, but the exceeding loveliness of the country has caused the red man still to struggle for its possession. The country is now occupied by United States troops, in sufficient numbers to hold the Indian in check, and the country is rapidly filling with settlers.

No, Cather listened to the men and women who broke the land, like Captain Forrester. He rouses himself at a dinner party when his wife teasingly demands that he explain his "philosophy of life," and it is this: what one thinks of, plans for, one will get, even in spite of oneself. "Because . . . because a thing that is dreamed of in the way I mean, is already an accomplished fact. All our great West has been developed from such dreams; the homesteader's and the prospector's and the contractor's. We dreamed the railroads across the mountains . . ."

Cather loved to travel by train; but she abhorred much of what the railroad, inevitably, brought to the heartland, above all, the "rage for newness." In an article published in *The Nation* in 1923, Cather claimed that, with the first generation of pioneers, "the attainment of material prosperity was a moral victory, because it was wrung from hard conditions, was the result of a struggle that tested character." She went on: "The sons, the generation now in middle life . . . hates to make anything, wants to live and die in an automobile, scudding past those acres where the old men used to follow

the long corn-rows up and down." Nearly fifty years before Cather
rebuked "the sons," the writer of *The State of Nebraska as a Home
for Immigrants* (which was commissioned under the auspices of the
then governor, Silas Garber) issued a hortatory summons to "the
poor of all the world":

> Until the advent of the Millennium or some other radical
> changes in the elementary constitution of this planet, and the
> atmosphere around it, and the people who dwell therein,
> shall we be beset by losses, calamities and disappointments.
> It is circumstances like these, together with the toil and expo-
> sure incident to the labor of carving out new homes, erecting
> new societies, and assuming new relationships within and
> about them, that bring out the best physical, intellectual and
> moral qualities of men—that make them the true pioneer.

This, Cather would have seconded, with gusto. In her stories of the
transformation of the American frontier, she conveyed a sense of
place and character that resonates with mythic gravity and timeless
beauty.

PORTRAITS OF CATHER

This Collector's Edition includes four portraits, dating from 1905 to
1936, of the woman who, as biographer Mildred Bennett revealed,
did not like to be photographed:

> She particularly detested candid camera fans, until finally she
> hated the idea of photography in general. When someone
> wrote asking for the use of her picture to put on a calendar
> to be distributed at Christmas time, her disgust was devastat-
> ing, and she was unable to work all day. Like many famous
> writers, she seemed to forget that she had once been a re-

porter, dependent on brashness and interference with privacy for news, and that there had been a time when she herself had needed and wanted publicity.

Bennett is probably exaggerating a little, at least in terms of Cather's "hate" for photography, if not of her loathing for fans who jumped out of bushes with their Kodaks ready to fire. Edward Steichen's 1927 photographs of Cather, for example, show a very relaxed woman, almost sparkling before the camera. In contrast to Bennett's remarks, Floral Merrill, who interviewed Cather for the *New York World* in 1925, said that for the novelist it was "photographs or nothing." This dictum, Merrill explained, was the outcome of three afternoons Cather spent being subjected to the feverish scrutiny of a caricaturist while lunching at the Algonquin. The result, Cather insisted, made her look like "G. K. Chesterton without his mustache."

The earliest photograph of Cather in the present volume shows her at the dinner honoring Mark Twain on his seventieth birthday, which was held on December 5, 1905, at Delmonico's in New York City. Ten years earlier, she had published an article in the *Nebraska State Journal* in which she confidently—and some would say, impudently—asserted that Twain "is not and never will be part of literature." She later changed her mind. The three "great ones" of American literature, she told an interviewer in 1913, were Mark Twain, Henry James, and Sarah Orne Jewett.

The 1915 photograph of Cather by Hollinger was selected, no doubt by her, as the frontispiece to the Library Edition of *The Song of the Lark*, the second volume of *The Novels and Stories of Willa Cather*, which was brought out by Houghton Mifflin, Cather's first publisher, in 1937. The author was very much involved in the production of the Library Edition, for which she made substantial cuts in *The Song of the Lark*. It was a handsome production, designed by the great Bruce Rogers, intended for collectors; but, according to Alfred A. Knopf, she "was not keen about it, and seemed to take a

Portrait photograph of Willa Cather, taken by Carl Van Vechten in the office of her publisher, Alfred A. Knopf, on January 22, 1936.

genuine satisfaction in the failure of the set to do very well." Still, Cather must have liked the Hollinger portrait, though the hat may come as a surprise to those who tend to envision Cather as some kind of indomitable frontierswoman, whose sole enjoyment in life was, say, camping in the Mesa Verde.

Writing in 1924, journalist Burton Rascoe decried the fact that, for him, all pictures he had seen of Cather amounted "almost to libels, for they portray a faintly sullen expression about her mouth, and such an expression she is not guilty of, I believe, ever. Hers is a mouth capable of sternness, severity, stubbornness, perhaps, but not sullenness." The 1917 and 1936 portrait photographs of Cather included in this collection certainly show her as very serious, perhaps even rather somber, especially the latter portrait by Carl Van Vechten. Missing from these is any flash of the very witty woman who possessed, as one interviewer discovered to her delight, "rare good sense," which she drove home "with a well-wrought mallet of humor." But both portraits give a suggestion of the woman who liked beautiful and expensive clothes, and whose fondness for bright colors, embroidery, and rich materials occasionally startled anyone who had been expecting Alexandra Bergson to walk into the room. "She has," said *Arts and Decoration* in 1924, "the extraordinary courage to wear at the same time salmon and green, and she does it with complete success." The next year, a writer for the *Cleveland Press* gasped that Cather had breezed into town "in a bright green and gray fur coat with gold and black velvet toque, and bright green bag to match." But, the readers of the *Press* were assured, "she's no Bohemian!"

A final portrait, written down from loving memory, is likely all the more true to life. In *Willa Cather: A Memoir*, Elizabeth Sergeant recalled her first meeting with the dynamic *McClure's* editor, who seemed to have brought something of the majestic, invigorating expansiveness of the Nebraska prairie land with her to New York City, and who of course would one day open up that country to imaginations of the world:

Her eyes were sailor-blue, her cheeks were rosy, her hair was red-brown, parted in the middle like a child's. As she shook hands, I felt the freshness and brusqueness, too, of an ocean breeze. Her boyish, enthusiastic manner was disarming, and as she led me through the jostle of the outer office, I was affected by the resonance of her Western voice, and by the informality of her clothes—it was as if she rebelled against urban conformities.

O PIONEERS!
and OTHER TALES
OF THE PRAIRIE

THE
BOHEMIAN
GIRL

"*The transcontinental express swung along the windings of the Sand River Valley . . .*" — "*The Bohemian Girl*"

I

THE TRANSCONTINENTAL EXPRESS swung along the windings of the Sand River Valley, and in the rear seat of the observation car a young man sat greatly at his ease, not in the least discomfited by the fierce sunlight which beat in upon his brown face and neck and strong back. There was a look of relaxation and of great passivity about his broad shoulders, which seemed almost too heavy until he stood up and squared them. He wore a pale flannel shirt and a blue silk necktie with loose ends. His trousers were wide and belted at the waist, and his short sack coat hung open. His heavy shoes had seen good service. His reddish-brown hair, like his clothes, had a foreign cut. He had deep-set, dark blue eyes under heavy reddish eyebrows. His face was kept clean only by close shaving, and even the sharpest razor left a glint of yellow in the smooth brown of his skin. His teeth and the palms of his hands were very white. His head, which looked hard and stubborn, lay indolently in the green cushion of the wicker chair, and as he looked out at the ripe summer country a teasing, not unkindly smile played over his lips. Once, as he basked thus comfortably, a quick light flashed in his eyes, curiously dilating the pupils, and his mouth became a hard, straight line, gradually relaxing into its former smile of rather kindly mockery.

He told himself, apparently, that there was no point in getting excited; and he seemed a master hand at taking his ease when he could. Neither the sharp whistle of the locomotive nor the brakeman's call disturbed him. It was not until after the train had stopped that he rose, put on a Panama hat, took from the rack a small valise and a flute case, and stepped deliberately to the station platform. The baggage was already unloaded, and the stranger presented a check for a battered sole-leather steamer trunk.

"Can you keep it here for a day or two?" he asked the agent. "I may send for it, and I may not."

"Depends on whether you like the country, I suppose?" demanded the agent in a challenging tone.

"Just so."

The agent shrugged his shoulders, looked scornfully at the small trunk, which was marked "N.E.," and handed out a claim check without further comment. The stranger watched him as he caught one end of the trunk and dragged it into the express room. The agent's manner seemed to remind him of something amusing. "Doesn't seem to be a very big place," he remarked, looking about.

"It's big enough for us," snapped the agent, as he banged the trunk into a corner.

That remark, apparently, was what Nils Ericson had wanted. He chuckled quietly as he took a leather strap from his pocket and swung his valise around his shoulder. Then he settled his Panama securely on his head, turned up his trousers, tucked the flute case under his arm, and started off across the fields. He gave the town, as he would have said, a wide berth, and cut through a great fenced pasture, emerging, when he rolled under the barbed wire at the farther corner, upon a white dusty road which ran straight up from the river valley to the high prairies, where the ripe wheat stood yellow and the tin roofs and weathercocks were twinkling in the fierce sunlight. By the time Nils had done three miles, the sun was sinking and the farm wagons on their way home from town came rattling by, covering him with dust and making him sneeze. When one of the farmers pulled up and offered to give him a lift, he clambered in willingly. The driver was a thin, grizzled old man with a long lean neck and a foolish sort of beard, like a goat's. "How fur ye goin'?" he asked, as he clucked to his horses and started off.

"Do you go by the Ericson place?"

"Which Ericson?" The old man drew in his reins as if he expected to stop again.

"Preacher Ericson's."

"Oh, the Old Lady Ericson's!" He turned and looked at Nils. "La, me! If you're goin' out there you might 'a' rid out in the automobile. That's a pity, now. The Old Lady Ericson was in town with her auto. You might 'a' heard it snortin' anywhere about the post office er the butcher shop."

"Has she a motor?" asked the stranger absently.

" 'Deed an' she has! She runs into town every night about this time for her mail and meat for supper. Some folks say she's afraid her auto won't get exercise enough, but I say that's jealousy."

"Aren't there any other motors about here?"

"Oh, yes! we have fourteen in all. But nobody else gets around like the Old Lady Ericson. She's out, rain er shine, over the whole county, chargin' into town and out amongst her farms, an' up to her sons' places. Sure you ain't goin' to the wrong place?" He craned his neck and looked at Nils' flute case with eager curiosity. "The old woman ain't got any piany that I knows on. Olaf, he has a grand. His wife's musical; took lessons in Chicago."

"I'm going up there tomorrow," said Nils imperturbably. He saw that the driver took him for a piano tuner.

"Oh, I see!" The old man screwed up his eyes mysteriously. He was a little dashed by the stranger's noncommunicativeness, but he soon broke out again.

"I'm one o' Mis' Ericson's tenants. Look after one of her places. I did own the place myself oncet, but I lost it a while back, in the bad years just after the World's Fair. Just as well, too, I say. Lets you out o' payin' taxes. The Ericsons do own most of the county now. I remember the old preacher's fav'rite text used to be, 'To them that hath shall be given.' They've spread something wonderful—run over this here country like bindweed. But I ain't one that begretches it to 'em. Folks is entitled to what they kin git; and they're hustlers. Olaf, he's in the Legislature now, and a likely man fur Congress. Listen, if that ain't the old woman comin' now. Want I should stop her?"

Nils shook his head. He heard the deep chug-chug of a motor vibrating steadily in the clear twilight behind them. The pale lights of the car swam over the hill, and the old man slapped his reins and turned clear out of the road, ducking his head at the first of three angry snorts from behind. The motor was running at a hot, even speed, and passed without turning an inch from its course. The driver was a stalwart woman who sat at ease in the front seat and drove her car bareheaded. She left a cloud of dust and a trail of gasoline behind her. Her tenant threw back his head and sneezed.

"Whew! I sometimes say I'd as lief be *before* Mrs. Ericson as behind her. She does beat all! Nearly seventy, and never lets another soul touch that car. Puts it into commission herself every morning, and keeps it tuned up by the hitch-bar all day. I never stop work for a drink o' water that I don't hear her a-churnin' up the road. I reckon her darter-in-laws never sets down easy nowadays. Never know when she'll pop in. Mis' Otto, she says to me: 'We're so afraid that thing'll blow up and do Ma some injury yet, she's so turrible venturesom.' Says I: 'I wouldn't stew, Mis' Otto; the old lady'll drive that car to the funeral of every darter-in-law she's got.' That was after the old woman had jumped a turrible bad culvert."

The stranger heard vaguely what the old man was saying. Just now he was experiencing something very much like homesickness, and he was wondering what had brought it about. The mention of a name or two, perhaps; the rattle of a wagon along a dusty road; the rank, resinous smell of sunflowers and ironweed, which the night damp brought up from the draws and low places; perhaps, more than all, the dancing lights of the motor that had plunged by. He squared his shoulders with a comfortable sense of strength.

The wagon, as it jolted westward, climbed a pretty steady upgrade. The country, receding from the rough river valley, swelled more and more gently, as if it had been smoothed out by the wind. On one of the last of the rugged ridges, at the end of a branch road, stood a grim square house with a tin roof and double porches. Behind the house stretched a row of broken, wind-racked poplars, and down the hill slope to the left straggled the sheds and stables. The old man stopped his horses where the Ericsons' road branched across a dry sand creek that wound about the foot of the hill.

"That's the old lady's place. Want I should drive in?"

"No, thank you. I'll roll out here. Much obliged to you. Good night."

His passenger stepped down over the front wheel, and the old man drove on reluctantly, looking back as if he would like to see how the stranger would be received.

As Nils was crossing the dry creek he heard the restive tramp of a horse coming toward him down the hill. Instantly he flashed out of the road and stood behind a thicket of wild plum bushes that grew in the sandy bed. Peering through the dusk, he saw a light horse, under tight rein, descending the hill at a sharp walk. The rider was a slender woman—barely visible against the dark hillside—wearing an old-fashioned derby hat and a long riding skirt. She sat lightly in the saddle, with her chin high, and seemed to be looking into the distance. As she passed the plum thicket her horse snuffed the air and shied. She struck him, pulling him in sharply, with an angry exclamation, *"Blázne!"* in Bohemian. Once in the main road, she let him out into a lope, and they soon emerged upon the crest of high land, where they moved along the skyline, silhouetted against the band of faint color that lingered in the west. This horse and rider, with their free, rhythmical gallop, were the only moving things to be seen on the face of the flat country. They seemed, in the last sad light of evening, not to be there accidentally, but as an inevitable detail of the landscape.

Nils watched them until they had shrunk to a mere moving speck against the sky, then he crossed the sand creek and climbed the hill. When he reached the gate the front of the house was dark, but a light was shining from the side windows. The pigs were squealing in the hog corral, and Nils could see a tall boy, who carried two big wooden buckets, moving about among them. Halfway between the barn and the house, the windmill wheezed lazily. Following the path that ran around to the back porch, Nils stopped to look through the screen door into the lamplit kitchen. The kitchen was the largest room in the house; Nils remembered that his older brothers used to give dances there when he was a boy. Beside the stove stood a little girl with two light yellow braids and a broad, flushed face, peering anxiously into a frying pan. In the dining room beyond, a large, broad-shouldered woman was moving about the table. She walked with an active, springy step. Her face was heavy and florid, almost without wrinkles, and her hair was black at seventy. Nils felt proud of her as he watched her deliberate activity; never a momentary hesitation, or a movement that did not tell. He waited until she came out into the kitchen and, brushing the child aside, took her place at the stove. Then he tapped on the screen door and entered.

"It's nobody but Nils, Mother. I expect you weren't looking for me."

Mrs. Ericson turned away from the stove and stood staring at him. "Bring the lamp, Hilda, and let me look."

Nils laughed and unslung his valise. "What's the matter, Mother? Don't you know me?"

Mrs. Ericson put down the lamp. "You must be Nils. You don't look very different, anyway."

"Nor you, Mother. You hold your own. Don't you wear glasses yet?"

"Only to read by. Where's your trunk, Nils?"

"Oh, I left that in town. I thought it might not be convenient for you to have company so near threshing-time."

"Don't be foolish, Nils." Mrs. Ericson turned back to the stove. "I don't thresh now. I hitched the wheat land onto the next farm and have a tenant. Hilda, take some hot water up to the company room, and go call little Eric."

The tow-haired child, who had been standing in mute amazement, took up the tea kettle and withdrew, giving Nils a long, admiring look from the door of the kitchen stairs.

"Who's the youngster?" Nils asked, dropping down on the bench behind the kitchen stove.

"One of your Cousin Henrik's."

"How long has Cousin Henrik been dead?"

"Six years. There are two boys. One stays with Peter and one with Anders. Olaf is their guardeen."

There was a clatter of pails on the porch, and a tall, lanky boy peered wonderingly in through the screen door. He had a fair, gentle face and big gray eyes, and wisps of soft yellow hair hung down under his cap. Nils sprang up and pulled him into the kitchen, hugging him and slapping him on the shoulders. "Well, if it isn't my kid! Look at the size of him! Don't you know me, Eric?"

The boy reddened under his sunburn and freckles, and hung his head. "I guess it's Nils," he said shyly.

"You're a good guesser," laughed Nils giving the lad's hand a swing. To himself he was thinking: "That's why the little girl looked so friendly. He's taught her to like me. He was only six when I went away, and he's remembered for twelve years."

Eric stood fumbling with his cap and smiling. "You look just like I thought you would," he ventured.

"Go wash your hands, Eric," called Mrs. Ericson. "I've got cob corn for supper, Nils. You used to like it. I guess you don't get much of that in the old country. Here's Hilda; she'll take you up to your room. You'll want to get the dust off you before you eat."

Mrs. Ericson went into the dining room to lay another plate, and the little girl came up and nodded to Nils as if to let him know that his room was ready. He put out his hand and she took it, with a startled glance up at his face. Little Eric dropped his towel, threw an arm about Nils and one about Hilda, gave them a clumsy squeeze, and then stumbled out to the porch.

During supper Nils heard exactly how much land each of his eight grown brothers farmed, how their crops were coming on, and how much live stock they were feeding. His mother watched him narrowly as she talked. "You've got better looking, Nils," she remarked abruptly, whereupon he grinned and the children giggled. Eric, although he was eighteen and as tall as Nils, was always accounted a child, being the last of so many sons. His face seemed childlike, too, Nils thought, and he had the open, wandering eyes of a little boy. All the others had been men at his age.

After supper Nils went out to the front porch and sat down on the step to smoke a pipe. Mrs. Ericson drew a rocking chair up near him and began to knit busily. It was one of the few Old World customs she had kept up, for she could not bear to sit with idle hands.

"Where's little Eric, Mother?"

"He's helping Hilda with the dishes. He does it of his own will; I don't like a boy to be too handy about the house."

"He seems like a nice kid."

"He's very obedient."

Nils smiled a little in the dark. It was just as well to shift the line of conversation. "What are you knitting there, Mother?"

"Baby stockings. The boys keep me busy." Mrs. Ericson chuckled and clicked her needles.

"How many grandchildren have you?"

"Only thirty-one now. Olaf lost his three. They were sickly, like their mother."

"I supposed he had a second crop by this time!"

"His second wife has no children. She's too proud. She tears about on horseback all the time. But she'll get caught up with, yet.

She sets herself very high, though nobody knows what for. They were low enough Bohemians she came of. I never thought much of Bohemians; always drinking."

Nils puffed away at his pipe in silence, and Mrs. Ericson knitted on. In a few moments she added grimly: "She was down here tonight, just before you came. She'd like to quarrel with me and come between me and Olaf, but I don't give her the chance. I suppose you'll be bringing a wife home some day."

"I don't know. I've never thought much about it."

"Well, perhaps it's best as it is," suggested Mrs. Ericson hopefully. "You'd never be contented tied down to the land. There was roving blood in your father's family, and it's come out in you. I expect your own way of life suits you best." Mrs. Ericson had dropped into a blandly agreeable tone which Nils well remembered. It seemed to amuse him a good deal and his white teeth flashed behind his pipe. His mother's strategies had always diverted him, even when he was a boy—they were so flimsy and patent, so illy proportioned to her vigor and force. "They've been waiting to see which way I'd jump," he reflected. He felt that Mrs. Ericson was pondering his case deeply as she sat clicking her needles.

"I don't suppose you've ever got used to steady work," she went on presently. "Men ain't apt to if they roam around too long. It's a pity you didn't come back the year after the World's Fair. Your father picked up a good bit of land cheap then, in the hard times, and I expect maybe he'd have give you a farm. It's too bad you put off comin' back so long, for I always thought he meant to do something by you."

Nils laughed and shook the ashes out of his pipe. "I'd have missed a lot if I had come back then. But I'm sorry I didn't get back to see father."

"Well, I suppose we have to miss things at one end or the other. Perhaps you are as well satisfied with your own doings, now, as you'd have been with a farm," said Mrs. Ericson reassuringly.

"Land's a good thing to have," Nils commented, as he lit another match and sheltered it with his hand.

His mother looked sharply at his face until the match burned out. "Only when you stay on it!" she hastened to say.

Eric came round the house by the path just then, and Nils rose, with a yawn. "Mother, if you don't mind, Eric and I will take a little tramp before bedtime. It will make me sleep."

"Very well; only don't stay long. I'll sit up and wait for you. I like to lock up myself."

Nils put his hand on Eric's shoulder, and the two tramped down the hill and across the sand creek into the dusty highroad beyond. Neither spoke. They swung along at an even gait, Nils puffing at his pipe. There was no moon, and the white road and the wide fields lay faint in the starlight. Over everything was darkness and thick silence, and the smell of dust and sunflowers. The brothers followed the road for a mile or more without finding a place to sit down. Finally, Nils perched on a stile over the wire fence, and Eric sat on the lower step.

"I began to think you never would come back, Nils," said the boy softly.

"Didn't I promise you I would?"

"Yes; but people don't bother about promises they make to babies. Did you really know you were going away for good when you went to Chicago with the cattle that time?"

"I thought it very likely, if I could make my way."

"I don't see how you did it, Nils. Not many fellows could." Eric rubbed his shoulder against his brother's knee.

"The hard thing was leaving home—you and father. It was easy enough, once I got beyond Chicago. Of course I got awful homesick; used to cry myself to sleep. But I'd burned my bridges."

"You had always wanted to go, hadn't you?"

"Always. Do you still sleep in our little room? Is that cottonwood still by the window?"

Eric nodded eagerly and smiled up at his brother in the gray darkness.

"You remember how we always said the leaves were whispering when they rustled at night? Well, they always whispered to me about the sea. Sometimes they said names out of the geography books. In a high wind they had a desperate sound, like something trying to tear loose."

"How funny, Nils," said Eric dreamily, resting his chin on his hand. "That tree still talks like that, and 'most always it talks to me about you."

They sat a while longer, watching the stars. At last Eric whispered anxiously: "Hadn't we better go back now? Mother will get tired waiting for us." They rose and took a short cut home, through the pasture.

I I

THE NEXT MORNING Nils woke with the first flood of light that came with dawn. The white-plastered walls of his room reflected the glare that shone through the thin window shades, and he found it impossible to sleep. He dressed hurriedly and slipped down the hall and up the back stairs to the half-story room which he used to share with his little brother. Eric, in a skimpy nightshirt, was sitting on the edge of the bed, rubbing his eyes, his pale yellow hair standing up in tufts all over his head. When he saw Nils, he murmured something confusedly and hustled his long legs into his trousers. "I didn't expect you'd be up so early, Nils," he said, as his head emerged from his blue shirt.

"Oh, you thought I was a dude, did you?" Nils gave him a playful tap which bent the tall boy up like a clasp knife. "See here; I must teach you to box." Nils thrust his hands into his pockets and walked about. "You haven't changed things much up here. Got most of my old traps, haven't you?"

He took down a bent, withered piece of sapling that hung over the dresser. "If this isn't the stick Lou Sandberg killed himself with!"

The boy looked up from his shoe-lacing.

"Yes; you never used to let me play with that. Just how did he do it, Nils? You were with father when he found Lou, weren't you?"

"Yes. Father was going off to preach somewhere, and, as we drove along, Lou's place looked sort of forlorn, and we thought we'd stop and cheer him up. When we found him father said he'd been dead a couple of days. He'd tied a piece of binding twine round his neck, made a noose in each end, fixed the nooses over the ends of a bent stick, and let the stick spring straight; strangled himself."

"What made him kill himself such a silly way?"

The simplicity of the boy's question set Nils laughing. He clapped little Eric on the shoulder. "What made him such a silly as to kill himself at all, I should say!"

"Oh, well! But his hogs had the cholera, and all up and died on him, didn't they?"

"Sure they did; but he didn't have cholera; and there were plenty of hogs left in the world, weren't there?"

"Well, but, if they weren't his, how could they do him any good?" Eric asked, in astonishment.

"Oh, scat! He could have had lots of fun with other people's hogs. He was a chump, Lou Sandberg. To kill yourself for a pig— think of that, now!" Nils laughed all the way downstairs, and quite embarrassed little Eric, who fell to scrubbing his face and hands at the tin basin. While he was parting his wet hair at the kitchen looking glass, a heavy tread sounded on the stairs. The boy dropped his comb. "Gracious, there's Mother. We must have talked too long." He hurried out to the shed, slipped on his overalls, and disappeared with the milking pails.

Mrs. Ericson came in, wearing a clean white apron, her black hair shining from the application of a wet brush.

"Good morning, Mother. Can't I make the fire for you?"

"No, thank you, Nils. It's no trouble to make a cob fire, and I like to manage the kitchen stove myself." Mrs. Ericson paused with a shovel full of ashes in her hand. "I expect you will be wanting to see your brothers as soon as possible. I'll take you up to Anders' place this morning. He's threshing, and most of our boys are over there."

"Will Olaf be there?"

Mrs. Ericson went on taking out the ashes, and spoke between shovels. "No; Olaf's wheat is all in, put away in his new barn. He got six thousand bushel this year. He's going to town today to get men to finish roofing his barn."

"So Olaf is building a new barn?" Nils asked absently.

"Biggest one in the county, and almost done. You'll likely be here for the barn-raising. He's going to have a supper and a dance as soon as everybody's done threshing. Says it keeps the voters in a good humor. I tell him that's all nonsense; but Olaf has a long head for politics."

"Does Olaf farm all Cousin Henrik's land?"

Mrs. Ericson frowned as she blew into the faint smoke curling up about the cobs. "Yes; he holds it in trust for the children, Hilda and her brothers. He keeps strict account of everything he raises on it, and puts the proceeds out at compound interest for them."

Nils smiled as he watched the little flames shoot up. The door of the back stairs opened, and Hilda emerged, her arms behind her, buttoning up her long gingham apron as she came. He nodded to her gaily, and she twinkled at him out of her little blue eyes, set far apart over her wide cheekbones.

"There, Hilda, you grind the coffee—and just put in an extra handful; I expect your Cousin Nils likes his strong," said Mrs. Ericson, as she went out to the shed.

Nils turned to look at the little girl, who gripped the coffee grinder between her knees and ground so hard that her two braids bobbed and her face flushed under its broad spattering of freckles. He noticed on her middle finger something that had not been there last night, and that had evidently been put on for company: a tiny gold ring with a clumsily set garnet stone. As her hand went round and round he touched the ring with the tip of his finger, smiling.

Hilda glanced toward the shed door through which Mrs. Ericson had disappeared. "My Cousin Clara gave me that," she whispered bashfully. "She's Cousin Olaf's wife."

III

MRS. OLAF ERICSON—Clara Vavrika, as many people still called her—was moving restlessly about her big bare house that morning. Her husband had left for the county town before his wife was out of bed—her lateness in rising was one of the many things the Ericson family had against her. Clara seldom came downstairs before eight o'clock, and this morning she was even later, for she had dressed with unusual care. She put on, however, only a tight-fitting black dress, which people thereabouts thought very plain. She was a tall, dark woman of thirty, with a rather sallow complexion and a touch of dull salmon red in her cheeks, where the blood seemed to burn under her brown skin. Her hair, parted evenly above her low forehead, was so black that there were distinctly blue lights in it. Her black eyebrows were delicate half-moons and her lashes were long and heavy. Her eyes slanted a little, as if she had a strain of Tartar or gypsy blood, and were sometimes full of fiery determination and sometimes dull and opaque. Her expression was never altogether amiable; was often, indeed, distinctly sullen, or, when she was animated, sarcastic. She was most attractive in profile, for then one saw to advantage her small, well-shaped head and delicate ears, and felt at once that here was a very positive, if not an altogether pleasing, personality.

The entire management of Mrs. Olaf's household devolved upon her aunt, Johanna Vavrika, a superstitious, doting woman of fifty. When Clara was a little girl her mother died, and Johanna's life had been spent in ungrudging service to her niece. Clara, like many self-willed and discontented persons, was really very apt, without knowing it, to do as other people told her, and to let her destiny be decided for her by intelligences much below her own. It was her Aunt Johanna who had humored and spoiled her in her girlhood, who had got her off to Chicago to study piano, and who had finally persuaded her to marry Olaf Ericson as the best match she would be likely to make in that part of the country. Johanna Vavrika had been deeply scarred by smallpox in the old country. She was short and fat, homely and jolly and sentimental. She was so broad, and took such short steps when she walked, that her brother, Joe Vavrika, always called her his duck. She adored her niece because of her talent, because of her good looks and masterful ways, but most of all because of her selfishness.

Clara's marriage with Olaf Ericson was Johanna's particular triumph. She was inordinately proud of Olaf's position, and she found a sufficiently exciting career in managing Clara's house, in keeping it above the criticism of the Ericsons, in pampering Olaf to keep him from finding fault with his wife, and in concealing from every one Clara's domestic infelicities. While Clara slept of a morning, Johanna Vavrika was bustling about, seeing that Olaf and the men had their breakfast, and that the cleaning or the butter-making or the washing was properly begun by the two girls in the kitchen. Then, at about eight o'clock, she would take Clara's coffee up to her, and chat with her while she drank it, telling her what was going on in the house. Old Mrs. Ericson frequently said that her daughter-in-law would not know what day of the week it was if Johanna did not tell her every morning. Mrs. Ericson despised and pitied Johanna, but did not wholly dislike her. The one thing she hated in her daughter-in-law above everything else was the way in which Clara could come it over people. It enraged her that the affairs of her son's big, barnlike house went on as well as they did, and she used to feel that in this world we have to wait overlong to see the guilty punished. "Suppose Johanna Vavrika died or got sick?" the old lady used to say to Olaf. "Your wife wouldn't know where to look for her own dish-cloth." Olaf only shrugged his shoulders. The fact remained that Johanna did not die, and, although Mrs. Ericson often told her she was looking poorly, she was never ill. She seldom left the house, and she slept in a little room off the kitchen. No Ericson, by night or day, could come prying about there to find fault without her knowing it. Her one weakness was that she was an incurable talker, and she sometimes made trouble without meaning to.

This morning Clara was tying a wine-colored ribbon about her throat when Johanna appeared with her coffee. After putting the tray on a sewing table, she began to make Clara's bed, chattering the while in Bohemian.

"Well, Olaf got off early, and the girls are baking. I'm going down presently to make some poppy-seed bread for Olaf. He asked for prune preserves at breakfast, and I told him I was out of them, and to bring some prunes and honey and cloves from town."

Clara poured her coffee. "Ugh! I don't see how men can eat so much sweet stuff. In the morning, too!"

Her aunt chuckled knowingly. "Bait a bear with honey, as we say in the old country."

"Was he cross?" her niece asked indifferently.

"Olaf? Oh, no! He was in fine spirits. He's never cross if you know how to take him. I never knew a man to make so little fuss about bills. I gave him a list of things to get a yard long, and he didn't say a word; just folded it up and put it in his pocket."

"I can well believe he didn't say a word," Clara remarked with a shrug. "Some day he'll forget how to talk."

"Oh, but they say he's a grand speaker in the Legislature. He knows when to keep quiet. That's why he's got such influence in politics. The people have confidence in him." Johanna beat up a pillow and held it under her fat chin while she slipped on the case. Her niece laughed.

"Maybe we could make people believe we were wise, Aunty, if we held our tongues. Why did you tell Mrs. Ericson that Norman threw me again last Saturday and turned my foot? She's been talking to Olaf."

Johanna fell into great confusion. "Oh, but, my precious, the old lady asked for you, and she's always so angry if I can't give an excuse. Anyhow, she needn't talk; she's always tearing up something with that motor of hers."

When her aunt clattered down to the kitchen, Clara went to dust the parlor. Since there was not much there to dust, this did not take very long. Olaf had built the house new for her before their marriage, but her interest in furnishing it had been short-lived. It went, indeed, little beyond a bathtub and her piano. They had disagreed about almost every other article of furniture, and Clara had said she would rather have her house empty than full of things she didn't want. The house was set in a hillside, and the west windows of the parlor looked out above the kitchen yard thirty feet below. The east windows opened directly into the front yard. At one of the latter, Clara, while she was dusting, heard a low whistle. She did not turn at once, but listened intently as she drew her cloth slowly along the round of a chair. Yes, there is was:

I dreamt that I dwelt in ma-a-arble halls.

She turned and saw Nils Ericson laughing in the sunlight, his hat in his hand, just outside the window. As she crossed the room he leaned against the wire screen. "Aren't you at all surprised to see me, Clara Vavrika?"

"No; I was expecting to see you. Mother Ericson telephoned Olaf last night that you were here."

Nils squinted and gave a long whistle. "Telephoned? That must have been while Eric and I were out walking. Isn't she enterprising? Lift this screen, won't you?"

Clara lifted the screen, and Nils swung his leg across the window sill. As he stepped into the room she said: "You didn't think you were going to get ahead of your mother, did you?"

He threw his hat on the piano. "Oh, I do sometimes. You see, I'm ahead of her now. I'm supposed to be in Anders' wheat field. But, as we were leaving, Mother ran her car into a soft place beside the road and sank up to the hubs. While they were going for horses to pull her out, I cut away behind the stacks and escaped." Nils chuckled. Clara's dull eyes lit up as she looked at him admiringly.

"You've got them guessing already. I don't know what your mother said to Olaf over the telephone, but he came back looking as if he'd seen a ghost, and he didn't go to bed until a dreadful hour— ten o'clock, I should think. He sat out on the porch in the dark like a graven image. It had been one of his talkative days, too." They both laughed, easily and lightly, like people who have laughed a great deal together; but they remained standing.

"Anders and Otto and Peter looked as if they had seen ghosts, too, over in the threshing field. What's the matter with them all?"

Clara gave him a quick, searching look. "Well, for one thing, they've always been afraid you have the other will."

Nils looked interested. "The other will?"

"Yes. A later one. They knew your father made another, but they never knew what he did with it. They almost tore the old house to pieces looking for it. They always suspected that he carried on a clandestine correspondence with you, for the one thing he would do was to get his own mail himself. So they thought he might have sent the new will to you for safekeeping. The old one, leaving everything to your mother, was made long before you went away, and it's understood among them that it cuts you out—that she will leave all the property to the others. Your father made the second will to prevent that. I've been hoping you had it. It would be such fun to spring it on them." Clara laughed mirthfully, a thing she did not often do now.

Nils shook his head reprovingly. "Come, now, you're malicious."

"No, I'm not. But I'd like something to happen to stir them all up, just for once. There never was such a family for having nothing ever happen to them but dinner and threshing. I'd almost be willing to die, just to have a funeral. *You* wouldn't stand it for three weeks."

Nils bent over the piano and began pecking at the keys with the finger of one hand. "I wouldn't? My dear young lady, how do you know what I can stand? *You* wouldn't wait to find out."

Clara flushed darkly and frowned. "I didn't believe you would ever come back—" she said defiantly.

"Eric believed I would, and he was only a baby when I went away. However, all's well that ends well, and I haven't come back to be a skeleton at the feast. We mustn't quarrel. Mother will be here with a search warrant pretty soon." He swung round and faced her, thrusting his hands into his coat pockets. "Come, you ought to be glad to see me, if you want something to happen. I'm something, even without a will. We can have a little fun, can't we? I think we can!"

She echoed him, "I think we can!" They both laughed and their eyes sparkled. Clara Vavrika looked ten years younger than when she had put the velvet ribbon about her throat that morning.

"You know, I'm so tickled to see mother," Nils went on. "I didn't know I was so proud of her. A regular pile driver. How about little pigtails, down at the house? Is Olaf doing the square thing by those children?"

Clara frowned pensively. "Olaf has to do something that looks like the square thing, now that he's a public man!" She glanced drolly at Nils. "But he makes a good commission out of it. On Sundays they all get together here and figure. He lets Peter and Anders put in big bills for the keep of the two boys, and he pays them out of the estate. They are always having what they call accountings. Olaf gets something out of it, too. I don't know just how they do it, but it's entirely a family matter, as they say. And when the Ericsons say that—" Clara lifted her eyebrows.

Just then the angry *honk-honk* of an approaching motor sounded from down the road. Their eyes met and they began to laugh. They laughed as children do when they can not contain themselves, and can not explain the cause of their mirth to grown people, but share it perfectly together. When Clara Vavrika sat down at the piano after he was gone, she felt that she had laughed away a dozen years. She practised as if the house were burning over her head.

When Nils greeted his mother and climbed into the front seat of the motor beside her, Mrs. Ericson looked grim, but she made no comment upon his truancy until she had turned her car and was retracing her revolutions along the road that ran by Olaf's big pasture. Then she remarked dryly:

"If I were you I wouldn't see too much of Olaf's wife while you are here. She's the kind of woman who can't see much of men without getting herself talked about. She was a good deal talked about before he married her."

"Hasn't Olaf tamed her?" Nils asked indifferently.

Mrs. Ericson shrugged her massive shoulders. "Olaf don't seem to have much luck, when it comes to wives. The first one was meek enough, but she was always ailing. And this one has her own way. He says if he quarreled with her she'd go back to her father, and then he'd lose the Bohemian vote. There are a great many Bohunks in this district. But when you find a man under his wife's thumb you can always be sure there's a soft spot in him somewhere."

Nils thought of his own father, and smiled. "She brought him a good deal of money, didn't she, besides the Bohemian vote?"

Mrs. Ericson sniffed. "Well, she has a fair half section in her own name, but I can't see as that does Olaf much good. She will have a good deal of property some day, if old Vavrika don't marry again. But I don't consider a saloonkeeper's money as good as other people's money."

Nils laughed outright. "Come, Mother, don't let your prejudices carry you that far. Money's money. Old Vavrika's a mighty decent sort of saloonkeeper. Nothing rowdy about him."

Mrs. Ericson spoke up angrily: "Oh, I know you always stood up for them! But hanging around there when you were a boy never did you any good, Nils, nor any of the other boys who went there. There weren't so many after her when she married Olaf, let me tell you. She knew enough to grab her chance."

Nils settled back in his seat. "Of course I liked to go there, Mother, and you were always cross about it. You never took the trouble to find out that it was the one jolly house in this country for a boy to go to. All the rest of you were working yourselves to death, and the houses were mostly a mess, full of babies and washing and flies. Oh, it was all right—I understand that; but you are young only once, and I happened to be young then. Now, Vavrika's was always jolly. He played the violin, and I used to take my flute, and Clara played the piano, and Johanna used to sing Bohemian songs. She always had a big supper for us—herrings and pickles and poppy-seed bread, and lots of cake and preserves. Old Joe had been in the army in the old country, and he could tell lots of good stories. I can see him cutting bread, at the head of the table, now. I don't know what I'd have done when I was a kid if it hadn't been for the Vavrikas, really."

"And all the time he was taking money that other people had worked hard in the fields for," Mrs. Ericson observed.

"So do the circuses, Mother, and they're a good thing. People ought to get fun for some of their money. Even father liked old Joe."

"Your father," Mrs. Ericson said grimly, "liked everybody."

As they crossed the sand creek and turned into her own place, Mrs. Ericson observed, "There's Olaf's buggy. He's stopped on his way from town." Nils shook himself and prepared to greet his brother, who was waiting on the porch.

Olaf was a big, heavy Norwegian, slow of speech and movement. His head was large and square, like a block of wood. When Nils, at a distance, tried to remember what his brother looked like, he could recall only his heavy head, high forehead, large nostrils, and pale blue eyes, set far apart. Olaf's features were rudimentary: the thing one noticed was the face itself, wide and flat and pale, devoid of any expression, betraying his fifty years as little as it betrayed anything else, and powerful by reason of its very stolidness. When Olaf shook hands with Nils he looked at him from under his light eyebrows, but Nils felt that no one could ever say what that pale look might mean. The one thing he had always felt in Olaf was a heavy stubbornness, like the unyielding stickiness of wet loam against the plow. He had always found Olaf the most difficult of his brothers.

"How do you do, Nils? Expect to stay with us long?"

"Oh, I may stay forever," Nils answered gaily. "I like this country better than I used to."

"There's been some work put into it since you left," Olaf remarked.

"Exactly. I think it's about ready to live in now—and I'm about ready to settle down." Nils saw his brother lower his big head. ("Exactly like a bull," he thought.) "Mother's been persuading me to slow down now, and go in for farming," he went on lightly.

Olaf made a deep sound in his throat. "Farming ain't learned in a day," he brought out, still looking at the ground.

"Oh, I know! But I pick things up quickly." Nils had not meant to antagonize his brother, and he did not know now why he was doing it. "Of course," he went on, "I shouldn't expect to make a big success, as you fellows have done. But then, I'm not ambitious. I won't want much. A little land, and some cattle, maybe."

Olaf still stared at the ground, his head down. He wanted to ask Nils what he had been doing all these years, that he didn't have a business somewhere he couldn't afford to leave; why he hadn't more pride than to come back with only a little sole-leather trunk to show for himself, and to present himself as the only failure in the family. He did not ask one of these questions, but he made them all felt distinctly.

"Humph!" Nils thought. "No wonder the man never talks, when he can butt his ideas into you like that without ever saying a word. I suppose he used that kind of smokeless powder on his wife all the time. But I guess she has her innings." He chuckled, and Olaf looked up. "Never mind me, Olaf. I laugh without knowing why, like little Eric. He's another cheerful dog."

"Eric," said Olaf slowly, "is a spoiled kid. He's just let his mother's best cow go dry because he don't milk her right. I was hoping you'd take him away somewhere and put him into business. If he don't do any good among strangers, he never will." This was a long speech for Olaf, and as he finished it he climbed into his buggy.

Nils shrugged his shoulders. "Same old tricks," he thought. "Hits from behind you every time. What a whale of a man!" He turned and went round to the kitchen, where his mother was scolding little Eric for letting the gasoline get low.

I V

JOE VAVRIKA'S SALOON was not in the county seat, where Olaf and Mrs. Ericson did their trading, but in a cheerfuller place, a little Bohemian settlement which lay at the other end of the county, ten level miles north of Olaf's farm. Clara rode up to see her father almost every day. Vavrika's house was, so to speak, in the back yard of his saloon. The garden between the two buildings was inclosed

by a high board fence as tight as a partition, and in summer Joe kept
beer tables and wooden benches among the gooseberry bushes under his little cherry tree. At one of these tables Nils Ericson was
seated in the late afternoon, three days after his return home. Joe
had gone in to serve a customer, and Nils was lounging on his
elbows, looking rather mournfully into his half-emptied pitcher,
when he heard a laugh across the little garden. Clara, in her riding
habit, was standing at the back door of the house, under the grape-
vine trellis that old Joe had grown there long ago. Nils rose.

"Come out and keep your father and me company. We've been
gossiping all afternoon. Nobody to bother us but the flies."

She shook her head. "No, I never come out here any more. Olaf
doesn't like it. I must live up to my position, you know."

"You mean to tell me you never come out and chat with the
boys, as you used to? He *has* tamed you! Who keeps up these flower
beds?"

"I come out on Sundays, when father is alone, and read the
Bohemian papers to him. But I am never here when the bar is open.
What have you two been doing?"

"Talking, as I told you. I've been telling him about my travels. I
find I can't talk much at home, not even to Eric."

Clara reached up and poked with her riding-whip at a white
moth that was fluttering in the sunlight among the vine leaves. "I
suppose you will never tell me about all those things."

"Where can I tell them? Not in Olaf's house, certainly. What's
the matter with our talking here?" He pointed persuasively with his
hat to the bushes and the green table, where the flies were singing
lazily above the empty beer glasses.

Clara shook her head weakly. "No, it wouldn't do. Besides, I
am going now."

"I'm on Eric's mare. Would you be angry if I overtook you?"

Clara looked back and laughed. "You might try and see. I can
leave you if I don't want you. Eric's mare can't keep up with
Norman."

Nils went into the bar and attempted to pay his score. Big Joe, six feet four, with curly yellow hair and mustache, clapped him on the shoulder. "Not a God-damn a your money go in my drawer, you hear? Only next time you bring your flute, te-te-te-te-te-ty." Joe wagged his fingers in imitation of the flute player's position. "My Clara, she come all-a-time Sundays an' play for me. She not like to play at Ericson's place." He shook his yellow curls and laughed. "Not a God-damn a fun at Ericson's. You come a Sunday. You like-a fun. No forget de flute." Joe talked very rapidly and always tumbled over his English. He seldom spoke it to his customers, and had never learned much.

Nils swung himself into the saddle and trotted to the west end of the village, where the houses and gardens scattered into prairie land and the road turned south. Far ahead of him, in the declining light, he saw Clara Vavrika's slender figure, loitering on horseback. He touched his mare with the whip, and shot along the white, level road, under the reddening sky. When he overtook Olaf's wife he saw that she had been crying. "What's the matter, Clara Vavrika?" he asked kindly.

"Oh, I get blue sometimes. It was awfully jolly living there with father. I wonder why I ever went away."

Nils spoke in a low, kind tone that he sometimes used with women: "That's what I've been wondering these many years. You were the last girl in the country I'd have picked for a wife for Olaf. What made you do it, Clara?"

"I suppose I really did it to oblige the neighbors"—Clara tossed her head. "People were beginning to wonder."

"To wonder?"

"Yes—why I didn't get married. I suppose I didn't like to keep them in suspense. I've discovered that most girls marry out of consideration for the neighborhood."

Nils bent his head toward her and his white teeth flashed. "I'd have gambled that one girl I knew would say, 'Let the neighborhood be damned.' "

Clara shook her head mournfully. "You see, they have it on you, Nils; that is, if you're a woman. They say you're beginning to go off. That's what makes us get married: we can't stand the laugh."

Nils looked sidewise at her. He had never seen her head droop before. Resignation was the last thing he would have expected of her. "In your case, there wasn't something else?"

"Something else?"

"I mean, you didn't do it to spite somebody? Somebody who didn't come back?"

Clara drew herself up. "Oh, I never thought you'd come back. Not after I stopped writing to you, at least. *That* was all over, long before I married Olaf."

"It never occurred to you, then, that the meanest thing you could do to me was to marry Olaf?"

Clara laughed. "No; I didn't know you were so fond of Olaf."

Nils smoothed his horse's mane with his glove. "You know, Clara Vavrika, you are never going to stick it out. You'll cut away some day, and I've been thinking you might as well cut away with me."

Clara threw up her chin. "Oh, you don't know me as well as you think. I won't cut away. Sometimes, when I'm with father, I feel like it. But I can hold out as long as the Ericsons can. They've never got the best of me yet, and one can live, so long as one isn't beaten. If I go back to father, it's all up with Olaf in politics. He knows that, and he never goes much beyond sulking. I've as much wit as the Ericsons. I'll never leave them unless I can show them a thing or two."

"You mean unless you can come it over them?"

"Yes—unless I go away with a man who is cleverer than they are, and who has more money."

Nils whistled. "Dear me, you are demanding a good deal. The Ericsons, take the lot of them, are a bunch to beat. But I should think the excitement of tormenting them would have worn off by this time."

"It has, I'm afraid," Clara admitted mournfully.

"Then why don't you cut away? There are more amusing games than this in the world. When I came home I thought it might amuse me to bully a few quarter sections out of the Ericsons; but I've almost decided I can get more fun for my money somewhere else."

Clara took in her breath sharply. "Ah, you have got the other will! That was why you came home!"

"No, it wasn't. I came home to see how you were getting on with Olaf."

Clara struck her horse with the whip, and in a bound she was far ahead of him. Nils dropped one word, "Damn!" and whipped after her; but she leaned forward in her saddle and fairly cut the wind. Her long riding skirt rippled in the still air behind her. The sun was just sinking behind the stubble in a vast, clear sky, and the shadows drew across the fields so rapidly that Nils could scarcely keep in sight the dark figure on the road. When he overtook her he caught her horse by the bridle. Norman reared, and Nils was frightened for her; but Clara kept her seat.

"Let me go, Nils Ericson!" she cried. "I hate you more than any of them. You were created to torture me, the whole tribe of you—to make me suffer in every possible way."

She struck her horse again and galloped away from him. Nils set his teeth and looked thoughtful. He rode slowly home along the deserted road, watching the stars come out in the clear violet sky. They flashed softly into the limpid heavens, like jewels let fall into clear water. They were a reproach, he felt, to a sordid world. As he turned across the sand creek, he looked up at the North Star and smiled, as if there were an understanding between them. His mother scolded him for being late for supper.

V

ON SUNDAY AFTERNOON Joe Vavrika, in his shirtsleeves and carpet slippers, was sitting in his garden, smoking a long-tasseled porcelain pipe with a hunting scene painted on the bowl. Clara sat under the cherry tree, reading aloud to him from the weekly Bohemian papers. She had worn a white muslin dress under her riding habit, and the leaves of the cherry tree threw a pattern of sharp shadows over her skirt. The black cat was dozing in the sunlight at her feet, and Joe's dachshund was scratching a hole under the scarlet geraniums and dreaming of badgers. Joe was filling his pipe for the third time since dinner, when he heard a knocking on the fence. He broke into a loud guffaw and unlatched the little door that led into the street. He did not call Nils by name, but caught him by the hand and dragged him in. Clara stiffened and the color deepened under her dark skin. Nils, too, felt a little awkward. He had not seen her since the night when she rode away from him and left him alone on the level road between the fields. Joe dragged him to the wooden bench beside the green table.

"You bring de flute," he cried, tapping the leather case under Nils' arm. "Ah, das-a good! Now we have some liddle fun like old times. I got somet'ing good for you." Joe shook his finger at Nils and winked his blue eye, a bright clear eye, full of fire, though the tiny bloodvessels on the ball were always a little distended. "I got somet'ing for you from"—he paused and waved his hand—"Hongarie. You know Hongarie? You wait!" He pushed Nils down on the bench, and went through the back door of his saloon.

Nils looked at Clara, who sat frigidly with her white skirts drawn tight about her. "He didn't tell you he had asked me to come, did he? He wanted a party and proceeded to arrange it. Isn't he fun? Don't be cross; let's give him a good time."

Clara smiled and shook out her skirt. "Isn't that like father? And he has sat here so meekly all day. Well, I won't pout. I'm glad you came. He doesn't have very many good times now any more. There are so few of his kind left. The second generation are a tame lot."

Joe came back with a flask in one hand and three wine glasses caught by the stems between the fingers of the other. These he placed on the table with an air of ceremony, and going behind Nils, held the flask between him and the sun, squinting into it admiringly. "You know dis, Tokai? A great friend of mine, he bring dis to me, a present out of Hongarie. You know how much it cost, dis wine? Chust so much what it weigh in gold. Nobody but de nobles drink him in Bohemie. Many, many years I save him up, dis Tokai." Joe whipped out his official corkscrew and delicately removed the cork. "De old man die what bring him to me, an' dis wine he lay on his belly in my cellar an' sleep. An' now," carefully pouring out the heavy yellow wine, "an' now he wake up; and maybe he wake us up, too!" He carried one of the glasses to his daughter and presented it with great gallantry.

Clara shook her head, but seeing her father's disappointment, relented. "You taste it first. I don't want so much."

Joe sampled it with a beatific expression, and turned to Nils. "You drink him slow, dis wine. He very soft, but he go down hot. You see!"

After a second glass Nils declared that he couldn't take any more without getting sleepy. "Now get your fiddle, Vavrika," he said as he opened his flute case.

But Joe settled back in his wooden rocker and wagged his big carpet slipper. "No-no-no-no-no-no-no! No play fiddle now any more: too much ache in de finger," waving them, "all-a-time rheumatiz. You play de flute, te-tety-te-tety-te. Bohemie songs."

"I've forgotten all the Bohemian songs I used to play with you and Johanna. But here's one that will make Clara pout. You remember how her eyes used to snap when we called her the Bohemian Girl?" Nils lifted his flute and began "When Other Lips and Other Hearts," and Joe hummed the air in a husky baritone, waving his carpet slipper. "Oh-h-h, das-a fine music," he cried, clapping his hands as Nils finished. "Now 'Marble Halls, Marble Halls'! Clara, you sing him."

Clara smiled and leaned back in her chair, beginning softly:

> *"I dreamt that I dwelt in ma-a-arble halls,*
> *With vassals and serfs at my knee,"*

and Joe hummed like a big bumblebee.

"There's one more you always played," Clara said quietly: "I remember that best." She locked her hands over her knee and began "The Heart Bowed Down," and sang it through without groping for the words. She was singing with a good deal of warmth when she came to the end of the old song:

> *"For memory is the only friend*
> *That grief can call its own."*

Joe flashed out his red silk handkerchief and blew his nose, shaking his head. "No-no-no-no-no-no-no! Too sad, too sad! I not like-a dat. Play quick somet'ing gay now."

Nils put his lips to the instrument, and Joe lay back in his chair, laughing and singing, "Oh, Evelina, Sweet Evelina!" Clara laughed, too. Long ago, when she and Nils went to high school, the model student of their class was a very homely girl in thick spectacles. Her name was Evelina Oleson; she had a long, swinging walk which somehow suggested the measure of that song, and they used mercilessly to sing it at her.

"Dat ugly Oleson girl, she teach in de school," Joe gasped, "an' she still walk chust like dat, yup-a, yup-a, yup-a, chust like a camel she go! Now, Nils, we have some more li'l drink. Oh, yes-yes-yes-yes-yes-yes-*yes!* Dis time you haf to drink, and Clara she haf to, so she show she not jealous. So, we all drink to your girl. You not tell her name, eh? No-no-no, I no make you tell. She pretty, eh? She make good sweetheart? I bet!" Joe winked and lifted his glass. "How soon you get married?"

Nils screwed up his eyes. "That I don't know. When she says."

Joe threw out his chest. "Das-a way boys talks. No way for mans. Mans say, 'You come to de church, an' get a hurry on you.' Das-a way mans talks."

"Maybe Nils hasn't got enough to keep a wife," put in Clara ironically. "How about that, Nils?" she asked him frankly, as if she wanted to know.

Nils looked at her coolly, raising one eyebrow. "Oh, I can keep her, all right."

"The way she wants to be kept?"

"With my wife, I'll decide that," replied Nils calmly. "I'll give her what's good for her."

Clara made a wry face. "You'll give her the strap, I expect, like old Peter Oleson gave his wife."

"When she needs it," said Nils lazily, locking his hands behind his head and squinting up through the leaves of the cherry tree. "Do you remember the time I squeezed the cherries all over your clean dress, and Aunt Johanna boxed my ears for me? My gracious, weren't you mad! You had both hands full of cherries, and I squeezed 'em and made the juice fly all over you. I liked to have fun with you; you'd get so mad."

"We *did* have fun, didn't we? None of the other kids ever had so much fun. We knew how to play."

Nils dropped his elbows on the table and looked steadily across at her. "I've played with lots of girls since, but I haven't found one who was such good fun."

Clara laughed. The late afternoon sun was shining full in her face, and deep in the back of her eyes there shone something fiery, like the yellow drops of Tokai in the brown glass bottle. "Can you still play, or are you only pretending?"

"I can play better than I used to, and harder."

"Don't you ever work, then?" She had not intended to say it. It slipped out because she was confused enough to say just the wrong thing.

"I work between times." Nils' steady gaze still beat upon her. "Don't you worry about my working, Mrs. Ericson. You're getting like all the rest of them." He reached his brown, warm hand across the table and dropped it on Clara's, which was cold as an icicle. "Last call for play, Mrs. Ericson!" Clara shivered, and suddenly her hands and cheeks grew warm. Her fingers lingered in his a moment, and they looked at each other earnestly. Joe Vavrika had put the mouth of the bottle to his lips and was swallowing the last drops of the Tokai, standing. The sun, just about to sink behind his shop, glistened on the bright glass, on his flushed face and curly yellow hair. "Look," Clara whispered; "that's the way I want to grow old."

VI

ON THE DAY of Olaf Ericson's barn-raising, his wife, for once in a way, rose early. Johanna Vavrika had been baking cakes and frying and boiling and spicing meats for a week beforehand, but it was not until the day before the party was to take place that Clara showed any interest in it. Then she was seized with one of her fitful spasms of energy, and took the wagon and little Eric and spent the day on Plum Creek, gathering vines and swamp goldenrod to decorate the barn.

By four o'clock in the afternoon buggies and wagons began to arrive at the big unpainted building in front of Olaf's house. When Nils and his mother came at five, there were more than fifty people in the barn, and a great drove of children. On the ground floor stood six long tables, set with the crockery of seven flourishing Ericson families, lent for the occasion. In the middle of each table was a big yellow pumpkin, hollowed out and filled with woodbine.

In one corner of the barn, behind a pile of green-and-white-striped watermelons, was a circle of chairs for the old people: the younger guests sat on bushel measures or barbed-wire spools, and the children tumbled about in the haymow. The box stalls Clara had converted into booths. The framework was hidden by goldenrod and sheaves of wheat, and the partitions were covered with wild grape-vines full of fruit. At one of these Johanna Vavrika watched over her cooked meats, enough to provision an army; and at the next her kitchen girls had ranged the ice-cream freezers, and Clara was already cutting pies and cakes against the hour of serving. At the third stall, little Hilda, in a bright pink lawn dress, dispensed lemonade throughout the afternoon. Olaf, as a public man, had thought it inadvisable to serve beer in his barn; but Joe Vavrika had come over with two demijohns concealed in his buggy, and after his arrival the wagon shed was much frequented by the men.

"Hasn't Cousin Clara fixed things lovely?" little Hilda whispered, when Nils went up to her stall and asked for lemonade.

Nils leaned against the booth, talking to the excited little girl and watching the people. The barn faced the west, and the sun, pouring in at the big doors, filled the whole interior with a golden light, through which filtered fine particles of dust from the haymow, where the children were romping. There was a great chattering from the stall where Johanna Vavrika exhibited to the admiring women her platters heaped with fried chicken, her roasts of beef, boiled tongues, and baked hams with cloves stuck in the crisp brown fat and garnished with tansy and parsley. The older women, having assured themselves that there were twenty kinds of cake, not counting cookies, and three dozen fat pies, repaired to the corner behind the pile of watermelons, put on their white aprons, and fell to their knitting and fancywork. They were a fine company of old women, and a Dutch painter would have loved to find them there together, where the sun made bright patches on the floor and sent long, quivering shafts of gold through the dusky shade up among the rafters. There were fat, rosy old women who looked hot in their

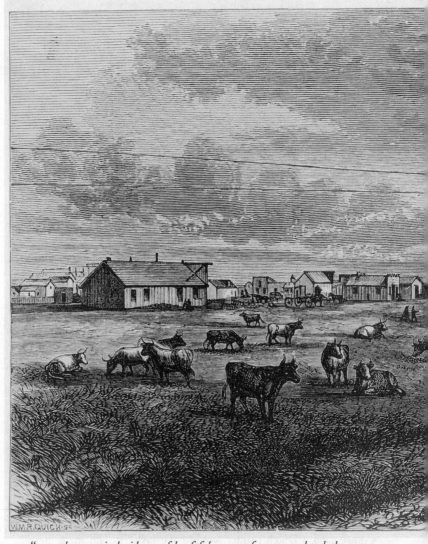

". . . she was seized with one of her fitful spasms of energy, and took the wagon and little Eric and spent the day on Plum Creek, gathering vines and swamp goldenrod to decorate the barn." —"The Bohemian Girl" (This rendering of the village of Plum Creek dates from 1875.)

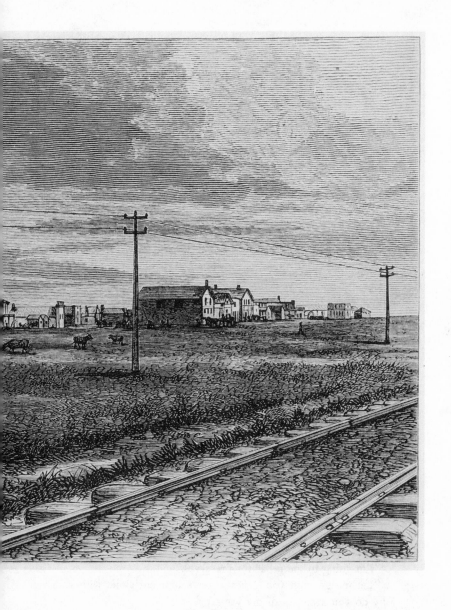

best black dresses; spare, alert old women with brown, dark-veined hands; and several of almost heroic frame, not less massive than old Mrs. Ericson herself. Few of them wore glasses, and old Mrs. Svendsen, a Danish woman, who was quite bald, wore the only cap among them. Mrs. Oleson, who had twelve big grandchildren, could still show two braids of yellow hair as thick as her own wrists. Among all these grandmothers there were more brown heads than white. They all had a pleased, prosperous air, as if they were more than satisfied with themselves and with life. Nils, leaning against Hilda's lemonade stand, watched them as they sat chattering in four languages, their fingers never lagging behind their tongues.

"Look at them over there," he whispered, detaining Clara as she passed him. "Aren't they the Old Guard? I've just counted thirty hands. I guess they've wrung many a chicken's neck and warmed many a boy's jacket for him in their time."

In reality he fell into amazement when he thought of the Herculean labors those fifteen pairs of hands had performed: of the cows they had milked, the butter they had made, the gardens they had planted, the children and grandchildren they had tended, the brooms they had worn out, the mountains of food they had cooked. It made him dizzy. Clara Vavrika smiled a hard, enigmatical smile at him and walked rapidly away. Nils' eyes followed her white figure as she went toward the house. He watched her walking alone in the sunlight, looked at her slender, defiant shoulders and her little hard-set head with its coils of blue-black hair. "No," he reflected; "she'd never be like them, not if she lived here a hundred years. She'd only grow more bitter. You can't tame a wild thing; you can only chain it. People aren't all alike. I mustn't lose my nerve." He gave Hilda's pigtail a parting tweak and set out after Clara. "Where to?" he asked, as he came upon her in the kitchen.

"I'm going to the cellar for preserves."

"Let me go with you. I never get a moment alone with you. Why do you keep out of my way?"

Clara laughed. "I don't usually get in anybody's way."

Nils followed her down the stairs and to the far corner of the cellar, where a basement window let in a stream of light. From a swinging shelf Clara selected several glass jars, each labeled in Johanna's careful hand. Nils took up a brown flask. "What's this? It looks good."

"It is. It's some French brandy father gave me when I was married. Would you like some? Have you a corkscrew? I'll get glasses."

When she brought them, Nils took them from her and put them down on the window sill. "Clara Vavrika, do you remember how crazy I used to be about you?"

Clara shrugged her shoulders. "Boys are always crazy about somebody or other. I dare say some silly has been crazy about Evelina Oleson. You got over it in a hurry."

"Because I didn't come back, you mean? I had to get on, you know, and it was hard sledding at first. Then I heard you'd married Olaf."

"And then you stayed away from a broken heart," Clara laughed.

"And then I began to think about you more than I had since I first went away. I began to wonder if you were really as you had seemed to me when I was a boy. I thought I'd like to see. I've had lots of girls, but no one ever pulled me the same way. The more I thought about you, the more I remembered how it used to be—like hearing a wild tune you can't resist, calling you out at night. It had been a long while since anything had pulled me out of my boots, and I wondered whether anything ever could again." Nils thrust his hands into his coat pockets and squared his shoulders, as his mother sometimes squared hers, as Olaf, in a clumsier manner, squared his. "So I thought I'd come back and see. Of course the family have tried to do me, and I rather thought I'd bring out father's will and make a fuss. But they can have their old land; they've put enough sweat into it." He took the flask and filled the two glasses carefully to the brim. "I've found out what I want from the Ericsons. Drink *skoal*, Clara." He lifted his glass, and Clara took hers with downcast eyes. "Look at me, Clara Vavrika. *Skoal!*"

She raised her burning eyes and answered fiercely: *"Skoal!"*

The barn supper began at six o'clock and lasted for two hilarious hours. Yense Nelson had made a wager that he could eat two whole fried chickens, and he did. Eli Swanson stowed away two whole custard pies, and Nick Hermanson ate a chocolate layer cake to the last crumb. There was even a cooky contest among the children, and one thin, slablike Bohemian boy consumed sixteen and won the prize, a gingerbread pig which Johanna Vavrika had carefully decorated with red candies and burnt sugar. Fritz Sweiheart, the German carpenter, won in the pickle contest, but he disappeared soon after supper and was not seen for the rest of the evening. Joe Vavrika said that Fritz could have managed the pickles all right, but he had sampled the demijohn in his buggy too often before sitting down to the table.

While the supper was being cleared away the two fiddlers began to tune up for the dance. Clara was to accompany them on her old upright piano, which had been brought down from her father's. By this time Nils had renewed old acquaintances. Since his interview with Clara in the cellar, he had been busy telling all the old women how young they looked, and all the young ones how pretty they were, and assuring the men that they had here the best farmland in the world. He had made himself so agreeable that old Mrs. Ericson's friends began to come up to her and tell how lucky she was to get her smart son back again, and please to get him to play his flute. Joe Vavrika, who could still play very well when he forgot that he had rheumatism, caught up a fiddle from Johnny Oleson and played a crazy Bohemian dance tune that set the wheels going. When he dropped the bow every one was ready to dance.

Olaf, in a frock coat and a solemn made-up necktie, led the grand march with his mother. Clara had kept well out of *that* by sticking to the piano. She played the march with a pompous solemnity which greatly amused the prodigal son, who went over and stood behind her.

"Oh, aren't you rubbing it into them, Clara Vavrika? And aren't you lucky to have me here, or all your wit would be thrown away."

"I'm used to being witty for myself. It saves my life."

The fiddles struck up a polka, and Nils convulsed Joe Vavrika by leading out Evelina Oleson, the homely schoolteacher. His next partner was a very fat Swedish girl, who, although she was an heiress, had not been asked for the first dance, but had stood against the wall in her tight, high-heeled shoes, nervously fingering a lace handkerchief. She was soon out of breath, so Nils led her, pleased and panting, to her seat, and went over to the piano, from which Clara had been watching his gallantry. "Ask Olena Yenson," she whispered. "She waltzes beautifully."

Olena, too, was rather inconveniently plump, handsome in a smooth, heavy way, with a fine color and good-natured, sleepy eyes. She was redolent of violet sachet powder, and had warm, soft, white hands, but she danced divinely, moving as smoothly as the tide coming in. "There, that's something like," Nils said as he released her. "You'll give me the next waltz, won't you? Now I must go and dance with my little cousin."

Hilda was greatly excited when Nils went up to her stall and held out his arm. Her little eyes sparkled, but she declared that she could not leave her lemonade. Old Mrs. Ericson, who happened along at this moment, said she would attend to that, and Hilda came out, as pink as her pink dress. The dance was a schottische, and in a moment her yellow braids were fairly standing on end. "Bravo!" Nils cried encouragingly. "Where did you learn to dance so nicely?"

"My Cousin Clara taught me," the little girl panted.

Nils found Eric sitting with a group of boys who were too awkward or too shy to dance, and told him that he must dance the next waltz with Hilda.

The boy screwed up his shoulders. "Aw, Nils, I can't dance. My feet are too big; I look silly."

"Don't be thinking about yourself. It doesn't matter how boys look."

Nils had never spoken to him so sharply before, and Eric made haste to scramble out of his corner and brush the straw from his coat.

Clara nodded approvingly. "Good for you, Nils. I've been trying to get hold of him. They dance very nicely together; I sometimes play for them."

"I'm obliged to you for teaching him. There's no reason why he should grow up to be a lout."

"He'll never be that. He's more like you than any of them. Only he hasn't your courage." From her slanting eyes Clara shot forth one of those keen glances, admiring and at the same time challenging, which she seldom bestowed on any one, and which seemed to say, "Yes, I admire you, but I am your equal."

Clara was proving a much better host than Olaf, who, once the supper was over, seemed to feel no interest in anything but the lanterns. He had brought a locomotive headlight from town to light the revels, and he kept skulking about it as if he feared the mere light from it might set his new barn on fire. His wife, on the contrary, was cordial to every one, was animated and even gay. The deep salmon color in her cheeks burned vividly, and her eyes were full of life. She gave the piano over to the fat Swedish heiress, pulled her father away from the corner where he sat gossiping with his cronies, and made him dance a Bohemian dance with her. In his youth Joe had been a famous dancer, and his daughter got him so limbered up that every one sat round and applauded them. The old ladies were particularly delighted, and made them go through the dance again. From their corner where they watched and commented, the old women kept time with their feet and hands, and whenever the fiddles struck up a new air old Mrs. Svendsen's white cap would begin to bob.

Clara was waltzing with little Eric when Nils came up to them, brushed his brother aside, and swung her out among the dancers. "Remember how we used to waltz on rollers at the old skating rink in town? I suppose people don't do that any more. We used to keep it up for hours. You know, we never did moon around as other boys and girls did. It was dead serious with us from the beginning. When we were most in love with each other, we used to fight. You were always pinching people; your fingers were like little nippers. A regular snapping turtle, you were. Lord, how you'd like Stockholm! Sit out in the streets in front of cafés and talk all night in summer. Just like a reception—officers and ladies and funny English people. Jolliest people in the world, the Swedes, once you get them going. Always drinking things—champagne and stout mixed, half-and-half; serve it out of big pitchers, and serve plenty. Slow pulse, you know; they can stand a lot. Once they light up, they're glowworms, I can tell you."

"All the same, you don't really like gay people."

"*I* don't?"

"No; I could see that when you were looking at the old women there this afternoon. They're the kind you really admire, after all; women like your mother. And that's the kind you'll marry."

"Is it, Miss Wisdom? You'll see who I'll marry, and she won't have a domestic virtue to bless herself with. She'll be a snapping turtle, and she'll be a match for me. All the same, they're a fine bunch of old dames over there. You admire them yourself."

"No, I don't; I detest them."

"You won't, when you look back on them from Stockholm or Budapest. Freedom settles all that. Oh, but you're the real Bohemian Girl, Clara Vavrika!" Nils laughed down at her sullen frown and began mockingly to sing:

> "*Oh, how could a poor gypsy maiden like me*
> *Expect the proud bride of a baron to be?*"

Clara clutched his shoulder. "Hush, Nils; every one is looking at you."

"I don't care. They can't gossip. It's all in the family, as the Ericsons say when they divide up little Hilda's patrimony amongst them. Besides, we'll give them something to talk about when we hit the trail. Lord, it will be a godsend to them! They haven't had anything so interesting to chatter about since the grasshopper year. It'll give them a new lease of life. And Olaf won't lose the Bohemian vote, either. They'll have the laugh on him so that they'll vote two apiece. They'll send him to Congress. They'll never forget his barn party, or us. They'll always remember us as we're dancing together now. We're making a legend. Where's my waltz, boys?" he called as they whirled past the fiddlers.

The musicians grinned, looked at each other, hesitated, and began a new air; and Nils sang with them, as the couples fell from a quick waltz to a long, slow glide:

> *"When other lips and other hearts*
> *Their tale of love shall tell,*
> *In language whose excess imparts*
> *The power they feel so well."*

The old women applauded vigorously. "What a gay one he is, that Nils!" And old Mrs. Svendsen's cap lurched dreamily from side to side to the following measure of the dance.

> *"Of days that have as ha-a-p-py been,*
> *And you'll remember me."*

VII

THE MOONLIGHT flooded that great, silent land. The reaped fields lay yellow in it. The straw stacks and poplar windbreaks threw sharp black shadows. The roads were white rivers of dust. The sky was a deep, crystalline blue, and the stars were few and faint. Everything seemed to have succumbed, to have sunk to sleep, under the great, golden, tender, midsummer moon. The splendor of it seemed to transcend human life and human fate. The senses were too feeble to take it in, and every time one looked up at the sky one felt unequal to it, as if one were sitting deaf under the waves of a great river of melody. Near the road, Nils Ericson was lying against a straw stack in Olaf's wheat field. His own life seemed strange and unfamiliar to him, as if it were something he had read about, or dreamed, and forgotten. He lay very still, watching the white road that ran in front of him, lost itself among the fields, and then, at a distance, reappeared over a little hill. At last, against this white band he saw something moving rapidly, and he got up and walked to the edge of the field. "She is passing the row of poplars now," he thought. He heard the padded beat of hoofs along the dusty road, and as she came into sight he stepped out and waved his arms. Then, for fear of frightening the horse, he drew back and waited. Clara had seen him, and she came up at a walk. Nils took the horse by the bit and stroked his neck.

"What are you doing out so late, Clara Vavrika? I went to the house, but Johanna told me you had gone to your father's."

"Who can stay in the house on a night like this? Aren't you out yourself?"

"Ah, but that's another matter."

Nils turned the horse into the field.

"What are you doing. Where are you taking Norman?"

"Not far, but I want to talk to you tonight; I have something to say to you. I can't talk to you at the house, with Olaf sitting there on the porch, weighing a thousand tons."

Clara laughed. "He won't be sitting there now. He's in bed by this time, and asleep—weighing a thousand tons."

Nils plodded on across the stubble. "Are you really going to spend the rest of your life like this, night after night, summer after summer? Haven't you anything better to do on a night like this than to wear yourself and Norman out tearing across the country to your father's and back? Besides, your father won't live forever, you know. His little place will be shut up or sold, and then you'll have nobody but the Ericsons. You'll have to fasten down the hatches for the winter then."

Clara moved her head restlessly. "Don't talk about that. I try never to think of it. If I lost father I'd lose everything, even my hold over the Ericsons."

"Bah! You'd lose a good deal more than that. You'd lose your race, everything that makes you yourself. You've lost a good deal of it now."

"Of what?"

"Of your love of life, your capacity for delight."

Clara put her hands up to her face. "I haven't, Nils Ericson, I haven't! Say anything to me but that. I won't have it!" she declared vehemently.

Nils led the horse up to a straw stack, and turned to Clara, looking at her intently, as he had looked at her that Sunday afternoon at Vavrika's. "But why do you fight for that so? What good is the power to enjoy, if you never enjoy? Your hands are cold again; what are you afraid of all the time? Ah, you're afraid of losing it; that's what's the matter with you! And you will, Clara Vavrika, you will! When I used to know you—listen; you've caught a wild bird in your hand, haven't you, and felt its heart beat so hard that you were afraid it would shatter its little body to pieces? Well, you used to be just like that, a slender, eager thing with a wild delight inside you. That is how I remembered you. And I come back and find you—a bitter woman. This is a perfect ferret fight here; you live by biting and being bitten. Can't you remember what life used to be?

Can't you remember that old delight? I've never forgotten it, or known its like, on land or sea."

He drew the horse under the shadow of the straw stack. Clara felt him take her foot out of the stirrup, and she slid softly down into his arms. He kissed her slowly. He was a deliberate man, but his nerves were steel when he wanted anything. Something flashed out from him like a knife out of a sheath. Clara felt everything slipping away from her; she was flooded by the summer night. He thrust his hand into his pocket, and then held it out at arm's length. "Look," he said. The shadow of the straw stack fell sharp across his wrist, and in the palm of his hand she saw a silver dollar shining. "That's my pile," he muttered; "will you go with me?"

Clara nodded, and dropped her forehead on his shoulder.

Nils took a deep breath. "Will you go with me tonight?"

"Where?" she whispered softly.

"To town, to catch the midnight flyer."

Clara lifted her head and pulled herself together. "Are you crazy, Nils? We couldn't go away like that."

"That's the only way we ever will go. You can't sit on the bank and think about it. You have to plunge. That's the way I've always done, and it's the right way for people like you and me. There's nothing so dangerous as sitting still. You've only got one life, one youth, and you can let it slip through your fingers if you want to; nothing easier. Most people do that. You'd be better off tramping the roads with me than you are here." Nils held back her head and looked into her eyes. "But I'm not that kind of a tramp, Clara. You won't have to take in sewing. I'm with a Norwegian shipping line; came over on business with the New York offices, but now I'm going straight back to Bergen. I expect I've got as much money as the Ericsons. Father sent me a little to get started. They never knew about that. There, I hadn't meant to tell you; I wanted you to come on your own nerve."

Clara looked off across the fields. "It isn't that, Nils, but some-

"Clara looked off across the fields. 'It isn't that, Nils, but something seems to hold me. I'm afraid to pull against it. It comes out of the ground, I think." —"The Bohemian Girl"

thing seems to hold me. I'm afraid to pull against it. It comes out of the ground, I think."

"I know all about that. One has to tear loose. You're not needed here. Your father will understand; he's made like us. As for Olaf, Johanna will take better care of him than ever you could. It's now or never, Clara Vavrika. My bag's at the station; I smuggled it there yesterday."

Clara clung to him and hid her face against his shoulder. "Not tonight," she whispered. "Sit here and talk to me tonight. I don't want to go anywhere tonight. I may never love you like this again."

Nils laughed through his teeth. "You can't come that on me. That's not my way, Clara Vavrika. Eric's mare is over there behind the stacks, and I'm off on the midnight. It's goodbye, or off across the world with me. My carriage won't wait. I've written a letter to Olaf; I'll mail it in town. When he reads it he won't bother us—not if I know him. He'd rather have the land. Besides, I could demand an investigation of his administration of Cousin Henrik's estate, and

that would be bad for a public man. You've no clothes, I know; but you can sit up tonight, and we can get everything on the way. Where's your old dash, Clara Vavrika? What's become of your Bohemian blood? I used to think you had courage enough for anything. Where's your nerve—what are you waiting for?"

Clara drew back her head, and he saw the slumberous fire in her eyes. "For you to say one thing, Nils Ericson."

"I never say that thing to any woman, Clara Vavrika." He leaned back, lifted her gently from the ground, and whispered through his teeth: "But I'll never, never let you go, not to any man on earth but me! Do you understand me? Now, wait here."

Clara sank down on a sheaf of wheat and covered her face with her hands. She did not know what she was going to do—whether she would go or stay. The great, silent country seemed to lay a spell upon her. The ground seemed to hold her as if by roots. Her knees were soft under her. She felt as if she could not bear separation from her old sorrows, from her old discontent. They were dear to her, they had kept her alive, they were a part of her. There would be nothing left of her if she were wrenched away from them. Never could she pass beyond that skyline against which her restlessness had beat so many times. She felt as if her soul had built itself a nest there on that horizon at which she looked every morning and every evening, and it was dear to her, inexpressibly dear. She pressed her fingers against her eyeballs to shut it out. Beside her she heard the tramping of horses in the soft earth. Nils said nothing to her. He put his hands under her arms and lifted her lightly to her saddle. Then he swung himself into his own.

"We shall have to ride fast to catch the midnight train. A last gallop, Clara Vavrika. Forward!"

There was a start, a thud of hoofs along the moonlit road, two dark shadows going over the hill; and then the great, still land stretched untroubled under the azure night. Two shadows had passed.

VIII

A YEAR after the flight of Olaf Ericson's wife, the night train was steaming across the plains of Iowa. The conductor was hurrying through one of the day coaches, his lantern on his arm, when a lank, fair-haired boy sat up in one of the plush seats and tweaked him by the coat.

"What is the next stop, please, sir?"

"Red Oak, Iowa. But you go through to Chicago, don't you?" He looked down, and noticed that the boy's eyes were red and his face was drawn, as if he were in trouble.

"Yes. But I was wondering whether I could get off at the next place and get a train back to Omaha."

"Well, I suppose you could. Live in Omaha?"

"No. In the western part of the State. How soon do we get to Red Oak?"

"Forty minutes. You'd better make up your mind, so I can tell the baggageman to put your trunk off."

"Oh, never mind about that! I mean, I haven't got any," the boy added, blushing.

"Run away," the conductor thought, as he slammed the coach door behind him.

Eric Ericson crumpled down in his seat and put his brown hand to his forehead. He had been crying, and he had had no supper, and his head was aching violently. "Oh, what shall I do?" he thought, as he looked dully down at his big shoes. "Nils will be ashamed of me; I haven't got any spunk."

Ever since Nils had run away with his brother's wife, life at home had been hard for little Eric. His mother and Olaf both suspected him of complicity. Mrs. Ericson was harsh and faultfinding, constantly wounding the boy's pride; and Olaf was always setting her against him.

Joe Vavrika heard often from his daughter. Clara had always been fond of her father, and happiness made her kinder. She wrote him long accounts of the voyage to Bergen, and of the trip she and Nils took through Bohemia to the little town where her father had grown up and where she herself was born. She visited all her kinsmen there, and sent her father news of his brother, who was a priest; of his sister, who had married a horsebreeder—of their big farm and their many children. These letters Joe always managed to read to little Eric. They contained messages for Eric and Hilda. Clara sent presents, too, which Eric never dared to take home and which poor little Hilda never even saw, though she loved to hear Eric tell about them when they were out getting the eggs together. But Olaf once saw Eric coming out of Vavrika's house—the old man had never asked the boy to come into his saloon—and Olaf went straight to his mother and told her. That night Mrs. Ericson came to Eric's room after he was in bed and made a terrible scene. She could be very terrifying when she was really angry. She forbade him ever to speak to Vavrika again, and after that night she would not allow him to go to town alone. So it was a long while before Eric got any more news of his brother. But old Joe suspected what was going on, and he carried Clara's letters about in his pocket. One Sunday he drove out to see a German friend of his, and chanced to catch sight of Eric, sitting by the cattle pond in the big pasture. They went together into Fritz Oberlies' barn, and read the letters and talked things over. Eric admitted that things were getting hard for him at home. That very night old Joe sat down and laboriously penned a statement of the case to his daughter.

Things got no better for Eric. His mother and Olaf felt that, however closely he was watched, he still, as they said, "heard." Mrs. Ericson could not admit neutrality. She had sent Johanna Vavrika packing back to her brother's, though Olaf would much rather have kept her than Anders' eldest daughter, whom Mrs. Ericson installed in her place. He was not so highhanded as his mother, and he once sulkily told her that she might better have taught her granddaughter to cook before she sent Johanna away. Olaf could have borne a good deal for the sake of prunes spiced in honey, the secret of which Johanna had taken away with her.

At last two letters came to Joe Vavrika: one from Nils, inclosing a postal order for money to pay Eric's passage to Bergen, and one from Clara, saying that Nils had a place for Eric in the offices of his company, that he was to live with them, and that they were only waiting for him to come. He was to leave New York on one of the boats of Nils' own line; the captain was one of their friends, and Eric was to make himself known at once.

Nils' directions were so explicit that a baby could have followed them, Eric felt. And here he was, nearing Red Oak, Iowa, and rocking backward and forward in despair. Never had he loved his brother so much, and never had the big world called to him so hard. But there was a lump in his throat which would not go down. Ever since nightfall he had been tormented by the thought of his mother, alone in that big house that had sent forth so many men. Her unkindness now seemed so little, and her loneliness so great. He remembered everything she had ever done for him: how frightened she had been when he tore his hand in the cornsheller, and how she wouldn't let Olaf scold him. When Nils went away he didn't leave his mother all alone, or he would never have gone. Eric felt sure of that.

The train whistled. The conductor came in, smiling not unkindly. "Well, young man, what are you going to do? We stop at Red Oak in three minutes."

"Yes, thank you. I'll let you know." The conductor went out, and the boy doubled up with misery. He couldn't let his one chance go like this. He felt for his breast pocket and crackled Nils' kind letter to give him courage. He didn't want Nils to be ashamed of him. The train stopped. Suddenly he remembered his brother's kind, twinkling eyes, that always looked at you as if from far away. The lump in his throat softened. "Ah, but Nils, Nils would *understand!*" he thought. "That's just it about Nils; he always understands."

A lank, pale boy with a canvas telescope stumbled off the train to the Red Oak siding, just as the conductor called, "All aboard!"

The next night Mrs. Ericson was sitting alone in her wooden rocking chair on the front porch. Little Hilda had been sent to bed and had cried herself to sleep. The old woman's knitting was in her lap, but her hands lay motionless on top of it. For more than an hour she had not moved a muscle. She simply sat, as only the Ericsons and the mountains can sit. The house was dark, and there was no sound but the croaking of the frogs down in the pond of the little pasture.

Eric did not come home by the road, but across the fields, where no one could see him. He set his telescope down softly in the kitchen shed, and slipped noiselessly along the path to the front porch. He sat down on the step without saying anything. Mrs. Ericson made no sign, and the frogs croaked on. At last the boy spoke timidly.

"I've come back, Mother."

"Very well," said Mrs. Ericson.

"Eric did not come home by the road, but across the fields, where no one could see him." —"The Bohemian Girl"

Eric leaned over and picked up a little stick out of the grass.

"How about the milking?" he faltered.

"That's been done, hours ago."

"Who did you get?"

"Get? I did it myself. I can milk as good as any of you."

Eric slid along the step near to her. "Oh, Mother, why did you?" he asked sorrowfully. "Why didn't you get one of Otto's boys?"

"I didn't want anybody to know I was in need of a boy," said Mrs. Ericson bitterly. She looked straight in front of her and her mouth tightened. "I always meant to give you the home farm," she added.

The boy started and slid closer. "Oh, Mother," he faltered, "I don't care about the farm. I came back because I thought you might be needing me, maybe." He hung his head and got no further.

"Very well," said Mrs. Ericson. Her hand went out from her suddenly and rested on his head. Her fingers twined themselves in his soft, pale hair. His tears splashed down on the boards; happiness filled his heart.

O PIONEERS!

To the memory of
SARAH ORNE JEWETT
in whose beautiful and delicate work
there is the perfection
that endures

Those fields, colored by various grain!
—MICKIEWICZ

PRAIRIE SPRING

Evening and the flat land,
Rich and sombre and always silent;
The miles of fresh-plowed soil,
Heavy and black, full of strength and harshness;
The growing wheat, the growing weeds,
The toiling horses, the tired men;
The long empty roads,
Sullen fires of sunset, fading,
The eternal, unresponsive sky.
Against all this, Youth,
Flaming like the wild roses,
Singing like the larks over the plowed fields,
Flashing like a star out of the twilight;
Youth with its insupportable sweetness,
Its fierce necessity,
Its sharp desire,
Singing and singing,
Out of the lips of silence,
Out of the earthy dusk.

PART ONE

———

THE WILD LAND

"A pioneer should have imagination, should be able to enjoy the idea of things more than the things themselves." —O Pioneers!

I

ONE JANUARY DAY, thirty years ago, the little town of Hanover, anchored on a windy Nebraska tableland, was trying not to be blown away. A mist of fine snowflakes was curling and eddying about the cluster of low drab buildings huddled on the gray prairie, under a gray sky. The dwelling-houses were set about haphazard on the tough prairie sod; some of them looked as if they had been moved in overnight, and others as if they were straying off by themselves, headed straight for the open plain. None of them had any appearance of permanence, and the howling wind blew under them as well as over them. The main street was a deeply rutted road, now frozen hard, which ran from the squat red railway station and the grain "elevator" at the north end of the town to the lumber yard and the horse pond at the south end. On either side of this road straggled two uneven rows of wooden buildings; the general merchandise stores, the two banks, the drug store, the feed store, the saloon, the post-office. The board sidewalks were gray with trampled snow, but at two o'clock in the afternoon the shopkeepers, having come back from dinner, were keeping well behind their frosty windows. The children were all in school, and there was nobody abroad in the streets but a few rough-looking countrymen in coarse overcoats, with their long caps pulled down to their noses. Some of them had brought their wives to town, and now and then a red or a plaid shawl flashed out of one store into the shelter of another. At the hitch-bars along the street a few heavy work-horses, harnessed to farm wagons, shivered under their blankets. About the station everything was quiet, for there would not be another train in until night.

On the sidewalk in front of one of the stores sat a little Swede boy, crying bitterly. He was about five years old. His black cloth coat was much too big for him and made him look like a little old man. His shrunken brown flannel dress had been washed many times and left a long stretch of stocking between the hem of his skirt and the tops of his clumsy, copper-toed shoes. His cap was pulled down over his ears; his nose and his chubby cheeks were chapped and red with cold. He cried quietly, and the few people who hurried by did not notice him. He was afraid to stop any one, afraid to go into the store and ask for help, so he sat wringing his long sleeves and looking up a telegraph pole beside him, whimpering, "My kitten, oh, my kitten! Her will fweeze!" At the top of the pole crouched a shivering gray kitten, mewing faintly and clinging desperately to the wood with her claws. The boy had been left at the store while his sister went to the doctor's office, and in her absence a dog had chased his kitten up the pole. The little creature had never been so high before, and she was too frightened to move. Her master was sunk in despair. He was a little country boy, and this village was to him a very strange and perplexing place, where people wore fine clothes and had hard hearts. He always felt shy and awkward here, and wanted to hide behind things for fear some one might laugh at him. Just now, he was too unhappy to care who laughed. At last he seemed to see a ray of hope: his sister was coming, and he got up and ran toward her in his heavy shoes.

His sister was a tall, strong girl, and she walked rapidly and resolutely, as if she knew exactly where she was going and what she was going to do next. She wore a man's long ulster (not as if it were an affliction, but as if it were very comfortable and belonged to her; carried it like a young soldier), and a round plush cap, tied down with a thick veil. She had a serious, thoughtful face, and her clear, deep blue eyes were fixed intently on the distance, without seeming to see anything, as if she were in trouble. She did not notice the little boy until he pulled her by the coat. Then she stopped short and stooped down to wipe his wet face.

"Why, Emil! I told you to stay in the store and not to come out. What is the matter with you?"

"My kitten, sister, my kitten! A man put her out, and a dog chased her up there." His forefinger, projecting from the sleeve of his coat, pointed up to the wretched little creature on the pole.

"Oh, Emil! Didn't I tell you she'd get us into trouble of some kind, if you brought her? What made you tease me so? But there, I ought to have known better myself." She went to the foot of the pole and held out her arms, crying, "Kitty, kitty, kitty," but the kitten only mewed and faintly waved its tail. Alexandra turned away decidedly. "No, she won't come down. Somebody will have to go up after her. I saw the Linstrums' wagon in town. I'll go and see if I can find Carl. Maybe he can do something. Only you must stop crying, or I won't go a step. Where's your comforter? Did you leave it in the store? Never mind. Hold still, till I put this on you."

She unwound the brown veil from her head and tied it about his throat. A shabby little traveling man, who was just then coming out of the store on his way to the saloon, stopped and gazed stupidly at the shining mass of hair she bared when she took off her veil; two thick braids, pinned about her head in the German way, with a fringe of reddish-yellow curls blowing out from under her cap. He took his cigar out of his mouth and held the wet end between the fingers of his woolen glove. "My God, girl, what a head of hair!" he exclaimed, quite innocently and foolishly. She stabbed him with a glance of Amazonian fierceness and drew in her lower lip—most unnecessary severity. It gave the little clothing drummer such a start that he actually let his cigar fall to the sidewalk and went off weakly in the teeth of the wind to the saloon. His hand was still unsteady when he took his glass from the bartender. His feeble flirtatious instincts had been crushed before, but never so mercilessly. He felt cheap and ill-used, as if some one had taken advantage of him. When a drummer had been knocking about in little drab towns and crawling across the wintry country in dirty smoking-cars, was he to be blamed if, when he chanced upon a fine human creature, he suddenly wished himself more of a man?

While the little drummer was drinking to recover his nerve, Alexandra hurried to the drug store as the most likely place to find Carl Linstrum. There he was, turning over a portfolio of chromo "studies" which the druggist sold to the Hanover women who did china-painting. Alexandra explained her predicament, and the boy followed her to the corner, where Emil still sat by the pole.

"I'll have to go up after her, Alexandra. I think at the depot they have some spikes I can strap on my feet. Wait a minute." Carl thrust his hands into his pockets, lowered his head, and darted up the street against the north wind. He was a tall boy of fifteen, slight and narrow-chested. When he came back with the spikes, Alexandra asked him what he had done with his overcoat.

"I left it in the drug store. I couldn't climb in it, anyhow. Catch me if I fall, Emil," he called back as he began his ascent. Alexandra watched him anxiously; the cold was bitter enough on the ground. The kitten would not budge an inch. Carl had to go to the very top of the pole, and then had some difficulty in tearing her from her hold. When he reached the ground, he handed the cat to her tearful little master. "Now go into the store with her, Emil, and get warm." He opened the door for the child. "Wait a minute, Alexandra. Why can't I drive for you as far as our place? It's getting colder every minute. Have you seen the doctor?"

"Yes. He is coming over to-morrow. But he says father can't get better; can't get well." The girl's lip trembled. She looked fixedly up the bleak street as if she were gathering her strength to face something, as if she were trying with all her might to grasp a situation which, no matter how painful, must be met and dealt with somehow. The wind flapped the skirts of her heavy coat about her.

Carl did not say anything, but she felt his sympathy. He, too, was lonely. He was a thin, frail boy, with brooding dark eyes, very quiet in all his movements. There was a delicate pallor in his thin face, and his mouth was too sensitive for a boy's. The lips had already a little curl of bitterness and skepticism. The two friends stood for a few moments on the windy street corner, not speaking a word, as two travelers, who have lost their way, sometimes stand and admit their perplexity in silence. When Carl turned away he said, "I'll see to your team." Alexandra went into the store to have her purchases packed in the egg-boxes, and to get warm before she set out on her long cold drive.

When she looked for Emil, she found him sitting on a step of the staircase that led up to the clothing and carpet department. He was playing with a little Bohemian girl, Marie Tovesky, who was tying her handkerchief over the kitten's head for a bonnet. Marie was a stranger in the country, having come from Omaha with her mother to visit her uncle, Joe Tovesky. She was a dark child, with brown curly hair, like a brunette doll's, a coaxing little red mouth, and round, yellow-brown eyes. Every one noticed her eyes; the brown iris had golden glints that made them look like gold-stone, or, in softer lights, like that Colorado mineral called tiger-eye.

The country children thereabouts wore their dresses to their shoe-tops, but this city child was dressed in what was then called the "Kate Greenaway" manner, and her red cashmere frock, gathered full from the yoke, came almost to the floor. This, with her poke bonnet, gave her the look of a quaint little woman. She had a white fur tippet about her neck and made no fussy objections when Emil fingered it admiringly. Alexandra had not the heart to take him away from so pretty a playfellow, and she let them tease the kitten together until Joe Tovesky came in noisily and picked up his little niece, setting her on his shoulder for every one to see. His children were all boys, and he adored this little creature. His cronies formed a circle about him, admiring and teasing the little girl, who took their jokes with great good nature. They were all delighted with her, for they seldom saw so pretty and carefully nurtured a child. They told her that she must choose one of them for a sweetheart, and each began pressing his suit and offering her bribes: candy, and little pigs, and spotted calves. She looked archly into the big, brown, mustached faces, smelling of spirits and tobacco, then she ran her tiny forefinger delicately over Joe's bristly chin and said, "Here is my sweetheart."

The Bohemians roared with laughter, and Marie's uncle hugged her until she cried, "Please don't, Uncle Joe! You hurt me." Each of Joe's friends gave her a bag of candy, and she kissed them all around, though she did not like country candy very well. Perhaps that was why she bethought herself of Emil. "Let me down, Uncle Joe," she said, "I want to give some of my candy to that nice little boy I found." She walked graciously over to Emil, followed by her lusty admirers, who formed a new circle and teased the little boy until he hid his face in his sister's skirts, and she had to scold him for being such a baby.

The farm people were making preparations to start for home. The women were checking over their groceries and pinning their big red shawls about their heads. The men were buying tobacco and candy with what money they had left, were showing each other new boots and gloves and blue flannel shirts. Three big Bohemians were drinking raw alcohol, tinctured with oil of cinnamon. This was said to fortify one effectually against the cold, and they smacked their lips after each pull at the flask. Their volubility drowned every other noise in the place, and the overheated store sounded of their spirited language as it reeked of pipe smoke, damp woolens, and kerosene.

Carl came in, wearing his overcoat and carrying a wooden box with a brass handle. "Come," he said, "I've fed and watered your team, and the wagon is ready." He carried Emil out and tucked him down in the straw in the wagon-box. The heat had made the little boy sleepy, but he still clung to his kitten.

"You were awful good to climb so high and get my kitten, Carl. When I get big I'll climb and get little boys' kittens for them," he murmured drowsily. Before the horses were over the first hill, Emil and his cat were both fast asleep.

Although it was only four o'clock, the winter day was fading. The road led southwest, toward the streak of pale, watery light that glimmered in the leaden sky. The light fell upon the two sad young faces that were turned mutely toward it: upon the eyes of the girl, who seemed to be looking with such anguished perplexity into the future; upon the sombre eyes of the boy, who seemed already to be looking into the past. The little town behind them had vanished as if it had never been, had fallen behind the swell of the prairie, and the stern frozen country received them into its bosom. The homesteads were few and far apart; here and there a windmill gaunt against the sky, a sod house crouching in a hollow. But the great fact was the land itself, which seemed to overwhelm the little beginnings of human society that struggled in its sombre wastes. It was from facing this vast hardness that the boy's mouth had become so bitter; because he felt that men were too weak to make any mark here, that the land wanted to be let alone, to preserve its own fierce strength, its peculiar, savage kind of beauty, its uninterrupted mournfulness.

The wagon jolted along over the frozen road. The two friends had less to say to each other than usual, as if the cold had somehow penetrated to their hearts.

"Did Lou and Oscar go to the Blue to cut wood today?" Carl asked.

"Yes. I'm almost sorry I let them go, it's turned so cold. But mother frets if the wood gets low." She stopped and put her hand to her forehead, brushing back her hair. "I don't know what is to become of us, Carl, if father has to die. I don't dare to think about it. I wish we could all go with him and let the grass grow back over everything."

Carl made no reply. Just ahead of them was the Norwegian graveyard, where the grass had, indeed, grown back over everything, shaggy and red, hiding even the wire fence. Carl realized that he was not a very helpful companion, but there was nothing he could say.

"Of course," Alexandra went on, steadying her voice a little, "the boys are strong and work hard, but we've always depended so on father that I don't see how we can go ahead. I almost feel as if there were nothing to go ahead for."

"Does your father know?"

"Yes, I think he does. He lies and counts on his fingers all day. I think he is trying to count up what he is leaving for us. It's a comfort to him that my chickens are laying right on through the cold weather and bringing in a little money. I wish we could keep his mind off such things, but I don't have much time to be with him now."

"I wonder if he'd like to have me bring my magic lantern over some evening?"

Alexandra turned her face toward him. "Oh, Carl! Have you got it?"

"Yes. It's back there in the straw. Didn't you notice the box I was carrying? I tried it all morning in the drug-store cellar, and it worked ever so well, makes fine big pictures."

"What are they about?"

"Oh, hunting pictures in Germany, and Robinson Crusoe and funny pictures about cannibals. I'm going to paint some slides for it on glass, out of the Hans Andersen book."

Alexandra seemed actually cheered. There is often a good deal of the child left in people who have had to grow up too soon. "Do bring it over, Carl. I can hardly wait to see it, and I'm sure it will please father. Are the pictures colored? Then I know he'll like them. He likes the calendars I get him in town. I wish I could get more. You must leave me here, mustn't you? It's been nice to have company."

Carl stopped the horses and looked dubiously up at the black sky. "It's pretty dark. Of course the horses will take you home, but I think I'd better light your lantern, in case you should need it."

He gave her the reins and climbed back into the wagon-box, where he crouched down and made a tent of his overcoat. After a dozen trials he succeeded in lighting the lantern, which he placed in front of Alexandra, half covering it with a blanket so that the light would not shine in her eyes. "Now, wait until I find my box. Yes, here it is. Good-night, Alexandra. Try not to worry." Carl sprang to the ground and ran off across the fields toward the Linstrum homestead. "Hoo, hoo-o-o-o!" he called back as he disappeared over a ridge and dropped into a sand gully. The wind answered him like an echo, "Hoo, hoo-o-o-o-o-o!" Alexandra drove off alone. The rattle of her wagon was lost in the howling of the wind, but her lantern, held firmly between her feet, made a moving point of light along the highway, going deeper and deeper into the dark country.

I I

ON ONE of the ridges of that wintry waste stood the low log house in which John Bergson was dying. The Bergson homestead was easier to find than many another, because it overlooked Norway Creek, a shallow, muddy stream that sometimes flowed, and sometimes stood still, at the bottom of a winding ravine with steep, shelving sides overgrown with brush and cottonwoods and dwarf ash. This creek gave a sort of identity to the farms that bordered upon it. Of all the bewildering things about a new country, the absence of human landmarks is one of the most depressing and disheartening. The houses on the Divide were small and were usually tucked away in low places; you did not see them until you came directly upon them. Most of them were built of the sod itself, and were only the unescapable ground in another form. The roads were but faint tracks in the grass, and the fields were scarcely noticeable. The record of the plow was insignificant, like the feeble scratches on stone left by prehistoric races, so indeterminate that they may, after all, be only the markings of glaciers, and not a record of human strivings.

In eleven long years John Bergson had made but little impression upon the wild land he had come to tame. It was still a wild thing that had its ugly moods; and no one knew when they were likely to come, or why. Mischance hung over it. Its Genius was unfriendly to man. The sick man was feeling this as he lay looking out of the window, after the doctor had left him, on the day following Alexandra's trip to town. There it lay outside his door, the same land, the same lead-colored miles. He knew every ridge and draw and gully between him and the horizon. To the south, his plowed fields; to the east, the sod stables, the cattle corral, the pond,—and then the grass.

Bergson went over in his mind the things that had held him back. One winter his cattle had perished in a blizzard. The next summer one of his plow horses broke its leg in a prairie-dog hole and had to be shot. Another summer he lost his hogs from cholera, and a valuable stallion died from a rattlesnake bite. Time and again his crops had failed. He had lost two children, boys, that came between Lou and Emil, and there had been the cost of sickness and death. Now, when he had at last struggled out of debt, he was going to die himself. He was only forty-six, and had, of course, counted upon more time.

Bergson had spent his first five years on the Divide getting into debt, and the last six getting out. He had paid off his mortgages and had ended pretty much where he began, with the land. He owned exactly six hundred and forty acres of what stretched outside his door; his own original homestead and timber claim, making three hundred and twenty acres, and the half-section adjoining, the homestead of a younger brother who had given up the fight, gone back to Chicago to work in a fancy bakery and distinguish himself in a Swedish athletic club. So far John had not attempted to cultivate the second half-section, but used it for pasture land, and one of his sons rode herd there in open weather.

John Bergson had the Old-World belief that land, in itself, is desirable. But this land was an enigma. It was like a horse that no one knows how to break to harness, that runs wild and kicks things to pieces. He had an idea that no one understood how to farm it

properly, and this he often discussed with Alexandra. Their neighbors, certainly, knew even less about farming than he did. Many of
them had never worked on a farm until they took up their homesteads. They had been *handwerkers* at home; tailors, locksmiths,
joiners, cigar-makers, etc. Bergson himself had worked in a ship-
yard.

For weeks, John Bergson had been thinking about these things.
His bed stood in the sitting-room, next to the kitchen. Through the
day, while the baking and washing and ironing were going on, the
father lay and looked up at the roof beams that he himself had
hewn, or out at the cattle in the corral. He counted the cattle over
and over. It diverted him to speculate as to how much weight each
of the steers would probably put on by spring. He often called his
daughter in to talk to her about this. Before Alexandra was twelve
years old she had begun to be a help to him, and as she grew older
he had come to depend more and more upon her resourcefulness
and good judgment. His boys were willing enough to work, but
when he talked with them they usually irritated him. It was Alexandra who read the papers and followed the markets, and who learned
by the mistakes of their neighbors. It was Alexandra who could
always tell about what it had cost to fatten each steer, and who
could guess the weight of a hog before it went on the scales closer
than John Bergson himself. Lou and Oscar were industrious, but he
could never teach them to use their heads about their work.

Alexandra, her father often said to himself, was like her grandfather; which was his way of saying that she was intelligent. John
Bergson's father had been a shipbuilder, a man of considerable force
and of some fortune. Late in life he married a second time, a Stockholm woman of questionable character, much younger than he, who
goaded him into every sort of extravagance. On the shipbuilder's
part, this marriage was an infatuation, the despairing folly of a
powerful man who cannot bear to grow old. In a few years his
unprincipled wife warped the probity of a lifetime. He speculated,
lost his own fortune and funds entrusted to him by poor seafaring

men, and died disgraced, leaving his children nothing. But when all was said, he had come up from the sea himself, had built up a proud little business with no capital but his own skill and foresight, and had proved himself a man. In his daughter, John Bergson recognized the strength of will, and the simple direct way of thinking things out, that had characterized his father in his better days. He would much rather, of course, have seen this likeness in one of his sons, but it was not a question of choice. As he lay there day after day he had to accept the situation as it was, and to be thankful that there was one among his children to whom he could entrust the future of his family and the possibilities of his hard-won land.

The winter twilight was fading. The sick man heard his wife strike a match in the kitchen, and the light of a lamp glimmered through the cracks of the door. It seemed like a light shining far away. He turned painfully in his bed and looked at his white hands, with all the work gone out of them. He was ready to give up, he felt. He did not know how it had come about, but he was quite willing to go deep under his fields and rest, where the plow could not find him. He was tired of making mistakes. He was content to leave the tangle to other hands; he thought of his Alexandra's strong ones.

"Dotter," he called feebly, *"dotter!"* He heard her quick step and saw her tall figure appear in the doorway, with the light of the lamp behind her. He felt her youth and strength, how easily she moved and stooped and lifted. But he would not have had it again if he could, not he! He knew the end too well to wish to begin again. He knew where it all went to, what it all became.

His daughter came and lifted him up on his pillows. She called him by an old Swedish name that she used to call him when she was little and took his dinner to him in the shipyard.

"Tell the boys to come here, daughter. I want to speak to them."

"They are feeding the horses, father. They have just come back from the Blue. Shall I call them?"

He sighed. "No, no. Wait until they come in. Alexandra, you will have to do the best you can for your brothers. Everything will come on you."

"I will do all I can, father."

"Don't let them get discouraged and go off like Uncle Otto. I want them to keep the land."

"We will, father. We will never lose the land."

There was a sound of heavy feet in the kitchen. Alexandra went to the door and beckoned to her brothers, two strapping boys of seventeen and nineteen. They came in and stood at the foot of the bed. Their father looked at them searchingly, though it was too dark to see their faces; they were just the same boys, he told himself, he had not been mistaken in them. The square head and heavy shoulders belonged to Oscar, the elder. The younger boy was quicker, but vacillating.

"Boys," said the father wearily, "I want you to keep the land together and to be guided by your sister. I have talked to her since I have been sick, and she knows all my wishes. I want no quarrels among my children, and so long as there is one house there must be one head. Alexandra is the oldest, and she knows my wishes. She will do the best she can. If she makes mistakes, she will not make so many as I have made. When you marry, and want a house of your own, the land will be divided fairly, according to the courts. But for the next few years you will have it hard, and you must all keep together. Alexandra will manage the best she can."

Oscar, who was usually the last to speak, replied because he was the older, "Yes, father. It would be so anyway, without your speaking. We will all work the place together."

"And you will be guided by your sister, boys, and be good brothers to her, and good sons to your mother? That is good. And Alexandra must not work in the fields any more. There is no necessity now. Hire a man when you need help. She can make much more with her eggs and butter than the wages of a man. It was one of my mistakes that I did not find that out sooner. Try to break a little more land every year; sod corn is good for fodder. Keep turning the land, and always put up more hay than you need. Don't grudge your mother a little time for plowing her garden and setting out fruit trees, even if it comes in a busy season. She has been a good mother to you, and she has always missed the old country."

When they went back to the kitchen the boys sat down silently at the table. Throughout the meal they looked down at their plates and did not lift their red eyes. They did not eat much, although they had been working in the cold all day, and there was a rabbit stewed in gravy for supper, and prune pies.

John Bergson had married beneath him, but he had married a good housewife. Mrs. Bergson was a fair-skinned, corpulent woman, heavy and placid like her son, Oscar, but there was something comfortable about her; perhaps it was her own love of comfort. For eleven years she had worthily striven to maintain some semblance of household order amid conditions that made order very difficult. Habit was very strong with Mrs. Bergson, and her unremitting efforts to repeat the routine of her old life among new surroundings had done a great deal to keep the family from disintegrating morally and getting careless in their ways. The Bergsons had a log house, for instance, only because Mrs. Bergson would not live in a sod house. She missed the fish diet of her own country, and twice every summer she sent the boys to the river, twenty miles to the southward, to fish for channel cat. When the children were little she used to load them all into the wagon, the baby in its crib, and go fishing herself.

Alexandra often said that if her mother were cast upon a desert island, she would thank God for her deliverance, make a garden, and find something to preserve. Preserving was almost a mania with Mrs. Bergson. Stout as she was, she roamed the scrubby banks of Norway Creek looking for fox grapes and goose plums, like a wild creature in search of prey. She made a yellow jam of the insipid ground-cherries that grew on the prairie, flavoring it with lemon peel; and she made a sticky dark conserve of garden tomatoes. She had experimented even with the rank buffalo-pea, and she could not see a fine bronze cluster of them without shaking her head and murmuring, "What a pity!" When there was nothing more to preserve, she began to pickle. The amount of sugar she used in these processes was sometimes a serious drain upon the family resources. She was a good mother, but she was glad when her children were old enough not to be in her way in the kitchen. She had never quite forgiven John Bergson for bringing her to the end of the earth; but, now that she was there, she wanted to be let alone to reconstruct her old life insofar as that was possible. She could still take some comfort in the world if she had bacon in the cave, glass jars on the shelves, and sheets in the press. She disapproved of all her neighbors because of their slovenly housekeeping, and the women thought her very proud. Once when Mrs. Bergson, on her way to Norway Creek, stopped to see old Mrs. Lee, the old woman hid in the haymow "for fear Mis' Bergson would catch her barefoot."

III

ONE SUNDAY AFTERNOON in July, six months after John Bergson's death, Carl was sitting in the doorway of the Linstrum kitchen, dreaming over an illustrated paper, when he heard the rattle of a wagon along the hill road. Looking up he recognized the Bergsons' team, with two seats in the wagon, which meant they were off for a pleasure excursion. Oscar and Lou, on the front seat, wore their cloth hats and coats, never worn except on Sundays, and Emil, on the second seat with Alexandra, sat proudly in his new trousers, made from a pair of his father's, and a pink-striped shirt, with a wide ruffled collar. Oscar stopped the horses and waved to Carl, who caught up his hat and ran through the melon patch to join them.

"Want to go with us?" Lou called. "We're going to Crazy Ivar's to buy a hammock."

"Sure." Carl ran up panting, and clambering over the wheel sat down beside Emil. "I've always wanted to see Ivar's pond. They say it's the biggest in all the country. Aren't you afraid to go to Ivar's in that new shirt, Emil? He might want it and take it right off your back."

Emil grinned. "I'd be awful scared to go," he admitted, "if you big boys weren't along to take care of me. Did you ever hear him howl, Carl? People say sometimes he runs about the country howling at night because he is afraid the Lord will destroy him. Mother thinks he must have done something awful wicked."

Lou looked back and winked at Carl. "What would you do, Emil, if you was out on the prairie by yourself and seen him coming?"

Emil stared. "Maybe I could hide in a badger-hole," he suggested doubtfully.

"But suppose there wasn't any badger-hole," Lou persisted. "Would you run?"

"No, I'd be too scared to run," Emil admitted mournfully, twisting his fingers. "I guess I'd sit right down on the ground and say my prayers."

The big boys laughed, and Oscar brandished his whip over the broad backs of the horses.

"He wouldn't hurt you, Emil," said Carl persuasively. "He came to doctor our mare when she ate green corn and swelled up most as big as the water-tank. He petted her just like you do your cats. I couldn't understand much he said, for he don't talk any English, but he kept patting her and groaning as if he had the pain himself, and saying, 'There now, sister, that's easier, that's better!' "

Lou and Oscar laughed, and Emil giggled delightedly and looked up at his sister.

"I don't think he knows anything at all about doctoring," said Oscar scornfully. "They say when horses have distemper he takes the medicine himself, and then prays over the horses."

Alexandra spoke up. "That's what the Crows said, but he cured their horses, all the same. Some days his mind is cloudy, like. But if you can get him on a clear day, you can learn a great deal from him. He understands animals. Didn't I see him take the horn off the Berquist's cow when she had torn it loose and went crazy? She was tearing all over the place, knocking herself against things. And at last she ran out on the roof of the old dugout and her legs went through and there she stuck, bellowing. Ivar came running with his white bag, and the moment he got to her she was quiet and let him saw her horn off and daub the place with tar."

Emil had been watching his sister, his face reflecting the sufferings of the cow. "And then didn't it hurt her any more?" he asked.

Alexandra patted him. "No, not any more. And in two days they could use her milk again."

The road to Ivar's homestead was a very poor one. He had settled in the rough country across the county line, where no one lived but some Russians,—half a dozen families who dwelt together in one long house, divided off like barracks. Ivar had explained his choice by saying that the fewer neighbors he had, the fewer temptations. Nevertheless, when one considered that his chief business was horse-doctoring, it seemed rather short-sighted of him to live in the most inaccessible place he could find. The Bergson wagon lurched along over the rough hummocks and grass banks, followed the bottom of winding draws, or skirted the margin of wide lagoons, where the golden coreopsis grew up out of the clear water and the wild ducks rose with a whirr of wings.

Lou looked after them helplessly. "I wish I'd brought my gun, anyway, Alexandra," he said fretfully. "I could have hidden it under the straw in the bottom of the wagon."

"Then we'd have had to lie to Ivar. Besides, they say he can smell dead birds. And if he knew, we wouldn't get anything out of him, not even a hammock. I want to talk to him, and he won't talk sense if he's angry. It makes him foolish."

Lou sniffed. "Whoever heard of him talking sense, anyhow! I'd rather have ducks for supper than Crazy Ivar's tongue."

Emil was alarmed. "Oh, but, Lou, you don't want to make him mad! He might howl!"

They all laughed again, and Oscar urged the horses up the crumbling side of a clay bank. They had left the lagoons and the red grass behind them. In Crazy Ivar's country the grass was short and gray, the draws deeper than they were in the Bergsons' neighborhood, and the land was all broken up into hillocks and clay ridges. The wild flowers disappeared, and only in the bottom of the draws and gullies grew a few of the very toughest and hardiest: shoestring, and ironweed, and snow-on-the-mountain.

"Look, look, Emil, there's Ivar's big pond!" Alexandra pointed to a shining sheet of water that lay at the bottom of a shallow draw. At one end of the pond was an earthen dam, planted with green willow bushes, and above it a door and a single window were set into the hillside. You would not have seen them at all but for the reflection of the sunlight upon the four panes of window-glass. And that was all you saw. Not a shed, not a corral, not a well, not even a path broken in the curly grass. But for the piece of rusty stovepipe sticking up through the sod, you could have walked over the roof of Ivar's dwelling without dreaming that you were near a human habitation. Ivar had lived for three years in the clay bank, without defiling the face of nature any more than the coyote that had lived there before him had done.

When the Bergsons drove over the hill, Ivar was sitting in the doorway of his house, reading the Norwegian Bible. He was a queerly shaped old man, with a thick, powerful body set on short bow-legs. His shaggy white hair, falling in a thick mane about his ruddy cheeks, made him look older than he was. He was barefoot, but he wore a clean shirt of unbleached cotton, open at the neck. He always put on a clean shirt when Sunday morning came round, though he never went to church. He had a peculiar religion of his own and could not get on with any of the denominations. Often he did not see anybody from one week's end to another. He kept a calendar, and every morning he checked off a day, so that he was never in any doubt as to which day of the week it was. Ivar hired himself out in threshing and corn-husking time, and he doctored sick animals when he was sent for. When he was at home, he made hammocks out of twine and committed chapters of the Bible to memory.

Ivar found contentment in the solitude he had sought out for himself. He disliked the litter of human dwellings: the broken food, the bits of broken china, the old wash-boilers and tea-kettles thrown into the sunflower patch. He preferred the cleanness and tidiness of the wild sod. He always said that the badgers had cleaner houses than people, and that when he took a housekeeper her name would be Mrs. Badger. He best expressed his preference for his wild homestead by saying that his Bible seemed truer to him there. If one stood in the doorway of his cave, and looked off at the rough land, the smiling sky, the curly grass white in the hot sunlight; if one listened to the rapturous song of the lark, the drumming of the quail, the burr of the locust against that vast silence, one understood what Ivar meant.

On this Sunday afternoon his face shone with happiness. He closed the book on his knee, keeping the place with his horny finger, and repeated softly:—

> *"He sendeth the springs into the valleys, which run*
> *among the hills;*
> *They give drink to every beast of the field; the wild*
> *asses quench their thirst.*
> *The trees of the Lord are full of sap; the cedars of*
> *Lebanon which he hath planted;*
> *Where the birds make their nests: as for the stork,*
> *the fir trees are her house.*
> *The high hills are a refuge for the wild goats; and the*
> *rocks for the conies."*

Before he opened his Bible again, Ivar heard the Bergsons' wagon approaching, and he sprang up and ran toward it.

"No guns, no guns!" he shouted, waving his arms distractedly.

"No, Ivar, no guns," Alexandra called reassuringly.

He dropped his arms and went up to the wagon, smiling amiably and looking at them out of his pale blue eyes.

"We want to buy a hammock, if you have one," Alexandra

explained, "and my little brother, here, wants to see your big pond, where so many birds come."

Ivar smiled foolishly, and began rubbing the horses' noses and feeling about their mouths behind the bits. "Not many birds just now. A few ducks this morning; and some snipe come to drink. But there was a crane last week. She spent one night and came back the next evening. I don't know why. It is not her season, of course. Many of them go over in the fall. Then the pond is full of strange voices every night."

Alexandra translated for Carl, who looked thoughtful. "Ask him, Alexandra, if it is true that a sea gull came here once. I have heard so."

She had some difficulty in making the old man understand.

He looked puzzled at first, then smote his hands together as he remembered. "Oh, yes, yes! A big white bird with long wings and pink feet. My! what a voice she had! She came in the afternoon and kept flying about the pond and screaming until dark. She was in trouble of some sort, but I could not understand her. She was going over to the other ocean, maybe, and did not know how far it was. She was afraid of never getting there. She was more mournful than our birds here; she cried in the night. She saw the light from my window and darted up to it. Maybe she thought my house was a boat, she was such a wild thing. Next morning, when the sun rose, I went out to take her food, but she flew up into the sky and went on her way." Ivar ran his fingers through his thick hair. "I have many strange birds stop with me here. They come from very far away and are great company. I hope you boys never shoot wild birds?"

Lou and Oscar grinned, and Ivar shook his bushy head. "Yes, I know boys are thoughtless. But these wild things are God's birds. He watches over them and counts them, as we do our cattle; Christ says so in the New Testament."

"Now, Ivar," Lou asked, "may we water our horses at your pond and give them some feed? It's a bad road to your place."

"Yes, yes, it is." The old man scrambled about and began to

loose the tugs. "A bad road, eh, girls? And the bay with a colt at home!"

Oscar brushed the old man aside. "We'll take care of the horses, Ivar. You'll be finding some disease on them. Alexandra wants to see your hammocks."

Ivar led Alexandra and Emil to his little cave house. He had but one room, neatly plastered and whitewashed, and there was a wooden floor. There was a kitchen stove, a table covered with oilcloth, two chairs, a clock, a calendar, a few books on the window-shelf; nothing more. But the place was as clean as a cupboard.

"But where do you sleep, Ivar?" Emil asked, looking about.

Ivar unslung a hammock from a hook on the wall; in it was rolled a buffalo robe. "There, my son. A hammock is a good bed, and in winter I wrap up in this skin. Where I go to work, the beds are not half so easy as this."

By this time Emil had lost all his timidity. He thought a cave a very superior kind of house. There was something pleasantly unusual about it and about Ivar. "Do the birds know you will be kind to them, Ivar? Is that why so many come?" he asked.

Ivar sat down on the floor and tucked his feet under him. "See, little brother, they have come from a long way, and they are very tired. From up there where they are flying, our country looks dark and flat. They must have water to drink and to bathe in before they can go on with their journey. They look this way and that, and far below them they see something shining, like a piece of glass set in the dark earth. That is my pond. They come to it and are not disturbed. Maybe I sprinkle a little corn. They tell the other birds, and next year more come this way. They have their roads up there, as we have down here."

Emil rubbed his knees thoughtfully. "And is that true, Ivar, about the head ducks falling back when they are tired, and the hind ones taking their place?"

"Yes. The point of the wedge gets the worst of it; they cut the wind. They can only stand it there a little while—half an hour, maybe. Then they fall back and the wedge splits a little, while the rear ones come up the middle to the front. Then it closes up and they fly on, with a new edge. They are always changing like that, up in the air. Never any confusion; just like soldiers who have been drilled."

Alexandra had selected her hammock by the time the boys came up from the pond. They would not come in, but sat in the shade of the bank outside while Alexandra and Ivar talked about the birds and about his housekeeping, and why he never ate meat, fresh or salt.

Alexandra was sitting on one of the wooden chairs, her arms resting on the table. Ivar was sitting on the floor at her feet. "Ivar," she said suddenly, beginning to trace the pattern on the oilcloth with her forefinger, "I came to-day more because I wanted to talk to you than because I wanted to buy a hammock."

"Yes?" The old man scraped his bare feet on the plank floor.

"We have a big bunch of hogs, Ivar. I wouldn't sell in the spring, when everybody advised me to, and now so many people are losing their hogs that I am frightened. What can be done?"

Ivar's little eyes began to shine. They lost their vagueness.

"You feed them swill and such stuff? Of course! And sour milk? Oh, yes! And keep them in a stinking pen? I tell you, sister, the hogs of this country are put upon! They become unclean, like the hogs in the Bible. If you kept your chickens like that, what would happen? You have a little sorghum patch, maybe? Put a fence around it, and turn the hogs in. Build a shed to give them shade, a thatch on poles. Let the boys haul water to them in barrels, clean water, and plenty. Get them off the old stinking ground, and do not let them go back there until winter. Give them only grain and clean feed, such as you would give horses or cattle. Hogs do not like to be filthy."

The boys outside the door had been listening. Lou nudged his brother. "Come, the horses are done eating. Let's hitch up and get out of here. He'll fill her full of notions. She'll be for having the pigs sleep with us, next."

Oscar grunted and got up. Carl, who could not understand what Ivar said, saw that the two boys were displeased. They did not mind hard work, but they hated experiments and could never see the use of taking pains. Even Lou, who was more elastic than his older brother, disliked to do anything different from their neighbors. He felt that it made them conspicuous and gave people a chance to talk about them.

Once they were on the homeward road, the boys forgot their ill-humor and joked about Ivar and his birds. Alexandra did not propose any reforms in the care of the pigs, and they hoped she had forgotten Ivar's talk. They agreed that he was crazier than ever, and would never be able to prove up on his land because he worked it so little. Alexandra privately resolved that she would have a talk with Ivar about this and stir him up. The boys persuaded Carl to stay for supper and go swimming in the pasture pond after dark.

That evening, after she had washed the supper dishes, Alexandra sat down on the kitchen doorstep, while her mother was mixing the bread. It was a still, deep-breathing summer night, full of the smell of the hay fields. Sounds of laughter and splashing came up from the pasture, and when the moon rose rapidly above the bare rim of the prairie, the pond glittered like polished metal, and she could see the flash of white bodies as the boys ran about the edge, or jumped into the water. Alexandra watched the shimmering pool dreamily, but eventually her eyes went back to the sorghum patch south of the barn, where she was planning to make her new pig corral.

I V

FOR THE FIRST three years after John Bergson's death, the affairs of his family prospered. Then came the hard times that brought every one on the Divide to the brink of despair; three years of drouth and failure, the last struggle of a wild soil against the encroaching plowshare. The first of these fruitless summers the Bergson boys bore courageously. The failure of the corn crop made labor cheap. Lou and Oscar hired two men and put in bigger crops than ever before. They lost everything they spent. The whole country was discouraged. Farmers who were already in debt had to give up their land. A few foreclosures demoralized the country. The settlers sat about on the wooden sidewalks in the little town and told each other that the country was never meant for men to live in; the thing to do was to get back to Iowa, to Illinois, to any place that had been proved habitable. The Bergson boys, certainly, would have been happier with their uncle Otto, in the bakery shop in Chicago. Like most of their neighbors, they were meant to follow in paths already marked out for them, not to break trails in a new country. A steady job, a few holidays, nothing to think about, and they would have been very happy. It was no fault of theirs that they had been dragged into the wilderness when they were little boys. A pioneer should have imagination, should be able to enjoy the idea of things more than the things themselves.

The second of these barren summers was passing. One September afternoon Alexandra had gone over to the garden across the draw to dig sweet potatoes—they had been thriving upon the weather that was fatal to everything else. But when Carl Linstrum came up the garden rows to find her, she was not working. She was standing lost in thought, leaning upon her pitchfork, her sunbonnet lying beside her on the ground. The dry garden patch smelled of drying vines and was strewn with yellow seed-cucumbers and pumpkins and citrons. At one end, next to the rhubarb, grew feathery asparagus, with red berries. Down the middle of the garden was a row of gooseberry and currant bushes. A few tough zenias and marigolds and a row of scarlet sage bore witness to the buckets of water that Mrs. Bergson had carried there after sundown, against the prohibition of her sons. Carl came quietly and slowly up the garden path, looking intently at Alexandra. She did not hear him. She was standing perfectly still, with that serious ease so characteristic of her. Her thick, reddish braids, twisted about her head, fairly burned in the sunlight. The air was cool enough to make the warm sun pleasant on one's back and shoulders, and so clear that the eye could follow a hawk up and up, into the blazing blue depths of the sky. Even Carl, never a very cheerful boy, and considerably darkened by these last two bitter years, loved the country on days like this, felt something strong and young and wild come out of it, that laughed at care.

"Alexandra," he said as he approached her, "I want to talk to you. Let's sit down by the gooseberry bushes." He picked up her sack of potatoes and they crossed the garden. "Boys gone to town?" he asked as he sank down on the warm, sun-baked earth. "Well, we have made up our minds at last, Alexandra. We are really going away."

She looked at him as if she were a little frightened. "Really, Carl? Is it settled?"

"Yes, father has heard from St. Louis, and they will give him back his old job in the cigar factory. He must be there by the first of November. They are taking on new men then. We will sell the place for whatever we can get, and auction the stock. We haven't enough to ship. I am going to learn engraving with a German engraver there, and then try to get work in Chicago."

Alexandra's hands dropped in her lap. Her eyes became dreamy and filled with tears.

Carl's sensitive lower lip trembled. He scratched in the soft earth beside him with a stick. "That's all I hate about it, Alexandra," he said slowly. "You've stood by us through so much and helped father out so many times, and now it seems as if we were running off and leaving you to face the worst of it. But it isn't as if we could really ever be of any help to you. We are only one more drag, one more thing you look out for and feel responsible for. Father was never meant for a farmer, you know that. And I hate it. We'd only get in deeper and deeper."

"Yes, yes, Carl, I know. You are wasting your life here. You are able to do much better things. You are nearly nineteen now, and I wouldn't have you stay. I've always hoped you would get away. But I can't help feeling scared when I think how I will miss you—more than you will ever know." She brushed the tears from her cheeks, not trying to hide them.

"But, Alexandra," he said sadly and wistfully, "I've never been any real help to you, beyond sometimes trying to keep the boys in a good humor."

Alexandra smiled and shook her head. "Oh, it's not that. Nothing like that. It's by understanding me, and the boys, and mother, that you've helped me. I expect that is the only way one person ever really can help another. I think you are about the only one that ever helped me. Somehow it will take more courage to bear your going than everything that has happened before."

Carl looked at the ground. "You see, we've all depended so on you," he said, "even father. He makes me laugh. When anything comes up he always says, 'I wonder what the Bergsons are going to do about that? I guess I'll go and ask her.' I'll never forget that time, when we first came here, and our horse had the colic, and I ran over to your place—your father was away, and you came home with me and showed father how to let the wind out of the horse. You were only a little girl then, but you knew ever so much more about farm work than poor father. You remember how homesick I used to get, and what long talks we used to have coming from school? We've someway always felt alike about things."

"Yes, that's it; we've liked the same things and we've liked them together, without anybody else knowing. And we've had good times, hunting for Christmas trees and going for ducks and making our plum wine together every year. We've never either of us had any other close friend. And now"—Alexandra wiped her eyes with the corner of her apron—"and now I must remember that you are going where you will have many friends, and will find the work you were meant to do. But you'll write to me, Carl? That will mean a great deal to me here."

"I'll write as long as I live," cried the boy impetuously. "And I'll be working for you as much as for myself, Alexandra. I want to do something you'll like and be proud of. I'm a fool here, but I know I can do something!" He sat up and frowned at the red grass.

Alexandra sighed. "How discouraged the boys will be when they hear. They always come home from town discouraged, anyway. So many people are trying to leave the country, and they talk to our boys and make them low-spirited. I'm afraid they are beginning to feel hard toward me because I won't listen to any talk about going. Sometimes I feel like I'm getting tired of standing up for this country."

"I won't tell the boys yet, if you'd rather not."

"Oh, I'll tell them myself, to-night, when they come home. They'll be talking wild, anyway, and no good comes of keeping bad news. It's all harder on them than it is on me. Lou wants to get married, poor boy, and he can't until times are better. See, there goes the sun, Carl. I must be getting back. Mother will want her potatoes. It's chilly already, the moment the light goes."

Alexandra rose and looked about. A golden afterglow throbbed in the west, but the country already looked empty and mournful. A dark moving mass came over the western hill, the Lee boy was bringing in the herd from the other half-section. Emil ran from the windmill to open the corral gate. From the log house, on the little rise across the draw, the smoke was curling. The cattle lowed and bellowed. In the sky the pale half-moon was slowly silvering. Alexandra and Carl walked together down the potato rows. "I have to keep telling myself what is going to happen," she said softly. "Since you have been here, ten years now, I have never really been lonely. But I can remember what it was like before. Now I shall have nobody but Emil. But he is my boy, and he is tender-hearted."

That night, when the boys were called to supper, they sat down moodily. They had worn their coats to town, but they ate in their striped shirts and suspenders. They were grown men now, and, as Alexandra said, for the last few years they had been growing more and more like themselves. Lou was still the slighter of the two, the quicker and more intelligent, but apt to go off at half-cock. He had a lively blue eye, a thin, fair skin (always burned red to the neckband of his shirt in summer), stiff, yellow hair that would not lie down on his head, and a bristly little yellow mustache, of which he was very proud. Oscar could not grow a mustache; his pale face was as bare as an egg, and his white eyebrows gave it an empty look. He was a man of powerful body and unusual endurance; the sort of man you could attach to a corn-sheller as you would an engine. He would turn it all day, without hurrying, without slowing down. But he was as indolent of mind as he was unsparing of his body. His love of routine amounted to a vice. He worked like an insect, always doing the same thing over in the same way, regardless of whether it was best or not. He felt that there was a sovereign virtue in mere bodily toil, and he rather liked to do things in the hardest way. If a field had once been in corn, he couldn't bear to put it into wheat. He liked to begin his corn-planting at the same time every year, whether the season were backward or forward. He seemed to feel that by his own irreproachable regularity he would clear himself of blame and reprove the weather. When the wheat crop failed, he threshed the straw at a dead loss to demonstrate how little grain there was, and thus prove his case against Providence.

Lou, on the other hand, was fussy and flighty; always planned to get through two days' work in one, and often got only the least important things done. He liked to keep the place up, but he never got round to doing odd jobs until he had to neglect more pressing work to attend to them. In the middle of the wheat harvest, when the grain was over-ripe and every hand was needed, he would stop to mend fences or to patch the harness; then dash down to the field and overwork and be laid up in bed for a week. The two boys balanced each other, and they pulled well together. They had been good friends since they were children. One seldom went anywhere, even to town, without the other.

To-night, after they sat down to supper, Oscar kept looking at Lou as if he expected him to say something, and Lou blinked his eyes and frowned at his plate. It was Alexandra herself who at last opened the discussion.

"The Linstrums," she said calmly, as she put another plate of hot biscuit on the table, "are going back to St. Louis. The old man is going to work in the cigar factory again."

At this Lou plunged in. "You see, Alexandra, everybody who can crawl out is going away. There's no use of us trying to stick it out, just to be stubborn. There's something in knowing when to quit."

"Where do you want to go, Lou?"

"Any place where things will grow," said Oscar grimly.

Lou reached for a potato. "Chris Arnson has traded his half-section for a place down on the river."

"Who did he trade with?"

"Charley Fuller, in town."

"Fuller the real estate man? You see, Lou, that Fuller has a head on him. He's buying and trading for every bit of land he can get up here. It'll make him a rich man, some day."

"He's rich now, that's why he can take a chance."

"Why can't we? We'll live longer than he will. Some day the land itself will be worth more than all we can ever raise on it."

Lou laughed. "It could be worth that, and still not be worth much. Why, Alexandra, you don't know what you're talking about. Our place wouldn't bring now what it would six years ago. The fellows that settled up here just made a mistake. Now they're beginning to see this high land wasn't never meant to grow nothing on, and everybody who ain't fixed to graze cattle is trying to crawl out. It's too high to farm up here. All the Americans are skinning out. That man Percy Adams, north of town, told me that he was going to let Fuller take his land and stuff for four hundred dollars and a ticket to Chicago."

"There's Fuller again!" Alexandra exclaimed. "I wish that man would take me for a partner. He's feathering his nest! If only poor people could learn a little from rich people! But all these fellows who are running off are bad farmers, like poor Mr. Linstrum. They couldn't get ahead even in good years, and they all got into debt while father was getting out. I think we ought to hold on as long as we can on father's account. He was so set on keeping this land. He must have seen harder times than this, here. How was it in the early days, mother?"

Mrs. Bergson was weeping quietly. These family discussions always depressed her, and made her remember all that she had been torn away from. "I don't see why the boys are always taking on about going away," she said, wiping her eyes. "I don't want to move again; out to some raw place, maybe, where we'd be worse off than we are here, and all to do over again. I won't move! If the rest of you go, I will ask some of the neighbors to take me in, and stay and be buried by father. I'm not going to leave him by himself on the prairie, for cattle to run over." She began to cry more bitterly.

The boys looked angry. Alexandra put a soothing hand on her mother's shoulder. "There's no question of that, mother. You don't have to go if you don't want to. A third of the place belongs to you by American law, and we can't sell without your consent. We only want you to advise us. How did it use to be when you and father first came? Was it really as bad as this, or not?"

"Oh, worse! Much worse," moaned Mrs. Bergson. "Drouth, chince-bugs, hail, everything! My garden all cut to pieces like sauerkraut. No grapes on the creek, no nothing. The people all lived just like coyotes."

Oscar got up and tramped out of the kitchen. Lou followed him. They felt that Alexandra had taken an unfair advantage in turning their mother loose on them. The next morning they were silent and reserved. They did not offer to take the women to church, but went down to the barn immediately after breakfast and stayed there all day. When Carl Linstrum came over in the afternoon, Alexandra winked to him and pointed toward the barn. He understood her and went down to play cards with the boys. They believed that a very wicked thing to do on Sunday, and it relieved their feelings.

Alexandra stayed in the house. On Sunday afternoon Mrs. Bergson always took a nap, and Alexandra read. During the week she read only the newspaper, but on Sunday, and in the long evenings of winter, she read a good deal; read a few things over a great many times. She knew long portions of the *Frithjof Saga* by heart, and, like most Swedes who read at all, she was fond of Longfellow's verse,—the ballads and the "Golden Legend" and "The Spanish Student." To-day she sat in the wooden rocking-chair with the Swedish Bible open on her knees, but she was not reading. She was looking thoughtfully away at the point where the upland road disappeared over the rim of the prairie. Her body was in an attitude of perfect repose, such as it was apt to take when she was thinking earnestly. Her mind was slow, truthful, steadfast. She had not the least spark of cleverness.

All afternoon the sitting-room was full of quiet and sunlight. Emil was making rabbit traps in the kitchen shed. The hens were clucking and scratching brown holes in the flower beds, and the wind was teasing the prince's feather by the door.

That evening Carl came in with the boys to supper.

"Emil," said Alexandra, when they were all seated at the table, "how would you like to go traveling? Because I am going to take a trip, and you can go with me if you want to."

The boys looked up in amazement; they were always afraid of Alexandra's schemes. Carl was interested.

"I've been thinking, boys," she went on, "that maybe I am too set against making a change. I'm going to take Brigham and the buckboard to-morrow and drive down to the river country and spend a few days looking over what they've got down there. If I find anything good, you boys can go down and make a trade."

"Nobody down there will trade for anything up here," said Oscar gloomily.

"That's just what I want to find out. Maybe they are just as discontented down there as we are up here. Things away from home often look better than they are. You know what your Hans Andersen book says, Carl, about the Swedes liking to buy Danish bread and the Danes liking to buy Swedish bread, because people always think the bread of another country is better than their own. Anyway, I've heard so much about the river farms, I won't be satisfied till I've seen for myself."

Lou fidgeted. "Look out! Don't agree to anything. Don't let them fool you."

Lou was apt to be fooled himself. He had not yet learned to keep away from the shell-game wagons that followed the circus.

After supper Lou put on a necktie and went across the fields to court Annie Lee, and Carl and Oscar sat down to a game of checkers, while Alexandra read *The Swiss Family Robinson* aloud to her mother and Emil. It was not long before the two boys at the table neglected their game to listen. They were all big children together, and they found the adventures of the family in the tree house so absorbing that they gave them their undivided attention.

V

A LEXANDRA AND EMIL spent five days down among the river farms, driving up and down the valley. Alexandra talked to the men about their crops and to the women about their poultry. She spent a whole day with one young farmer who had been away at school, and who was experimenting with a new kind of clover hay. She learned a great deal. As they drove along, she and Emil talked and planned. At last, on the sixth day, Alexandra turned Brigham's head northward and left the river behind.

"There's nothing in it for us down there, Emil. There are a few fine farms, but they are owned by the rich men in town, and couldn't be bought. Most of the land is rough and hilly. They can always scrape along down there, but they can never do anything big. Down there they have a little certainty, but up with us there is a big chance. We must have faith in the high land, Emil: I want to hold on harder than ever, and when you're a man you'll thank me." She urged Brigham forward.

When the road began to climb the first long swells of the Divide, Alexandra hummed an old Swedish hymn, and Emil wondered why his sister looked so happy. Her face was so radiant that he felt shy about asking her. For the first time, perhaps, since that land emerged from the waters of geologic ages, a human face was set toward it with love and yearning. It seemed beautiful to her, rich and strong and glorious. Her eyes drank in the breadth of it, until her tears blinded her. Then the Genius of the Divide, the great, free spirit which breathes across it, must have bent lower than it ever bent to a human will before. The history of every country begins in the heart of a man or a woman.

Alexandra reached home in the afternoon. That evening she held a family council and told her brothers all that she had seen and heard.

"I want you boys to go down yourselves and look it over. Nothing will convince you like seeing with your own eyes. The river land was settled before this, and so they are a few years ahead of us, and have learned more about farming. The land sells for three times as much as this, but in five years we will double it. The rich men down there own all the best land, and they are buying all they can get. The thing to do is to sell our cattle and what little old corn we have, and buy the Linstrum place. Then the next thing to do is to take out two loans on our half-sections, and buy Peter Crow's place; raise every dollar we can, and buy every acre we can."

"Mortgage the homestead again?" Lou cried. He sprang up and began to wind the clock furiously. "I won't slave to pay off another mortgage. I'll never do it. You'd just as soon kill us all, Alexandra, to carry out some scheme!"

Oscar rubbed his high, pale forehead. "How do you propose to pay off your mortgages?"

Alexandra looked from one to the other and bit her lip. They had never seen her so nervous. "See here," she brought out at last. "We borrow the money for six years. Well, with the money we buy a half-section from Linstrum and a half from Crow, and a quarter from Struble, maybe. That will give us upwards of fourteen hundred acres, won't it? You won't have to pay off your mortgages for six years. By that time, any of this land will be worth thirty dollars an acre—it will be worth fifty, but we'll say thirty; then you can sell a garden patch anywhere, and pay off a debt of sixteen hundred dollars. It's not the principal I'm worried about, it's the interest and taxes. We'll have to strain to meet the payments. But as sure as we are sitting here to-night, we can sit down here ten years from now independent landowners, not struggling farmers any longer. The chance that father was always looking for has come."

Lou was pacing the floor. "But how do you *know* that land is going to go up enough to pay the mortgages and—"

"And make us rich besides?" Alexandra put in firmly. "I can't explain that, Lou. You'll have to take my word for it. I *know*, that's all. When you drive about over the country you can feel it coming."

Oscar had been sitting with his head lowered, his hands hanging between his knees. "But we can't work so much land," he said dully, as if he were talking to himself. "We can't even try. It would just lie there and we'd work ourselves to death." He sighed, and laid his calloused fist on the table.

Alexandra's eyes filled with tears. She put her hand on his shoulder. "You poor boy, you won't have to work it. The men in town who are buying up other people's land don't try to farm it. They are the men to watch, in a new country. Let's try to do like the shrewd ones and not like these stupid fellows. I don't want you boys always to have to work like this. I want you to be independent, and Emil to go to school."

Lou held his head as if it were splitting. "Everybody will say we are crazy. It must be crazy, or everybody would be doing it."

"If they were, we wouldn't have much chance. No, Lou, I was talking about that with the smart young man who is raising the new kind of clover. He says the right thing is usually just what everybody don't do. Why are we better fixed than any of our neighbors? Because father had more brains. Our people were better people than these in the old country. We *ought* to do more than they do, and see further ahead. Yes, mother, I'm going to clear the table now."

Alexandra rose. The boys went to the stable to see to the stock, and they were gone a long while. When they came back Lou played on his *dragharmonika* and Oscar sat figuring at his father's secretary all evening. They said nothing more about Alexandra's project, but she felt sure now that they would consent to it. Just before bedtime Oscar went out for a pail of water. When he did not come back, Alexandra threw a shawl over her head and ran down the path to the windmill. She found him sitting there with his head in his hands, and she sat down beside him.

"Don't do anything you don't want to do, Oscar," she whispered. She waited a moment, but he did not stir. "I won't say any more about it, if you'd rather not. What makes you so discouraged?"

"I dread signing my name to them pieces of paper," he said slowly. "All the time I was a boy we had a mortgage hanging over us."

"Then don't sign one. I don't want you to, if you feel that way."

Oscar shook his head. "No, I can see there's a chance that way. I've thought a good while there might be. We're in so deep now, we might as well go deeper. But it's hard work pulling out of debt. Like pulling a threshing-machine out of the mud; breaks your back. Me and Lou's worked hard, and I can't see it's got us ahead much."

"Nobody knows about that as well as I do, Oscar. That's why I want to try an easier way. I don't want you to have to grub for every dollar."

"Yes, I know what you mean. Maybe it'll come out right. But signing papers is signing papers. There ain't no maybe about that." He took his pail and trudged up the path to the house.

Alexandra drew her shawl closer about her and stood leaning against the frame of the mill, looking at the stars which glittered so keenly through the frosty autumn air. She always loved to watch them, to think of their vastness and distance, and of their ordered march. It fortified her to reflect upon the great operations of nature, and when she thought of the law that lay behind them, she felt a sense of personal security. That night she had a new consciousness of the country, felt almost a new relation to it. Even her talk with the boys had not taken away the feeling that had overwhelmed her when she drove back to the Divide that afternoon. She had never known before how much the country meant to her. The chirping of the insects down in the long grass had been like the sweetest music. She had felt as if her heart were hiding down there, somewhere, with the quail and the plover and all the little wild things that crooned or buzzed in the sun. Under the long shaggy ridges, she felt the future stirring.

PART TWO

NEIGHBORING FIELDS

"The Divide is now thickly populated. The rich soil yields heavy harvests; the dry, bracing climate and the smoothness of the land make labor easy for men and beasts." —O Pioneers!

I

IT IS SIXTEEN YEARS since John Bergson died. His wife now lies beside him, and the white shaft that marks their graves gleams across the wheatfields. Could he rise from beneath it, he would not know the country under which he has been asleep. The shaggy coat of the prairie, which they lifted to make him a bed, has vanished forever. From the Norwegian graveyard one looks out over a vast checker-board, marked off in squares of wheat and corn; light and dark, dark and light. Telephone wires hum along the white roads, which always run at right angles. From the graveyard gate one can count a dozen gayly painted farmhouses; the gilded weather-vanes on the big red barns wink at each other across the green and brown and yellow fields. The light steel windmills tremble throughout their frames and tug at their moorings, as they vibrate in the wind that often blows from one week's end to another across that high, active, resolute stretch of country.

The Divide is now thickly populated. The rich soil yields heavy harvests; the dry, bracing climate and the smoothness of the land make labor easy for men and beasts. There are few scenes more gratifying than a spring plowing in that country, where the furrows of a single field often lie a mile in length, and the brown earth, with such a strong, clean smell, and such a power of growth and fertility in it, yields itself eagerly to the plow; rolls away from the shear, not even dimming the brightness of the metal, with a soft, deep sigh of happiness. The wheat-cutting sometimes goes on all night as well as all day, and in good seasons there are scarcely men and horses enough to do the harvesting. The grain is so heavy that it bends toward the blade and cuts like velvet.

There is something frank and joyous and young in the open face of the country. It gives itself ungrudgingly to the moods of the season, holding nothing back. Like the plains of Lombardy, it seems to rise a little to meet the sun. The air and the earth are curiously mated and intermingled, as if the one were the breath of the other. You feel in the atmosphere the same tonic, puissant quality that is in the tilth, the same strength and resoluteness.

One June morning a young man stood at the gate of the Norwegian graveyard, sharpening his scythe in strokes unconsciously timed to the tune he was whistling. He wore a flannel cap and duck trousers, and the sleeves of his white flannel shirt were rolled back to the elbow. When he was satisfied with the edge of his blade, he slipped the whetstone into his hip pocket and began to swing his scythe, still whistling, but softly, out of respect to the quiet folk about him. Unconscious respect, probably, for he seemed intent upon his own thoughts, and, like the Gladiator's, they were far away. He was a splendid figure of a boy, tall and straight as a young pine tree, with a handsome head, and stormy gray eyes, deeply set under a serious brow. The space between his two front teeth, which were unusually far apart, gave him the proficiency in whistling for which he was distinguished at college. (He also played the cornet in the University band.)

When the grass required his close attention, or when he had to stoop to cut about a headstone, he paused in his lively air,—the "Jewel" song,—taking it up where he had left it when his scythe swung free again. He was not thinking about the tired pioneers over whom his blade glittered. The old wild country, the struggle in which his sister was destined to succeed while so many men broke their hearts and died, he can scarcely remember. That is all among the dim things of childhood and has been forgotten in the brighter pattern life weaves to-day, in the bright facts of being captain of the track team, and holding the interstate record for the high jump, in the all-suffusing brightness of being twenty-one. Yet sometimes, in the pauses of his work, the young man frowned and looked at the ground with an intentness which suggested that even twenty-one might have its problems.

When he had been mowing the better part of an hour, he heard the rattle of a light cart on the road behind him. Supposing that it was his sister coming back from one of her farms, he kept on with his work. The cart stopped at the gate and a merry contralto voice called, "Almost through, Emil?" He dropped his scythe and went toward the fence, wiping his face and neck with his handkerchief. In the cart sat a young woman who wore driving gauntlets and a wide shade hat, trimmed with red poppies. Her face, too, was rather like a poppy, round and brown, with rich color in her cheeks and lips, and her dancing yellow-brown eyes bubbled with gayety. The wind was flapping her big hat and teasing a curl of her chestnut-colored hair. She shook her head at the tall youth.

"What time did you get over here? That's not much of a job for an athlete. Here I've been to town and back. Alexandra lets you sleep late. Oh, I know! Lou's wife was telling me about the way she spoils you. I was going to give you a lift, if you were done." She gathered up her reins.

"But I will be, in a minute. Please wait for me, Marie," Emil coaxed. "Alexandra sent me to mow our lot, but I've done half a dozen others, you see. Just wait till I finish off the Kourdnas'. By the way, they were Bohemians. Why aren't they up in the Catholic graveyard?"

"Free-thinkers," replied the young woman laconically.

"Lots of the Bohemian boys at the University are," said Emil, taking up his scythe again. "What did you ever burn John Huss for, anyway? It's made an awful row. They still jaw about it in history classes."

"We'd do it right over again, most of us," said the young woman hotly. "Don't they ever teach you in your history classes that you'd all be heathen Turks if it hadn't been for the Bohemians?"

Emil had fallen to mowing. "Oh, there's no denying you're a spunky little bunch, you Czechs," he called back over his shoulder.

Marie Shabata settled herself in her seat and watched the rhythmical movement of the young man's long arms, swinging her foot as if in time to some air that was going through her mind. The minutes passed. Emil mowed vigorously and Marie sat sunning herself and watching the long grass fall. She sat with the ease that belongs to persons of an essentially happy nature, who can find a comfortable spot almost anywhere; who are supple, and quick in adapting themselves to circumstances. After a final swish, Emil snapped the gate and sprang into the cart, holding his scythe well out over the wheel. "There," he sighed. "I gave old man Lee a cut or so, too. Lou's wife needn't talk. I never see Lou's scythe over here."

Marie clucked to her horse. "Oh, you know Annie!" She looked at the young man's bare arms. "How brown you've got since you came home. I wish I had an athlete to mow my orchard. I get wet to my knees when I go down to pick cherries."

"You can have one, any time you want him. Better wait until after it rains." Emil squinted off at the horizon as if he were looking for clouds.

"Will you? Oh, there's a good boy!" She turned her head to him with a quick, bright smile. He felt it rather than saw it. Indeed, he had looked away with the purpose of not seeing it. "I've been up looking at Angélique's wedding clothes," Marie went on, "and I'm so excited I can hardly wait until Sunday. Amédée will be a handsome bridegroom. Is anybody but you going to stand up with him? Well, then it will be a handsome wedding party." She made a droll face at Emil, who flushed. "Frank," Marie continued, flicking her horse, "is cranky at me because I loaned his saddle to Jan Smirka, and I'm terribly afraid he won't take me to the dance in the evening. Maybe the supper will tempt him. All Angélique's folks are baking for it, and all Amédée's twenty cousins. There will be barrels of beer. If once I get Frank to the supper, I'll see that I stay for the dance. And by the way, Emil, you mustn't dance with me but once or twice. You must dance with all the French girls. It hurts their feelings if you don't. They think you're proud because you've been away to school or something."

Emil sniffed. "How do you know they think that?"

"Well, you didn't dance with them much at Raoul Marcel's party, and I could tell how they took it by the way they looked at you—and at me."

"All right," said Emil shortly, studying the glittering blade of his scythe.

They drove westward toward Norway Creek, and toward a big white house that stood on a hill, several miles across the fields. There were so many sheds and outbuildings grouped about it that the place looked not unlike a tiny village. A stranger, approaching it, could not help noticing the beauty and fruitfulness of the outlying fields. There was something individual about the great farm, a most unusual trimness and care for detail. On either side of the road, for a mile before you reached the foot of the hill, stood tall osage orange hedges, their glossy green marking off the yellow fields. South of the hill, in a low, sheltered swale, surrounded by a mulberry hedge, was the orchard, its fruit trees knee-deep in timothy grass. Any one thereabouts would have told you that this was one of the richest farms on the Divide, and that the farmer was a woman, Alexandra Bergson.

If you go up the hill and enter Alexandra's big house, you will find that it is curiously unfinished and uneven in comfort. One room is papered, carpeted, over-furnished; the next is almost bare. The pleasantest rooms in the house are the kitchen—where Alexandra's three young Swedish girls chatter and cook and pickle and preserve all summer long—and the sitting-room, in which Alexandra has brought together the old homely furniture that the Bergsons used in their first log house, the family portraits, and the few things her mother brought from Sweden.

When you go out of the house into the flower garden, there you feel again the order and fine arrangement manifest all over the great farm; in the fencing and hedging, in the windbreaks and sheds, in the symmetrical pasture ponds, planted with scrub willows to give shade to the cattle in fly-time. There is even a white row of beehives in the orchard, under the walnut trees. You feel that, properly, Alexandra's house is the big out-of-doors, and that it is in the soil that she expresses herself best.

I I

E MIL REACHED HOME a little past noon, and when he went into the kitchen Alexandra was already seated at the head of the long table, having dinner with her men, as she always did unless there were visitors. He slipped into his empty place at his sister's right. The three pretty young Swedish girls who did Alexandra's house-work were cutting pies, refilling coffee-cups, placing platters of bread and meat and potatoes upon the red tablecloth, and continu-ally getting in each other's way between the table and the stove. To be sure they always wasted a good deal of time getting in each other's way and giggling at each other's mistakes. But, as Alexandra had pointedly told her sisters-in-law, it was to hear them giggle that she kept three young things in her kitchen; the work she could do herself, if it were necessary. These girls, with their long letters from home, their finery, and their love-affairs, afforded her a great deal of entertainment, and they were company for her when Emil was away at school.

Of the youngest girl, Signa, who has a pretty figure, mottled pink cheeks, and yellow hair, Alexandra is very fond, though she keeps a sharp eye upon her. Signa is apt to be skittish at mealtime, when the men are about, and to spill the coffee or upset the cream.

It is supposed that Nelse Jensen, one of the six men at the dinner-table, is courting Signa, though he has been so careful not to commit himself that no one in the house, least of all Signa, can tell just how far the matter has progressed. Nelse watches her glumly as she waits upon the table, and in the evening he sits on a bench behind the stove with his *dragharmonika*, playing mournful airs and watching her as she goes about her work. When Alexandra asked Signa whether she thought Nelse was in earnest, the poor child hid her hands under her apron and murmured, "I don't know, ma'm. But he scolds me about everything, like as if he wanted to have me!"

At Alexandra's left sat a very old man, barefoot and wearing a long blue blouse, open at the neck. His shaggy head is scarcely whiter than it was sixteen years ago, but his little blue eyes have become pale and watery, and his ruddy face is withered, like an apple that has clung all winter to the tree. When Ivar lost his land through mismanagement a dozen years ago, Alexandra took him in, and he has been a member of her household ever since. He is too old to work in the fields, but he hitches and unhitches the work-teams and looks after the health of the stock. Sometimes of a winter evening Alexandra calls him into the sitting-room to read the Bible aloud to her, for he still reads very well. He dislikes human habitations, so Alexandra has fitted him up a room in the barn, where he is very comfortable, being near the horses and, as he says, further from temptations. No one has ever found out what his temptations are. In cold weather he sits by the kitchen fire and makes hammocks or mends harness until it is time to go to bed. Then he says his prayers at great length behind the stove, puts on his buffalo-skin coat and goes out to his room in the barn.

Alexandra herself has changed very little. Her figure is fuller, and she has more color. She seems sunnier and more vigorous than she did as a young girl. But she still has the same calmness and deliberation of manner, the same clear eyes, and she still wears her hair in two braids wound round her head. It is so curly that fiery ends escape from the braids and make her head look like one of the big double sunflowers that fringe her vegetable garden. Her face is always tanned in summer, for her sunbonnet is oftener on her arm than on her head. But where her collar falls away from her neck, or where her sleeves are pushed back from her wrist, the skin is of such smoothness and whiteness as none but Swedish women ever possess; skin with the freshness of the snow itself.

Alexandra did not talk much at the table, but she encouraged her men to talk, and she always listened attentively, even when they seemed to be talking foolishly.

To-day Barney Flinn, the big red-headed Irishman who had been with Alexandra for five years and who was actually her foreman, though he had no such title, was grumbling about the new silo she had put up that spring. It happened to be the first silo on the Divide, and Alexandra's neighbors and her men were skeptical about it. "To be sure, if the thing don't work, we'll have plenty of feed without it, indeed," Barney conceded.

Nelse Jensen, Signa's gloomy suitor, had his word. "Lou, he says he wouldn't have no silo on his place if you'd give it to him. He says the feed outen it gives the stock the bloat. He heard of somebody lost four head of horses, feedin' 'em that stuff."

Alexandra looked down the table from one to another. "Well, the only way we can find out is to try. Lou and I have different notions about feeding stock, and that's a good thing. It's bad if all the members of a family think alike. They never get anywhere. Lou can learn by my mistakes and I can learn by his. Isn't that fair, Barney?"

The Irishman laughed. He had no love for Lou, who was always uppish with him and who said that Alexandra paid her hands too much. "I've not thought but to give the thing an honest try, mum. 'T would be only right, after puttin' so much expense into it. Maybe Emil will come out an' have a look at it wid me." He pushed back his chair, took his hat from the nail, and marched out with Emil, who, with his university ideas, was supposed to have instigated the silo. The other hands followed them, all except old Ivar. He had been depressed throughout the meal and had paid no heed to the talk of the men, even when they mentioned cornstalk bloat, upon which he was sure to have opinions.

"Did you want to speak to me, Ivar?" Alexandra asked as she rose from the table. "Come into the sitting-room."

The old man followed Alexandra, but when she motioned him to a chair he shook his head. She took up her workbasket and waited for him to speak. He stood looking at the carpet, his bushy head bowed, his hands clasped in front of him. Ivar's bandy legs seemed to have grown shorter with years, and they were completely misfitted to his broad, thick body and heavy shoulders.

"Well, Ivar, what is it?" Alexandra asked after she had waited longer than usual.

Ivar had never learned to speak English and his Norwegian was quaint and grave, like the speech of the more old-fashioned people. He always addressed Alexandra in terms of the deepest respect, hoping to set a good example to the kitchen girls, whom he thought too familiar in their manners.

"Mistress," he began faintly, without raising his eyes, "the folk have been looking coldly at me of late. You know there has been talk."

"Talk about what, Ivar?"

"About sending me away; to the asylum."

Alexandra put down her sewing-basket. "Nobody has come to me with such talk," she said decidedly. "Why need you listen? You know I would never consent to such a thing."

Ivar lifted his shaggy head and looked at her out of his little eyes. "They say that you cannot prevent it if the folk complain of me, if your brothers complain to the authorities. They say that your brothers are afraid—God forbid!—that I may do you some injury when my spells are on me. Mistress, how can any one think that?— that I could bite the hand that fed me!" The tears trickled down on the old man's beard.

Alexandra frowned. "Ivar, I wonder at you, that you should come bothering me with such nonsense. I am still running my own house, and other people have nothing to do with either you or me. So long as I am suited with you, there is nothing to be said."

Ivar pulled a red handkerchief out of the breast of his blouse and wiped his eyes and beard. "But I should not wish you to keep me if, as they say, it is against your interests, and if it is hard for you to get hands because I am here."

Alexandra made an impatient gesture, but the old man put out his hand and went on earnestly:—

"Listen, mistress, it is right that you should take these things into account. You know that my spells come from God, and that I would not harm any living creature. You believe that every one should worship God in the way revealed to him. But that is not the way of this country. The way here is for all to do alike. I am despised because I do not wear shoes, because I do not cut my hair, and because I have visions. At home, in the old country, there were many like me, who had been touched by God, or who had seen things in the graveyard at night and were different afterward. We thought nothing of it, and let them alone. But here, if a man is different in his feet or in his head, they put him in the asylum. Look at Peter Kralik; when he was a boy, drinking out of a creek, he swallowed a snake, and always after that he could eat only such food as the creature liked, for when he ate anything else, it became enraged and gnawed him. When he felt it whipping about in him, he drank alcohol to stupefy it and get some ease for himself. He could work as good as any man, and his head was clear, but they locked him up for being different in his stomach. That is the way; they have built the asylum for people who are different, and they will not even let us live in the holes with the badgers. Only your great prosperity has protected me so far. If you had had ill-fortune, they would have taken me to Hastings long ago."

As Ivar talked, his gloom lifted. Alexandra had found that she could often break his fasts and long penances by talking to him and letting him pour out the thoughts that troubled him. Sympathy always cleared his mind, and ridicule was poison to him.

"There is a great deal in what you say, Ivar. Like as not they will be wanting to take me to Hastings because I have built a silo; and then I may take you with me. But at present I need you here. Only don't come to me again telling me what people say. Let people go on talking as they like, and we will go on living as we think best. You have been with me now for twelve years, and I have gone to you for advice oftener than I have ever gone to any one. That ought to satisfy you."

Ivar bowed humbly. "Yes, mistress, I shall not trouble you with their talk again. And as for my feet, I have observed your wishes all these years, though you have never questioned me; washing them every night, even in winter."

Alexandra laughed. "Oh, never mind about your feet, Ivar. We can remember when half our neighbors went barefoot in summer. I expect old Mrs. Lee would love to slip her shoes off now sometimes, if she dared. I'm glad I'm not Lou's mother-in-law."

Ivar looked about mysteriously and lowered his voice almost to a whisper. "You know what they have over at Lou's house? A great white tub, like the stone water-troughs in the old country, to wash themselves in. When you sent me over with the strawberries, they were all in town but the old woman Lee and the baby. She took me in and showed me the thing, and she told me it was impossible to wash yourself clean in it, because, in so much water, you could not make a strong suds. So when they fill it up and send her in there, she pretends, and makes a splashing noise. Then, when they are all asleep, she washes herself in a little wooden tub she keeps under her bed."

Alexandra shook with laughter. "Poor old Mrs. Lee! They won't let her wear nightcaps, either. Never mind; when she comes to visit me, she can do all the old things in the old way, and have as much beer as she wants. We'll start an asylum for old-time people, Ivar."

Ivar folded his big handkerchief carefully and thrust it back into his blouse. "This is always the way, mistress. I come to you sorrowing, and you send me away with a light heart. And will you be so good as to tell the Irishman that he is not to work the brown gelding until the sore on its shoulder is healed?"

"That I will. Now go and put Emil's mare to the cart. I am going to drive up to the north quarter to meet the man from town who is to buy my alfalfa hay."

III

ALEXANDRA was to hear more of Ivar's case, however. On Sunday her married brothers came to dinner. She had asked them for that day because Emil, who hated family parties, would be absent, dancing at Amédée Chevalier's wedding, up in the French country. The table was set for company in the dining-room, where highly varnished wood and colored glass and useless pieces of china were conspicuous enough to satisfy the standards of the new prosperity. Alexandra had put herself into the hands of the Hanover furniture dealer, and he had conscientiously done his best to make her dining-room look like his display window. She said frankly that she knew nothing about such things, and she was willing to be governed by the general conviction that the more useless and utterly unusable objects were, the greater their virtue as ornament. That seemed reasonable enough. Since she liked plain things herself, it was all the more necessary to have jars and punchbowls and candlesticks in the company rooms for people who did appreciate them. Her guests liked to see about them these reassuring emblems of prosperity.

The family party was complete except for Emil, and Oscar's wife who, in the country phrase, "was not going anywhere just now." Oscar sat at the foot of the table and his four tow-headed little boys, aged from twelve to five, were ranged at one side. Neither Oscar nor Lou has changed much; they have simply, as Alexandra said of them long ago, grown to be more and more like themselves. Lou now looks the older of the two; his face is thin and shrewd and wrinkled about the eyes, while Oscar's is thick and dull. For all his dullness, however, Oscar makes more money than his brother, which adds to Lou's sharpness and uneasiness and tempts him to make a show. The trouble with Lou is that he is tricky, and his neighbors have found out that, as Ivar says, he has not a fox's face for nothing. Politics being the natural field for such talents, he neglects his farm to attend conventions and to run for county offices.

Lou's wife, formerly Annie Lee, has grown to look curiously like her husband. Her face has become longer, sharper, more aggressive. She wears her yellow hair in a high pompadour, and is bedecked with rings and chains and "beauty pins." Her tight, high-heeled shoes give her an awkward walk, and she is always more or less preoccupied with her clothes. As she sat at the table, she kept telling her youngest daughter to "be careful now, and not drop anything on mother."

The conversation at the table was all in English. Oscar's wife, from the malaria district of Missouri, was ashamed of marrying a foreigner, and his boys do not understand a word of Swedish. Annie and Lou sometimes speak Swedish at home, but Annie is almost as much afraid of being "caught" at it as ever her mother was of being caught barefoot. Oscar still has a thick accent, but Lou speaks like anybody from Iowa.

"When I was in Hastings to attend the convention," he was saying, "I saw the superintendent of the asylum, and I was telling him about Ivar's symptoms. He says Ivar's case is one of the most dangerous kind, and it's a wonder he hasn't done something violent before this."

Alexandra laughed good-humoredly. "Oh, nonsense, Lou! The

doctors would have us all crazy if they could. Ivar's queer, certainly, but he has more sense than half the hands I hire."

Lou flew at his fried chicken. "Oh, I guess the doctor knows his business, Alexandra. He was very much surprised when I told him how you'd put up with Ivar. He says he's likely to set fire to the barn any night, or to take after you and the girls with an axe."

Little Signa, who was waiting on the table, giggled and fled to the kitchen. Alexandra's eyes twinkled. "That was too much for Signa, Lou. We all know that Ivar's perfectly harmless. The girls would as soon expect me to chase them with an axe."

Lou flushed and signaled to his wife. "All the same, the neighbors will be having a say about it before long. He may burn anybody's barn. It's only necessary for one property-owner in the township to make complaint, and he'll be taken up by force. You'd better send him yourself and not have any hard feelings."

Alexandra helped one of her little nephews to gravy. "Well, Lou, if any of the neighbors try that, I'll have myself appointed Ivar's guardian and take the case to court, that's all. I am perfectly satisfied with him."

"Pass the preserves, Lou," said Annie in a warning tone. She had reasons for not wishing her husband to cross Alexandra too openly. "But don't you sort of hate to have people see him around here, Alexandra?" she went on with persuasive smoothness. "He *is* a disgraceful object, and you're fixed up so nice now. It sort of makes people distant with you, when they never know when they'll hear him scratching about. My girls are afraid as death of him, aren't you, Milly, dear?"

Milly was fifteen, fat and jolly and pompadoured, with a creamy complexion, square white teeth, and a short upper lip. She looked like her grandmother Bergson, and had her comfortable and comfort-loving nature. She grinned at her aunt, with whom she was a great deal more at ease than she was with her mother. Alexandra winked a reply.

"Milly needn't be afraid of Ivar. She's an especial favorite of his. In my opinion Ivar has just as much right to his own way of dressing and thinking as we have. But I'll see that he doesn't bother other people. I'll keep him at home, so don't trouble any more about him, Lou. I've been wanting to ask you about your new bathtub. How does it work?"

Annie came to the fore to give Lou time to recover himself. "Oh, it works something grand! I can't keep him out of it. He washes himself all over three times a week now, and uses all the hot water. I think it's weakening to stay in as long as he does. You ought to have one, Alexandra."

"I'm thinking of it. I might have one put in the barn for Ivar, if it will ease people's minds. But before I get a bathtub, I'm going to get a piano for Milly."

Oscar, at the end of the table, looked up from his plate. "What does Milly want of a pianny? What's the matter with her organ? She can make some use of that, and play in church."

Annie looked flusterd. She had begged Alexandra not to say anything about this plan before Oscar, who was apt to be jealous of what his sister did for Lou's children. Alexandra did not get on with Oscar's wife at all. "Milly can play in church just the same, and she'll still play on the organ. But practicing on it so much spoils her touch. Her teacher says so," Annie brought out with spirit.

Oscar rolled his eyes. "Well, Milly must have got on pretty good if she's got past the organ. I know plenty of grown folks that ain't," he said bluntly.

Annie threw up her chin. "She has got on good, and she's going to play for her commencement when she graduates in town next year."

"Yes," said Alexandra firmly, "I think Milly deserves a piano. All the girls around here have been taking lessons for years, but Milly is the only one of them who can ever play anything when you ask her. I'll tell you when I first thought I would like to give you a piano, Milly, and that was when you learned that book of old Swedish songs that your grandfather used to sing. He had a sweet tenor voice, and when he was a young man he loved to sing. I can remember hearing him singing with the sailors down in the ship-yard, when I was no bigger than Stella here," pointing to Annie's younger daughter.

Milly and Stella both looked through the door into the sitting-room, where a crayon portrait of John Bergson hung on the wall. Alexandra had had it made from a little photograph, taken for his friends just before he left Sweden; a slender man of thirty-five, with soft hair curling about his high forehead, a drooping mustache, and wondering, sad eyes that looked forward into the distance, as if they already beheld the New World.

After dinner Lou and Oscar went to the orchard to pick cher-ries—they had neither of them had the patience to grow an orchard of their own—and Annie went down to gossip with Alexandra's kitchen girls while they washed the dishes. She could always find out more about Alexandra's domestic economy from the prattling maids than from Alexandra herself, and what she discovered she used to her own advantage with Lou. On the Divide, farmers' daughters no longer went out into service, so Alexandra got her girls from Sweden, by paying their fare over. They stayed with her until they married, and were replaced by sisters or cousins from the old country.

Alexandra took her three nieces into the flower garden. She was fond of the little girls, especially of Milly, who came to spend a week with her aunt now and then, and read aloud to her from the old books about the house, or listened to stories about the early days on the Divide. While they were walking among the flower beds, a buggy drove up the hill and stopped in front of the gate. A man got out and stood talking to the driver. The little girls were delighted at the advent of a stranger, some one from very far away, they knew by his clothes, his gloves, and the sharp, pointed cut of his dark beard. The girls fell behind their aunt and peeped out at him from among the castor beans. The stranger came up to the gate and stood holding his hat in his hand, smiling, while Alexandra advanced slowly to meet him. As she approached he spoke in a low, pleasant voice.

"Don't you know me, Alexandra? I would have known you, anywhere."

Alexandra shaded her eyes with her hand. Suddenly she took a quick step forward. "Can it be!" she exclaimed with feeling; "can it be that it is Carl Linstrum? Why, Carl, it is!" She threw out both her hands and caught his across the gate. "Sadie, Milly, run tell your father and Uncle Oscar that our old friend Carl Linstrum is here. Be quick! Why, Carl, how did it happen? I can't believe this!" Alexandra shook the tears from her eyes and laughed.

The stranger nodded to his driver, dropped his suitcase inside the fence, and opened the gate. "Then you are glad to see me, and you can put me up overnight? I couldn't go through this country without stopping off to have a look at you. How little you have changed! Do you know, I was sure it would be like that. You simply couldn't be different. How fine you are!" He stepped back and looked at her admiringly.

Alexandra blushed and laughed again. "But you yourself, Carl—with that beard—how could I have known you? You went away a little boy." She reached for his suitcase and when he intercepted her she threw up her hands. "You see, I give myself away. I have only women come to visit me, and I do not know how to behave. Where is your trunk?"

"It's in Hanover. I can stay only a few days. I am on my way to the coast."

They started up the path. "A few days? After all these years!" Alexandra shook her finger at him. "See this, you have walked into a trap. You do not get away so easy." She put her hand affectionately on his shoulder. "You owe me a visit for the sake of old times. Why must you go to the coast at all?"

"Oh, I must! I am a fortune hunter. From Seattle I go on to Alaska."

"Alaska?" She looked at him in astonishment. "Are you going to paint the Indians?"

"Paint?" the young man frowned. "Oh! I'm not a painter, Alexandra. I'm an engraver. I have nothing to do with painting."

"But on my parlor wall I have the paintings—"

He interrupted nervously. "Oh, water-color sketches—done for amusement. I sent them to remind you of me, not because they were good. What a wonderful place you have made of this, Alexandra." He turned and looked back at the wide, map-like prospect of field and hedge and pasture. "I would never have believed it could be done. I'm disappointed in my own eye, in my imagination."

At this moment Lou and Oscar came up the hill from the orchard. They did not quicken their pace when they saw Carl; indeed, they did not openly look in his direction. They advanced distrustfully, and as if they wished the distance were longer.

Alexandra beckoned to them. "They think I am trying to fool them. Come, boys, it's Carl Linstrum, our old Carl!"

Lou gave the visitor a quick, sidelong glance and thrust out his hand. "Glad to see you." Oscar followed with "How d' do." Carl could not tell whether their offishness came from unfriendliness or from embarrassment. He and Alexandra led the way to the porch.

"Carl," Alexandra explained, "is on his way to Seattle. He is going to Alaska."

Oscar studied the visitor's yellow shoes. "Got business there?" he asked.

Carl laughed. "Yes, very pressing business. I'm going there to get rich. Engraving's a very interesting profession, but a man never makes any money at it. So I'm going to try the goldfields."

Alexandra felt that this was a tactful speech, and Lou looked up with some interest. "Ever done anything in that line before?"

"No, but I'm going to join a friend of mine who went out from New York and has done well. He has offered to break me in."

"Turrible cold winters, there, I hear," remarked Oscar. "I thought people went up there in the spring."

"They do. But my friend is going to spend the winter in Seattle and I am to stay with him there and learn something about prospecting before we start north next year."

Lou looked skeptical. "Let's see, how long have you been away from here?"

"Sixteen years. You ought to remember that, Lou, for you were married just after we went away."

"Going to stay with us some time?" Oscar asked.

"A few days, if Alexandra can keep me."

"I expect you'll be wanting to see your old place," Lou observed more cordially. "You won't hardly know it. But there's a few chunks of your old sod house left. Alexandra wouldn't never let Frank Shabata plough over it."

Annie Lee, who, ever since the visitor was announced, had been touching up her hair and settling her lace and wishing she had worn another dress, now emerged with her three daughters and introduced them. She was greatly impressed by Carl's urban appearance, and in her excitement talked very loud and threw her head about. "And you ain't married yet? At your age, now! Think of that! You'll have to wait for Milly. Yes, we've got a boy, too. The youngest. He's at home with his grandma. You must come over to see mother and hear Milly play. She's the musician of the family. She does pyrography, too. That's burnt wood, you know. You wouldn't believe what she can do with her poker. Yes, she goes to school in town, and she is the youngest in her class by two years."

Milly looked uncomfortable and Carl took her hand again. He liked her creamy skin and happy, innocent eyes, and he could see that her mother's way of talking distressed her. "I'm sure she's a clever little girl," he murmured, looking at her thoughtfully. "Let me see— Ah, it's your mother that she looks like, Alexandra. Mrs. Bergson must have looked just like this when she was a little girl.

Does Milly run about over the country as you and Alexandra used to, Annie?"

Milly's mother protested. "Oh, my, no! Things has changed since we was girls. Milly has it very different. We are going to rent the place and move into town as soon as the girls are old enough to go out into company. A good many are doing that here now. Lou is going into business."

Lou grinned. "That's what she says. You better go get your things on. Ivar's hitching up," he added, turning to Annie.

Young farmers seldom address their wives by name. It is always "you," or "she."

Having got his wife out of the way, Lou sat down on the step and began to whittle. "Well, what do folks in New York think of William Jennings Bryan?" Lou began to bluster, as he always did when he talked politics. "We gave Wall Street a scare in ninety-six, all right, and we're fixing another to hand them. Silver wasn't the only issue," he nodded mysteriously. "There's a good many things got to be changed. The West is going to make itself heard."

Carl laughed. "But, surely, it did do that, if nothing else."

Lou's thin face reddened up to the roots of his bristly hair. "Oh, we've only begun. We're waking up to a sense of our responsibilities, out here, and we ain't afraid, neither. You fellows back there must be a tame lot. If you had any nerve you'd get together and march down to Wall Street and blow it up. Dynamite it, I mean," with a threatening nod.

He was so much in earnest that Carl scarcely knew how to answer him. "That would be a waste of powder. The same business would go on in another street. The street doesn't matter. But what have you fellows out here got to kick about? You have the only safe place there is. Morgan himself couldn't touch you. One only has to drive through this country to see that you're all as rich as barons."

"We have a good deal more to say than we had when we were poor," said Lou threateningly. "We're getting on to a whole lot of things."

As Ivar drove a double carriage up to the gate, Annie came out in a hat that looked like the model of a battleship. Carl rose and took her down to the carriage, while Lou lingered for a word with his sister.

"What do you suppose he's come for?" he asked, jerking his head toward the gate.

"Why, to pay us a visit. I've been begging him to for years."

Oscar looked at Alexandra. "He didn't let you know he was coming?"

"No. Why should he? I told him to come at any time."

Lou shrugged his shoulders. "He doesn't seem to have done much for himself. Wandering around this way!"

Oscar spoke solemnly, as from the depths of a cavern. "He never was much account."

Alexandra left them and hurried down to the gate where Annie was rattling on to Carl about her new dining-room furniture. "You must bring Mr. Linstrum over real soon, only be sure to telephone me first," she called back, as Carl helped her into the carriage. Old Ivar, his white head bare, stood holding the horses. Lou came down the path and climbed into the front seat, took up the reins, and drove off without saying anything further to any one. Oscar picked up his youngest boy and trudged off down the road, the other three trotting after him. Carl, holding the gate open for Alexandra, began to laugh. "Up and coming on the Divide, eh, Alexandra?" he cried gayly.

IV

CARL HAD CHANGED, Alexandra felt, much less than one might have expected. He had not become a trim, self-satisfied city man. There was still something homely and wayward and definitely personal about him. Even his clothes, his Norfolk coat and his very high collars, were a little unconventional. He seemed to shrink into himself as he used to do; to hold himself away from things, as if he were afraid of being hurt. In short, he was more self-conscious than a man of thirty-five is expected to be. He looked older than his years and not very strong. His black hair, which still hung in a triangle over his pale forehead, was thin at the crown, and there were fine, relentless lines about his eyes. His back, with its high, sharp shoulders, looked like the back of an overworked German professor off on his holiday. His face was intelligent, sensitive, unhappy.

That evening after supper, Carl and Alexandra were sitting by the clump of castor beans in the middle of the flower garden. The gravel paths glittered in the moonlight, and below them the fields lay white and still.

"Do you know, Alexandra," he was saying, "I've been thinking how strangely things work out. I've been away engraving other men's pictures, and you've stayed at home and made your own." He pointed with his cigar toward the sleeping landscape. "How in the world have you done it? How have your neighbors done it?"

"We hadn't any of us much to do with it, Carl. The land did it. It had its little joke. It pretended to be poor because nobody knew how to work it right; and then, all at once, it worked itself. It woke up out of its sleep and stretched itself, and it was so big, so rich, that we suddenly found we were rich, just from sitting still. As for me, you remember when I began to buy land. For years after that I was always squeezing and borrowing until I was ashamed to show my face in the banks. And then, all at once, men began to come to me offering to lend me money—and I didn't need it! Then I went ahead and built this house. I really built it for Emil. I want you to see Emil, Carl. He is so different from the rest of us!"

"How different?"

"Oh, you'll see! I'm sure it was to have sons like Emil, and to give them a chance, that father left the old country. It's curious, too; on the outside Emil is just like an American boy,—he graduated from the State University in June, you know,—but underneath he is more Swedish than any of us. Sometimes he is so like father that he frightens me; he is so violent in his feelings like that."

"Is he going to farm here with you?"

"He shall do whatever he wants to," Alexandra declared warmly. "He is going to have a chance, a whole chance; that's what I've worked for. Sometimes he talks about studying law, and sometimes, just lately, he's been talking about going out into the sand hills and taking up more land. He has his sad times, like father. But I hope he won't do that. We have land enough, at last!" Alexandra laughed.

"How about Lou and Oscar? They've done well, haven't they?"

"Yes, very well; but they are different, and now that they have farms of their own I do not see so much of them. We divided the land equally when Lou married. They have their own way of doing things, and they do not altogether like my way, I am afraid. Perhaps they think me too independent. But I have had to think for myself a good many years and am not likely to change. On the whole, though, we take as much comfort in each other as most brothers and sisters do. And I am very fond of Lou's oldest daughter."

"I think I liked the old Lou and Oscar better, and they probably feel the same about me. I even, if you can keep a secret,"—Carl leaned forward and touched her arm, smiling,—"I even think I liked the old country better. This is all very splendid in its way, but there was something about this country when it was a wild old beast that has haunted me all these years. Now, when I come back to all this milk and honey, I feel like the old German song, 'Wo bist du, wo bist du, mein geliebtest Land?'—Do you ever feel like that, I wonder?"

"Yes, sometimes, when I think about father and mother and those who are gone; so many of our old neighbors." Alexandra paused and looked up thoughtfully at the stars. "We can remember the graveyard when it was wild prairie, Carl, and now—"

"And now the old story has begun to write itself over there," said Carl softly. "Isn't it queer: there are only two or three human stories, and they go on repeating themselves as fiercely as if they had never happened before; like the larks in this country, that have been singing the same five notes over for thousands of years."

"Oh, yes! The young people, they live so hard. And yet I sometimes envy them. There is my little neighbor, now; the people who bought your old place. I wouldn't have sold it to any one else, but I was always fond of that girl. You must remember her, little Marie Tovesky, from Omaha, who used to visit here? When she was eighteen she ran away from the convent school and got married, crazy child! She came out here a bride, with her father and husband. He had nothing, and the old man was willing to buy them a place and set them up. Your farm took her fancy, and I was glad to have her so near me. I've never been sorry, either. I even try to get along with Frank on her account."

"Is Frank her husband?"

"Yes. He's one of these wild fellows. Most Bohemians are good-natured, but Frank thinks we don't appreciate him here, I guess. He's jealous about everything, his farm and his horses and his pretty wife. Everybody likes her, just the same as when she was little. Sometimes I go up to the Catholic church with Emil, and it's funny to see Marie standing there laughing and shaking hands with people, looking so excited and gay, with Frank sulking behind her as if he could eat everybody alive. Frank's not a bad neighbor, but to get on with him you've got to make a fuss over him and act as if you thought he was a very important person all the time, and different from other people. I find it hard to keep that up from one year's end to another."

"I shouldn't think you'd be very successful at that kind of thing, Alexandra." Carl seemed to find the idea amusing.

"Well," said Alexandra firmly, "I do the best I can, on Marie's account. She has it hard enough, anyway. She's too young and pretty for this sort of life. We're all ever so much older and slower. But she's the kind that won't be downed easily. She'll work all day and go to a Bohemian wedding and dance all night, and drive the hay wagon for a cross man next morning. I could stay by a job, but I never had the go in me that she has, when I was going my best. I'll have to take you over to see her to-morrow."

Carl dropped the end of his cigar softly among the castor beans and sighed. "Yes, I suppose I must see the old place. I'm cowardly about things that remind me of myself. It took courage to come at all, Alexandra. I wouldn't have, if I hadn't wanted to see you very, very much."

Alexandra looked at him with her calm, deliberate eyes. "Why do you dread things like that, Carl?" she asked earnestly. "Why are you dissatisfied with yourself?"

Her visitor winced. "How direct you are, Alexandra! Just like you used to be. Do I give myself away so quickly? Well, you see, for one thing, there's nothing to look forward to in my profession. Wood-engraving is the only thing I care about, and that had gone out before I began. Everything's cheap metal work nowadays, touching up miserable photographs, forcing up poor drawings, and spoiling good ones. I'm absolutely sick of it all." Carl frowned. "Alexandra, all the way out from New York I've been planning how I could deceive you and make you think me a very enviable fellow, and here I am telling you the truth the first night. I waste a lot of time pretending to people, and the joke of it is, I don't think I ever deceive any one. There are too many of my kind; people know us on sight."

Carl paused. Alexandra pushed her hair back from her brow with a puzzled, thoughtful gesture. "You see," he went on calmly, "measured by your standards here, I'm a failure. I couldn't buy even one of your cornfields. I've enjoyed a great many things, but I've got nothing to show for it all."

"But you show for it yourself, Carl. I'd rather have had your freedom than my land."

Carl shook his head mournfully. "Freedom so often means that one isn't needed anywhere. Here you are an individual, you have a background of your own, you would be missed. But off there in the cities there are thousands of rolling stones like me. We are all alike; we have no ties, we know nobody, we own nothing. When one of us dies, they scarcely know where to bury him. Our landlady and the delicatessen man are our mourners, and we leave nothing behind us but a frock-coat and a fiddle, or an easel, or a typewriter, or whatever tool we got our living by. All we have ever managed to do is to pay our rent, the exorbitant rent that one has to pay for a few square feet of space near the heart of things. We have no house, no place, no people of our own. We live in the streets, in the parks, in the theatres. We sit in restaurants and concert halls and look about at the hundreds of our own kind and shudder."

Alexandra was silent. She sat looking at the silver spot the moon made on the surface of the pond down in the pasture. He knew that she understood what he meant. At last she said slowly, "And yet I would rather have Emil grow up like that than like his two brothers.

We pay a high rent, too, though we pay differently. We grow hard and heavy here. We don't move lightly and easily as you do, and our minds get stiff. If the world were no wider than my cornfields, if there were not something beside this, I wouldn't feel that it was much worthwhile to work. No, I would rather have Emil like you than like them. I felt that as soon as you came."

"I wonder why you feel like that?" Carl mused.

"I don't know. Perhaps I am like Carrie Jensen, the sister of one of my hired men. She had never been out of the cornfields, and a few years ago she got despondent and said life was just the same thing over and over, and she didn't see the use of it. After she had tried to kill herself once or twice, her folks got worried and sent her over to Iowa to visit some relations. Ever since she's come back she's been perfectly cheerful, and she says she's contented to live and work in a world that's so big and interesting. She said that anything as big as the bridges over the Platte and the Missouri reconciled her. And it's what goes on in the world that reconciles me."

V

ALEXANDRA did not find time to go to her neighbor's the next day, nor the next. It was a busy season on the farm, with the corn-plowing going on, and even Emil was in the field with a team and cultivator. Carl went about over the farms with Alexandra in the morning, and in the afternoon and evening they found a great deal to talk about. Emil, for all his track practice, did not stand up under farmwork very well, and by night he was too tired to talk or even to practice on his cornet.

On Wednesday morning Carl got up before it was light, and stole downstairs and out of the kitchen door just as old Ivar was making his morning ablutions at the pump. Carl nodded to him and hurried up the draw, past the garden, and into the pasture where the milking cows used to be kept.

The dawn in the east looked like the light from some great fire that was burning under the edge of the world. The color was reflected in the globules of dew that sheathed the short gray pasture grass. Carl walked rapidly until he came to the crest of the second hill, where the Bergson pasture joined the one that had belonged to his father. There he sat down and waited for the sun to rise. It was just there that he and Alexandra used to do their milking together,

"Carl walked rapidly until he came to the crest of the second hill, where the Bergson pasture joined the one that had belonged to his father." —O Pioneers!

he on his side of the fence, she on hers. He could remember exactly how she looked when she came over the close-cropped grass, her skirts pinned up, her head bare, a bright tin pail in either hand, and the milky light of the early morning all about her. Even as a boy he used to feel, when he saw her coming with her free step, her upright head and calm shoulders, that she looked as if she had walked straight out of the morning itself. Since then, when he had happened to see the sun come up in the country or on the water, he had often remembered the young Swedish girl and her milking pails.

Carl sat musing until the sun leaped above the prairie, and in the grass about him all the small creatures of day began to tune their tiny instruments. Birds and insects without number began to chirp, to twitter, to snap and whistle, to make all manner of fresh shrill noises. The pasture was flooded with light; every clump of iron-weed and snow-on-the-mountain threw a long shadow, and the golden light seemed to be rippling through the curly grass like the tide racing in.

He crossed the fence into the pasture that was now the Shabatas' and continued his walk toward the pond. He had not gone far, however, when he discovered that he was not the only person abroad. In the draw below, his gun in his hands, was Emil, advancing cautiously, with a young woman beside him. They were moving softly, keeping close together, and Carl knew that they expected to find ducks on the pond. At the moment when they came in sight of the bright spot of water, he heard a whirr of wings and the ducks shot up into the air. There was a sharp crack from the gun, and five of the birds fell to the ground. Emil and his companion laughed delightedly, and Emil ran to pick them up. When he came back, dangling the ducks by their feet, Marie held her apron and he dropped them into it. As she stood looking down at them, her face changed. She took up one of the birds, a rumpled ball of feathers with the blood dripping slowly from its mouth, and looked at the live color that still burned on its plumage.

As she let it fall, she cried in distress, "Oh, Emil, why did you?"

"I like that!" the boy exclaimed indignantly. "Why, Marie, you asked me to come yourself."

"Yes, yes, I know," she said tearfully, "but I didn't think. I hate to see them when they are first shot. They were having such a good time, and we've spoiled it all for them."

Emil gave a rather sore laugh. "I should say we had! I'm not going hunting with you any more. You're as bad as Ivar. Here, let me take them." He snatched the ducks out of her apron.

"Don't be cross, Emil. Only—Ivar's right about wild things. They're too happy to kill. You can tell just how they felt when they flew up. They were scared, but they didn't really think anything could hurt them. No, we won't do that any more."

"All right," Emil assented. "I'm sorry I made you feel bad." As he looked down into her tearful eyes, there was a curious, sharp young bitterness in his own.

Carl watched them as they moved slowly down the draw. They had not seen him at all. He had not overheard much of their dialogue, but he felt the import of it. It made him, somehow, unreasonably mournful to find two young things abroad in the pasture in the early morning. He decided that he needed his breakfast.

VI

A T DINNER that day Alexandra said she thought they must really manage to go over to the Shabatas' that afternoon. "It's not often I let three days go by without seeing Marie. She will think I have forsaken her, now that my old friend has come back."

After the men had gone back to work, Alexandra put on a white dress and her sun-hat, and she and Carl set forth across the fields. "You see we have kept up the old path, Carl. It has been so nice for me to feel that there was a friend at the other end of it again."

Carl smiled a little ruefully. "All the same, I hope it hasn't been *quite* the same."

Alexandra looked at him with surprise. "Why, no, of course not. Not the same. She could not very well take your place, if that's what you mean. I'm friendly with all my neighbors, I hope. But Marie is really a companion, some one I can talk to quite frankly. You wouldn't want me to be more lonely than I have been, would you?"

Carl laughed and pushed back the triangular lock of hair with the edge of his hat. "Of course I don't. I ought to be thankful that this path hasn't been worn by—well, by friends with more pressing errands than your little Bohemian is likely to have." He paused to give Alexandra his hand as she stepped over the stile. "Are you the least bit disappointed in our coming together again?" he asked abruptly. "Is it the way you hoped it would be?"

Alexandra smiled at this. "Only better. When I've thought about your coming, I've sometimes been a little afraid of it. You have lived where things move so fast, and everything is slow here; the people slowest of all. Our lives are like the years, all made up of weather and crops and cows. How you hated cows!" She shook her head and laughed to herself.

"I didn't when we milked together. I walked up to the pasture corners this morning. I wonder whether I shall ever be able to tell you all that I was thinking about up there. It's a strange thing, Alexandra; I find it easy to be frank with you about everything under the sun except—yourself!"

"You are afraid of hurting my feelings, perhaps." Alexandra looked at him thoughtfully.

"No, I'm afraid of giving you a shock. You've seen yourself for so long in the dull minds of the people about you, that if I were to tell you how you seem to me, it would startle you. But you must see that you astonish me. You must feel when people admire you."

Alexandra blushed and laughed with some confusion. "I felt that you were pleased with me, if you mean that."

"And you've felt when other people were pleased with you?" he insisted.

"Well, sometimes. The men in town, at the banks and the county offices, seem glad to see me. I think, myself, it is more pleasant to do business with people who are clean and healthy-looking," she admitted blandly.

Carl gave a little chuckle as he opened the Shabatas' gate for her. "Oh, do you?" he asked dryly.

There was no sign of life about the Shabatas' house except a big yellow cat, sunning itself on the kitchen doorstep.

Alexandra took the path that led to the orchard. "She often sits there and sews. I didn't telephone her we were coming, because I didn't want her to go to work and bake cake and freeze ice-cream.

She'll always make a party if you give her the least excuse. Do you recognize the apple trees, Carl?"

Linstrum looked about him. "I wish I had a dollar for every bucket of water I've carried for those trees. Poor father, he was an easy man, but he was perfectly merciless when it came to watering the orchard."

"That's one thing I like about Germans; they make an orchard grow if they can't make anything else. I'm so glad these trees belong to some one who takes comfort in them. When I rented this place, the tenants never kept the orchard up, and Emil and I used to come over and take care of it ourselves. It needs mowing now. There she is, down in the corner. Maria-a-a!" she called.

A recumbent figure started up from the grass and came running toward them through the flickering screen of light and shade.

"Look at her! Isn't she like a little brown rabbit?" Alexandra laughed.

Marie ran up panting and threw her arms about Alexandra. "Oh, I had begun to think you were not coming at all, maybe. I knew you were so busy. Yes, Emil told me about Mr. Linstrum being here. Won't you come up to the house?"

"Why not sit down there in your corner? Carl wants to see the orchard. He kept all these trees alive for years, watering them with his own back."

Marie turned to Carl. "Then I'm thankful to you, Mr. Linstrum. We'd never have bought the place if it hadn't been for this orchard, and then I wouldn't have had Alexandra, either." She gave Alexandra's arm a little squeeze as she walked beside her. "How nice your dress smells, Alexandra; you put rosemary leaves in your chest, like I told you."

She led them to the northwest corner of the orchard, sheltered on one side by a thick mulberry hedge and bordered on the other by a wheatfield, just beginning to yellow. In this corner the ground dipped a little, and the bluegrass, which the weeds had driven out in the upper part of the orchard, grew thick and luxuriant. Wild roses were flaming in the tufts of bunchgrass along the fence. Under a white mulberry tree there was an old wagon-seat. Beside it lay a book and a workbasket.

"You must have the seat, Alexandra. The grass would stain your dress," the hostess insisted. She dropped down on the ground at Alexandra's side and tucked her feet under her. Carl sat at a little distance from the two women, his back to the wheatfield, and watched them. Alexandra took off her shade-hat and threw it on the ground. Marie picked it up and played with the white ribbons, twisting them about her brown fingers as she talked. They made a pretty picture in the strong sunlight, the leafy pattern surrounding them like a net; the Swedish woman so white and gold, kindly and amused, but armored in calm, and the alert brown one, her full lips parted, points of yellow light dancing in her eyes as she laughed and chattered. Carl had never forgotten little Marie Tovesky's eyes, and he was glad to have an opportunity to study them. The brown iris, he found, was curiously slashed with yellow, the color of sunflower honey, or of old amber. In each eye one of these streaks must have been larger than the others, for the effect was that of two dancing points of light, two little yellow bubbles, such as rise in a glass of champagne. Sometimes they seemed like the sparks from a forge. She seemed so easily excited, to kindle with a fierce little flame if one but breathed upon her. "What a waste," Carl reflected. "She ought to be doing all that for a sweetheart. How awkwardly things come about!"

It was not very long before Marie sprang up out of the grass again. "Wait a moment. I want to show you something." She ran away and disappeared behind the low-growing apple trees.

"What a charming creature," Carl murmured. "I don't wonder that her husband is jealous. But can't she walk? Does she always run?"

Alexandra nodded. "Always. I don't see many people, but I don't believe there are many like her, anywhere."

Marie came back with a branch she had broken from an apricot tree, laden with pale-yellow, pink-cheeked fruit. She dropped it beside Carl. "Did you plant those, too? They are such beautiful little trees."

Carl fingered the blue-green leaves, porous like blotting-paper and shaped like birch leaves, hung on waxen red stems. "Yes, I think I did. Are these the circus trees, Alexandra?"

"Shall I tell her about them?" Alexandra asked. "Sit down like a good girl, Marie, and don't ruin my poor hat, and I'll tell you a story. A long time ago, when Carl and I were, say, sixteen and twelve, a circus came to Hanover and we went to town in our wagon, with Lou and Oscar, to see the parade. We hadn't money enough to go to the circus. We followed the parade out to the circus grounds and hung around until the show began and the crowd went inside the tent. Then Lou was afraid we looked foolish standing outside in the pasture, so we went back to Hanover feeling very sad. There was a man in the streets selling apricots, and we had never seen any before. He had driven down from somewhere up in the French country, and he was selling them twenty-five cents a peck. We had a little money our fathers had given us for candy, and I bought two pecks and Carl bought one. They cheered us a good deal, and we saved all the seeds and planted them. Up to the time Carl went away, they hadn't borne at all."

"And now he's come back to eat them," cried Marie, nodding at Carl. "That *is* a good story. I can remember you a little, Mr. Linstrum. I used to see you in Hanover sometimes, when Uncle Joe took me to town. I remember you because you were always buying pencils and tubes of paint at the drug store. Once, when my uncle left me at the store, you drew a lot of little birds and flowers for me on a piece of wrapping-paper. I kept them for a long while. I thought you were very romantic because you could draw and had such black eyes."

Carl smiled. "Yes, I remember that time. Your uncle bought you some kind of a mechanical toy, a Turkish lady sitting on an ottoman and smoking a hookah, wasn't it? And she turned her head backwards and forwards."

"Oh, yes! Wasn't she splendid! I knew well enough I ought not to tell Uncle Joe I wanted it, for he had just come back from the saloon and was feeling good. You remember how he laughed? She tickled him, too. But when we got home, my aunt scolded him for buying toys when she needed so many things. We wound our lady up every night, and when she began to move her head my aunt used to laugh as hard as any of us. It was a music-box, you know, and the Turkish lady played a tune while she smoked. That was how she made you feel so jolly. As I remember her, she was lovely, and had a gold crescent on her turban."

Half an hour later, as they were leaving the house, Carl and Alexandra were met in the path by a strapping fellow in overalls and a blue shirt. He was breathing hard, as if he had been running, and was muttering to himself.

Marie ran forward, and, taking him by the arm, gave him a little push toward her guests. "Frank, this is Mr. Linstrum."

Frank took off his broad straw hat and nodded to Alexandra. When he spoke to Carl, he showed a fine set of white teeth. He was burned a dull red down to his neckband, and there was a heavy three-days' stubble on his face. Even in his agitation he was handsome, but he looked a rash and violent man.

Barely saluting the callers, he turned at once to his wife and began, in an outraged tone, "I have to leave my team to drive the old woman Hiller's hogs out-a my wheat. I go to take dat old woman to de court if she ain't careful, I tell you!"

His wife spoke soothingly. "But, Frank, she has only her lame boy to help her. She does the best she can."

Alexandra looked at the excited man and offered a suggestion. "Why don't you go over there some afternoon and hog-tight her fences? You'd save time for yourself in the end."

Frank's neck stiffened. "Not-a-much, I won't. I keep my hogs home. Other peoples can do like me. See? If that Louis can mend shoes, he can mend fence."

"Maybe," said Alexandra placidly; "but I've found it sometimes pays to mend other people's fences. Good-bye, Marie. Come to see me soon."

Alexandra walked firmly down the path and Carl followed her.

Frank went into the house and threw himself on the sofa, his face to the wall, his clenched fist on his hip. Marie, having seen her guests off, came in and put her hand coaxingly on his shoulder.

"Poor Frank! You've run until you've made your head ache, now haven't you? Let me make you some coffee."

"What else am I to do?" he cried hotly in Bohemian. "Am I to let any old woman's hogs root up my wheat? Is that what I work myself to death for?"

"Don't worry about it, Frank. I'll speak to Mrs. Hiller again. But, really, she almost cried last time they got out, she was so sorry."

Frank bounced over on his other side. "That's it; you always side with them against me. They all know it. Anybody here feels free to borrow the mower and break it, or turn their hogs in on me. They know you won't care!"

Marie hurried away to make his coffee. When she came back, he was fast asleep. She sat down and looked at him for a long while, very thoughtfully. When the kitchen clock struck six she went out to get supper, closing the door gently behind her. She was always sorry for Frank when he worked himself into one of these rages, and she was sorry to have him rough and quarrelsome with his neighbors. She was perfectly aware that the neighbors had a good deal to put up with, and that they bore with Frank for her sake.

VII

MARIE'S FATHER, Albert Tovesky, was one of the more intelligent Bohemians who came West in the early seventies. He settled in Omaha and became a leader and adviser among his people there. Marie was his youngest child, by a second wife, and was the apple of his eye. She was barely sixteen, and was in the graduating class of the Omaha High School, when Frank Shabata arrived from the old country and set all the Bohemian girls in a flutter. He was easily the buck of the beer-gardens, and on Sunday he was a sight to see, with his silk hat and tucked shirt and blue frock-coat, wearing gloves and carrying a little wisp of a yellow cane. He was tall and fair, with splendid teeth and close-cropped yellow curls, and he wore a slightly disdainful expression, proper for a young man with high connections, whose mother had a big farm in the Elbe valley. There was often an interesting discontent in his blue eyes, and every Bohemian girl he met imagined herself the cause of that unsatisfied expression. He had a way of drawing out his cambric handkerchief slowly, by one corner, from his breast-pocket, that was melancholy and romantic in the extreme. He took a little flight with each of the more eligible Bohemian girls, but it was when he was with little Marie Tovesky that he drew his handkerchief out most slowly, and, after he had lit a fresh cigar, dropped the match most despairingly. Any one could see, with half an eye, that his proud heart was bleeding for somebody.

One Sunday, late in the summer after Marie's graduation, she met Frank at a Bohemian picnic down the river and went rowing with him all the afternoon. When she got home that evening she went straight to her father's room and told him that she was engaged to Shabata. Old Tovesky was having a comfortable pipe before he went to bed. When he heard his daughter's announcement, he first prudently corked his beer bottle and then leaped to his feet and had a turn of temper. He characterized Frank Shabata by a Bohemian expression which is the equivalent of stuffed shirt.

"Why don't he go to work like the rest of us did? His farm in the Elbe valley, indeed! Ain't he got plenty brothers and sisters? It's his mother's farm, and why don't he stay at home and help her? Haven't I seen his mother out in the morning at five o'clock with her ladle and her big bucket on wheels, putting liquid manure on the cabbages? Don't I know the look of old Eva Shabata's hands? Like an old horse's hoofs they are—and this fellow wearing gloves and rings! Engaged, indeed! You aren't fit to be out of school, and that's what's the matter with you. I will send you off to the Sisters of the Sacred Heart in St. Louis, and they will teach you some sense, *I* guess!"

Accordingly, the very next week, Albert Tovesky took his daughter, pale and tearful, down the river to the convent. But the way to make Frank want anything was to tell him he couldn't have it. He managed to have an interview with Marie before she went away, and whereas he had been only half in love with her before, he now persuaded himself that he would not stop at anything. Marie took with her to the convent, under the canvas lining of her trunk, the results of a laborious and satisfying morning on Frank's part; no less than a dozen photographs of himself, taken in a dozen different love-lorn attitudes. There was a little round photograph for her watch-case, photographs for her wall and dresser, and even long narrow ones to be used as bookmarks. More than once the handsome gentleman was torn to pieces before the French class by an indignant nun.

Marie pined in the convent for a year, until her eighteenth birthday was passed. Then she met Frank Shabata in the Union Station in St. Louis and ran away with him. Old Tovesky forgave his daughter because there was nothing else to do, and bought her a farm in the country that she had loved so well as a child. Since then her story had been a part of the history of the Divide. She and Frank had been living there for five years when Carl Linstrum came back to pay his long deferred visit to Alexandra. Frank had, on the whole, done better than one might have expected. He had flung himself at the soil with savage energy. Once a year he went to Hastings or to Omaha, on a spree. He stayed away for a week or two, and then came home and worked like a demon. He did work; if he felt sorry for himself, that was his own affair.

VIII

ON THE EVENING of the day of Alexandra's call at the Shabatas',
a heavy rain set in. Frank sat up until a late hour reading the
Sunday newspapers. One of the Goulds was getting a divorce, and
Frank took it as a personal affront. In printing the story of the
young man's marital troubles, the knowing editor gave a sufficiently
colored account of his career, stating the amount of his income and
the manner in which he was supposed to spend it. Frank read
English slowly, and the more he read about this divorce case, the
angrier he grew. At last he threw down the page with a snort. He
turned to his farm-hand who was reading the other half of the
paper.

"By God! If I have that young feller in de hayfield once, I show
him somet'ing. Listen here what he do wit his money." And Frank
began the catalogue of the young man's reputed extravagances.

Marie sighed. She thought it hard that the Goulds, for whom she
had nothing but good will, should make her so much trouble. She
hated to see the Sunday newspapers come into the house. Frank was
always reading about the doings of rich people and feeling outraged. He had an inexhaustible stock of stories about their crimes
and follies, how they bribed the courts and shot down their butlers

with impunity whenever they chose. Frank and Lou Bergson had very similar ideas, and they were two of the political agitators of the country.

The next morning broke clear and brilliant, but Frank said the ground was too wet to plough, so he took the cart and drove over to Sainte-Agnes to spend the day at Moses Marcel's saloon. After he was gone, Marie went out to the back porch to begin her butter-making. A brisk wind had come up and was driving puffy white clouds across the sky. The orchard was sparkling and rippling in the sun. Marie stood looking toward it wistfully, her hand on the lid of the churn, when she heard a sharp ring in the air, the merry sound of the whetstone on the scythe. That invitation decided her. She ran into the house, put on a short skirt and a pair of her husband's boots, caught up a tin pail and started for the orchard. Emil had already begun work and was mowing vigorously. When he saw her coming, he stopped and wiped his brow. His yellow canvas leggings and khaki trousers were splashed to the knees.

"Don't let me disturb you, Emil. I'm going to pick cherries. Isn't everything beautiful after the rain? Oh, but I'm glad to get this place mowed! When I heard it raining in the night, I thought maybe you would come and do it for me to-day. The wind wakened me. Didn't it blow dreadfully? Just smell the wild roses! They are always so spicy after a rain. We never had so many of them in here before. I suppose it's the wet season. Will you have to cut them, too?"

"If I cut the grass, I will," Emil said teasingly. "What's the matter with you? What makes you so flighty?"

"Am I flighty? I suppose that's the wet season, too, then. It's exciting to see everything growing so fast,—and to get the grass cut! Please leave the roses till last, if you must cut them. Oh, I don't mean all of them, I mean that low place down by my tree, where there are so many. Aren't you splashed! Look at the spider-webs all over the grass. Good-bye. I'll call you if I see a snake."

She tripped away and Emil stood looking after her. In a few

moments he heard the cherries dropping smartly into the pail, and he began to swing his scythe with that long, even stroke that few American boys ever learn. Marie picked cherries and sang softly to herself, stripping one glittering branch after another, shivering when she caught a shower of raindrops on her neck and hair. And Emil mowed his way slowly down toward the cherry trees.

That summer the rains had been so many and opportune that it was almost more than Shabata and his man could do to keep up with the corn; the orchard was a neglected wilderness. All sorts of weeds and herbs and flowers had grown up there; splotches of wild lark-spur, pale green-and-white spikes of hoarhound, plantations of wild cotton, tangles of foxtail and wild wheat. South of the apricot trees, cornering on the wheatfield, was Frank's alfalfa, where myriads of white and yellow butterflies were always fluttering above the purple blossoms. When Emil reached the lower corner by the hedge, Marie was sitting under her white mulberry tree, the pailful of cherries beside her, looking off at the gentle, tireless swelling of the wheat.

"Emil," she said suddenly—he was mowing quietly about under the tree so as not to disturb her—"what religion did the Swedes have away back, before they were Christians?"

Emil paused and straightened his back. "I don't know. About like the Germans', wasn't it?"

Marie went on as if she had not heard him. "The Bohemians, you know, were tree worshipers before the missionaries came. Fa-ther says the people in the mountains still do queer things, some-times,—they believe that trees bring good or bad luck."

Emil looked superior. "Do they? Well, which are the lucky trees? I'd like to know."

"I don't know all of them, but I know lindens are. The old people in the mountains plant lindens to purify the forest, and to do away with the spells that come from the old trees they say have lasted from heathen times. I'm a good Catholic, but I think I could get along with caring for trees, if I hadn't anything else."

"That's a poor saying," said Emil, stooping over to wipe his hands in the wet grass.

"Why is it? If I feel that way, I feel that way. I like trees because they seem more resigned to the way they have to live than other things do. I feel as if this tree knows everything I ever think of when I sit here. When I come back to it, I never have to remind it of anything; I begin just where I left off."

Emil had nothing to say to this. He reached up among the branches and began to pick the sweet, insipid fruit,—long ivory-colored berries, tipped with faint pink, like white coral, that fall to the ground unheeded all summer through. He dropped a handful into her lap.

"Do you like Mr. Linstrum?" Marie asked suddenly.

"Yes. Don't you?"

"Oh, ever so much; only he seems kind of staid and school-teachery. But, of course, he is older than Frank, even. I'm sure I don't want to live to be more than thirty, do you? Do you think Alexandra likes him very much?"

"I suppose so. They were old friends."

"Oh, Emil, you know what I mean!" Marie tossed her head impatiently. "Does she really care about him? When she used to tell me about him, I always wondered whether she wasn't a little in love with him."

"Who, Alexandra?" Emil laughed and thrust his hands into his trousers pockets. "Alexandra's never been in love, you crazy!" He laughed again. "She wouldn't know how to go about it. The idea!"

Marie shrugged her shoulders. "Oh, you don't know Alexandra as well as you think you do! If you had any eyes, you would see that she is very fond of him. It would serve you all right if she walked off with Carl. I like him because he appreciates her more than you do."

Emil frowned. "What are you talking about, Marie? Alexandra's all right. She and I have always been good friends. What more do you want? I like to talk to Carl about New York and what a fellow can do there."

"Oh, Emil! Surely you are not thinking of going off there?"

"Why not? I must go somewhere, mustn't I?" The young man took up his scythe and leaned on it. "Would you rather I went off in the sand hills and lived like Ivar?"

Marie's face fell under his brooding gaze. She looked down at his wet leggings. "I'm sure Alexandra hopes you will stay on here," she murmured.

"Then Alexandra will be disappointed," the young man said roughly. "What do I want to hang around here for? Alexandra can run the farm all right, without me. I don't want to stand around and look on. I want to be doing something on my own account."

"That's so," Marie sighed. "There are so many, many things you can do. Almost anything you choose."

"And there are so many, many things I can't do." Emil echoed her tone sarcastically. "Sometimes I don't want to do anything at all, and sometimes I want to pull the four corners of the Divide together"—he threw out his arm and brought it back with a jerk—"so, like a table-cloth. I get tired of seeing men and horses going up and down, up and down."

Marie looked up at his defiant figure and her face clouded. "I wish you weren't so restless, and didn't get so worked up over things," she said sadly.

"Thank you," he returned shortly.

She sighed despondently. "Everything I say makes you cross, don't it? And you never used to be cross to me."

Emil took a step nearer and stood frowning down at her bent head. He stood in an attitude of self-defense, his feet well apart, his hands clenched and drawn up at his sides, so that the cords stood out on his bare arms. "I can't play with you like a little boy any more," he said slowly. "That's what you miss, Marie. You'll have to get some other little boy to play with." He stopped and took a deep breath. Then he went on in a low tone, so intense that it was almost threatening: "Sometimes you seem to understand perfectly, and then sometimes you pretend you don't. You don't help things any by pretending. It's then that I want to pull the corners of the Divide together. If you *won't* understand, you know, I could make you!"

Marie clasped her hands and started up from her seat. She had grown very pale and her eyes were shining with excitement and distress. "But, Emil, if I understand, then all our good times are over, we can never do nice things together any more. We shall have to behave like Mr. Linstrum. And, anyhow, there's nothing to understand!" She struck the ground with her little foot fiercely. "That won't last. It will go away, and things will be just as they used to. I wish you were a Catholic. The Church helps people, indeed it does. I pray for you, but that's not the same as if you prayed yourself."

She spoke rapidly and pleadingly, looked entreatingly into his face. Emil stood defiant, gazing down at her.

"I can't pray to have the things I want," he said slowly, "and I won't pray not to have them, not if I'm damned for it."

Marie turned away, wringing her hands. "Oh, Emil, you won't try! Then all our good times are over."

"Yes, over. I never expect to have any more."

Emil gripped the hand-holds of his scythe and began to mow. Marie took up her cherries and went slowly toward the house, crying bitterly.

IX

ON SUNDAY AFTERNOON, a month after Carl Linstrum's arrival, he rode with Emil up into the French country to attend a Catholic fair. He sat for most of the afternoon in the basement of the church, where the fair was held, talking to Marie Shabata, or strolled about the gravel terrace, thrown up on the hillside in front of the basement doors, where the French boys were jumping and wrestling and throwing the discus. Some of the boys were in their white baseball suits; they had just come up from a Sunday practice game down in the ballgrounds. Amédée, the newly married, Emil's best friend, was their pitcher, renowned among the country towns for his dash and skill. Amédée was a little fellow, a year younger than Emil and much more boyish in appearance; very lithe and active and neatly made, with a clear brown and white skin, and flashing white teeth. The Sainte-Agnes boys were to play the Hastings nine in a fortnight, and Amédée's lightning balls were the hope of his team. The little Frenchman seemed to get every ounce there was in him behind the ball as it left his hand.

"You'd have made the battery at the University for sure, 'Médée," Emil said as they were walking from the ballgrounds back

"On Sunday afternoon, a month after Carl Linstrum's arrival, he rode with Emil up into the French country to attend a Catholic fair." —O Pioneers!

to the church on the hill. "You're pitching better than you did in the spring."

Amédée grinned. "Sure! A married man don't lose his head no more." He slapped Emil on the back as he caught step with him. "Oh, Emil, you wanna get married right off quick! It's the greatest thing ever!"

Emil laughed. "How am I going to get married without any girl?"

Amédée took his arm. "Pooh! There are plenty girls will have you. You wanna get some nice French girl, now. She treat you well; always be jolly. See"—he began checking off on his fingers—"there is Sévérine, and Alphosen, and Joséphine, and Hectorine, and Louise, and Malvina—why, I could love any of them girls! Why don't you get after them? Are you stuck up, Emil, or is anything the matter with you? I never did know a boy twenty-two years old before that didn't have no girl. You wanna be a priest, maybe? Not-a for me!" Amédée swaggered. "I bring many good Catholics into this world, I hope, and that's a way I help the Church."

Emil looked down and patted him on the shoulder. "Now you're windy, 'Médée. You Frenchies like to brag."

But Amédée had the zeal of the newly married, and he was not to be lightly shaken off. "Honest and true, Emil, don't you want *any* girl? Maybe there's some young lady in Lincoln, now, very grand"—Amédée waved his hand languidly before his face to denote the fan of heartless beauty—"and you lost your heart up there. Is that it?"

"Maybe," said Emil.

But Amédée saw no appropriate glow in his friend's face. "Bah!" he exclaimed in disgust. "I tell all the French girls to keep 'way from you. You gotta rock in there," thumping Emil on the ribs.

When they reached the terrace at the side of the church, Amédée, who was excited by his success on the ballgrounds, challenged Emil to a jumping-match, though he knew he would be beaten. They belted themselves up, and Raoul Marcel, the choir tenor and Father Duchesne's pet, and Jean Bordelau held the string over which they vaulted. All the French boys stood round, cheering and humping themselves up when Emil or Amédée went over the wire, as if they were helping in the lift. Emil stopped at five-feet-five, declaring that he would spoil his appetite for supper if he jumped any more.

Angélique, Amédée's pretty bride, as blonde and fair as her name, who had come out to watch the match, tossed her head at Emil and said:—

" 'Médée could jump much higher than you if he were as tall.

And anyhow, he is much more graceful. He goes over like a bird, and you have to hump yourself all up."

"Oh, I do, do I?" Emil caught her and kissed her saucy mouth squarely, while she laughed and struggled and called, " 'Médée! 'Médée!"

"There, you see your 'Médée isn't even big enough to get you away from me. I could run away with you right now and he could only sit down and cry about it. I'll show you whether I have to hump myself!" Laughing and panting, he picked Angélique up in his arms and began running about the rectangle with her. Not until he saw Marie Shabata's tiger eyes flashing from the gloom of the basement doorway did he hand the disheveled bride over to her husband. "There, go to your graceful; I haven't the heart to take you away from him."

Angélique clung to her husband and made faces at Emil over the white shoulder of Amédée's ball-shirt. Emil was greatly amused at her air of proprietorship and at Amédée's shameless submission to it. He was delighted with his friend's good fortune. He liked to see and to think about Amédée's sunny, natural, happy love.

He and Amédée had ridden and wrestled and larked together since they were lads of twelve. On Sundays and holidays they were always arm in arm. It seemed strange that now he should have to hide the thing that Amédée was so proud of, that the feeling which gave one of them such happiness should bring the other such despair. It was like that when Alexandra tested her seed-corn in the spring, he mused. From two ears that had grown side by side, the grains of one shot up joyfully into the light, projecting themselves into the future, and the grains from the other lay still in the earth and rotted; and nobody knew why.

X

WHILE EMIL AND CARL were amusing themselves at the fair, Alexandra was at home, busy with her account-books, which had been neglected of late. She was almost through with her figures when she heard a cart drive up to the gate, and looking out of the window she saw her two older brothers. They had seemed to avoid her ever since Carl Linstrum's arrival, four weeks ago that day, and she hurried to the door to welcome them. She saw at once that they had come with some very definite purpose. They followed her stiffly into the sitting-room. Oscar sat down, but Lou walked over to the window and remained standing, his hands behind him.

"You are by yourself?" he asked, looking toward the doorway into the parlor.

"Yes. Carl and Emil went up to the Catholic fair."

For a few moments neither of the men spoke.

Then Lou came out sharply. "How soon does he intend to go away from here?"

"I don't know, Lou. Not for some time, I hope." Alexandra spoke in an even, quiet tone that often exasperated her brothers. They felt that she was trying to be superior with them.

Oscar spoke up grimly. "We thought we ought to tell you that people have begun to talk," he said meaningly.

Alexandra looked at him. "What about?"

Oscar met her eyes blankly. "About you, keeping him here so long. It looks bad for him to be hanging on to a woman this way. People think you're getting taken in."

Alexandra shut her account-book firmly. "Boys," she said seriously, "don't let's go on with this. We won't come out anywhere. I can't take advice on such a matter. I know you mean well, but you must not feel responsible for me in things of this sort. If we go on with this talk it will only make hard feeling."

Lou whipped about from the window. "You ought to think a little about your family. You're making us all ridiculous."

"How am I?"

"People are beginning to say you want to marry the fellow."

"Well, and what is ridiculous about that?"

Lou and Oscar exchanged outraged looks. "Alexandra! Can't you see he's just a tramp and he's after your money? He wants to be taken care of, he does!"

"Well, suppose I want to take care of him? Whose business is it but my own?"

"Don't you know he'd get hold of your property?"

"He'd get hold of what I wished to give him, certainly."

Oscar sat up suddenly and Lou clutched at his bristly hair.

"Give him?" Lou shouted. "Our property, our homestead?"

"I don't know about the homestead," said Alexandra quietly. "I know you and Oscar have always expected that it would be left to your children, and I'm not sure but that you're right. But I'll do exactly as I please with the rest of my land, boys."

"The rest of your land!" cried Lou, growing more excited every minute. "Didn't all the land come out of the homestead? It was bought with money borrowed on the homestead, and Oscar and me worked ourselves to the bone paying interest on it."

"Yes, you paid the interest. But when you married we made a division of the land, and you were satisfied. I've made more on my farms since I've been alone than when we all worked together."

"Everything you've made has come out of the original land that us boys worked for, hasn't it? The farms and all that comes out of them belongs to us as a family."

Alexandra waved her hand impatiently. "Come now, Lou. Stick to the facts. You are talking nonsense. Go to the county clerk and ask him who owns my land, and whether my titles are good."

Lou turned to his brother. "This is what comes of letting a woman meddle in business," he said bitterly. "We ought to have taken things in our own hands years ago. But she liked to run things, and we humored her. We thought you had good sense, Alexandra. We never thought you'd do anything foolish."

Alexandra rapped impatiently on her desk with her knuckles. "Listen, Lou. Don't talk wild. You say you ought to have taken things into your own hands years ago. I suppose you mean before you left home. But how could you take hold of what wasn't there? I've got most of what I have now since we divided the property; I've built it up myself, and it has nothing to do with you."

Oscar spoke up solemnly. "The property of a family really belongs to the men of the family, no matter about the title. If anything goes wrong, it's the men that are held responsible."

"Yes, of course," Lou broke in. "Everybody knows that. Oscar and me have always been easy-going and we've never made any fuss. We were willing you should hold the land and have the good of it, but you got no right to part with any of it. We worked in the fields to pay for the first land you bought, and whatever's come out of it has got to be kept in the family."

Oscar reinforced his brother, his mind fixed on the one point he could see. "The property of a family belongs to the men of the family, because they are held responsible, and because they do the work."

Alexandra looked from one to the other, her eyes full of indignation. She had been impatient before, but now she was beginning to feel angry. "And what about my work?" she asked in an unsteady voice.

Lou looked at the carpet. "Oh, now, Alexandra, you always took it pretty easy! Of course we wanted you to. You liked to manage round, and we always humored you. We realize you were a great deal of help to us. There's no woman anywhere around that knows as much about business as you do, and we've always been proud of that, and thought you were pretty smart. But, of course, the real work always fell on us. Good advice is all right, but it don't get the weeds out of the corn."

"Maybe not, but it sometimes puts in the crop, and it sometimes keeps the fields for corn to grow in," said Alexandra dryly. "Why, Lou, I can remember when you and Oscar wanted to sell this homestead and all the improvements to old preacher Ericson for two thousand dollars. If I'd consented, you'd have gone down to the river and scraped along on poor farms for the rest of your lives. When I put in our first field of alfalfa you both opposed me, just because I first heard about it from a young man who had been to the University. You said I was being taken in then, and all the neighbors said so. You know as well as I do that alfalfa has been the salvation of this country. You all laughed at me when I said our land here was about ready for wheat, and I had to raise three big wheat crops before the neighbors quit putting all their land in corn. Why, I remember you cried, Lou, when we put in the first big wheat-planting, and said everybody was laughing at us."

Lou turned to Oscar. "That's the woman of it; if she tells you to put in a crop, she thinks she's put it in. It makes women conceited to meddle in business. I shouldn't think you'd want to remind us how hard you were on us, Alexandra, after the way you baby Emil."

"Hard on you? I never meant to be hard. Conditions were hard. Maybe I would never have been very soft, anyhow; but I certainly didn't choose to be the kind of girl I was. If you take even a vine and cut it back again and again, it grows hard, like a tree."

Lou felt that they were wandering from the point, and that in digression Alexandra might unnerve him. He wiped his forehead with a jerk of his handkerchief. "We never doubted you, Alexandra. We never questioned anything you did. You've always had your own way. But you can't expect us to sit like stumps and see you done out of the property by any loafer who happens along, and making yourself ridiculous into the bargain."

Oscar rose. "Yes," he broke in, "everybody's laughing to see you get took in; at your age, too. Everybody knows he's nearly five years younger than you, and is after your money. Why, Alexandra, you are forty years old!"

"All that doesn't concern anybody but Carl and me. Go to town and ask your lawyers what you can do to restrain me from disposing of my own property. And I advise you to do what they tell you; for the authority you can exert by law is the only influence you will ever have over me again." Alexandra rose. "I think I would rather not have lived to find out what I have to-day," she said quietly, closing her desk.

Lou and Oscar looked at each other questioningly. There seemed to be nothing to do but to go, and they walked out.

"You can't do business with women," Oscar said heavily as he clambered into the cart. "But anyhow, we've had our say, at last."

Lou scratched his head. "Talk of that kind might come too high, you know; but she's apt to be sensible. You hadn't ought to have said that about her age, though, Oscar. I'm afraid that hurt her feelings; and the worst thing we can do is to make her sore at us. She'd marry him out of contrariness."

"I only meant," said Oscar, "that she is old enough to know better, and she is. If she was going to marry, she ought to done it long ago, and not go making a fool of herself now."

Lou looked anxious, nevertheless. "Of course," he reflected hopefully and inconsistently. "Alexandra ain't much like other women-folks. Maybe it won't make her sore. Maybe she'd as soon be forty as not!"

X I

EMIL CAME HOME at about half-past seven o'clock that evening. Old Ivar met him at the windmill and took his horse, and the young man went directly into the house. He called to his sister and she answered from her bedroom, behind the sitting-room, saying that she was lying down.

Emil went to her door.

"Can I see you for a minute?" he asked. "I want to talk to you about something before Carl comes."

Alexandra rose quickly and came to the door. "Where is Carl?"

"Lou and Oscar met us and said they wanted to talk to him, so he rode over to Oscar's with them. Are you coming out?" Emil asked impatiently.

"Yes, sit down. I'll be dressed in a moment."

Alexandra closed her door, and Emil sank down on the old slat lounge and sat with his head in his hands. When his sister came out, he looked up, not knowing whether the interval had been short or long, and he was surprised to see that the room had grown quite dark. That was just as well; it would be easier to talk if he were not under the gaze of those clear, deliberate eyes, that saw so far in some directions and were so blind in others. Alexandra, too, was glad of the dusk. Her face was swollen from crying.

Emil started up and then sat down again. "Alexandra," he said slowly, in his deep young baritone, "I don't want to go away to law school this fall. Let me put it off another year. I want to take a year off and look around. It's awfully easy to rush into a profession you don't really like, and awfully hard to get out of it. Linstrum and I have been talking about that."

"Very well, Emil. Only don't go off looking for land." She came up and put her hand on his shoulder. "I've been wishing you could stay with me this winter."

"That's just what I don't want to do, Alexandra. I'm restless. I want to go to a new place. I want to go down to the City of Mexico to join one of the University fellows who's at the head of an electrical plant. He wrote me he could give me a little job, enough to pay my way, and I could look around and see what I want to do. I want to go as soon as harvest is over. I guess Lou and Oscar will be sore about it."

"I suppose they will." Alexandra sat down on the lounge beside him. "They are very angry with me, Emil. We have had a quarrel. They will not come here again."

Emil scarcely heard what she was saying; he did not notice the sadness of her tone. He was thinking about the reckless life he meant to live in Mexico.

"What about?" he asked absently.

"About Carl Linstrum. They are afraid I am going to marry him, and that some of my property will get away from them."

Emil shrugged his shoulders. "What nonsense!" he murmured. "Just like them."

Alexandra drew back. "Why nonsense, Emil?"

"Why, you've never thought of such a thing, have you? They always have to have something to fuss about."

"Emil," said his sister slowly, "you ought not to take things for granted. Do you agree with them that I have no right to change my way of living?"

Emil looked at the outline of his sister's head in the dim light. They were sitting close together and he somehow felt that she could hear his thoughts. He was silent for a moment, and then said in an embarrassed tone, "Why, no, certainly not. You ought to do whatever you want to. I'll always back you."

"But it would seem a little bit ridiculous to you if I married Carl?"

Emil fidgeted. The issue seemed to him too far-fetched to warrant discussion. "Why, no. I should be surprised if you wanted to. I can't see exactly why. But that's none of my business. You ought to do as you please. Certainly you ought not to pay any attention to what the boys say."

Alexandra sighed. "I had hoped you might understand, a little, why I do want to. But I suppose that's too much to expect. I've had a pretty lonely life, Emil. Besides Marie, Carl is the only friend I have ever had."

Emil was awake now; a name in her last sentence roused him. He put out his hand and took his sister's awkwardly. "You ought to do just as you wish, and I think Carl's a fine fellow. He and I would always get on. I don't believe any of the things the boys say about him, honest I don't. They are suspicious of him because he's intelligent. You know their way. They've been sore at me ever since you let me go away to college. They're always trying to catch me up. If I were you, I wouldn't pay any attention to them. There's nothing to get upset about. Carl's a sensible fellow. He won't mind them."

"I don't know. If they talk to him the way they did to me, I think he'll go away."

Emil grew more and more uneasy. "Think so? Well, Marie said it would serve us all right if you walked off with him."

"Did she? Bless her little heart! *She* would." Alexandra's voice broke.

Emil began unlacing his leggings. "Why don't you talk to her about it? There's Carl, I hear his horse. I guess I'll go upstairs and get my boots off. No, I don't want any supper. We had supper at five o'clock, at the fair."

Emil was glad to escape and get to his own room. He was a little ashamed for his sister, though he had tried not to show it. He felt that there was something indecorous in her proposal, and she did seem to him somewhat ridiculous. There was trouble enough in the world, he reflected, as he threw himself upon his bed, without people who were forty years old imagining they wanted to get married. In the darkness and silence Emil was not likely to think long about Alexandra. Every image slipped away but one. He had seen Marie in the crowd that afternoon. She sold candy at the fair. *Why* had she ever run away with Frank Shabata, and how could she go on laughing and working and taking an interest in things? Why did she like so many people, and why had she seemed pleased when all the French and Bohemian boys, and the priest himself, crowded round her candy stand? Why did she care about any one but him? Why could he never, never find the thing he looked for in her playful, affectionate eyes?

Then he fell to imagining that he looked once more and found it there, and what it would be like if she loved him,—she who, as Alexandra said, could give her whole heart. In that dream he could lie for hours, as if in a trance. His spirit went out of his body and crossed the fields to Marie Shabata.

At the University dances the girls had often looked wonderingly at the tall young Swede with the fine head, leaning against the wall and frowning, his arms folded, his eyes fixed on the ceiling or the floor. All the girls were a little afraid of him. He was distinguished-looking, and not the jollying kind. They felt that he was too intense and preoccupied. There was something queer about him. Emil's fraternity rather prided itself upon its dances, and sometimes he did his duty and danced every dance. But whether he was on the floor or brooding in a corner, he was always thinking about Marie Shabata. For two years the storm had been gathering in him.

XII

CARL CAME into the sitting-room while Alexandra was lighting the lamp. She looked up at him as she adjusted the shade. His sharp shoulders stooped as if he were very tired, his face was pale, and there were bluish shadows under his dark eyes. His anger had burned itself out and left him sick and disgusted.

"You have seen Lou and Oscar?" Alexandra asked.

"Yes." His eyes avoided hers.

Alexandra took a deep breath. "And now you are going away. I thought so."

Carl threw himself into a chair and pushed the dark lock back from his forehead with his white, nervous hand. "What a hopeless position you are in, Alexandra!" he exclaimed feverishly. "It is your fate to be always surrounded by little men. And I am no better than the rest. I am too little to face the criticism of even such men as Lou and Oscar. Yes, I am going away; to-morrow. I cannot even ask you to give me a promise until I have something to offer you. I thought, perhaps, I could do that; but I find I can't."

"What good comes of offering people things they don't need?" Alexandra asked sadly. "I don't need money. But I have needed you for a great many years. I wonder why I have been permitted to prosper, if it is only to take my friends away from me."

"I don't deceive myself," Carl said frankly. "I know that I am going away on my own account. I must make the usual effort. I must have something to show for myself. To take what you would give me, I should have to be either a very large man or a very small one, and I am only in the middle class."

Alexandra sighed. "I have a feeling that if you go away, you will not come back. Something will happen to one of us, or to both. People have to snatch at happiness when they can, in this world. It is always easier to lose than to find. What I have is yours, if you care enough about me to take it."

Carl rose and looked up at the picture of John Bergson. "But I can't, my dear, I can't! I will go North at once. Instead of idling about in California all winter, I shall be getting my bearings up there. I won't waste another week. Be patient with me, Alexandra. Give me a year!"

"As you will," said Alexandra wearily. "All at once, in a single day, I lose everything; and I do not know why. Emil, too, is going away." Carl was still studying John Bergson's face and Alexandra's eyes followed his. "Yes," she said, "if he could have seen all that would come of the task he gave me, he would have been sorry. I hope he does not see me now. I hope that he is among the old people of his blood and country, and that tidings do not reach him from the New World."

PART THREE

WINTER MEMORIES

I

WINTER HAS SETTLED down over the Divide again; the season in which Nature recuperates, in which she sinks to sleep between the fruitfulness of autumn and the passion of spring. The birds have gone. The teeming life that goes on down in the long grass is exterminated. The prairie-dog keeps his hole. The rabbits run shivering from one frozen garden patch to another and are hard put to it to find frost-bitten cabbage-stalks. At night the coyotes roam the wintry waste, howling for food. The variegated fields are all one color now; the pastures, the stubble, the roads, the sky are the same leaden gray. The hedgerows and trees are scarcely perceptible against the bare earth, whose slaty hue they have taken on. The ground is frozen so hard that it bruises the foot to walk in the roads or in the ploughed fields. It is like an iron country, and the spirit is oppressed by its rigor and melancholy. One could easily believe that in that dead landscape the germs of life and fruitfulness were extinct forever.

Alexandra has settled back into her old routine. There are weekly letters from Emil. Lou and Oscar she has not seen since Carl went away. To avoid awkward encounters in the presence of curious spectators, she has stopped going to the Norwegian Church and drives up to the Reform Church at Hanover, or goes with Marie Shabata to the Catholic Church, locally known as "the French Church." She has not told Marie about Carl, or her differences with her brothers. She was never very communicative about her own affairs, and when she came to the point, an instinct told her that about such things she and Marie would not understand one another.

Old Mrs. Lee had been afraid that family misunderstandings might deprive her of her yearly visit to Alexandra. But on the first day of December Alexandra telephoned Annie that to-morrow she would send Ivar over for her mother, and the next day the old lady arrived with her bundles. For twelve years Mrs. Lee had always entered Alexandra's sitting-room with the same exclamation, "Now we be yust-a like old times!" She enjoyed the liberty Alexandra gave her, and hearing her own language about her all day long. Here she could wear her nightcap and sleep with all her windows shut, listen to Ivar reading the Bible, and here she could run about among the stables in a pair of Emil's old boots. Though she was bent almost double, she was as spry as a gopher. Her face was as brown as if it had been varnished, and as full of wrinkles as a washerwoman's hands. She had three jolly old teeth left in the front of her mouth, and when she grinned she looked very knowing, as if when you found out how to take it, life wasn't half bad. While she and Alexandra patched and pieced and quilted, she talked incessantly about stories she read in a Swedish family paper, telling the plots in great detail; or about her life on a dairy farm in Gottland when she was a girl. Sometimes she forgot which were the printed stories and which were the real stories, it all seemed so far away. She loved to take a little brandy, with hot water and sugar, before she went to bed, and Alexandra always had it ready for her. "It sends good dreams," she would say with a twinkle in her eye.

When Mrs. Lee had been with Alexandra for a week, Marie Shabata telephoned one morning to say that Frank had gone to town for the day, and she would like them to come over for coffee in the afternoon. Mrs. Lee hurried to wash out and iron her new cross-stitched apron, which she had finished only the night before; a checked gingham apron worked with a design ten inches broad across the bottom; a hunting scene, with fir trees and a stag and dogs and huntsmen. Mrs. Lee was firm with herself at dinner, and refused a second helping of apple dumplings. "I ta-ank I save up," she said with a giggle.

At two o'clock in the afternoon Alexandra's cart drove up to the Shabatas' gate, and Marie saw Mrs. Lee's red shawl come bobbing up the path. She ran to the door and pulled the old woman into the house with a hug, helping her to take off her wraps while Alexandra blanketed the horse outside. Mrs. Lee had put on her best black satine dress—she abominated woolen stuffs, even in winter—and a crocheted collar, fastened with a big pale gold pin, containing faded daguerreotypes of her father and mother. She had not worn her apron for fear of rumpling it, and now she shook it out and tied it round her waist with a conscious air. Marie drew back and threw up her hands, exclaiming, "Oh, what a beauty! I've never seen this one before, have I, Mrs. Lee?"

The old woman giggled and ducked her head. "No, yust las' night I ma-ake. See dis tread; verra strong, no wa-ash out, no fade. My sister send from Sveden. I yust-a ta-ank you like dis."

Marie ran to the door again. "Come in, Alexandra. I have been looking at Mrs. Lee's apron. Do stop on your way home and show it to Mrs. Hiller. She's crazy about cross-stitch."

While Alexandra removed her hat and veil, Mrs. Lee went out to the kitchen and settled herself in a wooden rocking-chair by the stove, looking with great interest at the table, set for three, with a white cloth, and a pot of pink geraniums in the middle. "My, a-an't you gotta fine plants; such-a much flower. How you keep from freeze?"

She pointed to the window-shelves, full of blooming fuchsias and geraniums.

"I keep the fire all night, Mrs. Lee, and when it's very cold I put them all on the table, in the middle of the room. Other nights I only put newspapers behind them. Frank laughs at me for fussing, but when they don't bloom he says, 'What's the matter with the darned things?'—What do you hear from Carl, Alexandra?"

"He got to Dawson before the river froze, and now I suppose I won't hear any more until spring. Before he left California he sent me a box of orange flowers, but they didn't keep very well. I have brought a bunch of Emil's letters for you." Alexandra came out from the sitting-room and pinched Marie's cheek playfully. "You don't look as if the weather ever froze you up. Never have colds, do you? That's a good girl. She had dark red cheeks like this when she was a little girl, Mrs. Lee. She looked like some queer foreign kind of a doll. I've never forgot the first time I saw you in Mieklejohn's store, Marie, the time father was lying sick. Carl and I were talking about that before he went away."

"I remember, and Emil had his kitten along. When are you going to send Emil's Christmas box?"

"It ought to have gone before this. I'll have to send it by mail now, to get it there in time."

Marie pulled a dark purple silk necktie from her workbasket. "I knit this for him. It's a good color, don't you think? Will you please put it in with your things and tell him it's from me, to wear when he goes serenading."

Alexandra laughed. "I don't believe he goes serenading much. He says in one letter that the Mexican ladies are said to be very beautiful, but that don't seem to me very warm praise."

Marie tossed her head. "Emil can't fool me. If he's bought a guitar, he goes serenading. Who wouldn't, with all those Spanish girls dropping flowers down from their windows! I'd sing to them every night, wouldn't you, Mrs. Lee?"

The old lady chuckled. Her eyes lit up as Marie bent down and opened the oven door. A delicious hot fragrance blew out into the tidy kitchen. "My, somet'ing smell good!" She turned to Alexandra with a wink, her three yellow teeth making a brave show, "I ta-ank dat stop my yaw from ache no more!" she said contentedly.

Marie took out a pan of delicate little rolls, stuffed with stewed apricots, and began to dust them over with powdered sugar. "I hope you'll like these, Mrs. Lee; Alexandra does. The Bohemians always like them with their coffee. But if you don't, I have a coffee-cake with nuts and poppy seeds. Alexandra, will you get the cream jug? I put it in the window to keep cool."

"The Bohemians," said Alexandra, as they drew up to the table, "certainly know how to make more kinds of bread than any other people in the world. Old Mrs. Hiller told me once at the church supper that she could make seven kinds of fancy bread, but Marie could make a dozen."

Mrs. Lee held up one of the apricot rolls between her brown thumb and forefinger and weighed it critically. "Yust like-a fedders," she pronounced with satisfaction. "My, a-an't dis nice!" she exclaimed as she stirred her coffee. "I yust ta-ake a liddle yelly now, too, I ta-ank."

Alexandra and Marie laughed at her forehandedness, and fell to talking of their own affairs. "I was afraid you had a cold when I talked to you over the telephone the other night, Marie. What was the matter, had you been crying?"

"Maybe I had," Marie smiled guiltily. "Frank was out late that night. Don't you get lonely sometimes in the winter, when everybody has gone away?"

"I thought it was something like that. If I hadn't had company, I'd have run over to see for myself. If you get down-hearted, what will become of the rest of us?" Alexandra asked.

"I don't, very often. There's Mrs. Lee without any coffee!"

Later, when Mrs. Lee declared that her powers were spent, Marie and Alexandra went upstairs to look for some crochet patterns the old lady wanted to borrow. "Better put on your coat, Alexandra. It's cold up there, and I have no idea where those patterns are. I may have to look through my old trunks." Marie caught up a shawl and opened the stair door, running up the steps ahead of her guest. "While I go through the bureau drawers, you might look in those hat-boxes on the closet-shelf, over where Frank's clothes hang. There are a lot of odds and ends in them."

She began tossing over the contents of the drawers, and Alexandra went into the clothes-closet. Presently she came back, holding a slender elastic yellow stick in her hand.

"What in the world is this, Marie? You don't mean to tell me Frank ever carried such a thing?"

Marie blinked at it with astonishment and sat down on the floor. "Where did you find it? I didn't know he had kept it. I haven't seen it for years."

"It really is a cane, then?"

"Yes. One he brought from the old country. He used to carry it when I first knew him. Isn't it foolish? Poor Frank!"

Alexandra twirled the stick in her fingers and laughed. "He must have looked funny!"

Marie was thoughtful. "No, he didn't, really. It didn't seem out of place. He used to be awfully gay like that when he was a young man. I guess people always get what's hardest for them, Alexandra." Marie gathered the shawl closer about her and still looked hard at the cane. "Frank would be all right in the right place," she said reflectively. "He ought to have a different kind of wife, for one thing. Do you know, Alexandra, I could pick out exactly the right sort of woman for Frank—now. The trouble is you almost have to marry a man before you can find out the sort of wife he needs; and usually it's exactly the sort you are not. Then what are you going to do about it?" she asked candidly.

Alexandra confessed she didn't know. "However," she added, "it seems to me that you get along with Frank about as well as any woman I've ever seen or heard of could."

Marie shook her head, pursing her lips and blowing her warm breath softly out into the frosty air. "No; I was spoiled at home. I like my own way, and I have a quick tongue. When Frank brags, I say sharp things, and he never forgets. He goes over and over it in his mind; I can feel him. Then I'm too giddy. Frank's wife ought to be timid, and she ought not to care about another living thing in the world but just Frank! I didn't when I married him, but I suppose I was too young to stay like that." Marie sighed.

Alexandra had never heard Marie speak so frankly about her husband before, and she felt that it was wiser not to encourage her. No good, she reasoned, ever came from talking about such things, and while Marie was thinking aloud, Alexandra had been steadily searching the hat-boxes. "Aren't these the patterns, Marie?"

Marie sprang up from the floor. "Sure enough, we were looking for patterns, weren't we? I'd forgot about everything but Frank's other wife. I'll put that away."

She poked the cane behind Frank's Sunday clothes, and though she laughed, Alexandra saw there were tears in her eyes.

When they went back to the kitchen, the snow had begun to fall, and Marie's visitors thought they must be getting home. She went out to the cart with them, and tucked the robes about old Mrs. Lee while Alexandra took the blanket off her horse. As they drove away, Marie turned and went slowly back to the house. She took up the package of letters Alexandra had brought, but she did not read them. She turned them over and looked at the foreign stamps, and then sat watching the flying snow while the dusk deepened in the kitchen and the stove sent out a red glow.

Marie knew perfectly well that Emil's letters were written more for her than for Alexandra. They were not the sort of letters that a young man writes to his sister. They were both more personal and more painstaking; full of descriptions of the gay life in the old Mexican capital in the days when the strong hand of Porfirio Diaz was still strong. He told about bull-fights and cock-fights, churches and *fiestas,* the flower-markets and the fountains, the music and dancing, the people of all nations he met in the Italian restaurants on San Francisco Street. In short, they were the kind of letters a young man writes to a woman when he wishes himself and his life to seem interesting to her, when he wishes to enlist her imagination in his behalf.

Marie, when she was alone or when she sat sewing in the evening, often thought about what it must be like down there where Emil was; where there were flowers and street bands everywhere, and carriages rattling up and down, and where there was a little blind boot-black in front of the cathedral who could play any tune you asked for by dropping the lids of blacking-boxes on the stone steps. When everything is done and over for one at twenty-three, it is pleasant to let the mind wander forth and follow a young adventurer who has life before him. "And if it had not been for me," she thought, "Frank might still be free like that, and having a good time making people admire him. Poor Frank, getting married wasn't very good for him either. I'm afraid I do set people against him, as he says. I seem, somehow, to give him away all the time. Perhaps he would try to be agreeable to people again, if I were not around. It seems as if I always make him just as bad as he can be."

Later in the winter, Alexandra looked back upon that afternoon as the last satisfactory visit she had had with Marie. After that day the younger woman seemed to shrink more and more into herself. When she was with Alexandra she was not spontaneous and frank as she used to be. She seemed to be brooding over something, and holding something back. The weather had a good deal to do with their seeing less of each other than usual. There had not been such snowstorms in twenty years, and the path across the fields was drifted deep from Christmas until March. When the two neighbors went to see each other, they had to go round by the wagon-road, which was twice as far. They telephoned each other almost every night, though in January there was a stretch of three weeks when the wires were down, and when the postman did not come at all.

Marie often ran in to see her nearest neighbor, old Mrs. Hiller, who was crippled with rheumatism and had only her son, the lame shoemaker, to take care of her; and she went to the French Church, whatever the weather. She was a sincerely devout girl. She prayed for herself and for Frank, and for Emil, among the temptations of that gay, corrupt old city. She found more comfort in the Church that winter than ever before. It seemed to come closer to her, and to fill an emptiness that ached in her heart. She tried to be patient with her husband. He and his hired man usually played California Jack in the evening. Marie sat sewing or crocheting and tried to take a friendly interest in the game, but she was always thinking about the wide fields outside, where the snow was drifting over the fences; and about the orchard, where the snow was falling and packing, crust over crust. When she went out into the dark kitchen to fix her plants for the night, she used to stand by the window and look out at the white fields, or watch the currents of snow whirling over the orchard. She seemed to feel the weight of all the snow that lay down there. The branches had become so hard that they wounded your hand if you but tried to break a twig. And yet, down under the frozen crusts, at the roots of the trees, the secret of life was still safe, warm as the blood in one's heart; and the spring would come again! Oh, it would come again!

II

IF ALEXANDRA HAD had much imagination she might have guessed what was going on in Marie's mind, and she would have seen long before what was going on in Emil's. But that, as Emil himself had more than once reflected, was Alexandra's blind side, and her life had not been of the kind to sharpen her vision. Her training had all been toward the end of making her proficient in what she had undertaken to do. Her personal life, her own realization of herself, was almost a subconscious existence; like an underground river that came to the surface only here and there, at intervals months apart, and then sank again to flow on under her own fields. Nevertheless, the underground stream was there, and it was because she had so much personality to put into her enterprises and succeeded in putting it into them so completely, that her affairs prospered better than those of her neighbors.

There were certain days in her life, outwardly uneventful, which Alexandra remembered as peculiarly happy; days when she was close to the flat, fallow world about her, and felt, as it were, in her own body the joyous germination in the soil. There were days, too, which she and Emil had spent together, upon which she loved to look back. There had been such a day when they were down on the river in the dry year, looking over the land. They had made an early start one morning and had driven a long way before noon. When Emil said he was hungry, they drew back from the road, gave Brigham his oats among the bushes, and climbed up to the top of a grassy bluff to eat their lunch under the shade of some little elm trees. The river was clear there, and shallow, since there had been no rain, and it ran in ripples over the sparkling sand. Under the overhanging willows of the opposite bank there was an inlet where the water was deeper and flowed so slowly that it seemed to sleep in the sun. In this little bay a single wild duck was swimming and diving and preening her feathers, disporting herself very happily in the flickering light and shade. They sat for a long time, watching the solitary bird take its pleasure. No living thing had ever seemed to Alexandra as beautiful as that wild duck. Emil must have felt about it as she did, for afterward, when they were at home, he used sometimes to say, "Sister, you know our duck down there—" Alexandra remembered that day as one of the happiest in her life. Years afterward she thought of the duck as still there, swimming and diving all by herself in the sunlight, a kind of enchanted bird that did not know age or change.

Most of Alexandra's happy memories were as impersonal as this one; yet to her they were very personal. Her mind was a white book, with clear writing about weather and beasts and growing things. Not many people would have cared to read it; only a happy few. She had never been in love, she had never indulged in sentimental reveries. Even as a girl she had looked upon men as work-fellows. She had grown up in serious times.

There was one fancy indeed, which persisted through her girl-hood. It most often came to her on Sunday mornings, the one day in the week when she lay late abed listening to the familiar morning sounds; the windmill singing in the brisk breeze, Emil whistling as he blacked his boots down by the kitchen door. Sometimes, as she lay thus luxuriously idle, her eyes closed, she used to have an illusion of being lifted up bodily and carried lightly by some one

"Her training had all been toward the end of making her proficient in what she had undertaken to do. Her personal life, her own realization of herself, was almost a subconscious existence; like an underground river that came to the surface only here and there, at intervals months apart, and then sank again to flow on under her own fields." —O Pioneers!

very strong. It was a man, certainly, who carried her, but he was like no man she knew; he was much larger and stronger and swifter, and he carried her as easily as if she were a sheaf of wheat. She never saw him, but, with eyes closed, she could feel that he was yellow like the sunlight, and there was the smell of ripe cornfields about him. She could feel him approach, bend over her and lift her, and then she could feel herself being carried swiftly off across the fields. After such a reverie she would rise hastily, angry with her-

self, and go down to the bath-house that was partitioned off the kitchen shed. There she would stand in a tin tub and prosecute her bath with vigor, finishing it by pouring buckets of cold well-water over her gleaming white body which no man on the Divide could have carried very far.

As she grew older, this fancy more often came to her when she was tired than when she was fresh and strong. Sometimes, after she had been in the open all day, overseeing the branding of the cattle or the loading of the pigs, she would come in chilled, take a concoction of spices and warm home-made wine, and go to bed with her body actually aching with fatigue. Then, just before she went to sleep, she had the old sensation of being lifted and carried by a strong being who took from her all her bodily weariness.

PART FOUR

THE WHITE
MULBERRY TREE

I

THE FRENCH CHURCH, properly the Church of Sainte-Agnes, stood upon a hill. The high, narrow, red-brick building, with its tall steeple and steep roof, could be seen for miles across the wheatfields, though the little town of Sainte-Agnes was completely hidden away at the foot of the hill. The church looked powerful and triumphant there on its eminence, so high above the rest of the landscape, with miles of warm color lying at its feet, and by its position and setting it reminded one of some of the churches built long ago in the wheat-lands of middle France.

Late one June afternoon Alexandra Bergson was driving along one of the many roads that led through the rich French farming country to the big church. The sunlight was shining directly in her face, and there was a blaze of light all about the red church on the hill. Beside Alexandra lounged a strikingly exotic figure in a tall Mexican hat, a silk sash, and a black velvet jacket sewn with silver buttons. Emil had returned only the night before, and his sister was so proud of him that she decided at once to take him up to the church supper, and to make him wear the Mexican costume he had brought home in his trunk. "All the girls who have stands are going to wear fancy costumes," she argued, "and some of the boys. Marie is going to tell fortunes, and she sent to Omaha for a Bohemian dress her father brought back from a visit to the old country. If you wear those clothes, they will all be pleased. And you must take your guitar. Everybody ought to do what they can to help along, and we have never done much. We are not a talented family."

The supper was to be at six o'clock, in the basement of the church, and afterward there would be a fair, with charades and an auction. Alexandra had set out from home early, leaving the house to Signa and Nelse Jensen, who were to be married next week. Signa had shyly asked to have the wedding put off until Emil came home.

Alexandra was well satisfied with her brother. As they drove through the rolling French country toward the westering sun and the stalwart church, she was thinking of that time long ago when she and Emil drove back from the river valley to the still unconquered Divide. Yes, she told herself, it had been worthwhile; both Emil and the country had become what she had hoped. Out of her father's children there was one who was fit to cope with the world, who had not been tied to the plow, and who had a personality apart from the soil. And that, she reflected, was what she had worked for. She felt well satisfied with her life.

When they reached the church, a score of teams were hitched in front of the basement doors that opened from the hillside upon the sanded terrace, where the boys wrestled and had jumping-matches. Amédée Chevalier, a proud father of one week, rushed out and embraced Emil. Amédée was an only son,—hence he was a very rich young man,—but he meant to have twenty children himself, like his uncle Xavier. "Oh, Emil," he cried, hugging his old friend rapturously, "why ain't you been up to see my boy? You come to-morrow, sure? Emil, you wanna get a boy right off! It's the greatest thing ever! No, no, no! Angel not sick at all. Everything just fine. That boy he come into this world laughin', and he been laughin' ever since. You come an' see!" He pounded Emil's ribs to emphasize each announcement.

Emil caught his arms. "Stop, Amédée. You're knocking the wind out of me. I brought him cups and spoons and blankets and moccasins enough for an orphan asylum. I'm awful glad it's a boy, sure enough!"

The young men crowded round Emil to admire his costume and to tell him in a breath everything that had happened since he went away. Emil had more friends up here in the French country than down on Norway Creek. The French and Bohemian boys were spirited and jolly, liked variety, and were as much predisposed to favor anything new as the Scandinavian boys were to reject it. The Norwegian and Swedish lads were much more self-centered, apt to be egotistical and jealous. They were cautious and reserved with Emil because he had been away to college, and were prepared to take him down if he should try to put on airs with them. The French boys liked a bit of swagger, and they were always delighted to hear about anything new: new clothes, new games, new songs, new dances. Now they carried Emil off to show him the club room they had just fitted up over the post-office, down in the village. They ran down the hill in a drove, all laughing and chattering at once, some in French, some in English.

Alexandra went into the cool, whitewashed basement where the women were setting the tables. Marie was standing on a chair, building a little tent of shawls where she was to tell fortunes. She sprang down and ran toward Alexandra, stopping short and looking at her in disappointment. Alexandra nodded to her encouragingly.

"Oh, he will be here, Marie. The boys have taken him off to show him something. You won't know him. He is a man now, sure enough. I have no boy left. He smokes terrible-smelling Mexican cigarettes and talks Spanish. How pretty you look, child. Where did you get those beautiful earrings?"

"They belonged to father's mother. He always promised them to me. He sent them with the dress and said I could keep them."

Marie wore a short red skirt of stoutly woven cloth, a white bodice and kirtle, a yellow silk turban wound low over her brown curls, and long coral pendants in her ears. Her ears had been pierced against a piece of cork by her great-aunt when she was seven years old. In those germless days she had worn bits of broomstraw, plucked from the common sweeping-broom, in the lobes until the holes were healed and ready for little gold rings.

When Emil came back from the village, he lingered outside on the terrace with the boys. Marie could hear him talking and strumming on his guitar while Raoul Marcel sang falsetto. She was vexed with him for staying out there. It made her very nervous to hear him and not to see him; for, certainly, she told herself, she was not going out to look for him. When the supper bell rang and the boys came trooping in to get seats at the first table, she forgot all about her annoyance and ran to greet the tallest of the crowd, in his conspicuous attire. She didn't mind showing her embarrassment at all. She blushed and laughed excitedly as she gave Emil her hand, and looked delightedly at the black velvet coat that brought out his fair skin and fine blond head. Marie was incapable of being lukewarm about anything that pleased her. She simply did not know how to give a half-hearted response. When she was delighted, she was as likely as not to stand on her tip-toes and clap her hands. If people laughed at her, she laughed with them.

"Do the men wear clothes like that every day, in the street?" She caught Emil by his sleeve and turned him about. "Oh, I wish I lived where people wore things like that! Are the buttons real silver? Put on the hat, please. What a heavy thing! How do you ever wear it? Why don't you tell us about the bull-fights?"

She wanted to wring all his experiences from him at once, without waiting a moment. Emil smiled tolerantly and stood looking down at her with his old, brooding gaze, while the French girls fluttered about him in their white dresses and ribbons, and Alexandra watched the scene with pride. Several of the French girls, Marie knew, were hoping that Emil would take them to supper, and she was relieved when he took only his sister. Marie caught Frank's arm and dragged him to the same table, managing to get seats opposite the Bergsons, so that she could hear what they were talking about. Alexandra made Emil tell Mrs. Xavier Chevalier, the mother of the twenty, about how he had seen a famous matador killed in the bull-ring. Marie listened to every word, only taking her eyes from Emil to watch Frank's plate and keep it filled. When Emil finished his account,—bloody enough to satisfy Mrs. Xavier and to make her feel thankful that she was not a matador,—Marie broke out with a volley of questions. How did the women dress when they went to bull-fights? Did they wear mantillas? Did they never wear hats?

After supper the young people played charades for the amusement of their elders, who sat gossiping between their guesses. All the shops in Sainte-Agnes were closed at eight o'clock that night, so that the merchants and their clerks could attend the fair. The auction was the liveliest part of the entertainment, for the French boys always lost their heads when they began to bid, satisfied that their extravagance was in a good cause. After all the pincushions and sofa pillows and embroidered slippers were sold, Emil precipitated a panic by taking out one of his turquoise shirt studs, which every one had been admiring, and handing it to the auctioneer. All the French girls clamored for it, and their sweethearts bid against each other recklessly. Marie wanted it, too, and she kept making signals to Frank, which he took a sour pleasure in disregarding. He didn't see the use of making a fuss over a fellow just because he was dressed like a clown. When the turquoise went to Malvina Sauvage, the French banker's daughter, Marie shrugged her shoulders and betook herself to her little tent of shawls, where she began to shuffle her cards by the light of a tallow candle, calling out, "Fortunes, fortunes!"

The young priest, Father Duchesne, went first to have his fortune read. Marie took his long white hand, looked at it, and then began to run off her cards. "I see a long journey across water for you, Father. You will go to a town all cut up by water; built on islands, it seems to be, with rivers and green fields all about. And you will visit an old lady with a white cap and gold hoops in her ears, and you will be very happy there."

"Mais, oui," said the priest, with a melancholy smile. "C'est L'Isle-Adam, chez ma mère. Vous êtes trés savante, ma fille." He patted her yellow turban, calling, "Venez donc, mes garçons! Il y a ici une véritable clairvoyante!"

Marie was clever at fortune-telling, indulging in a light irony that amused the crowd. She told old Brunot, the miser, that he would lose all his money, marry a girl of sixteen, and live happily on a crust. Sholte, the fat Russian boy, who lived for his stomach, was to be disappointed in love, grow thin, and shoot himself from despondency. Amédée was to have twenty children, and nineteen of them were to be girls. Amédée slapped Frank on the back and asked him why he didn't see what the fortune-teller would promise him. But Frank shook off his friendly hand and grunted, "She tell my fortune long ago; bad enough!" Then he withdrew to a corner and sat glowering at his wife.

Frank's case was all the more painful because he had no one in particular to fix his jealousy upon. Sometimes he could have thanked the man who would bring him evidence against his wife. He had discharged a good farm-boy, Jan Smirka, because he thought Marie was fond of him; but she had not seemed to miss Jan when he was gone, and she had been just as kind to the next boy. The farm-hands would always do anything for Marie; Frank couldn't find one so surly that he would not make an effort to please her. At the bottom of his heart Frank knew well enough that if he could once give up his grudge, his wife would come back to him. But he could never in the world do that. The grudge was fundamental. Perhaps he could not have given it up if he had tried. Perhaps he got more satisfaction out of feeling himself abused than he would have got out of being loved. If he could once have made Marie thoroughly unhappy, he might have relented and raised her from the dust. But she had never humbled herself. In the first days of their love she had been his slave; she had admired him abandonedly. But the moment he began to bully her and to be unjust, she began to draw away; at first in tearful amazement, then in quiet, unspoken disgust. The distance between them had widened and hardened. It no longer contracted and brought them suddenly together. The spark of her life went somewhere else, and he was always watching to surprise it. He knew that somewhere she must get a feeling to live upon, for she was not a woman who could live without loving. He wanted to prove to himself the wrong he felt. What did she hide in her heart? Where did it go? Even Frank had his churlish delicacies; he never reminded her of how much she had once loved him. For that Marie was grateful to him.

While Marie was chattering to the French boys, Amédée called Emil to the back of the room and whispered to him that they were going to play a joke on the girls. At eleven o'clock, Amédée was to go up to the switchboard in the vestibule and turn off the electric lights, and every boy would have a chance to kiss his sweetheart before Father Duchesne could find his way up the stairs to turn the current on again. The only difficulty was the candle in Marie's tent; perhaps, as Emil had no sweetheart, he would oblige the boys by blowing out the candle. Emil said he would undertake to do that.

At five minutes to eleven he sauntered up to Marie's booth, and the French boys dispersed to find their girls. He leaned over the card-table and gave himself up to looking at her. "Do you think you could tell my fortune?" he murmured. It was the first word he had had alone with her for almost a year. "My luck hasn't changed any. It's just the same."

Marie had often wondered whether there was anyone else who could look his thoughts to you as Emil could. To-night, when she met his steady, powerful eyes, it was impossible not to feel the sweetness of the dream he was dreaming; it reached her before she could shut it out, and hid itself in her heart. She began to shuffle her cards furiously. "I'm angry with you, Emil," she broke out with petulance. "Why did you give them that lovely blue stone to sell? You might have known Frank wouldn't buy it for me, and I wanted it awfully!"

Emil laughed shortly. "People who want such little things surely ought to have them," he said dryly. He thrust his hand into the pocket of his velvet trousers and brought out a handful of uncut turquoises, as big as marbles. Leaning over the table he dropped them into her lap. "There, will those do? Be careful, don't let any one see them. Now, I suppose you want me to go away and let you play with them?"

Marie was gazing in rapture at the soft blue color of the stones. "Oh, Emil! Is everything down there beautiful like these? How could you ever come away?"

At that instant Amédée laid hands on the switchboard. There was a shiver and a giggle, and every one looked toward the red blur that Marie's candle made in the dark. Immediately that, too, was gone. Little shrieks and currents of soft laughter ran up and down the dark hall. Marie started up,—directly into Emil's arms. In the same instant she felt his lips. The veil that had hung uncertainly between them for so long was dissolved. Before she knew what she was doing, she had committed herself to that kiss that was at once a boy's and a man's, as timid as it was tender; so like Emil and so unlike any one else in the world. Not until it was over did she realize what it meant. And Emil, who had so often imagined the shock of this first kiss, was surprised at its gentleness and naturalness. It was like a sigh which they had breathed together; almost sorrowful, as if each were afraid of wakening something in the other.

When the lights came on again, everybody was laughing and shouting, and all the French girls were rosy and shining with mirth. Only Marie, in her little tent of shawls, was pale and quiet. Under her yellow turban the red coral pendants swung against white cheeks. Frank was still staring at her, but he seemed to see nothing.

Years ago, he himself had had the power to take the blood from her cheeks like that. Perhaps he did not remember—perhaps he had never noticed! Emil was already at the other end of the hall, walking about with the shoulder-motion he had acquired among the Mexicans, studying the floor with his intent, deep-set eyes. Marie began to take down and fold her shawls. She did not glance up again. The young people drifted to the other end of the hall where the guitar was sounding. In a moment she heard Emil and Raoul singing:

"Across the Rio Grand-e
There lies a sunny land-e,
My bright-eyed Mexico!"

Alexandra Bergson came up to the card booth. "Let me help you, Marie. You look tired."

She placed her hand on Marie's arm and felt her shiver. Marie stiffened under that kind, calm hand. Alexandra drew back, perplexed and hurt.

There was about Alexandra something of the impervious calm of the fatalist, always disconcerting to very young people, who cannot feel that the heart lives at all unless it is still at the mercy of storms; unless its strings can scream to the touch of pain.

I I

SIGNA'S WEDDING SUPPER was over. The guests, and the tiresome little Norwegian preacher who had performed the marriage ceremony, were saying good-night. Old Ivar was hitching the horses to the wagon to take the wedding presents and the bride and groom up to their new home, on Alexandra's north quarter. When Ivar drove up to the gate, Emil and Marie Shabata began to carry out the presents, and Alexandra went into her bedroom to bid Signa good-bye and to give her a few words of good counsel. She was surprised to find that the bride had changed her slippers for heavy shoes and was pinning up her skirts. At that moment Nelse appeared at the gate with the two milk cows that Alexandra had given Signa for a wedding present.

Alexandra began to laugh. "Why, Signa, you and Nelse are to ride home. I'll send Ivar over with the cows in the morning."

Signa hesitated and looked perplexed. When her husband called her, she pinned her hat on resolutely. "I ta-ank I better do yust like he say," she murmured in confusion.

Alexandra and Marie accompanied Signa to the gate and saw the party set off, old Ivar driving ahead in the wagon and the bride and groom following on foot, each leading a cow. Emil burst into a laugh before they were out of hearing.

"Those two will get on," said Alexandra as they turned back to the house. "They are not going to take any chances. They will feel safer with those cows in their own stable. Marie, I am going to send for an old woman next. As soon as I get the girls broken in, I marry them off."

"I've no patience with Signa, marrying that grumpy fellow!" Marie declared. "I wanted her to marry that nice Smirka boy who worked for us last winter. I think she liked him, too."

"Yes, I think she did," Alexandra assented, "but I suppose she was too much afraid of Nelse to marry any one else. Now that I think of it, most of my girls have married men they were afraid of. I believe there is a good deal of the cow in most Swedish girls. You high-strung Bohemians can't understand us. We're a terribly practical people, and I guess we think a cross man makes a good manager."

Marie shrugged her shoulders and turned to pin up a lock of hair that had fallen on her neck. Somehow Alexandra had irritated her of late. Everybody irritated her. She was tired of everybody. "I'm going home alone, Emil, so you needn't get your hat," she said as she wound her scarf quickly about her head. "Good-night, Alexandra," she called back in a strained voice, running down the gravel walk.

Emil followed with long strides until he overtook her. Then she began to walk slowly. It was a night of warm wind and faint starlight, and the fireflies were glimmering over the wheat.

"Marie," said Emil after they had walked for a while, "I wonder if you know how unhappy I am?"

Marie did not answer him. Her head, in its white scarf, drooped forward a little.

Emil kicked a clod from the path and went on:—

"I wonder whether you are really shallow-hearted, like you

seem? Sometimes I think one boy does just as well as another for you. It never seems to make much difference whether it is me or Raoul Marcel or Jan Smirka. Are you like that?"

"Perhaps I am. What do you want me to do? Sit around and cry all day? When I've cried until I can't cry any more, then—I must do something else."

"Are you sorry for me?" he persisted.

"No, I'm not. If I were big and free like you, I wouldn't let anything make me unhappy. As old Napoleon Brunot said at the fair, I wouldn't go lovering after no woman. I'd take the first train and go off and have all the fun there is."

"I tried that, but it didn't do any good. Everything reminded me. The nicer the place was, the more I wanted you." They had come to the stile and Emil pointed to it persuasively. "Sit down a moment, I want to ask you something." Marie sat down on the top step and Emil drew nearer. "Would you tell me something that's none of my business if you thought it would help me out? Well, then, tell me, *please* tell me, why you ran away with Frank Shabata!"

Marie drew back. "Because I was in love with him," she said firmly.

"Really?" he asked incredulously.

"Yes, indeed. Very much in love with him. I think I was the one who suggested our running away. From the first it was more my fault than his."

Emil turned away his face.

"And now," Marie went on, "I've got to remember that. Frank is just the same now as he was then, only then I would see him as I wanted him to be. I would have my own way. And now I pay for it."

"You don't do all the paying."

"That's it. When one makes a mistake, there's no telling where it will stop. But you can go away; you can leave all this behind you."

"Not everything. I can't leave you behind. Will you go away with me, Marie?"

Marie started up and stepped across the stile. "Emil! How wickedly you talk! I am not that kind of a girl, and you know it. But what am I going to do if you keep tormenting me like this!" she added plaintively.

"Marie, I won't bother you any more if you will tell me just one thing. Stop a minute and look at me. No, nobody can see us. Everybody's asleep. That was only a firefly. Marie, *stop* and tell me!"

Emil overtook her and catching her by the shoulders shook her gently, as if he were trying to awaken a sleepwalker.

Marie hid her face on his arm. "Don't ask me anything more. I don't know anything except how miserable I am. And I thought it would be all right when you came back. Oh, Emil," she clutched his sleeve and began to cry, "what am I to do if you don't go away? I can't go, and one of us must. Can't you see?"

Emil stood looking down at her, holding his shoulders stiff and stiffening the arm to which she clung. Her white dress looked gray in the darkness. She seemed like a troubled spirit, like some shadow out of the earth, clinging to him and entreating him to give her peace. Behind her the fireflies were weaving in and out over the wheat. He put his hand on her bent head. "On my honor, Marie, if you will say you love me, I will go away."

She lifted her face to his. "How could I help it? Didn't you know?"

Emil was the one who trembled, through all his frame. After he left Marie at her gate, he wandered about the fields all night, till morning put out the fireflies and the stars.

I I I

ONE EVENING, a week after Signa's wedding, Emil was kneeling before a box in the sitting-room, packing his books. From time to time he rose and wandered about the house, picking up stray volumes and bringing them listlessly back to his box. He was packing without enthusiasm. He was not very sanguine about his future. Alexandra sat sewing by the table. She had helped him pack his trunk in the afternoon. As Emil came and went by her chair with his books, he thought to himself that it had not been so hard to leave his sister since he first went away to school. He was going directly to Omaha, to read law in the office of a Swedish lawyer until October, when he would enter the law school at Ann Arbor. They had planned that Alexandra was to come to Michigan—a long journey for her—at Christmas time, and spend several weeks with him. Nevertheless, he felt that this leavetaking would be more final than his earlier ones had been; that it meant a definite break with his old home and the beginning of something new—he did not know what. His ideas about the future would not crystallize; the more he tried to think about it, the vaguer his conception of it became. But one thing was clear, he told himself; it was high time that he made good to Alexandra, and that ought to be incentive enough to begin with.

As he went about gathering up his books he felt as if he were uprooting things. At last he threw himself down on the old slat lounge where he had slept when he was little, and lay looking up at the familiar cracks in the ceiling.

"Tired, Emil?" his sister asked.

"Lazy," he murmured, turning on his side and looking at her. He studied Alexandra's face for a long time in the lamplight. It had never occurred to him that his sister was a handsome woman until Marie Shabata had told him so. Indeed, he had never thought of her as being a woman at all, only a sister. As he studied her bent head, he looked up at the picture of John Bergson above the lamp. "No," he thought to himself, "she didn't get it there. I suppose I am more like that."

"Alexandra," he said suddenly, "that old walnut secretary you use for a desk was father's, wasn't it?"

Alexandra went on stitching. "Yes. It was one of the first things he bought for the old log house. It was a great extravagance in those days. But he wrote a great many letters back to the old country. He had many friends there, and they wrote to him up to the time he died. No one ever blamed him for grandfather's disgrace. I can see him now, sitting there on Sundays, in his white shirt, writing pages and pages, so carefully. He wrote a fine, regular hand, almost like engraving. Yours is something like his, when you take pains."

"Grandfather was really crooked, was he?"

"He married an unscrupulous woman, and then—then I'm afraid he was really crooked. When we first came here father used to have dreams about making a great fortune and going back to Sweden to pay back to the poor sailors the money grandfather had lost."

Emil stirred on the lounge. "I say, that would have been worthwhile, wouldn't it? Father wasn't a bit like Lou or Oscar, was he? I can't remember much about him before he got sick."

"Oh, not at all!" Alexandra dropped her sewing on her knee.

"He had better opportunities; not to make money, but to make something of himself. He was a quiet man, but he was very intelligent. You would have been proud of him, Emil."

Alexandra felt that he would like to know there had been a man of his kin whom he could admire. She knew that Emil was ashamed of Lou and Oscar, because they were bigoted and self-satisfied. He never said much about them, but she could feel his disgust. His brothers had shown their disapproval of him ever since he first went away to school. The only thing that would have satisfied them would have been his failure at the University. As it was, they resented every change in his speech, in his dress, in his point of view; though the latter they had to conjecture, for Emil avoided talking to them about any but family matters. All his interests they treated as affectations.

Alexandra took up her sewing again. "I can remember father when he was quite a young man. He belonged to some kind of a musical society, a male chorus, in Stockholm. I can remember going with mother to hear them sing. There must have been a hundred of them, and they all wore long black coats and white neckties. I was used to seeing father in a blue coat, a sort of jacket, and when I recognized him on the platform, I was very proud. Do you remember that Swedish song he taught you, about the ship boy?"

"Yes. I used to sing it to the Mexicans. They like anything different." Emil paused. "Father had a hard fight here, didn't he?" he added thoughtfully.

"Yes, and he died in a dark time. Still, he had hope. He believed in the land."

"And in you, I guess," Emil said to himself. There was another period of silence; that warm, friendly silence, full of perfect understanding, in which Emil and Alexandra had spent many of their happiest half-hours.

At last Emil said abruptly, "Lou and Oscar would be better off if they were poor, wouldn't they?"

Alexandra smiled. "Maybe. But their children wouldn't. I have great hopes of Milly."

Emil shivered. "I don't know. Seems to me it gets worse as it goes on. The worst of the Swedes is that they're never willing to find out how much they don't know. It was like that at the University. Always so pleased with themselves! There's no getting behind that conceited Swedish grin. The Bohemians and Germans were so different."

"Come, Emil, don't go back on your own people. Father wasn't conceited, Uncle Otto wasn't. Even Lou and Oscar weren't when they were boys."

Emil looked incredulous, but he did not dispute the point. He turned on his back and lay still for a long time, his hands locked under his head, looking up at the ceiling. Alexandra knew that he was thinking of many things. She felt no anxiety about Emil. She had always believed in him, as she had believed in the land. He had been more like himself since he got back from Mexico; seemed glad to be at home, and talked to her as he used to do. She had no doubt that his wandering fit was over, and that he would soon be settled in life.

"Alexandra," said Emil suddenly, "do you remember the wild duck we saw down on the river that time?"

His sister looked up. "I often think of her. It always seems to me she's there still, just like we saw her."

"I know. It's queer what things one remembers and what things one forgets." Emil yawned and sat up. "Well, it's time to turn in." He rose, and going over to Alexandra stooped down and kissed her lightly on the cheek. "Good-night, sister. I think you did pretty well by us."

Emil took up his lamp and went upstairs. Alexandra sat finishing his new nightshirt, that must go in the top tray of his trunk.

◆ ◆ ◆ ◆ ◆ ◆ ◆ ◆ ◆ ◆ ◆ ◆ ◆ ◆ ◆ ◆ ◆

I V

THE NEXT MORNING Angélique, Amédée's wife, was in the kitchen baking pies, assisted by old Mrs. Chevalier. Between the mixing-board and the stove stood the old cradle that had been Amédée's, and in it was his black-eyed son. As Angélique, flushed and excited, with flour on her hands, stopped to smile at the baby, Emil Bergson rode up to the kitchen door on his mare and dismounted.

" 'Médée is out in the field, Emil," Angélique called as she ran across the kitchen to the oven. "He begins to cut his wheat to-day; the first wheat ready to cut anywhere about here. He bought a new header, you know, because all the wheat's so short this year. I hope he can rent it to the neighbors, it cost so much. He and his cousins bought a steam thresher on shares. You ought to go out and see that header work. I watched it an hour this morning, busy as I am with all the men to feed. He has a lot of hands, but he's the only one that knows how to drive the header or how to run the engine, so he has to be everywhere at once. He's sick, too, and ought to be in his bed."

Emil bent over Hector Baptiste, trying to make him blink his round, bead-like black eyes. "Sick? What's the matter with your daddy, kid? Been making him walk the floor with you?"

Angélique sniffed. "Not much! We don't have that kind of babies. It was his father that kept Baptiste awake. All night I had to be getting up and making mustard plasters to put on his stomach. He had an awful colic. He said he felt better this morning, but I don't think he ought to be out in the field, overheating himself."

Angélique did not speak with much anxiety, not because she was indifferent, but because she felt so secure in their good fortune. Only good things could happen to a rich, energetic, handsome young man like Amédée, with a new baby in the cradle and a new header in the field.

Emil stroked the black fuzz on Baptiste's head. "I say, Angélique, one of 'Médée's grandmothers, 'way back, must have been a squaw. This kid looks exactly like the Indian babies."

Angélique made a face at him, but old Mrs. Chevalier had been touched on a sore point, and she let out such a stream of fiery *patois* that Emil fled from the kitchen and mounted his mare.

Opening the pasture gate from the saddle, Emil rode across the field to the clearing where the thresher stood, driven by a stationary engine and fed from the header boxes. As Amédée was not on the engine, Emil rode on to the wheatfield, where he recognized, on the header, the slight, wiry figure of his friend, coatless, his white shirt puffed out by the wind, his straw hat stuck jauntily on the side of his head. The six big work-horses that drew, or rather pushed, the header, went abreast at a rapid walk, and as they were still green at the work they required a good deal of management on Amédée's part; especially when they turned the corners, where they divided, three and three, and then swung round into line again with a movement that looked as complicated as a wheel of artillery. Emil felt a new thrill of admiration for his friend, and with it the old pang of envy at the way in which Amédée could do with his might what his hand found to do, and feel that, whatever it was, it was the most important thing in the world. "I'll have to bring Alexandra up to see this thing work," Emil thought; "it's splendid!"

When he saw Emil, Amédée waved to him and called to one of his twenty cousins to take the reins. Stepping off the header without stopping it, he ran up to Emil who had dismounted. "Come along," he called. "I have to go over to the engine for a minute. I gotta green man running it, and I gotta keep an eye on him."

Emil thought the lad was unnaturally flushed and more excited than even the cares of managing a big farm at a critical time warranted. As they passed behind a last year's stack, Amédée clutched at his right side and sank down for a moment on the straw.

"Ouch! I got an awful pain in me, Emil. Something's the matter with my insides, for sure."

Emil felt his fiery cheek. "You ought to go straight to bed, 'Médée, and telephone for the doctor; that's what you ought to do."

Amédée staggered up with a gesture of despair. "How can I? I got no time to be sick. Three thousand dollars' worth of new machinery to manage, and the wheat so ripe it will begin to shatter next week. My wheat's short but it's gotta grand full berries. What's he slowing down for? We haven't got header boxes enough to feed the thresher, I guess."

Amédée started hot-foot across the stubble, leaning a little to the right as he ran, and waved to the engineer not to stop the engine.

Emil saw that this was no time to talk about his own affairs. He mounted his mare and rode on to Sainte-Agnes, to bid his friends there good-bye. He went first to see Raoul Marcel, and found him innocently practicing the "Gloria" for the big confirmation service on Sunday while he polished the mirrors of his father's saloon.

As Emil rode homewards at three o'clock in the afternoon, he saw Amédée staggering out of the wheatfield, supported by two of his cousins. Emil stopped and helped them put the boy to bed.

V

WHEN FRANK SHABATA came in from work at five o'clock that evening, old Moses Marcel, Raoul's father, telephoned him that Amédée had had a seizure in the wheatfield, and that Doctor Paradis was going to operate on him as soon as the Hanover doctor got there to help. Frank dropped a word of this at the table, bolted his supper, and rode off to Sainte-Agnes, where there would be sympathetic discussion of Amédée's case at Marcel's saloon.

As soon as Frank was gone, Marie telephoned Alexandra. It was a comfort to hear her friend's voice. Yes, Alexandra knew what there was to be known about Amédée. Emil had been there when they carried him out of the field, and had stayed with him until the doctors operated for appendicitis at five o'clock. They were afraid it was too late to do much good; it should have been done three days ago. Amédée was in a very bad way. Emil had just come home, worn out and sick himself. She had given him some brandy and put him to bed.

Marie hung up the receiver. Poor Amédée's illness had taken on a new meaning to her, now that she knew Emil had been with him. And it might so easily have been the other way—Emil who was ill and Amédée who was sad! Marie looked about the dusky sitting-room. She had seldom felt so utterly lonely. If Emil was asleep, there was not even a chance of his coming; and she could not go to Alexandra for sympathy. She meant to tell Alexandra everything, as soon as Emil went away. Then whatever was left between them would be honest.

But she could not stay in the house this evening. Where should she go? She walked slowly down through the orchard, where the evening air was heavy with the smell of wild cotton. The fresh, salty scent of the wild roses had given way before this more powerful perfume of midsummer. Wherever those ashes-of-rose balls hung on their milky stalks, the air about them was saturated with their breath. The sky was still red in the west and the evening star hung directly over the Bergsons' windmill. Marie crossed the fence at the wheatfield corner, and walked slowly along the path that led to Alexandra's. She could not help feeling hurt that Emil had not come to tell her about Amédée. It seemed to her most unnatural that he should not have come. If she were in trouble, certainly he was the one person in the world she would want to see. Perhaps he wished her to understand that for her he was as good as gone already.

Marie stole slowly, flutteringly, along the path, like a white night-moth out of the fields. The years seemed to stretch before her like the land; spring, summer, autumn, winter, spring; always the same patient fields, the patient little trees, the patient lives; always the same yearning, the same pulling at the chain—until the instinct to live had torn itself and bled and weakened for the last time, until the chain secured a dead woman, who might cautiously be released. Marie walked on, her face lifted toward the remote, inaccessible evening star.

When she reached the stile she sat down and waited. How terrible it was to love people when you could not really share their lives!

Yes, insofar as she was concerned, Emil was already gone. They couldn't meet any more. There was nothing for them to say. They had spent the last penny of their small change; there was nothing left but gold. The day of love-tokens was past. They had now only their hearts to give each other. And Emil being gone, what was her life to be like? In some ways, it would be easier. She would not, at least, live in perpetual fear. If Emil were once away and settled at work, she would not have the feeling that she was spoiling his life. With the memory he left her, she could be as rash as she chose. Nobody could be the worse for it but herself; and that, surely, did not matter. Her own case was clear. When a girl had loved one man, and then loved another while that man was still alive, everybody knew what to think of her. What happened to her was of little consequence, so long as she did not drag other people down with her. Emil once away, she could let everything else go and live a new life of perfect love.

Marie left the stile reluctantly. She had, after all, thought he might come. And how glad she ought to be, she told herself, that he was asleep. She left the path and went across the pasture. The moon was almost full. An owl was hooting somewhere in the fields. She had scarcely thought about where she was going when the pond glittered before her, where Emil had shot the ducks. She stopped and looked at it. Yes, there would be a dirty way out of life, if one chose to take it. But she did not want to die. She wanted to live and dream—a hundred years, forever! As long as this sweetness welled up in her heart, as long as her breast could hold this treasure of pain! She felt as the pond must feel when it held the moon like that; when it encircled and swelled with that image of gold.

In the morning, when Emil came downstairs, Alexandra met him in the sitting-room and put her hands on his shoulders. "Emil, I went to your room as soon as it was light, but you were sleeping so sound I hated to wake you. There was nothing you could do, so I let you sleep. They telephoned from Sainte-Agnes that Amédée died at three o'clock this morning."

V I

THE CHURCH has always held that life is for the living. On Saturday, while half the village of Sainte-Agnes was mourning for Amédée and preparing the funeral black for his burial on Monday, the other half was busy with white dresses and white veils for the great confirmation service to-morrow, when the bishop was to confirm a class of one hundred boys and girls. Father Duchesne divided his time between the living and the dead. All day Saturday the church was a scene of bustling activity, a little hushed by the thought of Amédée. The choir were busy rehearsing a mass of Rossini, which they had studied and practiced for this occasion. The women were trimming the altar, the boys and girls were bringing flowers.

On Sunday morning the bishop was to drive overland to Sainte-Agnes from Hanover, and Emil Bergson had been asked to take the place of one of Amédée's cousins in the cavalcade of forty French boys who were to ride across country to meet the bishop's carriage. At six o'clock on Sunday morning the boys met at the church. As they stood holding their horses by the bridle, they talked in low tones of their dead comrade. They kept repeating that Amédée had always been a good boy, glancing toward the red brick church which had played so large a part in Amédée's life, had been the scene of his most serious moments and of his happiest hours. He had played and wrestled and sung and courted under its shadow. Only three weeks ago he had proudly carried his baby there to be christened. They could not doubt that that invisible arm was still about Amédée; that through the church on earth he had passed to the church triumphant, the goal of the hopes and faith of so many hundred years.

When the word was given to mount, the young men rode at a walk out of the village; but once out among the wheatfields in the morning sun, their horses and their own youth got the better of them. A wave of zeal and fiery enthusiasm swept over them. They longed for a Jerusalem to deliver. The thud of their galloping hoofs interrupted many a country breakfast and brought many a woman and child to the door of the farmhouses as they passed. Five miles east of Sainte-Agnes they met the bishop in his open carriage, attended by two priests. Like one man the boys swung off their hats in a broad salute, and bowed their heads as the handsome old man lifted his two fingers in the episcopal blessing. The horsemen closed about the carriage like a guard, and whenever a restless horse broke from control and shot down the road ahead of the body, the bishop laughed and rubbed his plump hands together. "What fine boys!" he said to his priests. "The Church still has her cavalry."

As the troop swept past the graveyard half a mile east of the town,—the first frame church of the parish had stood there,—old Pierre Séguin was already out with his pick and spade, digging Amédée's grave. He knelt and uncovered as the bishop passed. The boys with one accord looked away from old Pierre to the red church on the hill, with the gold cross flaming on its steeple.

Mass was at eleven. While the church was filling, Emil Bergson waited outside, watching the wagons and buggies drive up the hill. After the bell began to ring, he saw Frank Shabata ride up on horseback and tie his horse to the hitch-bar. Marie, then, was not coming. Emil turned and went into the church. Amédée's was the only empty pew, and he sat down in it. Some of Amédée's cousins were there, dressed in black and weeping. When all the pews were full, the old men and boys packed the open space at the back of the church, kneeling on the floor. There was scarcely a family in town that was not represented in the confirmation class, by a cousin, at least. The new communicants, with their clear, reverent faces, were beautiful to look upon as they entered in a body and took the front benches reserved for them. Even before the Mass began, the air was charged with feeling. The choir had never sung so well and Raoul Marcel, in the "Gloria," drew even the bishop's eyes to the organ loft. For the offertory he sang Gounod's "Ave Maria,"—always spoken of in Sainte-Agnes as "the Ave Maria."

Emil began to torture himself with questions about Marie. Was she ill? Had she quarreled with her husband? Was she too unhappy to find comfort even here? Had she, perhaps, thought that he would come to her? Was she waiting for him? Overtaxed by excitement and sorrow as he was, the rapture of the service took hold upon his body and mind. As he listened to Raoul, he seemed to emerge from the conflicting emotions which had been whirling him about and sucking him under. He felt as if a clear light broke upon his mind, and with it a conviction that good was, after all, stronger than evil, and that good was possible to men. He seemed to discover that there was a kind of rapture in which he could love forever without faltering and without sin. He looked across the heads of the people at Frank Shabata with calmness. That rapture was for those who could feel it; for people who could not, it was non-existent. He coveted nothing that was Frank Shabata's. The spirit he had met in music was his own. Frank Shabata had never found it; would never find it if he lived beside it a thousand years; would have destroyed it if he had found it, as Herod slew the innocents, as Rome slew the martyrs.

"San—cta Mari-i-i-a,"

wailed Raoul from the organ loft;

"O—ra pro no-o-bis!"

And it did not occur to Emil that any one had ever reasoned thus before, that music had ever before given a man this equivocal revelation.

The confirmation service followed the Mass. When it was over, the congregation thronged about the newly confirmed. The girls, and even the boys, were kissed and embraced and wept over. All the aunts and grandmothers wept with joy. The housewives had much ado to tear themselves away from the general rejoicing and hurry back to their kitchens. The country parishioners were staying in town for dinner, and nearly every house in Sainte-Agnes entertained visitors that day. Father Duchesne, the bishop, and the visiting priests dined with Fabien Sauvage, the banker. Emil and Frank Shabata were both guests of old Moïse Marcel. After dinner Frank and old Moïse retired to the rear room of the saloon to play California Jack and drink their cognac, and Emil went over to the banker's with Raoul, who had been asked to sing for the bishop.

At three o'clock, Emil felt that he could stand it no longer. He slipped out under cover of "The Holy City," followed by Malvina's wistful eye, and went to the stable for his mare. He was at that height of excitement from which everything is foreshortened, from which life seems short and simple, death very near, and the soul seems to soar like an eagle. As he rode past the graveyard he looked at the brown hole in the earth where Amédée was to lie, and felt no horror. That, too, was beautiful, that simple doorway into forgetfulness. The heart, when it is too much alive, aches for that brown earth, and ecstasy has no fear of death. It is the old and the poor and the maimed who shrink from that brown hole; its wooers are found among the young, the passionate, the gallant-hearted. It was not until he had passed the graveyard that Emil realized where he was going. It was the hour for saying good-bye. It might be the last time that he would see her alone, and to-day he could leave her without rancor, without bitterness.

Everywhere the grain stood ripe and the hot afternoon was full of the smell of the ripe wheat, like the smell of bread baking in an oven. The breath of the wheat and the sweet clover passed him like pleasant things in a dream. He could feel nothing but the sense of diminishing distance. It seemed to him that his mare was flying, or running on wheels, like a railway train. The sunlight, flashing on the window-glass of the big red barns, drove him wild with joy. He was like an arrow shot from the bow. His life poured itself out along the road before him as he rode to the Shabata farm.

When Emil alighted at the Shabatas' gate, his horse was in a lather. He tied her in the stable and hurried to the house. It was empty. She might be at Mrs. Hiller's or with Alexandra. But anything that reminded him of her would be enough, the orchard, the mulberry tree . . . When he reached the orchard the sun was hanging low over the wheatfield. Long fingers of light reached through the apple branches as through a net; the orchard was riddled and shot with gold; light was the reality, the trees were merely interferences that reflected and refracted light. Emil went softly down between the cherry trees toward the wheatfield. When he came to the corner, he stopped short and put his hand over his mouth. Marie was lying on her side under the white mulberry tree, her face half hidden in the grass, her eyes closed, her hands lying limply where they had happened to fall. She had lived a day of her new life of perfect love, and it had left her like this. Her breast rose and fell faintly, as if she were asleep. Emil threw himself down beside her and took her in his arms. The blood came back to her cheeks, her amber eyes opened slowly, and in them Emil saw his own face and the orchard and the sun. "I was dreaming this," she whispered, hiding her face against him, "don't take my dream away!"

VII

WHEN FRANK SHABATA got home that night, he found Emil's mare in his stable. Such an impertinence amazed him. Like everybody else, Frank had had an exciting day. Since noon he had been drinking too much, and he was in a bad temper. He talked bitterly to himself while he put his own horse away, and as he went up the path and saw that the house was dark he felt an added sense of injury. He approached quietly and listened on the doorstep. Hearing nothing, he opened the kitchen door and went softly from one room to another. Then he went through the house again, up-stairs and down, with no better result. He sat down on the bottom step of the box stairway and tried to get his wits together. In that unnatural quiet there was no sound but his own heavy breathing. Suddenly an owl began to hoot out in the fields. Frank lifted his head. An idea flashed into his mind, and his sense of injury and outrage grew. He went into his bedroom and took his murderous 405 Winchester from the closet.

When Frank took up his gun and walked out of the house, he had not the faintest purpose of doing anything with it. He did not believe that he had any real grievance. But it gratified him to feel like a desperate man. He had got into the habit of seeing himself always in desperate straits. His unhappy temperament was like a cage; he could never get out of it; and he felt that other people, his wife in particular, must have put him there. It had never more than dimly occurred to Frank that he made his own unhappiness. Though he took up his gun with dark projects in his mind, he would have been paralyzed with fright had he known that there was the slightest probability of his ever carrying any of them out.

Frank went slowly down to the orchard gate, stopped and stood for a moment lost in thought. He retraced his steps and looked through the barn and the hayloft. Then he went out to the road, where he took the footpath along the outside of the orchard hedge. The hedge was twice as tall as Frank himself, and so dense that one could see through it only by peering closely between the leaves. He could see the empty path a long way in the moonlight. His mind traveled ahead to the stile, which he always thought of as haunted by Emil Bergson. But why had he left his horse?

At the wheatfield corner, where the orchard hedge ended and the path led across the pasture to the Bergsons', Frank stopped. In the warm, breathless night air he heard a murmuring sound, perfectly inarticulate, as low as the sound of water coming from a spring, where there is no fall, and where there are no stones to fret it. Frank strained his ears. It ceased. He held his breath and began to tremble. Resting the butt of his gun on the ground, he parted the mulberry leaves softly with his fingers and peered through the hedge at the dark figures on the grass, in the shadow of the mulberry tree. It seemed to him that they must feel his eyes, that they must hear him breathing. But they did not. Frank, who had always wanted to see things blacker than they were, for once wanted to believe less than he saw. The woman lying in the shadow might so easily be one of the Bergsons' farm-girls. . . . Again the murmur, like water welling out of the ground. This time he heard it more distinctly, and his blood was quicker than his brain. He began to act, just as a man who falls into the fire begins to act. The gun sprang to his shoulder, he sighted mechanically and fired three times without stopping, stopped without knowing why. Either he shut his eyes or he had vertigo. He did not see anything while he was firing. He thought he heard a cry simultaneous with the second report, but he was not sure. He peered again through the hedge, at the two dark figures under the tree. They had fallen a little apart from each other, and were perfectly still— No, not quite; in a white patch of light, where the moon shone through the branches, a man's hand was plucking spasmodically at the grass.

Suddenly the woman stirred and uttered a cry, then another, and another. She was living! She was dragging herself toward the hedge! Frank dropped his gun and ran back along the path, shaking, stumbling, gasping. He had never imagined such horror. The cries followed him. They grew fainter and thicker, as if she were choking. He dropped on his knees beside the hedge and crouched like a rabbit, listening; fainter, fainter; a sound like a whine; again—a moan—another—silence. Frank scrambled to his feet and ran on, groaning and praying. From habit he went toward the house, where he was used to being soothed when he had worked himself into a frenzy, but at the sight of the black, open door, he started back. He knew that he had murdered somebody, that a woman was bleeding and moaning in the orchard, but he had not realized before that it was his wife. The gate stared him in the face. He threw his hands over his head. Which way to turn? He lifted his tormented face and looked at the sky. "Holy Mother of God, not to suffer! She was a good girl—not to suffer!"

Frank had been wont to see himself in dramatic situations; but now, when he stood by the windmill, in the bright space between the barn and the house, facing his own black doorway, he did not see himself at all. He stood like the hare when the dogs are approaching from all sides. And he ran like a hare, back and forth about that moonlit space, before he could make up his mind to go into the dark stable for a horse. The thought of going into a doorway was terrible to him. He caught Emil's horse by the bit and led it out. He could not have buckled a bridle on his own. After two or three attempts, he lifted himself into the saddle and started for Hanover. If he could catch the one o'clock train, he had money enough to get as far as Omaha.

While he was thinking dully of this in some less sensitized part of his brain, his acuter faculties were going over and over the cries he had heard in the orchard. Terror was the only thing that kept him from going back to her, terror that she might still be she, that she might still be suffering. A woman, mutilated and bleeding in his orchard—it was because it was a woman that he was so afraid. It was inconceivable that he should have hurt a woman. He would rather be eaten by wild beasts than see her move on the ground as she had moved in the orchard. Why had she been so careless? She knew he was like a crazy man when he was angry. She had more than once taken that gun away from him and held it, when he was angry with other people. Once it had gone off while they were struggling over it! She was never afraid. But, when she knew him, why hadn't she been more careful? Didn't she have all summer before her to love Emil Bergson in, without taking such chances? Probably she had met the Smirka boy, too, down there in the orchard. He didn't care. She could have met all the men on the Divide there, and welcome, if only she hadn't brought this horror on him.

There was a wrench in Frank's mind. He did not honestly believe that of her. He knew that he was doing her wrong. He stopped his horse to admit this to himself the more directly, to think it out the more clearly. He knew that he was to blame. For three years he had been trying to break her spirit. She had a way of making the best of things that seemed to him a sentimental affectation. He wanted his wife to resent that he was wasting his best years among these stupid and unappreciative people; but she had seemed to find the people quite good enough. If he ever got rich he meant to buy her pretty clothes and take her to California in a Pullman car, and treat her like a lady; but in the meantime he wanted her to feel that life was as ugly and as unjust as he felt it. He had tried to make her life ugly. He had refused to share any of the little pleasures she was so plucky about making for herself. She could be gay about the least thing in the world; but she must be gay! When she first came to him, her faith in him, her adoration—Frank struck the mare with his fist. Why had Marie made him do this thing; why had she brought this upon him? He was overwhelmed by sickening misfortune. All at once he heard her cries again—he had forgotten for a moment. "Marie," he sobbed aloud, "Marie!"

When Frank was halfway to Hanover, the motion of his horse brought on a violent attack of nausea. After it had passed, he rode on again, but he could think of nothing except his physical weakness and his desire to be comforted by his wife. He wanted to get into his own bed! Had his wife been at home, he would have turned and gone back to her meekly enough.

VIII

WHEN OLD IVAR climbed down from his loft at four o'clock the next morning, he came upon Emil's mare, jaded and lather-stained, her bridle broken, chewing the scattered tufts of hay outside the stable door. The old man was thrown into a fright at once. He put the mare in her stall, threw her a measure of oats, and then set out as fast as his bow-legs could carry him on the path to the nearest neighbor.

"Something is wrong with that boy. Some misfortune has come upon us. He would never have used her so, in his right senses. It is not his way to abuse his mare," the old man kept muttering, as he scuttled through the short, wet pasture grass on his bare feet.

While Ivar was hurrying across the fields, the first long rays of the sun were reaching down between the orchard boughs to those two dew-drenched figures. The story of what had happened was written plainly on the orchard grass, and on the white mulberries that had fallen in the night and were covered with dark stain. For Emil the chapter had been short. He was shot in the heart, and had rolled over on his back and died. His face was turned up to the sky and his brows were drawn in a frown, as if he had realized that something had befallen him. But for Marie Shabata it had not been so easy. One ball had torn through her right lung, another had shattered the carotid artery. She must have started up and gone toward the hedge, leaving a trail of blood. There she had fallen and bled. From that spot there was another trail, heavier than the first, where she must have dragged herself back to Emil's body. Once there, she seemed not to have struggled any more. She had lifted her head to her lover's breast, taken his hand in both her own, and bled quietly to death. She was lying on her right side in an easy and natural position, her cheek on Emil's shoulder. On her face there was a look of ineffable content. Her lips were parted a little; her eyes were lightly closed, as if in a day-dream or a light slumber. After she lay down there, she seemed not to have moved an eyelash. The hand she held was covered with dark stains, where she had kissed it.

But the stained, slippery grass, the darkened mulberries, told only half the story. Above Marie and Emil, two white butterflies from Frank's alfalfa-field were fluttering in and out among the interlacing shadows; diving and soaring, now close together, now far apart; and in the long grass by the fence the last wild roses of the year opened their pink hearts to die.

When Ivar reached the path by the hedge, he saw Shabata's rifle lying in the way. He turned and peered through the branches, falling upon his knees as if his legs had been mowed from under him. "Merciful God!" he groaned; "merciful, merciful God!"

Alexandra, too, had risen early that morning, because of her anxiety about Emil. She was in Emil's room upstairs when, from the window, she saw Ivar coming along the path that led from the Shabatas'. He was running like a spent man, tottering and lurching from side to side. Ivar never drank, and Alexandra thought at once that one of his spells had come upon him, and that he must be in a very bad way indeed. She ran downstairs and hurried out to meet him, to hide his infirmity from the eyes of her household. The old man fell in the road at her feet and caught her hand, over which he bowed his shaggy head. "Mistress, mistress," he sobbed, "it has fallen! Sin and death for the young ones! God have mercy upon us!"

PART FIVE

ALEXANDRA

"Fortunate country, that is one day to receive hearts like Alexandra's into its bosom, to give them out again in the yellow wheat, in the rustling corn, in the shining eyes of youth!" —O Pioneers!

◆ ◆ ◆ ◆ ◆ ◆ ◆ ◆ ◆ ◆ ◆ ◆ ◆ ◆ ◆ ◆ ◆ ◆ ◆

I

IVAR WAS SITTING at a cobbler's bench in the barn, mending harness by the light of a lantern and repeating to himself the 101st Psalm. It was only five o'clock of a mid-October day, but a storm had come up in the afternoon, bringing black clouds, a cold wind and torrents of rain. The old man wore his buffalo-skin coat, and occasionally stopped to warm his fingers at the lantern. Suddenly a woman burst into the shed, as if she had been blown in, accompanied by a shower of rain-drops. It was Signa, wrapped in a man's overcoat and wearing a pair of boots over her shoes. In time of trouble Signa had come back to stay with her mistress, for she was the only one of the maids from whom Alexandra would accept much personal service. It was three months now since the news of the terrible thing that had happened in Frank Shabata's orchard had first run like a fire over the Divide. Signa and Nelse were staying on with Alexandra until winter.

"Ivar," Signa exclaimed as she wiped the rain from her face, "do you know where she is?"

The old man put down his cobbler's knife. "Who, the mistress?"

"Yes. She went away about three o'clock. I happened to look out of the window and saw her going across the fields in her thin dress and sun-hat. And now this storm has come on. I thought she was going to Mrs. Hiller's and I telephoned as soon as the thunder stopped, but she had not been there. I'm afraid she is out somewhere and will get her death of cold."

Ivar put on his cap and took up the lantern. "*Ja, ja,* we will see. I will hitch the boy's mare to the cart and go."

Signa followed him across the wagon-shed to the horses' stable. She was shivering with cold and excitement. "Where do you suppose she can be, Ivar?"

The old man lifted a set of single harness carefully from its peg. "How should I know?"

"But you think she is at the graveyard, don't you?" Signa persisted. "So do I. Oh, I wish she would be more like herself! I can't believe it's Alexandra Bergson come to this, with no head about anything. I have to tell her when to eat and when to go to bed."

"Patience, patience, sister," muttered Ivar as he settled the bit in the horse's mouth. "When the eyes of the flesh are shut, the eyes of the spirit are open. She will have a message from those who are gone, and that will bring her peace. Until then we must bear with her. You and I are the only ones who have weight with her. She trusts us."

"How awful it's been these last three months." Signa held the lantern so that he could see to buckle the straps. "It don't seem right that we must all be so miserable. Why do we all have to be punished? Seems to me like good times would never come again."

Ivar expressed himself in a deep sigh, but said nothing. He stooped and took a sandburr from his toe.

"Ivar," Signa asked suddenly, "will you tell me why you go barefoot? All the time I lived here in the house I wanted to ask you. Is it for a penance, or what?"

"No, sister. It is for the indulgence of the body. From my youth up I have had a strong, rebellious body, and have been subject to every kind of temptation. Even in age my temptations are prolonged. It was necessary to make some allowances; and the feet, as I understand it, are free members. There is no divine prohibition for them in the Ten Commandments. The hands, the tongue, the eyes, the heart, all the bodily desires we are commanded to subdue; but the feet are free members. I indulge them without harm to any one, even to trampling in filth when my desires are low. They are quickly cleaned again."

Signa did not laugh. She looked thoughtful as she followed Ivar out to the wagon-shed and held the shafts up for him, while he backed in the mare and buckled the hold-backs. "You have been a good friend to the mistress, Ivar," she murmured.

"And you, God be with you," replied Ivar as he clambered into the cart and put the lantern under the oilcloth lap-cover. "Now for a ducking, my girl," he said to the mare, gathering up the reins.

As they emerged from the shed, a stream of water, running off the thatch, struck the mare on the neck. She tossed her head indignantly, then struck out bravely on the soft ground, slipping back again and again as she climbed the hill to the main road. Between the rain and the darkness Ivar could see very little, so he let Emil's mare have the rein, keeping her head in the right direction. When the ground was level, he turned her out of the dirt road upon the sod, where she was able to trot without slipping.

Before Ivar reached the graveyard, three miles from the house, the storm had spent itself, and the downpour had died into a soft, dripping rain. The sky and the land were a dark smoke color, and seemed to be coming together, like two waves. When Ivar stopped at the gate and swung out his lantern, a white figure rose from beside John Bergson's white stone.

The old man sprang to the ground and shuffled toward the gate calling, "Mistress, mistress!"

Alexandra hurried to meet him and put her hand on his shoulder. "*Tyst!* Ivar. There's nothing to be worried about. I'm sorry if I've scared you all. I didn't notice the storm till it was on me, and I couldn't walk against it. I'm glad you've come. I am so tired I didn't know how I'd ever get home!"

Ivar swung the lantern up so that it shone in her face. *"Gud!* You are enough to frighten us, mistress. You look like a drowned woman. How could you do such a thing!"

Groaning and mumbling he led her out of the gate and helped her into the cart, wrapping her in the dry blankets on which he had been sitting.

Alexandra smiled at his solicitude. "Not much use in that, Ivar. You will only shut the wet in. I don't feel so cold now; but I'm heavy and numb. I'm glad you came."

Ivar turned the mare and urged her into a sliding trot. Her feet sent back a continual spatter of mud.

Alexandra spoke to the old man as they jogged along through the sullen gray twilight of the storm. "Ivar, I think it has done me good to get cold clear through like this, once. I don't believe I shall suffer so much any more. When you get so near the dead, they seem more real than the living. Worldly thoughts leave one. Ever since Emil died, I've suffered so when it rained. Now that I've been out in it with him, I shan't dread it. After you once get cold clear through, the feeling of the rain on you is sweet. It seems to bring back feelings you had when you were a baby. It carries you back into the dark, before you were born; you can't see things, but they come to you, somehow, and you know them and aren't afraid of them. Maybe it's like that with the dead. If they feel anything at all, it's the old things, before they were born, that comfort people like the feeling of their own bed does when they are little."

"Mistress," said Ivar reproachfully, "those are bad thoughts. The dead are in Paradise."

Then he hung his head, for he did not believe that Emil was in Paradise.

When they got home, Signa had a fire burning in the sitting-room stove. She undressed Alexandra and gave her a hot footbath, while Ivar made ginger tea in the kitchen. When Alexandra was in bed, wrapped in hot blankets, Ivar came in with his tea and saw that she drank it. Signa asked permission to sleep on the slat lounge outside her door. Alexandra endured their attentions patiently, but she was glad when they put out the lamp and left her. As she lay alone in the dark, it occurred to her for the first time that perhaps she was actually tired of life. All the physical operations of life seemed difficult and painful. She longed to be free from her own body, which ached and was so heavy. And longing itself was heavy: she yearned to be free of that.

As she lay with her eyes closed, she had again, more vividly than for many years, the old illusion of her girlhood, of being lifted and carried lightly by some one very strong. He was with her a long while this time, and carried her very far, and in his arms she felt free from pain. When he laid her down on her bed again, she opened her eyes, and, for the first time in her life, she saw him, saw him clearly, though the room was dark, and his face was covered. He was standing in the doorway of her room. His white cloak was thrown over his face, and his head was bent a little forward. His shoulders seemed as strong as the foundations of the world. His right arm, bared from the elbow, was dark and gleaming, like bronze, and she knew at once that it was the arm of the mightiest of all lovers. She knew at last for whom it was she had waited, and where he would carry her. That, she told herself, was very well. Then she went to sleep.

Alexandra wakened in the morning with nothing worse than a hard cold and a stiff shoulder. She kept her bed for several days, and it was during that time that she formed a resolution to go to Lincoln to see Frank Shabata. Ever since she last saw him in the courtroom, Frank's haggard face and wild eyes had haunted her. The trial had lasted only three days. Frank had given himself up to the police in Omaha and pleaded guilty of killing without malice and without premeditation. The gun was, of course, against him, and the judge had given him the full sentence,—ten years. He had now been in the State Penitentiary for a month.

Frank was the only one, Alexandra told herself, for whom anything could be done. He had been less in the wrong than any of them, and he was paying the heaviest penalty. She often felt that she herself had been more to blame than poor Frank. From the time the Shabatas had first moved to the neighboring farm, she had omitted no opportunity of throwing Marie and Emil together. Because she knew Frank was surly about doing little things to help his wife, she was always sending Emil over to spade or plant or carpenter for Marie. She was glad to have Emil see as much as possible of an intelligent, city-bred girl like their neighbor; she noticed that it improved his manners. She knew that Emil was fond of Marie, but it had never occurred to her that Emil's feeling might be different from her own. She wondered at herself now, but she had never thought of danger in that direction. If Marie had been unmarried,— oh, yes! Then she would have kept her eyes open. But the mere fact that she was Shabata's wife, for Alexandra, settled everything. That she was beautiful, impulsive, barely two years older than Emil, these facts had had no weight with Alexandra. Emil was a good boy, and only bad boys ran after married women.

Now, Alexandra could in a measure realize that Marie was, after all, Marie; not merely a "married woman." Sometimes, when Alexandra thought of her, it was with an aching tenderness. The moment she had reached them in the orchard that morning, everything was clear to her. There was something about those two lying in the grass, something in the way Marie had settled her cheek on Emil's shoulder, that told her everything. She wondered then how they could have helped loving each other; how she could have helped knowing that they must. Emil's cold, frowning face, the girl's content—Alexandra had felt awe of them, even in the first shock of her grief.

The idleness of those days in bed, the relaxation of body which attended them, enabled Alexandra to think more calmly than she had done since Emil's death. She and Frank, she told herself, were left out of that group of friends who had been overwhelmed by disaster. She must certainly see Frank Shabata. Even in the court-room her heart had grieved for him. He was in a strange country, he had no kinsmen or friends, and in a moment he had ruined his life. Being what he was, she felt, Frank could not have acted otherwise. She could understand his behavior more easily than she could understand Marie's. Yes, she must go to Lincoln to see Frank Shabata.

The day after Emil's funeral, Alexandra had written to Carl Linstrum; a single page of note-paper, a bare statement of what had happened. She was not a woman who could write much about such a thing, and about her own feelings she could never write very freely. She knew that Carl was away from post-offices, prospecting somewhere in the interior. Before he started he had written her where he expected to go, but her ideas about Alaska were vague. As the weeks went by and she heard nothing from him, it seemed to Alexandra that her heart grew hard against Carl. She began to wonder whether she would not do better to finish her life alone. What was left of life seemed unimportant.

I I

LATE IN THE AFTERNOON of a brilliant October day, Alexandra
Bergson, dressed in a black suit and traveling-hat, alighted at the
Burlington depot in Lincoln. She drove to the Lindell Hotel, where
she had stayed two years ago when she came up for Emil's Commencement. In spite of her usual air of sureness and self-possession,
Alexandra felt ill at ease in hotels, and she was glad, when she went
to the clerk's desk to register, that there were not many people in
the lobby. She had her supper early, wearing her hat and black
jacket down to the dining-room and carrying her handbag. After
supper she went out for a walk.

It was growing dark when she reached the university campus.
She did not go into the grounds, but walked slowly up and down
the stone walk outside the long iron fence, looking through at the
young men who were running from one building to another, at the
lights shining from the armory and the library. A squad of cadets
were going through their drill behind the armory, and the com-
mands of their young officer rang out at regular intervals, so sharp
and quick that Alexandra could not understand them. Two stalwart
girls came down the library steps and out through one of the iron
gates. As they passed her, Alexandra was pleased to hear them

speaking Bohemian to each other. Every few moments a boy would come running down the flagged walk and dash out into the street as if he were rushing to announce some wonder to the world. Alexandra felt a great tenderness for them all. She wished one of them would stop and speak to her. She wished she could ask them whether they had known Emil.

As she lingered by the south gate she actually did encounter one of the boys. He had on his drill cap and was swinging his books at the end of a long strap. It was dark by this time; he did not see her and ran against her. He snatched off his cap and stood bareheaded and panting. "I'm awfully sorry," he said in a bright, clear voice, with a rising inflection, as if he expected her to say something.

"Oh, it was my fault!" said Alexandra eagerly. "Are you an old student here, may I ask?"

"No, ma'am. I'm a Freshie, just off the farm. Cherry County. Were you hunting somebody?"

"No, thank you. That is——" Alexandra wanted to detain him. "That is, I would like to find some of my brother's friends. He graduated two years ago."

"Then you'd have to try the Seniors, wouldn't you? Let's see; I don't know any of them yet, but there'll be sure to be some of them around the library. That red building, right there," he pointed.

"Thank you, I'll try there," said Alexandra lingeringly.

"Oh, that's all right! Good-night." The lad clapped his cap on his head and ran straight down Eleventh Street. Alexandra looked after him wistfully.

She walked back to her hotel unreasonably comforted. "What a nice voice that boy had, and how polite he was. I know Emil was always like that to women." And again, after she had undressed and was standing in her nightgown, brushing her long, heavy hair by the electric light, she remembered him and said to herself: "I don't think I ever heard a nicer voice than that boy had. I hope he will get on well here. Cherry County; that's where the hay is so fine, and the coyotes can scratch down to water."

At nine o'clock the next morning Alexandra presented herself at the warden's office in the State Penitentiary. The warden was a German, a ruddy, cheerful-looking man who had formerly been a harness-maker. Alexandra had a letter to him from the German banker in Hanover. As he glanced at the letter, Mr. Schwartz put away his pipe.

"That big Bohemian, is it? Sure, he's gettin' along fine," said Mr. Schwartz cheerfully.

"I am glad to hear that. I was afraid he might be quarrelsome and get himself into more trouble. Mr. Schwartz, if you have time, I would like to tell you a little about Frank Shabata, and why I am interested in him."

The warden listened genially while she told him briefly something of Frank's history and character, but he did not seem to find anything unusual in her account.

"Sure, I'll keep an eye on him. We'll take care of him all right," he said, rising. "You can talk to him here, while I go to see to things in the kitchen. I'll have him sent in. He ought to be done washing out his cell by this time. We have to keep 'em clean, you know."

The warden paused at the door, speaking back over his shoulder to a pale young man in convicts' clothes who was seated at a desk in the corner, writing in a big ledger.

"Bertie, when 1037 is brought in, you just step out and give this lady a chance to talk."

The young man bowed his head and bent over his ledger again.

When Mr. Schwartz disappeared, Alexandra thrust her black-edged handkerchief nervously into her handbag. Coming out on the street-car she had not had the least dread of meeting Frank. But since she had been here the sounds and smells in the corridor, the look of the men in convicts' clothes who passed the glass door of the warden's office, affected her unpleasantly.

The warden's clock ticked, the young convict's pen scratched busily in the big book, and his sharp shoulders were shaken every few seconds by a loose cough which he tried to smother. It was easy to see that he was a sick man. Alexandra looked at him timidly, but he did not once raise his eyes. He wore a white shirt under his striped jacket, a high collar, and a necktie, very carefully tied. His hands were thin and white and well cared for, and he had a seal ring on his little finger. When he heard steps approaching in the corridor, he rose, blotted his book, put his pen in the rack, and left the room without raising his eyes. Through the door he opened a guard came in, bringing Frank Shabata.

"You the lady that wanted to talk to 1037? Here he is. Be on your good behavior, now. He can set down, lady," seeing that Alexandra remained standing. "Push that white button when you're through with him, and I'll come."

The guard went out and Alexandra and Frank were left alone.

Alexandra tried not to see his hideous clothes. She tried to look straight into his face, which she could scarcely believe was his. It was already bleached to a chalky gray. His lips were colorless, his fine teeth looked yellowish. He glanced at Alexandra sullenly, blinked as if he had come from a dark place, and one eyebrow twitched continually. She felt at once that this interview was a terrible ordeal to him. His shaved head, showing the conformation of his skull, gave him a criminal look which he had not had during the trial.

Alexandra held out her hand. "Frank," she said, her eyes filling suddenly, "I hope you'll let me be friendly with you. I understand how you did it. I don't feel hard toward you. They were more to blame than you."

Frank jerked a dirty blue handkerchief from his trousers pocket. He had begun to cry. He turned away from Alexandra. "I never did mean to do not'ing to dat woman," he muttered. "I never mean to do not'ing to dat boy. I ain't had not'ing ag'in' dat boy. I always like dat boy fine. An' then I find him—" He stopped. The feeling went out of his face and eyes. He dropped into a chair and sat looking stolidly at the floor, his hands hanging loosely between his knees, the handkerchief lying across his striped leg. He seemed to have stirred up in his mind a disgust that had paralyzed his faculties.

"I haven't come up here to blame you, Frank. I think they were more to blame than you." Alexandra, too, felt benumbed.

Frank looked up suddenly and stared out of the office window. "I guess dat place all go to hell what I work so hard on," he said with a slow, bitter smile. "I not care a damn." He stopped and rubbed the palm of his hand over the light bristles on his head with annoyance. "I no can t'ink without my hair," he complained. "I forget English. We not talk here, except swear."

Alexandra was bewildered. Frank seemed to have undergone a change of personality. There was scarcely anything by which she could recognize her handsome Bohemian neighbor. He seemed, somehow, not altogether human. She did not know what to say to him.

"You do not feel hard to me, Frank?" she asked at last.

Frank clenched his fist and broke out in excitement. "I not feel hard at no woman. I tell you I not that kind-a man. I never hit my wife. No, never I hurt her when she devil me something awful!" He struck his fist down on the warden's desk so hard that he afterward stroked it absently. A pale pink crept over his neck and face. "Two, t'ree years I know dat woman don' care no more 'bout me, Alexandra Bergson. I know she after some other man. I know her, oo-oo! An' I ain't never hurt her. I never would-a done dat, if I ain't had dat gun along. I don' know what in hell make me take dat gun. She always say I ain't no man to carry gun. If she been in dat house, where she ought-a been— But das a foolish talk."

Frank rubbed his head and stopped suddenly, as he had stopped before. Alexandra felt that there was something strange in the way he chilled off, as if something came up in him that extinguished his power of feeling or thinking.

"Yes, Frank," she said kindly. "I know you never meant to hurt Marie."

Frank smiled at her queerly. His eyes filled slowly with tears.

"You know, I most forgit dat woman's name. She ain't got no name for me no more. I never hate my wife, but dat woman what make me do dat— Honest to God, but I hate her! I no man to fight. I don' want to kill no boy and no woman. I not care how many men she take under dat tree. I no care for not'ing but dat fine boy I kill, Alexandra Bergson. I guess I go crazy sure 'nough."

Alexandra remembered the little yellow cane she had found in Frank's clothes-closet. She thought of how he had come to this country a gay young fellow, so attractive that the prettiest Bohemian girl in Omaha had run away with him. It seemed unreasonable that life should have landed him in such a place as this. She blamed Marie bitterly. And why, with her happy, affectionate nature, should she have brought destruction and sorrow to all who had loved her, even to poor old Joe Tovesky, the uncle who used to carry her about so proudly when she was a little girl? That was the strangest thing of all. Was there, then, something wrong in being warm-hearted and impulsive like that? Alexandra hated to think so. But there was Emil, in the Norwegian graveyard at home, and here was Frank Shabata. Alexandra rose and took him by the hand.

"Frank Shabata, I am never going to stop trying until I get you pardoned. I'll never give the Governor any peace. I know I can get you out of this place."

Frank looked at her distrustfully, but he gathered confidence from her face. "Alexandra," he said earnestly, "if I git out-a here, I not trouble dis country no more. I go back where I come from; see my mother."

Alexandra tried to withdraw her hand, but Frank held on to it nervously. He put out his finger and absently touched a button on her black jacket. "Alexandra," he said in a low tone, looking steadily at the button, "you ain' t'ink I use dat girl awful bad before—"

"No, Frank. We won't talk about that," Alexandra said, pressing his hand. "I can't help Emil now, so I'm going to do what I can for you. You know I don't go away from home often, and I came up here on purpose to tell you this."

The warden at the glass door looked in inquiringly. Alexandra nodded, and he came in and touched the white button on his desk. The guard appeared, and with a sinking heart Alexandra saw Frank led away down the corridor. After a few words with Mr. Schwartz, she left the prison and made her way to the street-car. She had refused with horror the warden's cordial invitation to "go through the institution." As the car lurched over its uneven roadbed, back toward Lincoln, Alexandra thought of how she and Frank had been wrecked by the same storm and of how, although she could come out into the sunlight, she had not much more left in her life than he. She remembered some lines from a poem she had liked in her schooldays:

> *Henceforth the world will only be*
> *A wider prison-house to me,—*

and sighed. A disgust of life weighed upon her heart; some such feeling as had twice frozen Frank Shabata's features while they talked together. She wished she were back on the Divide.

When Alexandra entered her hotel, the clerk held up one finger and beckoned her. As she approached his desk, he handed her a telegram. Alexandra took the yellow envelope and looked at it in perplexity, then stepped into the elevator without opening it. As she walked down the corridor toward her room, she reflected that she was, in a manner, immune from evil tidings. On reaching her room she locked the door, and sitting down on a chair by the dresser, opened the telegram. It was from Hanover, and it read:

Arrived Hanover last night. Shall wait here until you come. Please hurry.

CARL LINSTRUM.

Alexandra put her head down on the dresser and burst into tears.

◆ ◆ ◆ ◆ ◆ ◆ ◆ ◆ ◆ ◆ ◆ ◆ ◆ ◆ ◆ ◆ ◆ ◆ ◆

III

THE NEXT AFTERNOON Carl and Alexandra were walking across the fields from Mrs. Hiller's. Alexandra had left Lincoln after midnight, and Carl had met her at the Hanover station early in the morning. After they reached home, Alexandra had gone over to Mrs. Hiller's to leave a little present she had bought for her in the city. They stayed at the old lady's door but a moment, and then came out to spend the rest of the afternoon in the sunny fields.

Alexandra had taken off her black traveling-suit and put on a white dress; partly because she saw that her black clothes made Carl uncomfortable and partly because she felt oppressed by them herself. They seemed a little like the prison where she had worn them yesterday, and to be out of place in the open fields. Carl had changed very little. His cheeks were browner and fuller. He looked less like a tired scholar than when he went away a year ago, but no one, even now, would have taken him for a man of business. His soft, lustrous black eyes, his whimsical smile, would be less against him in the Klondike than on the Divide. There are always dreamers on the frontier.

Carl and Alexandra had been talking since morning. Her letter had never reached him. He had first learned of her misfortune from a San Francisco paper, four weeks old, which he had picked up in a saloon and which contained a brief account of Frank Shabata's trial. When he put down the paper, he had already made up his mind that he could reach Alexandra as quickly as a letter could; and ever since he had been on the way; day and night, by the fastest boats and trains he could catch. His steamer had been held back two days by rough weather.

As they came out of Mrs. Hiller's garden they took up their talk again where they had left it.

"But could you come away like that, Carl, without arranging things? Could you just walk off and leave your business?" Alexandra asked.

Carl laughed. "Prudent Alexandra! You see, my dear, I happen to have an honest partner. I trust him with everything. In fact, it's been his enterprise from the beginning, you know. I'm in it only because he took me in. I'll have to go back in the spring. Perhaps you will want to go with me then. We haven't turned up millions yet, but we've got a start that's worth following. But this winter I'd like to spend with you. You won't feel that we ought to wait longer, on Emil's account, will you, Alexandra?"

Alexandra shook her head. "No, Carl; I don't feel that way about it. And surely you needn't mind anything Lou and Oscar say now. They are much angrier with me about Emil, now, than about you. They say it was all my fault. That I ruined him by sending him to college."

"No, I don't care a button for Lou or Oscar. The moment I knew you were in trouble, the moment I thought you might need me, it all looked different. You've always been a triumphant kind of person." Carl hesitated, looking sidewise at her strong, full figure. "But you do need me now, Alexandra?"

She put her hand on his arm. "I needed you terribly when it happened, Carl. I cried for you at night. Then everything seemed to get hard inside of me, and I thought perhaps I should never care for you again. But when I got your telegram yesterday, then—then it was just as it used to be. You are all I have in the world, you know."

Carl pressed her hand in silence. They were passing the Shabatas' empty house now, but they avoided the orchard path and took one that led over by the pasture pond.

"Can you understand it, Carl?" Alexandra murmured. "I have had nobody but Ivar and Signa to talk to. Do talk to me. Can you understand it? Could you have believed that of Marie Tovesky? I would have been cut to pieces, little by little, before I would have betrayed her trust in me!"

Carl looked at the shining spot of water before them. "Maybe she was cut to pieces, too, Alexandra. I am sure she tried hard; they both did. That was why Emil went to Mexico, of course. And he was going away again, you tell me, though he had only been home three weeks. You remember that Sunday when I went with Emil up to the French Church fair? I thought that day there was some kind of feeling, something unusual, between them. I meant to talk to you about it. But on my way back I met Lou and Oscar and got so angry that I forgot everything else. You mustn't be hard on them, Alexandra. Sit down here by the pond a minute. I want to tell you something."

They sat down on the grass-tufted bank and Carl told her how he had seen Emil and Marie out by the pond that morning, more than a year ago, and how young and charming and full of grace they had seemed to him. "It happens like that in the world sometimes, Alexandra," he added earnestly. "I've seen it before. There are women who spread ruin around them through no fault of theirs, just by being too beautiful, too full of life and love. They can't help it. People come to them as people go to a warm fire in winter. I used to feel that in her when she was a little girl. Do you remember how all the Bohemians crowded round her in the store that day, when she gave Emil her candy? You remember those yellow sparks in her eyes?"

Alexandra sighed. "Yes. People couldn't help loving her. Poor

Frank does, even now, I think; though he's got himself in such a tangle that for a long time his love has been bitterer than his hate. But if you saw there was anything wrong, you ought to have told me, Carl."

Carl took her hand and smiled patiently. "My dear, it was something one felt in the air, as you feel the spring coming, or a storm in summer. I didn't *see* anything. Simply, when I was with those two young things, I felt my blood go quicker, I felt—how shall I say it?—an acceleration of life. After I got away, it was all too delicate, too intangible, to write about."

Alexandra looked at him mournfully. "I try to be more liberal about such things than I used to be. I try to realize that we are not all made alike. Only, why couldn't it have been Raoul Marcel, or Jan Smirka? Why did it have to be my boy?"

"Because he was the best there was, I suppose. They were both the best you had here."

The sun was dropping low in the west when the two friends rose and took the path again. The straw-stacks were throwing long shadows, the owls were flying home to the prairie-dog town. When they came to the corner where the pastures joined, Alexandra's twelve young colts were galloping in a drove over the brow of the hill.

"Carl," said Alexandra, "I should like to go up there with you in the spring. I haven't been on the water since we crossed the ocean, when I was a little girl. After we first came out here I used to dream sometimes about the shipyard where father worked, and a little sort of inlet, full of masts." Alexandra paused. After a moment's thought she said, "But you would never ask me to go away for good, would you?"

"Of course not, my dearest. I think I know how you feel about this country as well as you do yourself." Carl took her hand in both his own and pressed it tenderly.

"Yes, I still feel that way, though Emil is gone. When I was on the train this morning, and we got near Hanover, I felt something like I did when I drove back with Emil from the river that time, in the dry year. I was glad to come back to it. I've lived here a long time. There is great peace here, Carl, and freedom. . . . I thought when I came out of that prison, where poor Frank is, that I should never feel free again. But I do, here." Alexandra took a deep breath and looked off into the red west.

"You belong to the land," Carl murmured, "as you have always said. Now more than ever."

"Yes, now more than ever. You remember what you once said about the graveyard, and the old story writing itself over? Only it is we who write it, with the best we have."

They paused on the last ridge of the pasture, overlooking the house and the windmill and the stables that marked the site of John Bergson's homestead. On every side the brown waves of the earth rolled away to meet the sky.

"Lou and Oscar can't see those things," said Alexandra suddenly. "Suppose I do will my land to their children, what difference will that make? The land belongs to the future, Carl; that's the way it seems to me. How many of the names on the county clerk's plat will be there in fifty years? I might as well try to will the sunset over there to my brothers' children. We come and go, but the land is always here. And the people who love it and understand it are the people who own it—for a little while."

Carl looked at her wonderingly. She was still gazing into the west, and in her face there was that exalted serenity that sometimes came to her at moments of deep feeling. The level rays of the sinking sun shone in her clear eyes.

"Why are you thinking of such things now, Alexandra?"

"I had a dream before I went to Lincoln— But I will tell you about that afterward, after we are married. It will never come true, now, in the way I thought it might." She took Carl's arm and they walked toward the gate. "How many times we have walked this path together, Carl. How many times we will walk it again! Does it seem to you like coming back to your own place? Do you feel at peace with the world here? I think we shall be very happy. I haven't any fears. I think when friends marry, they are safe. We don't suffer like—those young ones." Alexandra ended with a sigh.

They had reached the gate. Before Carl opened it, he drew Alexandra to him and kissed her softly, on her lips and on her eyes.

She leaned heavily on his shoulder. "I am tired," she murmured. "I have been very lonely, Carl."

They went into the house together, leaving the Divide behind them, under the evening star. Fortunate country, that is one day to receive hearts like Alexandra's into its bosom, to give them out again in the yellow wheat, in the rustling corn, in the shining eyes of youth!

A
LOST LADY

Come, my coach!
Good night, ladies; good night, sweet ladies,
Good night, good night.

PART ONE

A stereoscopic view from October 1866 of Union Pacific officials on an excursion to the 100th meridian, then the westernmost point of railroad construction.

I

THIRTY OR FORTY years ago, in one of those gray towns along
the Burlington railroad, which are so much grayer today than
they were then, there was a house well known from Omaha to
Denver for its hospitality and for a certain charm of atmosphere.
Well known, that is to say, to the railroad aristocracy of that time;
men who had to do with the railroad itself, or with one of the "land
companies" which were its by-products. In those days it was
enough to say of a man that he was "connected with the Burlington." There were the directors, the general managers, vice-presi-
dents, superintendents, whose names we all knew; and their younger
brothers or nephews were auditors, freight agents, departmental
assistants. Everyone "connected" with the Road, even the large
cattle- and grain-shippers, had annual passes; they and their families
rode about over the line a great deal. There were then two distinct
social strata in the prairie States; the homesteaders and hand-work-
ers who were there to make a living, and the bankers and gentlemen
ranchers who came from the Atlantic seaboard to invest money and
to "develop our great West," as they used to tell us.

When the Burlington men were traveling back and forth on
business not very urgent, they found it agreeable to drop off the

express and spend a night in a pleasant house where their importance was delicately recognized; and no house was pleasanter than that of Captain Daniel Forrester, at Sweet Water. Captain Forrester was himself a railroad man, a contractor, who had built hundreds of miles of road for the Burlington,—over the sage brush and cattle country, and on up into the Black Hills.

The Forrester place, as every one called it, was not at all remarkable; the people who lived there made it seem much larger and finer than it was. The house stood on a low round hill, nearly a mile east of town; a white house with a wing, and sharp-sloping roofs to shed the snow. It was encircled by porches, too narrow for modern notions of comfort, supported by the fussy, fragile pillars of that time, when every honest stick of timber was tortured by the turning-lathe into something hideous. Stripped of its vines and denuded of its shrubbery, the house would probably have been ugly enough. It stood close into a fine cottonwood grove that threw sheltering arms to left and right and grew all down the hillside behind it. Thus placed on the hill, against its bristling grove, it was the first thing one saw on coming into Sweet Water by rail, and the last thing one saw on departing.

To approach Captain Forrester's property, you had first to get over a wide, sandy creek which flowed along the eastern edge of the town. Crossing this by the footbridge or the ford, you entered the Captain's private lane bordered by Lombardy poplars, with wide meadows lying on either side. Just at the foot of the hill on which the house sat, one crossed a second creek by the stout wooden roadbridge. This stream traced artless loops and curves through the broad meadows that were half pasture land, half marsh. Anyone but Captain Forrester would have drained the bottom land and made it into highly productive fields. But he had selected this place long ago because it looked beautiful to him, and he happened to like the way the creek wound through his pasture, with mint and joint-grass and twinkling willows along its banks. He was well off for those times, and he had no children. He could afford to humor his fancies.

"The Forrester place, as every one called it, was not at all remarkable; the people who lived there made it seem much larger and finer than it was." —A Lost Lady

When the Captain drove friends from Omaha or Denver over from the station in his democrat wagon, it gratified him to hear these gentlemen admire his fine stock, grazing in the meadows on either side of his lane. And when they reached the top of the hill, it gratified him to see men who were older than himself leap nimbly to the ground and run up the front steps as Mrs. Forrester came out on the porch to greet them. Even the hardest and coldest of his friends, a certain narrow-faced Lincoln banker, became animated when he took her hand, tried to meet the gay challenge in her eyes and to reply cleverly to the droll word of greeting on her lips.

She was always there, just outside the front door, to welcome their visitors, having been warned of their approach by the sound of hoofs and the rumble of wheels on the wooden bridge. If she happened to be in the kitchen, helping her Bohemian cook, she came out in her apron, waving a buttery iron spoon, or shook cherry-stained fingers at the new arrival. She never stopped to pin up a lock; she was attractive in dishabille, and she knew it. She had been known to rush to the door in her dressing-gown, brush in hand and her long black hair rippling over her shoulders, to welcome Cyrus Dalzell, president of the Colorado & Utah; and the great man had never felt more flattered. In his eyes, and in the eyes of the admiring middle-aged men who visited there, whatever Mrs. Forrester chose to do was "lady-like" because she did it. They could not imagine her in any dress or situation in which she would not be charming. Captain Forrester himself, a man of few words, told Judge Pommeroy that he had never seen her look more captivating than on the day when she was chased by the new bull in the pasture. She had forgotten about the bull and gone into the meadow to gather wild flowers. He heard her scream, and as he ran puffing down the hill, she was scudding along the edge of the marshes like a hare, beside herself with laughter, and stubbornly clinging to the crimson parasol that had made all the trouble.

Mrs. Forrester was twenty-five years younger than her husband, and she was his second wife. He married her in California and brought her to Sweet Water a bride. They called the place home even then, when they lived there but a few months out of each year. But later, after the Captain's terrible fall with his horse in the mountains, which broke him so that he could no longer build railroads, he and his wife retired to the house on the hill. He grew old there,—and even she, alas! grew older.

I I

B ut we will begin this story with a summer morning long ago, when Mrs. Forrester was still a young woman, and Sweet Water was a town of which great things were expected. That morning she was standing in the deep bay-window of her parlor, arranging old-fashioned blush roses in a glass bowl. Glancing up, she saw a group of little boys coming along the driveway, barefoot, with fishing-poles and lunch-baskets. She knew most of them; there was Niel Herbert, Judge Pommeroy's nephew, a handsome boy of twelve whom she liked; and polite George Adams, son of a gentleman rancher from Lowell, Massachusetts. The others were just little boys from the town; the butcher's red-headed son, the leading grocer's fat brown twins, Ed Elliott (whose flirtatious old father kept a shoe store and was the Don Juan of the lower world of Sweet Water), and the two sons of the German tailor,—pale, freckled lads with ragged clothes and ragged rust-colored hair, from whom she sometimes bought game or catfish when they appeared silent and spook-like at her kitchen door and thinly asked if she would "care for any fish this morning."

As the boys came up the hill she saw them hesitate and consult together. "You ask her, Niel."

"You'd better, George. She goes to your house all the time, and she barely knows me to speak to."

As they paused before the three steps which led up to the front porch, Mrs. Forrester came to the door and nodded graciously, one of the pink roses in her hand.

"Good-morning, boys. Off for a picnic?"

George Adams stepped forward and solemnly took off his big straw hat. "Good-morning, Mrs. Forrester. Please may we fish and wade down in the marsh and have our lunch in the grove?"

"Certainly. You have a lovely day. How long has school been out? Don't you miss it? I'm sure Niel does. Judge Pommeroy tells me he's very studious."

The boys laughed, and Niel looked unhappy.

"Run along, and be sure you don't leave the gate into the pasture open. Mr. Forrester hates to have the cattle get in on his blue grass."

The boys went quietly round the house to the gate into the grove, then ran shouting down the grassy slopes under the tall trees. Mrs. Forrester watched them from the kitchen window until they disappeared behind the roll of the hill. She turned to her Bohemian cook.

"Mary, when you are baking this morning, put in a pan of cookies for those boys. I'll take them down when they are having their lunch."

The round hill on which the Forrester house stood sloped gently down to the bridge in front, and gently down through the grove behind. But east of the house, where the grove ended, it broke steeply from high grassy banks, like bluffs, to the marsh below. It was thither the boys were bound.

When lunch time came they had done none of the things they meant to do. They had behaved like wild creatures all morning; shouting from the breezy bluffs, dashing down into the silvery marsh through the dewy cobwebs that glistened on the tall weeds, swishing among the pale tan cattails, wading in the sandy creek bed, chasing a striped water snake from the old willow stump where he was sunning himself, cutting sling-shot crotches, throwing themselves on their stomachs to drink at the cool spring that flowed out from under a bank into a thatch of dark watercress. Only the two German boys, Rheinhold and Adolph Blum, withdrew to a still pool where the creek was dammed by a reclining tree trunk, and, in spite of all the noise and splashing about them, managed to catch a few suckers.

The wild roses were wide open and brilliant, the blue-eyed grass was in purple flower, and the silvery milkweed was just coming on. Birds and butterflies darted everywhere. All at once the breeze died, the air grew very hot, the marsh steamed, and the birds disappeared. The boys found they were tired; their shirts stuck to their bodies and their hair to their foreheads. They left the sweltering marsh-meadows for the grove, lay down on the clean grass under the grateful shade of the tall cottonwoods, and spread out their lunch. The Blum boys never brought anything but rye bread and hunks of dry cheese,—their companions wouldn't have touched it on any account. But Thaddeus Grimes, the butcher's red-headed son, was the only one impolite enough to show his scorn. "You live on wienies to home, why don't you never bring none?" he bawled.

"Hush," said Niel Herbert. He pointed to a white figure coming rapidly down through the grove, under the flickering leaf shadows,—Mrs. Forrester, bareheaded, a basket on her arm, her blue-black hair shining in the sun. It was not until years afterward that she began to wear veils and sun hats, though her complexion was never one of her beauties. Her cheeks were pale and rather thin, slightly freckled in summer.

As she approached, George Adams, who had a particular mother, rose, and Niel followed his example.

"Here are some hot cookies for your lunch, boys." She took the napkin off the basket. "Did you catch anything?"

"We didn't fish much. Just ran about," said George.

"I know! You were wading and things." She had a nice way of

talking to boys, light and confidential. "I wade down there myself sometimes, when I go down to get flowers. I can't resist it. I pull off my stockings and pick up my skirts, and in I go!" She thrust out a white shoe and shook it.

"But you can swim, can't you, Mrs. Forrester," said George. "Most women can't."

"Oh yes, they can! In California everybody swims. But the Sweet Water doesn't tempt me,—mud and water snakes and blood-suckers—Ugh!" she shivered, laughing.

"We seen a water snake this morning and chased him. A whopper!" Thad Grimes put in.

"Why didn't you kill him? Next time I go wading he'll bite my toes! Now, go on with your lunch. George can leave the basket with Mary as you go out." She left them, and they watched her white figure drifting along the edge of the grove as she stopped here and there to examine the raspberry vines by the fence.

"These are good cookies, all right," said one of the giggly brown Weaver twins. The German boys munched in silence. They were all rather pleased that Mrs. Forrester had come down to them herself, instead of sending Mary. Even rough little Thad Grimes, with his red thatch and catfish mouth—the characteristic feature of all the Grimes brood—knew that Mrs. Forrester was a very special kind of person. George and Niel were already old enough to see for themselves that she was different from the other townswomen, and to reflect upon what it was that made her so. The Blum brothers regarded her humbly from under their pale, chewed-off hair, as one of the rich and great of the world. They realized, more than their companions, that such a fortunate and privileged class was an axiomatic fact in the social order.

The boys had finished their lunch and were lying on the grass talking about how Judge Pommeroy's water spaniel, Fanny, had been poisoned, and who had certainly done it, when they had a second visitor.

"Shut up, boys, there he comes now. That's Poison Ivy," said one of the Weaver twins. "Shut up, we don't want old Roger poisoned."

A well-grown boy of eighteen or nineteen, dressed in a shabby corduroy hunting suit, with a gun and gamebag, had climbed up from the marsh and was coming down the grove between the rows of trees. He walked with a rude, arrogant stride, kicking at the twigs, and carried himself with unnatural erectness, as if he had a steel rod down his back. There was something defiant and suspicious about the way he held his head. He came up to the group and addressed them in a superior, patronizing tone.

"Hullo, kids. What are *you* doing here?"

"Picnic," said Ed Elliott.

"I thought girls went on picnics. Did you bring teacher along? Ain't you kids old enough to hunt yet?"

George Adams looked at him scornfully. "Of course we are. I got a 22 Remington for my last birthday. But we know better than to bring guns over here. You better hide yours, Mr. Ivy, or Mrs. Forrester will come down and tell you to get out."

"She can't see us from the house. And anyhow, she can't say anything to me. I'm just as good as she is."

To this the boys made no reply. Such an assertion was absurd even to fish-mouthed Thad; his father's business depended upon some people being better than others, and ordering better cuts of meat in consequence. If everybody ate round steak like Ivy Peters' family, there would be nothing in the butcher's trade.

The visitor had put his gun and gamebag behind a tree, however, and stood stiffly upright, surveying the group out of his narrow beady eyes and making them all uncomfortable. George and Niel hated to look at Ivy,—and yet his face had a kind of fascination for them. It was red, and the flesh looked hard, as if it were swollen from bee-stings, or from an encounter with poison ivy. This nickname, however, was given him because it was well known that he had "made away" with several other dogs before he had poisoned the Judge's friendly water spaniel. The boys said he took a dislike to a dog and couldn't rest until he made an end of him.

Ivy's red skin was flecked with tiny freckles, like rust spots, and in each of his hard cheeks there was a curly indentation, like a knot in a tree-bole,—two permanent dimples which did anything but soften his countenance. His eyes were very small, and an absence of eyelashes gave his pupils the fixed, unblinking hardness of a snake's or a lizard's. His hands had the same swollen look as his face, were deeply creased across the back and knuckles, as if the skin were stretched too tight. He was an ugly fellow, Ivy Peters, and he liked being ugly.

He began telling the boys that it was too hot to hunt now, but later he meant to steal down to the marsh, where the ducks came at sundown, and bag a few. "I can make off across the corn fields before the old Cap sees me. He's not much on the run."

"He'll complain to your father."

"A whoop my father cares!" The speaker's restless eyes were looking up through the branches. "See that woodpecker tapping; don't mind us a bit. That's nerve!"

"They are protected here, so they're not afraid," said precise George.

"Hump! They'll spoil the old man's grove for him. That tree's full of holes already. Wouldn't he come down easy, now!"

Niel and George Adams sat up. "Don't you dare shoot here, you'll get us all into trouble."

"She'd come right down from the house," cried Ed Elliott.

"Let her come, stuck-up piece! Who's talking about shooting, anyway? There's more ways of killing dogs than choking them with butter."

At this effrontery the boys shot amazed glances at one another, and the brown Weaver twins broke simultaneously into giggles and rolled over on the turf. But Ivy seemed unaware that he was regarded as being especially resourceful where dogs were concerned.

He drew from his pocket a metal sling-shot and some round bits of gravel. "I won't kill it. I'll just surprise it, so we can have a look at it."

"Bet you won't hit it!"

"Bet I will!" He fitted the stone to the leather, squinted, and let fly. Sure enough, the woodpecker dropped at his feet. He threw his heavy black felt hat over it. Ivy never wore a straw hat, even in the hottest weather. "Now wait. He'll come to. You'll hear him flutter in a minute."

"It ain't a he, anyhow. It's a female. Anybody would know that," said Niel contemptuously, annoyed that this unpopular boy should come along and spoil their afternoon. He held the fate of his uncle's spaniel against Ivy Peters.

"All right, Miss Female," said Ivy carelessly, intent upon a project of his own. He took from his pocket a little red leather box, and when he opened it the boys saw that it contained curious little instruments: tiny sharp knife blades, hooks, curved needles, a saw, a blow-pipe, and scissors. "Some of these I got with a taxidermy outfit from the *Youth's Companion,* and some I made myself." He got stiffly down on his knees,—his joints seemed disinclined to bend at all,—and listened beside his hat. "She's as lively as a cricket," he announced. Thrusting his hand suddenly under the brim, he brought out the startled bird. It was not bleeding, and did not seem to be crippled.

"Now, you watch, and I'll show you something," said Ivy. He held the woodpecker's head in a vice made of his thumb and forefinger, enclosing its panting body with his palm. Quick as a flash, as if it were a practised trick, with one of those tiny blades he slit both the eyes that glared in the bird's stupid little head, and instantly released it.

The woodpecker rose in the air with a whirling, corkscrew motion, darted to the right, struck a tree trunk,—to the left, and struck another. Up and down, backward and forward among the tangle of branches it flew, raking its feathers, falling and recovering itself.

The boys stood watching it, indignant and uncomfortable, not knowing what to do. They were not especially sensitive; Thad was always on hand when there was anything doing at the slaughter house, and the Blum boys lived by killing things. They wouldn't have believed they could be so upset by a hurt woodpecker. There was something wild and desperate about the way the darkened creature beat its wings in the branches, whirling in the sunlight and never seeing it, always thrusting its head up and shaking it, as a bird does when it is drinking. Presently it managed to get its feet on the same limb where it had been struck, and seemed to recognize that perch. As if it had learned something by its bruises, it pecked and crept its way along the branch and disappeared into its own hole.

"There," Niel Herbert exclaimed between his teeth, "if I can get it now, I can kill it and put it out of its misery. Let me on your back, Rhein."

Rheinhold was the tallest, and he obediently bent his bony back. The trunk of a cottonwood tree is hard to climb; the bark is rough, and the branches begin a long way up. Niel tore his trousers and scratched his bare legs smartly before he got to the first fork. After recovering breath, he wound his way up toward the woodpecker's hole, which was inconveniently high. He was almost there, his companions below thought him quite safe, when he suddenly lost his balance, turned a somersault in the air, and bumped down on the grass at their feet. There he lay without moving.

"Run for water!"

"Run for Mrs. Forrester! Ask her for whiskey."

"No," said George Adams, "let's carry him up to the house. She will know what to do."

"That's sense," said Ivy Peters. As he was much bigger and stronger than any of the others, he lifted Niel's limp body and started up the hill. It had occurred to him that this would be a fine chance to get inside the Forresters' house and see what it was like, and this he had always wanted to do.

Mary, the cook, saw them coming from the kitchen window, and ran for her mistress. Captain Forrester was in Kansas City that day.

Mrs. Forrester came to the back door. "What's happened? It's Niel, too! Bring him in this way, please."

Ivy Peters followed her, keeping his eyes open, and the rest trooped after him,—all but the Blum boys, who knew that their place was outside the kitchen door. Mrs. Forrester led the way through the butler's pantry, the dining-room, the back parlor, to her own bedroom. She threw down the white counterpane, and Ivy laid Niel upon the sheets. Mrs. Forrester was concerned, but not frightened.

"Mary, will you bring the brandy from the sideboard. George, telephone Dr. Dennison to come over at once. Now you other boys run out on the front porch and wait quietly. There are too many of you in here." She knelt by the bed, putting brandy between Niel's white lips with a teaspoon. The little boys withdrew, only Ivy Peters remained standing in the back parlor, just outside the bedroom door, his arms folded across his chest, taking in his surroundings with bold, unblinking eyes.

Mrs. Forrester glanced at him over her shoulder. "Will you wait on the porch, please? You are older than the others, and if anything is needed I can call on you."

Ivy cursed himself, but he had to go. There was something final about her imperious courtesy,—high-and-mighty, he called it. He had intended to sit down in the biggest leather chair and cross his legs and make himself at home; but he found himself on the front porch, put out by that delicately modulated voice as effectually as if he had been kicked out by the brawniest tough in town.

Niel opened his eyes and looked wonderingly about the big, half-darkened room, full of heavy, old-fashioned walnut furniture. He was lying on a white bed with ruffled pillow shams, and Mrs. Forrester was kneeling beside him, bathing his forehead with cologne. Bohemian Mary stood behind her, with a basin of water.

"Ouch, my arm!" he muttered, and the perspiration broke out on his face.

"Yes, dear, I'm afraid it's broken. Don't move. Dr. Dennison will be here in a few minutes. It doesn't hurt very much, does it?"

"No'm," he said faintly. He was in pain, but he felt weak and contented. The room was cool and dusky and quiet. At his house everything was horrid when one was sick. . . . What soft fingers Mrs. Forrester had, and what a lovely lady she was. Inside the lace ruffle of her dress he saw her white throat rising and falling so quickly. Suddenly she got up to take off her glittering rings,—she had not thought of them before,—shed them off her fingers with a quick motion as if she were washing her hands, and dropped them into Mary's broad palm. The little boy was thinking that he would probably never be in so nice a place again. The windows went almost down to the baseboard, like doors, and the closed green shutters let in streaks of sunlight that quivered on the polished floor and the silver things on the dresser. The heavy curtains were looped back with thick cords, like ropes. The marble-topped wash-stand was as big as a sideboard. The massive walnut furniture was all inlaid with pale-colored woods. Niel had a scroll-saw, and this inlay interested him.

"There, he looks better now, doesn't he, Mary?" Mrs. Forrester ran her fingers through his black hair and lightly kissed him on the forehead. Oh, how sweet, how sweet she smelled!

"Wheels on the bridge; it's Doctor Dennison. Go and show him in, Mary."

Dr. Dennison set Niel's arm and took him home in his buggy. Home was not a pleasant place to go to; a frail egg-shell house, set off on the edge of the prairie where people of no consequence lived. Except for the fact that he was Judge Pommeroy's nephew, Niel would have been one of the boys to whom Mrs. Forrester merely nodded brightly as she passed. His father was a widower. A poor relation, a spinster from Kentucky, kept house for them, and Niel thought she was probably the worst housekeeper in the world.

Their house was usually full of washing in various stages of incompletion,—tubs sitting about with linen soaking,—and the beds were "aired" until any hour in the afternoon when Cousin Sadie happened to think of making them up. She liked to sit down after breakfast and read murder trials, or peruse a well-worn copy of "St. Elmo." Sadie was a good-natured thing and was always running off to help a neighbor, but Niel hated to have anyone come to see them. His father was at home very little, spent all his time at his office. He kept the county abstract books and made farm loans. Having lost his own property, he invested other people's money for them. He was a gentle, agreeable man, young, good-looking, with nice manners, but Niel felt there was an air of failure and defeat about his family. He clung to his maternal uncle, Judge Pommeroy, white-whiskered and portly, who was Captain Forrester's lawyer and a friend of all the great men who visited the Forresters. Niel was proud, like his mother; she died when he was five years old. She had hated the West, and used haughtily to tell her neighbors that she would never think of living anywhere but in Fayette County, Kentucky; that they had only come to Sweet Water to make investments and to "turn the crown into the pound." By that phrase she was still remembered, poor lady.

III

FOR THE NEXT few years Niel saw very little of Mrs. Forrester. She was an excitement that came and went with summer. She and her husband always spent the winter in Denver and Colorado Springs,—left Sweet Water soon after Thanksgiving and did not return until the first of May. He knew that Mrs. Forrester liked him, but she hadn't much time for growing boys. When she had friends staying with her, and gave a picnic supper for them, or a dance in the grove on a moonlit night, Niel was always invited. Coming and going along the road to the marsh with the Blum boys, he sometimes met the Captain driving visitors over in the democrat wagon, and he heard about these people from Black Tom, Judge Pommeroy's faithful negro servant, who went over to wait on the table for Mrs. Forrester when she had a dinner party.

Then came the accident which cut short the Captain's career as a roadbuilder. After that fall with his horse, he lay ill at the Antlers, in Colorado Springs, all winter. In the summer, when Mrs. Forrester brought him home to Sweet Water, he still walked with a cane. He had grown much heavier, seemed encumbered by his own bulk, and never suggested taking a contract for the railroad again. He was able to work in his garden, trimmed his snowball bushes and lilac hedges, devoted a great deal of time to growing roses. He and his wife still went away for the winter, but each year the period of their absence grew shorter.

All this while the town of Sweet Water was changing. Its future no longer looked bright. Successive crop failures had broken the spirit of the farmers. George Adams and his family had gone back to Massachusetts, disillusioned about the West. One by one the other gentlemen ranchers followed their example. The Forresters now had fewer visitors. The Burlington was "drawing in its horns," as people said, and the railroad officials were not stopping off at Sweet Water so often,—were more inclined to hurry past a town where they had sunk money that would never come back.

Niel Herbert's father was one of the first failures to be crowded to the wall. He closed his little house, sent his cousin Sadie back to Kentucky, and went to Denver to accept an office position. He left Niel behind to read law in the office with his uncle. Not that Niel had any taste for the law, but he liked being with Judge Pommeroy, and he might as well stay there as anywhere, for the present. The few thousand dollars his mother had left him would not be his until he was twenty-one.

Niel fitted up a room for himself behind the suite which the Judge retained for his law offices, on the second floor of the most pretentious brick block in town. There he lived with monastic cleanliness and severity, glad to be rid of his cousin and her inconsequential housewifery, and resolved to remain a bachelor, like his uncle. He took care of the offices, which meant that he did the janitor work, and arranged them exactly to suit his taste, making the rooms so attractive that all the Judge's friends, and especially Captain Forrester, dropped in there to talk oftener than ever.

The Judge was proud of his nephew. Niel was now nineteen, a tall, straight, deliberate boy. His features were clear-cut, his gray eyes, so dark that they looked black under his long lashes, were rather moody and challenging. The world did not seem over-bright to young people just then. His reserve, which did not come from embarrassment or vanity, but from a critical habit of mind, made him seem older than he was, and a little cold.

One winter afternoon, only a few days before Christmas, Niel sat writing in the back office, at the long table where he usually worked or trifled, surrounded by the Judge's fine law library and solemn steel engravings of statesmen and jurists. His uncle was at his desk in the front office, engaged in a friendly consultation with one of his country clients. Niel, greatly bored with the notes he was copying, was trying to invent an excuse for getting out on the street, when he became aware of light footsteps coming rapidly down the outside corridor. The door of the front office opened, he heard his uncle rise quickly to his feet, and, at the same moment, heard a woman's laugh,—a soft, musical laugh which rose and descended like a suave scale. He turned in his screw chair so that he could look over his shoulder through the double doors into the front room. Mrs. Forrester stood there, shaking her muff at the Judge and the bewildered Swede farmer. Her quick eye lighted upon a bottle of Bourbon and two glasses on the desk among the papers.

"Is that the way you prepare your cases, Judge? What an example for Niel!" She peeped through the door and nodded to the boy as he rose.

He remained in the back room, however, watching her while she declined the chair the Judge pushed toward her and made a sign of refusal when he politely pointed to the Bourbon. She stood beside his desk in her long sealskin coat and cap, a crimson scarf showing above the collar, a little brown veil with spots tied over her eyes. The veil did not in the least obscure those beautiful eyes, dark and full of light, set under a low white forehead and arching eyebrows. The frosty air had brought no color to her cheeks,—her skin had always the fragrant, crystalline whiteness of white lilacs. Mrs. Forrester looked at one, and one knew that she was bewitching. It was instantaneous, and it pierced the thickest hide. The Swede farmer was now grinning from ear to ear, and he, too, had shuffled to his feet. There could be no negative encounter, however slight, with Mrs. Forrester. If she merely bowed to you, merely looked at you, it constituted a personal relation. Something about her took hold of one in a flash; one became acutely conscious of her, of her fragility and grace, of her mouth which could say so much without words; of her eyes, lively, laughing, intimate, nearly always a little mocking.

"Will you and Niel dine with us tomorrow evening, Judge? And will you lend me Tom? We've just had a wire. The Ogdens are stopping over with us. They've been East to bring the girl home from school,—she's had mumps or something. They want to get home for Christmas, but they will stop off for two days. Probably Frank Ellinger will come on from Denver."

"No prospect can afford me such pleasure as that of dining with Mrs. Forrester," said the Judge ponderously.

"Thank you!" she bowed playfully and turned toward the double doors. "Niel, could you leave your work long enough to drive me home? Mr. Forrester has been detained at the bank."

Niel put on his wolfskin coat. Mrs. Forrester took him by his shaggy sleeve and went with him quickly down the long corridor and the narrow stairs to the street.

At the hitch-bar stood her cutter, looking like a painted toy among the country sleds and wagons. Niel tucked the buffalo robes about Mrs. Forrester, untied the ponies, and sprang in beside her. Without direction the team started down the frozen main street, where few people were abroad, crossed the creek on the ice, and trotted up the poplar-bordered lane toward the house on the hill. The late afternoon sun burned on the snow-crusted pastures. The poplars looked very tall and straight, pinched up and severe in their winter poverty. Mrs. Forrester chatted to Niel with her face turned toward him, holding her muff up to break the wind.

"I'm counting on you to help me entertain Constance Ogden. Can you take her off my hands day after tomorrow, come over in the afternoon? Your duties as a lawyer aren't very arduous yet?"

She smiled teasingly. "What can I do with a miss of nineteen? One who goes to college? I've no learned conversation for her!"

"Surely I haven't!" Niel exclaimed.

"Oh, but you're a boy! Perhaps you can interest her in lighter things. She's considered pretty."

"Do you think she is?"

"I haven't seen her lately. She was striking,—china blue eyes and heaps of yellow hair, not exactly yellow,—what they call an ashen blond, I believe."

Niel had noticed that in describing the charms of other women Mrs. Forrester always made fun of them a little.

They drew up in front of the house. Ben Keezer came round from the kitchen to take the team.

"You are to go back for Mr. Forrester at six, Ben. Niel, come in for a moment and get warm." She drew him through the little storm entry, which protected the front door in winter, into the hall. "Hang up your coat and come along." He followed her through the parlor into the sitting-room, where a little coal grate was burning under the black mantelpiece, and sat down in the big leather chair in which Captain Forrester dozed after his mid-day meal. It was a rather dark room, with walnut bookcases that had carved tops and glass doors. The floor was covered by a red carpet, and the walls were hung with large, old-fashioned engravings; "The House of the Poet on the Last Day of Pompeii," "Shakespeare Reading before Queen Elizabeth."

Mrs. Forrester left him and presently returned carrying a tray with a decanter and sherry glasses. She put it down on her husband's smoking-table, poured out a glass for Niel and one for herself, and perched on the arm of one of the stuffed chairs, where she sat sipping her sherry and stretching her tiny, silver-buckled slippers out toward the glowing coals.

"It's so nice to have you staying on until after Christmas," Niel observed. "You've only been here one other Christmas since I can remember."

"I'm afraid we're staying on all winter this year. Mr. Forrester thinks we can't afford to go away. For some reason, we are extraordinarily poor just now."

"Like everybody else," the boy commented grimly.

"Yes, like everybody else. However, it does no good to be glum about it, does it?" She refilled the two glasses. "I always take a little sherry at this time in the afternoon. At Colorado Springs some of my friends take tea, like the English. But I should feel like an old woman, drinking tea! Besides, sherry is good for my throat." Niel remembered some legend about a weak chest and occasional terrifying hemorrhages. But that seemed doubtful, as one looked at her,—fragile, indeed, but with such light, effervescing vitality. "Perhaps I do seem old to you, Niel, quite old enough for tea and a cap!"

He smiled gravely. "You seem always the same to me, Mrs. Forrester."

"Yes? And how is that?"

"Lovely. Just lovely."

As she bent forward to put down her glass she patted his cheek. "Oh, you'll do very well for Constance!" Then, seriously, "I'm glad if I do, though. I want you to like me well enough to come to see us often this winter. You shall come with your uncle to make a fourth at whist. Mr. Forrester must have his whist in the evening. Do you think he is looking any worse, Niel? It frightens me to see him getting a little uncertain. But there, we must believe in good luck!" She took up the half-empty glass and held it against the light.

Niel liked to see the firelight sparkle on her earrings, long pendants of garnets and seed-pearls in the shape of fleurs-de-lys. She was the only woman he knew who wore earrings; they hung naturally against her thin, triangular cheeks. Captain Forrester, although he had given her handsomer ones, liked to see her wear these, because they had been his mother's. It gratified him to have his wife wear jewels; it meant something to him. She never left off her beautiful rings unless she was in the kitchen.

"A winter in the country may do him good," said Mrs. Forrester, after a silence during which she looked intently into the fire, as if she were trying to read the outcome of their difficulties there. "He loves this place so much. But you and Judge Pommeroy must keep an eye on him when he is in town, Niel. If he looks tired or uncertain, make some excuse and bring him home. He can't carry a drink or two as he used,"—she glanced over her shoulder to see that the door into the dining-room was shut. "Once last winter he had been drinking with some old friends at the Antlers,—nothing unusual, just as he always did, as a man must be able to do,—but it was too much for him. When he came out to join me in the carriage, coming down that long walk, you know, he fell. There was no ice, he didn't slip. It was simply because he was unsteady. He had trouble getting up. I still shiver to think of it. To me, it was as if one of the mountains had fallen down."

A little later Niel went plunging down the hill, looking exultantly into the streak of red sunset. Oh, the winter would not be so bad, this year! How strange that she should be here at all, a woman like her among common people! Not even in Denver had he ever seen another woman so elegant. He had sat in the dining-room of the Brown Palace hotel and watched them as they came down to dinner,—fashionable women from "the East," on their way to California. But he had never found one so attractive and distinguished as Mrs. Forrester. Compared with her, other women were heavy and dull; even the pretty ones seemed lifeless,—they had not that something in their glance that made one's blood tingle. And never elsewhere had he heard anything like her inviting, musical laugh, that was like the distant measures of dance music, heard through opening and shutting doors.

He could remember the very first time he ever saw Mrs. Forrester, when he was a little boy. He had been loitering in front of the Episcopal church one Sunday morning, when a low carriage drove up to the door. Ben Keezer was on the front seat, and on the back seat was a lady, alone, in a black silk dress all puffs and ruffles, and a black hat, carrying a parasol with a carved ivory handle. As the carriage stopped she lifted her dress to alight; out of a swirl of foamy white petticoats she thrust a black, shiny slipper. She stepped lightly to the ground and with a nod to the driver went into the church. The little boy followed her through the open door, saw her enter a pew and kneel. He was proud now that at the first moment he had recognized her as belonging to a different world from any he had ever known.

Niel paused for a moment at the end of the lane to look up at the last skeleton poplar in the long row; just above its pointed tip hung the hollow, silver winter moon.

I V

IN PLEASANT WEATHER Judge Pommeroy walked to the Forresters', but on the occasion of the dinner for the Ogdens he engaged the liveryman to take him and his nephew over in one of the town hacks,—vehicles seldom used except for funerals and weddings. They smelled strongly of the stable and contained lap-robes as heavy as lead and as slippery as oiled paper. Niel and his uncle were the only townspeople asked to the Forresters' that evening; they rolled over the creek and up the hill in state, and emerged covered with horsehair.

Captain Forrester met them at the door, his burly figure buttoned up in a frock coat, a flat collar and black string tie under the heavy folds of his neck. He was always clean-shaven except for a drooping dun-colored moustache. The company stood behind him laughing while Niel caught up the whisk-broom and began dusting roan hairs off his uncle's broadcloth. Mrs. Forrester gave Niel a brushing in turn and then took him into the parlor and introduced him to Mrs. Ogden and her daughter.

The daughter was a rather pretty girl, Niel thought, in a pale pink evening dress which left bare her smooth arms and short, dimpled neck. Her eyes were, as Mrs. Forrester had said, a china blue, rather prominent and inexpressive. Her fleece of ashy-gold hair was bound about her head with silver bands. In spite of her fresh, rose-like complexion, her face was not altogether agreeable. Two dissatisfied lines reached from the corners of her short nose to the corners of her mouth. When she was displeased, even a little, these lines tightened, drew her nose back, and gave her a suspicious, injured expression. Niel sat down by her and did his best, but he found her hard to talk to. She seemed nervous and distracted, kept glancing over her shoulders, and crushing her handkerchief up in her hands. Her mind, clearly, was elsewhere. After a few moments he turned to the mother, who was more easily interested.

Mrs. Ogden was almost unpardonably homely. She had a pear-shaped face, and across her high forehead lay a row of flat, dry curls. Her bluish brown skin was almost the color of her violet dinner dress. A diamond necklace glittered about her wrinkled throat. Unlike Constance, she seemed thoroughly amiable, but as she talked she tilted her head and "used" her eyes, availing herself of those arch glances which he had supposed only pretty women indulged in. Probably she had long been surrounded by people to whom she was an important personage, and had acquired the manner of a spoiled darling. Niel thought her rather foolish at first, but in a few moments he had got used to her mannerisms and began to like her. He found himself laughing heartily and forgot the discouragement of his failure with the daughter.

Mr. Ogden, a short, weather-beaten man of fifty, with a cast in one eye, a stiff imperial, and twisted moustaches, was noticeably quieter and less expansive than when Niel had met him here on former occasions. He seemed to expect his wife to do the talking. When Mrs. Forrester addressed him, or passed near him, his good eye twinkled and followed her,—while the eye that looked askance remained unchanged and committed itself to nothing.

Suddenly everyone became more lively; the air warmed, and the lamplight seemed to brighten, as a fourth member of the Denver party came in from the dining-room with a glittering tray full of cocktails he had been making. Frank Ellinger was a bachelor of forty, six feet two, with long straight legs, fine shoulders, and a figure that still permitted his white waistcoat to button without a wrinkle under his conspicuously well-cut dinner coat. His black hair, coarse and curly as the filling of a mattress, was gray about the ears, his florid face showed little purple veins about his beaked nose,—a nose like the prow of a ship, with long nostrils. His chin was deeply cleft, his thick curly lips seemed very muscular, very much under his control, and, with his strong white teeth, irregular and curved, gave him the look of a man who could bite an iron rod in two with a snap of his jaws. His whole figure seemed very much alive under his clothes, with a restless, muscular energy that had something of the cruelty of wild animals in it. Niel was very much interested in this man, the hero of many ambiguous stories. He didn't know whether he liked him or not. He knew nothing bad about him, but he felt something evil.

The cocktails were the signal for general conversation, the company drew together in one group. Even Miss Constance seemed less dissatisfied. Ellinger drank his cocktail standing beside her chair, and offered her the cherry in his glass. They were old-fashioned whiskey cocktails. Nobody drank Martinis then; gin was supposed to be the consolation of sailors and inebriate scrub-women.

"Very good, Frank, very good," Captain Forrester pronounced, drawing out a fresh, cologne-scented handkerchief to wipe his moustache. "Are encores in order?" The Captain puffed slightly when he talked. His eyes, always somewhat suffused and bloodshot since his injury, blinked at his friends from under his heavy lids.

"One more round for everybody, Captain." Ellinger brought in from the sideboard a capacious shaker and refilled all the glasses except Miss Ogden's. At her he shook his finger, and offered her the little dish of Maraschino cherries.

"No, I don't want those. I want the one in your glass," she said with a pouty smile. "I like it to taste of something!"

"Constance!" said her mother reprovingly, rolling her eyes at Mrs. Forrester, as if to share with her the charm of such innocence.

"Niel," Mrs. Forrester laughed, "won't you give the child your cherry, too?"

Niel promptly crossed the room and proffered the cherry in the bottom of his glass. She took it with her thumb and fore-finger and dropped it into her own,—where, he was quick to observe, she left it when they went out to dinner. A stubborn piece of pink flesh, he decided, and certainly a fool about a man quite old enough to be her father. He sighed when he saw that he was placed next her at the dinner table.

Captain Forrester still made a commanding figure at the head of his own table, with his napkin tucked under his chin and the work of carving well in hand. Nobody could lay bare the bones of a brace of duck or a twenty-pound turkey more deftly. "What part of the turkey do you prefer, Mrs. Ogden?" If one had a preference, it was gratified, with all the stuffing and gravy that went with it, and the vegetables properly placed. When a plate left Captain Forrester's hands, it was a dinner; the recipient was served, and well served. He served Mrs. Forrester last of the ladies but before the men, and to her, too, he said, "Mrs. Forrester, what part of the turkey shall I give you this evening?" He was a man who did not vary his formulae or his manners. He was no more mobile than his countenance. Niel and Judge Pommeroy had often remarked how much Captain Forrester looked like the pictures of Grover Cleveland. His clumsy dignity covered a deep nature, and a conscience that had never been juggled with. His repose was like that of a mountain. When he laid his fleshy thick-fingered hand upon a frantic horse, an hysterical woman, an Irish workman out for blood, he brought them peace; something they could not resist. That had been the secret of his management of men. His sanity asked nothing, claimed nothing; it was so simple that it brought a hush over distracted creatures. In the old days, when he was building road in the Black Hills, trouble sometimes broke out in camp when he was absent, staying with Mrs. Forrester at Colorado Springs. He would put down the telegram that announced an insurrection and say to his wife, "Maidy, I must go to the men." And that was all he did,—he went to them.

While the Captain was intent upon his duties as host he talked very little, and Judge Pommeroy and Ellinger kept a lively cross-fire of amusing stories going. Niel, sitting opposite Ellinger, watched him closely. He still couldn't decide whether he liked him or not. In Denver Frank was known as a prince of good fellows; tactful, generous, resourceful, though apt to trim his sails to the wind; a man who good-humoredly bowed to the inevitable, or to the almost-inevitable. He had, when he was younger, been notoriously "wild," but that was not held against him, even by mothers with marriageable daughters, like Mrs. Ogden. Morals were different in those days. Niel had heard his uncle refer to Ellinger's youthful infatuation with a woman called Nell Emerald, a handsome and rather unusual woman who conducted a house properly licensed by the Denver police. Nell Emerald had told an old club man that though she had been out behind young Ellinger's new trotting horse, she "had no respect for a man who would go driving with a prostitute in broad daylight." This story and a dozen like it were often related of Ellinger, and the women laughed over them as heartily as the men. All the while that he was making a scandalous chronicle for himself, young Ellinger had been devotedly caring for an invalid mother, and he was described to strangers as a terribly fast young man and a model son. That combination pleased the taste of the time. Nobody thought the worse of him. Now that his mother was dead, he lived at the Brown Palace hotel, though he still kept her house at Colorado Springs.

When the roast was well under way, Black Tom, very formal in a white waistcoat and high collar, poured the champagne. Captain Forrester lifted his glass, the frail stem between his thick fingers, and glancing round the table at his guests and at Mrs. Forrester, said,

"Happy days!"

It was the toast he always drank at dinner, the invocation he was sure to utter when he took a glass of whiskey with an old friend. Whoever had heard him say it once, liked to hear him say it again. Nobody else could utter those two words as he did, with such gravity and high courtesy. It seemed a solemn moment, seemed to knock at the door of Fate; behind which all days, happy and otherwise, were hidden. Niel drank his wine with a pleasant shiver, thinking that nothing else made life seem so precarious, the future so cryptic and unfathomable, as that brief toast uttered by the massive man, "Happy days!"

Mrs. Ogden turned to the host with her most languishing smile: "Captain Forrester, I want you to tell Constance"—(She was an East Virginia woman, and what she really said was, "Cap'n Forrester, Ah wan' yew to tell, etc." Her vowels seemed to roll about in the same way her eyes did.)—"I want you to tell Constance about how you first found this lovely spot, 'way back in Indian times."

The Captain looked down the table between the candles at Mrs. Forrester, as if to consult her. She smiled and nodded, and her beautiful earrings swung beside her pale cheeks. She was wearing her diamonds tonight, and a black velvet gown. Her husband had archaic ideas about jewels; a man bought them for his wife in acknowledgment of things he could not gracefully utter. They must be costly; they must show that he was able to buy them, and that she was worthy to wear them.

With her approval the Captain began his narrative: a concise account of how he came West a young boy, after serving in the Civil War, and took a job as driver for a freighting company that carried supplies across the plains from Nebraska City to Cherry Creek, as Denver was then called. The freighters, after embarking in that sea of grass six hundred miles in width, lost all count of the days of the week and the month. One day was like another, and all were glorious; good hunting, plenty of antelope and buffalo, boundless sunny sky, boundless plains of waving grass, long fresh-water lagoons yellow with lagoon flowers, where the bison in their periodic migrations stopped to drink and bathe and wallow.

"An ideal life for a young man," the Captain pronounced. Once, when he was driven out of the trail by a wash-out, he rode south on his horse to explore, and found an Indian encampment near the Sweet Water, on this very hill where his house now stood. He was, he said, "greatly taken with the location," and made up his mind that he would one day have a house there. He cut down a young willow tree and drove the stake into the ground to mark the spot where he wished to build. He went away and did not come back for many years; he was helping to lay the first railroad across the plains.

"There were those that were dependent on me," he said. "I had sickness to contend with, and responsibilities. But in all those years I expect there was hardly a day passed that I did not remember the Sweet Water and this hill. When I came here a young man, I had planned it in my mind, pretty much as it is today; where I would dig my well, and where I would plant my grove and my orchard. I planned to build a house that my friends could come to, with a wife like Mrs. Forrester to make it attractive to them. I used to promise myself that some day I would manage it." This part of the story the Captain told not with embarrassment, but with reserve, choosing his words slowly, absently cracking English walnuts with his strong fingers and heaping a little hoard of kernels beside his plate. His friends understood that he was referring to his first marriage, to the poor invalid wife who had never been happy and who had kept his nose to the grindstone.

"When things looked most discouraging," he went on, "I came back here once and bought the place from the railroad company. They took my note. I found my willow stake,—it had rooted and grown into a tree,—and I planted three more to mark the corners of my house. Twelve years later Mrs. Forrester came here with me, shortly after our marriage, and we built our house." Captain Forrester puffed from time to time, but his clear account commanded attention. Something in the way he uttered his unornamented phrases gave them the impressiveness of inscriptions cut in stone.

Mrs. Forrester nodded at him from her end of the table. "And now, tell us your philosophy of life,—this is where it comes in," she laughed teasingly.

The Captain coughed and looked abashed. "I was intending to omit that tonight. Some of our guests have already heard it."

"No, no. It belongs at the end of the story, and if some of us have heard it, we can hear it again. Go on!"

"Well, then, my philosophy is that what you think of and plan for day by day, in spite of yourself, so to speak—you will get. You will get it more or less. That is, unless you are one of the people who get nothing in this world. There are such people. I have lived too much in mining works and construction camps not to know that." He paused as if, though this was too dark a chapter to be gone into, it must have its place, its moment of silent recognition. "If you are not one of those, Constance and Niel, you will accomplish what you dream of most."

"And why? That's the interesting part of it," his wife prompted him.

"Because," he roused himself from his abstraction and looked about at the company, "because a thing that is dreamed of in the way I mean, is already an accomplished fact. All our great West has been developed from such dreams; the homesteader's and the prospector's and the contractor's. We dreamed the railroads across the mountains, just as I dreamed my place on the Sweet Water. All these things will be everyday facts to the coming generation, but to us—" Captain Forrester ended with a sort of grunt. Something forbidding had come into his voice, the lonely, defiant note that is so often heard in the voices of old Indians.

Mrs. Ogden had listened to the story with such sympathy that Niel liked her better than ever, and even the preoccupied Constance seemed able to give it her attention. They rose from the dessert and went into the parlor to arrange the card tables. The Captain still played whist as well as ever. As he brought out a box of his best cigars, he paused before Mrs. Ogden and said, "Is smoke offensive to you, Mrs. Ogden?" When she protested that it was not, he crossed the room to where Constance was talking with Ellinger and asked with the same grave courtesy, "Is smoke offensive to you, Constance?" Had there been half a dozen women present, he would have asked that question of each, probably, and in the same words. It did not bother him to repeat a phrase. If an expression answered his purpose, he saw no reason for varying it.

Mrs. Forrester and Mr. Ogden were to play against Mrs. Ogden and the Captain. "Constance," said Mrs. Forrester as she sat down, "will you play with Niel? I'm told he's very good."

Miss Ogden's short nose flickered up, the lines on either side of it deepened, and she again looked injured. Niel was sure she detested him. He was not going to be done in by her.

"Miss Ogden," he said as he stood beside his chair, deliberately shuffling a pack of cards, "my uncle and I are used to playing together, and probably you are used to playing with Mr. Ellinger. Suppose we try that combination?"

She gave him a quick, suspicious glance from under her yellow eyelashes and flung herself into a chair without so much as answering him. Frank Ellinger came in from the dining-room, where he had been sampling the Captain's French brandy, and took the vacant seat opposite Miss Ogden. "So it's you and me, Connie? Good enough!" he exclaimed, cutting the pack Niel pushed toward him.

Just before midnight Black Tom opened the door and announced that the egg-nog was ready. The card players went into the dining-room, where the punch-bowl stood smoking on the table.

"Constance," said Captain Forrester, "do you sing? I like to hear one of the old songs with the egg-nog."

"Ah'm sorry, Cap'n Forrester. Ah really haven't any voice."

Niel noticed that whenever Constance spoke to the Captain she strained her throat, though he wasn't in the least deaf. He broke in over her refusal. "Uncle can start a song if you coax him, sir."

Judge Pommeroy, after smoothing his silver whiskers and coughing, began "Auld Lang Syne." The others joined in, but they hadn't got to the end of it when a hollow rumbling down on the bridge made them laugh, and everyone ran to the front windows to see the Judge's funeral coach come lurching up the hill, with only one of the side lanterns lit. Mrs. Forrester sent Tom out with a drink for the driver. While Niel and his uncle were putting on their overcoats in the hall, she came up to them and whispered coaxingly to the boy, "Remember, you are coming over tomorrow, at two? I am planning a drive, and I want you to amuse Constance for me."

Niel bit his lip and looked down into Mrs. Forrester's laughing, persuasive eyes. "I'll do it for you, but that's the only reason," he said threateningly.

"I understand, for me! I'll credit it to your account."

The Judge and his nephew rolled away on swaying springs. The Ogdens retired to their rooms upstairs. Mrs. Forrester went to help the Captain divest himself of his frock coat, and put it away for him. Ever since he was hurt he had to be propped high on pillows at night, and he slept in a narrow iron bed, in the alcove which had formerly been his wife's dressing-room. While he was undressing he breathed heavily and sighed, as if he were very tired. He fumbled with his studs, then blew on his fingers and tried again. His wife came to his aid and quickly unbuttoned everything. He did not thank her in words, but submitted gratefully.

When the iron bed creaked at receiving his heavy figure, she called from the big bedroom, "Good-night, Mr. Forrester," and drew the heavy curtains that shut off the alcove. She took off her rings and earrings and was beginning to unfasten her black velvet bodice when, at a tinkle of glass from without, she stopped short. Re-hooking the shoulder of her gown, she went to the dining-room, now faintly lit by the coal fire in the back parlor. Frank Ellinger was standing at the sideboard, taking a nightcap. The Forrester French brandy was old, and heavy like a cordial.

"Be careful," she murmured as she approached him. "I have a

distinct impression that there is someone on the enclosed stairway. There is a wide crack in the door. Ah, but kittens have claws, these days! Pour me just a little. Thank you. I'll have mine in by the fire."

He followed her into the next room, where she stood by the grate, looking at him in the light of the pale blue flames that ran over the fresh coal, put on to keep the fire.

"You've had a good many brandies, Frank," she said, studying his flushed, masterful face.

"Not too many. I'll need them . . . tonight," he replied meaningly.

She nervously brushed back a lock of hair that had come down a little. "It's not tonight. It's morning. Go to bed and sleep as late as you please. Take care, I heard silk stockings on the stairs. Goodnight." She put her hand on the sleeve of his coat; the white fingers clung to the black cloth as bits of paper cling to magnetized iron. Her touch, soft as it was, went through the man, all the feet and inches of him. His broad shoulders lifted on a deep breath. He looked down at her.

Her eyes fell. "Good-night," she said faintly. As she turned quickly away, the train of her velvet dress caught the leg of his broadcloth trousers and dragged with a friction that crackled and threw sparks. Both started. They stood looking at each other for a moment before she actually slipped through the door. Ellinger remained by the hearth, his arms folded tight over his chest, his curly lips compressed, frowning into the fire.

V

NIEL WENT UP the hill the next afternoon, just as the cutter with the two black ponies jingled round the driveway and stopped at the front door. Mrs. Forrester came out on the porch, dressed for a sleigh ride. Ellinger followed her, buttoned up in a long fur-lined coat, showily befrogged down the front, with a glossy astrachan collar. He looked even more powerful and bursting with vigor than last night. His highly-colored, well-visored countenance shone with a good opinion of himself and of the world.

Mrs. Forrester called to Niel gaily. "We are going down to the Sweet Water to cut cedar boughs for Christmas. Will you keep Constance company? She seems a trifle disappointed at being left behind, but we can't take the big sleigh,—the pole is broken. Be nice to her, there's a good boy!" She pressed his hand, gave him a meaning, confidential smile, and stepped into the sleigh. Ellinger sprang in beside her, and they glided down the hill with a merry tinkle of sleighbells.

Niel found Miss Ogden in the back parlor, playing solitaire by the fire. She was clearly out of humor.

"Come in, Mr. Herbert. I think they might have taken us along,

"The air was still and blue . . . When the strokes of the hatchet rang out from the ravine, he could see her eyelids flutter . . . soft shivers went through her body." —A Lost Lady

don't you? I want to see the river my own self. I hate bein' shut up in the house!"

"Let's go out, then. Wouldn't you like to see the town?"

Constance seemed not to hear him. She was wrinkling and un-wrinkling her short nose, and the restless lines about her mouth were fluttering. "What's to hinder us from getting a sleigh at the livery barn and going down to the Sweet Water? I don't suppose the river's private property?" She gave a nervous, angry laugh and looked hopefully at Niel.

"We couldn't get anything at this hour. The livery teams are all out," he said with firmness.

Constance glanced at him suspiciously, then sat down at the card table and leaned over it, drawing her plump shoulders together. Her fluffy yellow hair was wound round her head like a scarf and held in place by narrow bands of black velvet.

The ponies had crossed the second creek and were trotting down the high road toward the river. Mrs. Forrester expressed her feelings in a laugh full of mischief. "Is she running after us? Where did she get the idea that she was to come? What a relief to get away!" She lifted her chin and sniffed the air. The day was gray, without sun, and the air was still and dry, a warm cold. "Poor Mr. Ogden," she went on, "how much livelier he is without his ladies! They almost extinguish him. Now aren't you glad you never married?"

"I'm certainly glad I never married a homely woman. What does a man do it for, anyway? She had no money,—and he's always had it, or been on the way to it."

"Well, they're off tomorrow. And Connie! You've reduced her to a state of imbecility, really! What an afternoon Niel must be having!" She laughed as if the idea of his predicament delighted her.

"Who's this kid, anyway?" Ellinger asked her to take the reins for a moment while he drew a cigar from his pocket. "He's a trifle stiff. Does he make himself useful?"

"Oh, he's a nice boy, stranded here like the rest of us. I'm going to train him to be very useful. He's devoted to Mr. Forrester. Handsome, don't you think?"

"So-so." They turned into a by-road that wound along the Sweet Water. Ellinger held the ponies in a little and turned down his high astrachan collar. "Let's have a look at you, Marian."

Mrs. Forrester was holding her muff before her face, to catch the flying particles of snow the ponies kicked up. From behind it she glanced at him sidewise. "Well?" she said teasingly.

He put his arm through hers and settled himself low in the sleigh. "You ought to look at me better than that. It's been a devil of a long while since I've seen you."

"Perhaps it's been too long," she murmured. The mocking spark in her eyes softened perceptibly under the long pressure of his arm. "Yes, it's been long," she admitted lightly.

"You didn't answer the letter I wrote you on the eleventh."

"Didn't I? Well, at any rate I answered your telegram." She drew her head away as his face came nearer. "You'll really have to watch the ponies, my dear, or they'll tumble us out in the snow."

"I don't care. I wish they would!" he said between his teeth. "Why didn't you answer my letter?"

"Oh, I don't remember! You don't write so many."

"It's no satisfaction. You won't let me write you love letters. You say it's risky."

"So it is, and foolish. But now you needn't be so careful. Not too careful!" she laughed softly. "When I'm off in the country for a whole winter, alone, and growing older, I like to . . ." she put her hand on his, "to be reminded of pleasanter things."

Ellinger took off his glove with his teeth. His eyes, sweeping the winding road and the low, snow-covered bluffs, had something wolfish in them.

"Be careful, Frank. My rings! You hurt me!"

"Then why didn't you take them off? You used to. Are these your cedars, shall we stop here?"

"No, not here." She spoke very low. "The best ones are farther on, in a deep ravine that winds back into the hills."

Ellinger glanced at her averted head, and his heavy lips twitched in a smile at one corner. The quality of her voice had changed, and he knew the change. They went spinning along the curves of the winding road, saying not a word. Mrs. Forrester sat with her head bent forward, her face half hidden in her muff. At last she told him to stop. To the right of the road he saw a thicket. Behind it a dry watercourse wound into the bluffs. The tops of the dark, still cedars, just visible from the road, indicated its windings.

"Sit still," he said, "while I take out the horses."

———

When the blue shadows of approaching dusk were beginning to fall over the snow, one of the Blum boys, slipping quietly along through the timber in search of rabbits, came upon the empty cutter standing in the brush, and near it the two ponies, stamping impatiently where they were tied. Adolph slid back into the thicket and lay down behind a fallen log to see what would happen. Not much ever happened to him but weather.

Presently he heard low voices, coming nearer from the ravine. The big stranger who was visiting at the Forresters' emerged, carrying the buffalo robes on one arm; Mrs. Forrester herself was clinging to the other. They walked slowly, wholly absorbed by what they were saying to each other. When they came up to the sleigh, the man spread the robes on the seat and put his hands under Mrs. Forrester's arms to lift her in. But he did not lift her; he stood for a long while holding her crushed up against his breast, her face hidden in his black overcoat.

"What about those damned cedar boughs?" he asked, after he had put her in and covered her up. "Shall I go back and cut some?"

"It doesn't matter," she murmured.

He reached under the seat for a hatchet and went back to the ravine. Mrs. Forrester sat with her eyes closed, her cheek pillowed on her muff, a faint, soft smile on her lips. The air was still and blue; the Blum boy could almost hear her breathe. When the strokes of the hatchet rang out from the ravine, he could see her eyelids flutter . . . soft shivers went through her body.

The man came back and threw the evergreens into the sleigh. When he got in beside her, she slipped her hand through his arm and settled softly against him. "Drive slowly," she murmured, as if she were talking in her sleep. "It doesn't matter if we are late for dinner. Nothing matters." The ponies trotted off.

The pale Blum boy rose from behind his log and followed the

tracks up the ravine. When the orange moon rose over the bluffs, he was still sitting under the cedars, his gun on his knee. While Mrs. Forrester had been waiting there in the sleigh, with her eyes closed, feeling so safe, he could almost have touched her with his hand. He had never seen her before when her mocking eyes and lively manner were not between her and all the world. If it had been Thad Grimes who lay behind that log, now, or Ivy Peters?

But with Adolph Blum her secrets were safe. His mind was feudal; the rich and fortunate were also the privileged. These warm-blooded, quick-breathing people took chances,—followed impulses only dimly understandable to a boy who was wet and weather-chapped all the year; who waded in the mud fishing for cat, or lay in the marsh waiting for wild duck. Mrs. Forrester had never been too haughty to smile at him when he came to the back door with his fish. She never haggled about the price. She treated him like a human being. His little chats with her, her nod and smile when she passed him on the street, were among the pleasantest things he had to remember. She bought game of him in the closed season, and didn't give him away.

V I

IT WAS DURING that winter, the first one Mrs. Forrester had ever spent in the house on the hill, that Niel came to know her very well. For the Forresters that winter was a sort of isthmus between two estates; soon afterward came a change in their fortunes. And for Niel it was a natural turning-point, since in the autumn he was nineteen, and in the spring he was twenty,—a very great difference.

After the Christmas festivities were over, the whist parties settled into a regular routine. Three evenings a week Judge Pommeroy and his nephew sat down to cards with the Forresters. Sometimes they went over early and dined there. Sometimes they stayed for a late supper after the last rubber. Niel, who had been so content with a bachelor's life, and who had made up his mind that he would never live in a place that was under the control of women, found himself becoming attached to the comforts of a well-conducted house; to the pleasures of the table, to the soft chairs and soft lights and agreeable human voices at the Forresters'. On bitter, windy nights, sitting in his favorite blue chair before the grate, he used to wonder how he could manage to tear himself away, to plunge into the outer darkness, and run down the long frozen road and up the dead street of the town. Captain Forrester was experimenting with bulbs that winter, and had built a little glass conservatory on the south side of the house, off the back parlor. Through January and February the house was full of narcissus and Roman hyacinths, and their heavy, spring-like odor made a part of the enticing comfort of the fireside there.

Where Mrs. Forrester was, dullness was impossible, Niel believed. The charm of her conversation was not so much in what she said, though she was often witty, but in the quick recognition of her eyes, in the living quality of her voice itself. One could talk with her about the most trivial things, and go away with a high sense of elation. The secret of it, he supposed, was that she couldn't help being interested in people, even very commonplace people. If Mr. Ogden or Mr. Dalzell were not there to tell their best stories for her, then she could be amused by Ivy Peters' ruffianly manners, or the soft compliments of old man Elliott when he sold her a pair of winter shoes. She had a fascinating gift of mimicry. When she mentioned the fat iceman, or Thad Grimes at his meat block, or the Blum boys with their dead rabbits, by a subtle suggestion of their manner she made them seem more individual and vivid than they were in their own person. She often caricatured people to their faces, and they were not offended, but greatly flattered. Nothing pleased one more than to provoke her laughter. Then you felt you were getting on with her. It was her form of commenting, of agreeing with you and appreciating you when you said something interesting,—and it often told you a great deal that was both too direct and too elusive for words.

Long, long afterward, when Niel did not know whether Mrs. Forrester were living or dead, if her image flashed into his mind, it came with a brightness of dark eyes, her pale triangular cheeks with long earrings, and her many-colored laugh. When he was dull, dull and tired of everything, he used to think that if he could hear that long-lost lady laugh again, he could be gay.

The big storm of the winter came late that year; swept down over Sweet Water the first day of March and beat upon the town for three days and nights. Thirty inches of snow fell, and the cutting wind blew it into whirling drifts. The Forresters were snowed in. Ben Keezer, their man of all work, did not attempt to break a road or even to come over to the town himself. On the third day Niel went to the post-office, got the Captain's leather mail sack with its accumulation of letters, and set off across the creek, plunging into drifts up to his middle, sometimes up to his arm-pits. The fences along the lane were covered, but he broke his trail by keeping between the two lines of poplars. When at last he reached the front porch, Captain Forrester came to the door and let him in.

"Glad to see you, my boy, very glad. It's been a little lonesome for us. You must have had hard work getting over. I certainly appreciate it. Come to the sitting-room fire and dry yourself. We will talk quietly. Mrs. Forrester has gone upstairs to lie down; she's been complaining of a headache."

Niel stood before the fire in his rubber boots, drying his trousers. The Captain did not sit down but opened the glass door into his little conservatory.

"I've something pretty to show you, Niel. All my hyacinths are coming along at once, every color of the rainbow. The Roman hyacinths, I say, are Mrs. Forrester's. They seem to suit her."

Niel went to the door and looked with keen pleasure at the fresh, watery blossoms. "I was afraid you might lose them in this bitter weather, Captain."

"No, these things can stand a good deal of cold. They've been company for us." He stood looking out through the glass at the drifted shrubbery. Niel liked to see him look out over his place. A man's house is his castle, his look seemed to say. "Ben tells me the rabbits have come up to the barn to eat the hay, everything green is covered up. I had him throw a few cabbages out for them, so they won't suffer. Mrs. Forrester has been on the porch every day, feeding the snow birds," he went on, as if talking to himself.

The stair door opened, and Mrs. Forrester came down in her Japanese dressing-gown, looking very pale. The dark shadows under her eyes seemed to mean that she had been losing sleep.

"Oh, it's Niel! How nice of you. And you've brought the mail. Are there any letters for me?"

"Three. Two from Denver and one from California." Her husband gave them to her. "Did you sleep, Maidy?"

"No, but I rested. It's delightful up in the west room, the wind sings and whistles about the eaves. If you'll excuse me, I'll dress and glance at my letters. Stand closer to the fire, Niel. Are you very wet?" When she stopped beside him to feel his clothes, he smelled a sharp odor of spirits. Was she ill, he wondered, or merely so bored that she had been trying to dull herself?

When she came back she had dressed and rearranged her hair.

"Mrs. Forrester," said the Captain in a solicitous tone, "I believe I would like some tea and toast this afternoon, like your English friends, and it would be good for your head. We won't offer Niel anything else."

"Very well. Mary has gone to bed with a toothache, but I will make the tea. Niel can make the toast here by the fire while you read your paper."

She was cheerful now,—tied one of Mary's aprons about Niel's neck and set him down with the toasting fork. He noticed that the Captain, as he read his paper, kept his eye on the sideboard with a certain watchfulness, and when his wife brought the tray with tea, and no sherry, he seemed very much pleased. He drank three cups, and took a second piece of toast.

"You see, Mr. Forrester," she said lightly, "Niel has brought back my appetite. I ate no lunch today," turning to the boy, "I've been shut up too long. Is there anything in the papers?"

This meant was there any news concerning the people they knew. The Captain put on his silver-rimmed glasses again and read aloud about the doings of their friends in Denver and Omaha and Kansas City. Mrs. Forrester sat on a stool by the fire, eating toast and making humorous comments upon the subjects of those solemn paragraphs; the engagement of Miss Erma Salton-Smith, etc.

"At last, thank God! You remember her, Niel. She's been here. I think you danced with her."

"I don't think I do. What is she like?"

"She's exactly like her name. Don't you remember? Tall, very animated, glittering eyes, like the Ancient Mariner's?"

Niel laughed. "Don't you like bright eyes, Mrs. Forrester?"

"Not any others, I don't!" She joined in his laugh so gaily that the Captain looked out over his paper with an expression of satisfaction. He let the journal slowly crumple on his knees, and sat watching the two beside the grate. To him they seemed about the same age. It was a habit with him to think of Mrs. Forrester as very, very young.

She noticed that he was not reading. "Would you like me to light the lamp, Mr. Forrester?"

"No, thank you. The twilight is very pleasant."

It was twilight by now. They heard Mary come downstairs and begin stirring about the kitchen. The Captain, his slippers in the zone of firelight and his heavy shoulders in shadow, snored from time to time. As the room grew dusky, the windows were squares of clear, pale violet, and the shutters ceased to rattle. The wind was dying with the day. Everything was still, except when Bohemian Mary roughly clattered a pan. Mrs. Forrester whispered that she was out of sorts because her sweetheart, Joe Pucelik, hadn't been over to see her. Sunday night was his regular night, and Sunday was the first day of the blizzard. "When she's neglected, her tooth always begins to ache!"

"Well, now that I've got over, he'll have to come, or she will be in a temper."

"Oh, he'll come!" Mrs. Forrester shrugged. "I am blind and deaf, but I'm quite sure she makes it worth his while!" After a few moments she rose. "Come," she whispered, "Mr. Forrester is asleep. Let's run down the hill, there's no one to stop us. I'll slip on my rubber boots. No objections!" She put her fingers on his lips. "Not a word! I can't stand this house a moment longer."

They slipped quietly out of the front door into the cold air which tasted of new-fallen snow. A clear arc of blue and rose color painted the west, over the buried town. When they reached the rounded breast of the hill, blown almost bare, Mrs. Forrester stood still and drew in deep breaths, looking down over the drifted meadows and the stiff, blue poplars.

"Oh, but it is bleak!" she murmured. "Suppose we should have to stay here all next winter, too, . . . and the next! What will become of me, Niel?" There was fear, unmistakable fright in her voice. "You see there is nothing for me to do. I get no exercise. I don't skate; we didn't in California, and my ankles are weak. I've always danced in the winter, there's plenty of dancing at Colorado Springs. You wouldn't believe how I miss it. I shall dance till I'm eighty. . . . I'll be the waltzing grandmother! It's good for me, I need it."

They plunged down into the drifts and did not stop again until they reached the wooden bridge.

"See, even the creek is frozen! I thought running water never froze. How long will it be like this?"

"Not long now. In a month you'll see the green begin in the marsh and run over the meadows. It's lovely over here in the spring. And you'll be able to get out tomorrow, Mrs. Forrester. The clouds are thinning. Look, there's the new moon!"

She turned. "Oh, I saw it over the wrong shoulder!"

"No you didn't. You saw it over mine."

She sighed and took his arm. "My dear boy, your shoulders aren't broad enough."

Instantly before his eyes rose the image of a pair of shoulders that were very broad, objectionably broad, clad in a frogged overcoat with an astrachan collar. The intrusion of this third person annoyed him as they went slowly back up the hill.

Curiously enough, it was as Captain Forrester's wife that she most interested Niel, and it was in her relation to her husband that he most admired her. Given her other charming attributes, her comprehension of a man like the railroad-builder, her loyalty to him, stamped her more than anything else. That, he felt, was quality; something that could never become worn or shabby; steel of Damascus. His admiration of Mrs. Forrester went back to that, just as, he felt, she herself went back to it. He rather liked the stories, even the spiteful ones, about the gay life she led in Colorado, and the young men she kept dangling about her every winter. He sometimes thought of the life she might have been living ever since he had known her,—and the one she had chosen to live. From that disparity, he believed, came the subtlest thrill of her fascination. She mocked outrageously at the properties she observed, and inherited the magic of contradictions.

VII

O N T H E E V E N I N G S when there was no whist at the Forresters',
Niel usually sat in his room and read,—but not law, as he was
supposed to do. The winter before, when the Forresters were away,
and one dull day dragged after another, he had come upon a copi-
ous diversion, an almost inexhaustible resource. The high, narrow
bookcase in the back office, between the double doors and the wall,
was filled from top to bottom with rows of solemn-looking volumes
bound in dark cloth, which were kept apart from the law library; an
almost complete set of the Bohn classics, which Judge Pommeroy
had bought long ago when he was a student at the University of
Virginia. He had brought them West with him, not because he read
them a great deal, but because, in his day, a gentleman had such
books in his library, just as he had claret in his cellar. Among them
was a set of Byron in three volumes, and last winter, apropos of a
quotation which Niel didn't recognize, his uncle advised him to read
Byron,—all except *Don Juan*. That, the Judge remarked, with a
deep smile, he "could save until later." Niel, of course, began with
Don Juan. Then he read *Tom Jones* and *Wilhelm Meister* and raced
on until he came to Montaigne and a complete translation of Ovid.
He hadn't finished yet with these last,—always went back to them

after other experiments. These authors seemed to him to know their business. Even in *Don Juan* there was a little "fooling," but with these gentlemen none.

There were philosophical works in the collection, but he did no more than open and glance at them. He had no curiosity about what men had thought; but about what they had felt and lived, he had a great deal. If anyone had told him that these were classics and represented the wisdom of the ages, he would doubtless have let them alone. But ever since he had first found them for himself, he had been living a double life, with all its guilty enjoyments. He read the *Heroides* over and over, and felt that they were the most glowing love stories ever told. He did not think of these books as something invented to beguile the idle hour, but as living creatures, caught in the very behavior of living,—surprised behind their misleading severity of form and phrase. He was eavesdropping upon the past, being let into the great world that had plunged and glittered and sumptuously sinned long before little Western towns were dreamed of. Those rapt evenings beside the lamp gave him a long perspective, influenced his conception of the people about him, made him know just what he wished his own relations with these people to be. For some reason, his reading made him wish to become an architect. If the Judge had left his Bohn library behind him in Kentucky, his nephew's life might have turned out differently.

Spring came at last, and the Forrester place had never been so lovely. The Captain spent long, happy days among his flowering shrubs, and his wife used to say to visitors, "Yes, you can see Mr. Forrester in a moment; I will send the English gardener to call him."

Early in June, when the Captain's roses were just coming on, his pleasant labors were interrupted. One morning an alarming telegram reached him. He cut it open with his garden shears, came into the house, and asked his wife to telephone for Judge Pommeroy. A savings bank, one in which he was largely interested, had failed in Denver. That evening the Captain and his lawyer went west on the express. The Judge, when he was giving Niel final instructions about the office business, told him he was afraid the Captain was bound to lose a good deal of money.

Mrs. Forrester seemed unaware of any danger; she went to the station to see her husband off, spoke of his errand merely as a "business trip." Niel, however, felt a foreboding gloom. He dreaded poverty for her. She was one of the people who ought always to have money; any retrenchment of their generous way of living would be a hardship for her,—would be unfitting. She would not be herself in straitened circumstances.

Niel took his meals at the town hotel; on the third day after Captain Forrester's departure, he was annoyed to find Frank Ellinger's name on the hotel register. Ellinger did not appear at supper, which meant, of course, that he was dining with Mrs. Forrester, and that the lady herself would get his dinner. She had taken the occasion of the Captain's absence to let Bohemian Mary go to visit her mother on the farm for a week. Niel thought it very bad taste in Ellinger to come to Sweet Water when Captain Forrester was away. He must know that it would stir up the gossips.

Niel had meant to call on Mrs. Forrester that evening, but now he went back to the office instead. He read late, and after he went to bed, he slept lightly. He was awakened before dawn by the puffing of the switch engine down at the round house. He tried to muffle his ears in the sheet and go to sleep again, but the sound of escaping steam for some reason excited him. He could not shut out the feeling that it was summer, and that the dawn would soon be flaming gloriously over the Forresters' marsh. He had awakened with that intense, blissful realization of summer which sometimes comes to children in their beds. He rose and dressed quickly. He would get over to the hill before Frank Ellinger could intrude his unwelcome presence, while he was still asleep in the best bedroom of the Wimbleton hotel.

An impulse of affection and guardianship drew Niel up the poplar-bordered road in the early light,—though he did not go near the
house itself, but at the second bridge cut round through the meadow
and on to the marsh. The sky was burning with the soft pink and
silver of a cloudless summer dawn. The heavy, bowed grasses
splashed him to the knees. All over the marsh, snow-on-the-mountain, globed with dew, made cool sheets of silver, and the swamp
milk-weed spread its flat, raspberry-colored clusters. There was an
almost religious purity about the fresh morning air, the tender sky,
the grass and flowers with the sheen of early dew upon them. There
was in all living things something limpid and joyous—like the wet,
morning call of the birds, flying up through the unstained atmosphere. Out of the saffron east a thin, yellow, wine-like sunshine
began to gild the fragrant meadows and the glistening tops of the
grove. Niel wondered why he did not often come over like this, to
see the day before men and their activities had spoiled it, while the
morning was still unsullied, like a gift handed down from the heroic
ages.

Under the bluffs that overhung the marsh he came upon thickets
of wild roses, with flaming buds, just beginning to open. Where
they had opened, their petals were stained with that burning rose-
color which is always gone by noon,—a dye made of sunlight and
morning and moisture, so intense that it cannot possibly last . . .
must fade, like ecstasy. Niel took out his knife and began to cut the
stiff stems, crowded with red thorns.

He would make a bouquet for a lovely lady; a bouquet gathered
off the cheeks of morning . . . these roses, only half awake, in the
defenselessness of utter beauty. He would leave them just outside
one of the French windows of her bedroom. When she opened her
shutters to let in the light, she would find them,—and they would
perhaps give her a sudden distaste for coarse worldlings like Frank
Ellinger.

After tying his flowers with a twist of meadow grass, he went up
the hill through the grove and softly round the still house to the

north side of Mrs. Forrester's own room, where the door-like green shutters were closed. As he bent to place the flowers on the sill, he heard from within a woman's soft laughter; impatient, indulgent, teasing, eager. Then another laugh, very different, a man's. And it was fat and lazy,—ended in something like a yawn.

Niel found himself at the foot of the hill on the wooden bridge, his face hot, his temples beating, his eyes blind with anger. In his hand he still carried the prickly bunch of wild roses. He threw them over the wire fence into a mud-hole the cattle had trampled under the bank of the creek. He did not know whether he had left the house by the driveway or had come down through the shrubbery. In that instant between stooping to the window-sill and rising, he had lost one of the most beautiful things in his life. Before the dew dried, the morning had been wrecked for him; and all subsequent mornings, he told himself bitterly. This day saw the end of that admiration and loyalty that had been like a bloom on his existence. He could never recapture it. It was gone, like the morning freshness of the flowers.

"Lilies that fester," he muttered, *"lilies that fester smell far worse than weeds."*

Grace, variety, the lovely voice, the sparkle of fun and fancy in those dark eyes; all this was nothing. It was not a moral scruple she had outraged, but an aesthetic ideal. Beautiful women, whose beauty meant more than it said . . . was their brilliancy always fed by something coarse and concealed? Was that their secret?

VIII

NIEL MET his uncle and Captain Forrester when they alighted from the morning train, and drove over to the house with them. The business on which they had gone to Denver was not referred to until they were sitting with Mrs. Forrester in the front parlor. The windows were open, and the perfume of the mock-orange and of June roses was blowing in from the garden. Captain Forrester introduced the subject, after slowly unfolding his handkerchief and wiping his forehead, and his fleshy neck, around his low collar.

"Maidy," he said, not looking at her, "I've come home a poor man. It took about everything there was to square up. You'll have this place, unencumbered, and my pension; that will be about all. The live-stock will bring in something."

Niel saw that Mrs. Forrester grew very pale, but she smiled and brought her husband his cigar stand. "Oh, well! I expect we can manage, can't we?"

"We can just manage. Not much more. I'm afraid Judge Pommeroy considers I acted foolishly."

"Not at all, Mrs. Forrester," the Judge exclaimed. "He acted just as I hope I would have done in his place. But I am an unmarried man. There were certain securities, government bonds, which Captain Forrester could have turned over to you, but it would have been at the expense of the depositors."

"I've known men to do that," said the Captain heavily, "but I never considered they paid their wives a compliment. If Mrs. Forrester is satisfied, I shall never regret my decision." For the first time his tired, swollen eyes sought his wife's.

"I never question your decisions in business, Mr. Forrester. I know nothing about such things."

The Captain put down the cigar he had taken but not lighted, rose with an effort, and walked over to the bay window, where he stood gazing out over his meadows. "The place looks very nice, Maidy," he said presently. "I see you've watered the roses. They need it, this weather. Now, if you'll excuse me, I'll lie down for a while. I did not sleep well on the train. Niel and the Judge will stay for lunch." He opened the door into Mrs. Forrester's room and closed it behind him.

Judge Pommeroy began to explain to Mrs. Forrester the situation they had faced in Denver. The bank, about which Mrs. Forrester knew nothing but its name, was one which paid good interest on small deposits. The depositors were wage-earners; railroad employees, mechanics, and day laborers, many of whom had at some time worked for Captain Forrester. His was the only well-known name among the bank officers, it was the name which promised security and fair treatment to his old workmen and their friends. The other directors were promising young business men with many irons in the fire. But, the Judge said with evident chagrin, they had refused to come up to the scratch and pay their losses like gentlemen. They claimed that the bank was insolvent, not through unwise investments or mismanagement, but because of a nation-wide financial panic, a shrinking in values that no one could have foreseen. They argued that the fair thing was to share the loss with the depositors; to pay them fifty cents on the dollar, giving long-time notes for twenty-five per cent, settling on a basis of seventy-five per cent.

Captain Forrester had stood firm that not one of the depositors should lose a dollar. The promising young business men had listened to him respectfully, but finally told him they would settle only on their own terms; any additional refunding must be his affair. He sent to the vault for his private steel box, opened it in their presence, and sorted the contents on the table. The government bonds he turned in at once. Judge Pommeroy was sent out to sell the mining stocks and other securities in the open market.

At this part of his narrative the Judge rose and began to pace the floor, twisting the seals on his watch-chain. "That was what a man of honor was bound to do, Mrs. Forrester. With five of the directors backing down, he had either to lose his name or save it. The depositors had put their savings into that bank because Captain Forrester was president. To those men with no capital but their back and their two hands, his name meant safety. As he tried to explain to the directors, those deposits were above price; money saved to buy a home, or to take care of a man in sickness, or to send a boy to school. And those young men, bright fellows, well thought of in the community, sat there and looked down their noses and let your husband strip himself down to pledging his life insurance! There was a crowd in the street outside the bank all day, every day; Poles and Swedes and Mexicans, looking scared to death. A lot of them couldn't speak English,—seemed like the only English word they knew was 'Forrester.' As we went in and out we'd hear the Mexicans saying, 'Forrester, Forrester.' It was a torment for me, on your account, Ma'm, to see the Captain strip himself. But, 'pon my honor, I couldn't forbid him. As for those white-livered rascals that sat there,—" the Judge stopped before Mrs. Forrester and ruffled his bushy white hair with both hands, "By God, Madam, I think I've lived too long! In my day the difference between a business man and a scoundrel was bigger than the difference between a white man and a nigger. I wasn't the right one to go out there as the Captain's counsel. One of these smooth members of the bar, like Ivy Peters is getting ready to be, might have saved something for you out of the wreck. But I couldn't use my influence with your husband. To that crowd outside the bank doors his name meant a hundred cents on the dollar, and by God, they got it! I'm proud of him, Ma'm; proud of his acquaintance!"

It was the first time Niel had ever seen Mrs. Forrester flush. A quick pink swept over her face. Her eyes glistened with moisture. "You were quite right, Judge. I wouldn't for the world have had him do otherwise for me. He would never hold up his head again. You see, I know him." As she said this she looked at Niel, on the other side of the room, and her glance was like a delicate and very dignified rebuke to some discourtesy,—though he was not conscious of having shown her any.

When their hostess went out to see about lunch, Judge Pommeroy turned to his nephew. "Son, I'm glad you want to be an architect. I can't see any honorable career for a lawyer, in this new business world that's coming up. Leave the law to boys like Ivy Peters, and get into some clean profession. I wasn't the right man to go with Forrester." He shook his head sadly.

"Will they really be poor?"

"They'll be pinched. It's as he said; they've nothing left but this place."

Mrs. Forrester returned and went to waken her husband for lunch. When she opened the door into her room, they heard stertorous breathing, and she called to them to come quickly. The Captain was stretched upon his iron bed in the antechamber, and Mrs. Forrester was struggling to lift his head.

"Quick, Niel," she panted. "We must get pillows under him. Bring those from my bed."

Niel gently pushed her away. Sweat poured from his face as he got his strength under the Captain's shoulders. It was like lifting a wounded elephant. Judge Pommeroy hurried back to the sitting-room and telephoned Dr. Dennison that Captain Forrester had had a stroke.

A stroke could not finish a man like Daniel Forrester. He was kept in his bed for three weeks, and Niel helped Mrs. Forrester and Ben Keezer take care of him. Although he was at the house so much during that time, he never saw Mrs. Forrester alone,—scarcely saw her at all, indeed. With so much to attend to, she became ab-stracted, almost impersonal. There were many letters to answer, gifts of fruit and wine and flowers to be acknowledged. Solicitous inquiries came from friends scattered all the way from the Missouri to the mountains. When Mrs. Forrester was not in the Captain's room, or in the kitchen preparing special foods for him, she was at her desk.

One morning while she was seated there, a distinguished visitor arrived. Niel, waiting by the door for the letters he was to take to the post, saw a large, red-whiskered man in a rumpled pongee suit and a panama hat come climbing up the hill; Cyrus Dalzell, presi-dent of the Colorado & Utah, who had come over in his private car to enquire for the health of his old friend. Niel warned Mrs. For-rester, and she went to meet the visitor, just as he mounted the steps, wiping his face with a red silk bandanna.

He took both the lady's hands and exclaimed in a warm, deep voice, "Here she is, looking as fresh as a bride! May I claim an old privilege?" He bent his head and kissed her. "I won't be in your way, Marian," he said as they came into the house, "but I had to see for myself how he does, and how you do."

Mr. Dalzell shook hands with Niel, and as he talked he moved about the parlor clumsily and softly, like a brown bear. Mrs. For-rester stopped him to straighten his flowing yellow tie and pull down the back of his wrinkled coat. "It's easy to see that Kitty wasn't with you this morning when you dressed," she laughed.

"Thank you, thank you, my dear. I've got a green porter down there, and he doesn't seem to realize the extent of his duties. No, Kitty wanted to come, but we have two giddy nieces out from Portsmouth, visiting us, and she felt she couldn't. I just had my car hitched on to the tail of the Burlington flyer and came myself. Now tell me about Daniel. Was it a stroke?"

Mrs. Forrester sat down on the sofa beside him and told him about her husband's illness, while he interrupted with sympathetic questions and comments, taking her hand between his large, soft palms and patting it affectionately.

"And now I can go home and tell Kitty that he will soon be as good as ever,—and that you look like you were going to lead the ball tonight. You whisper to Daniel that I've got a couple cases of port down in my car that will build him up faster than anything the doctors give him. And I've brought along a dozen sherry, for a lady that knows a thing or two about wines. And next winter you are both coming out to stay with us at the Springs, for a change of air."

Mrs. Forrester shook her head gently. "Oh, that, I'm afraid, is a pretty dream. But we'll dream it, anyway!" Everything about her had brightened since Cyrus Dalzell came up the hill. Even the long garnet earrings beside her cheeks seemed to flash with a deeper color, Niel thought. She was a different woman from the one who sat there writing, half an hour ago. Her fingers, as they played on the sleeve of the pongee coat, were light and fluttery as butterfly wings.

"No dream at all, my dear. Kitty has arranged everything. You know how quickly she thinks things out. I am to come for you in my car. We'll get my old porter Jim as a valet for Daniel, and you can just play around and put fresh life into us all. We saw last winter that we couldn't do anything without our Lady Forrester. Nothing came off right without her. If we had a party, we sat down afterward and wondered what in hell we'd had it for. Oh, no, we can't manage without you!"

Tears flashed into her eyes. "That's very dear of you. It's sweet to be remembered when one is away." In her voice there was the heart-breaking sweetness one sometimes hears in lovely, gentle old songs.

I X

AFTER THREE WEEKS the Captain was up and around again. He dragged his left foot, and his left arm was uncertain. Though he recovered his speech, it was thick and clouded; some words he could not pronounce distinctly,—slid over them, dropped out a syllable. Therefore he avoided talking even more than was his habit. The doctor said that unless another brain lesion occurred, he might get on comfortably for some years yet.

In August Niel was to go to Boston to begin coaching for his entrance examinations at the Massachusetts Institute of Technology, where he meant to study architecture. He put off bidding the Forresters good-bye until the very day before he left. His last call was different from any he had ever made there before. Already they began to treat him like a young man. He sat rather stiffly in that parlor where he had been so much at home. The Captain was in his big chair in the bay window, in the full glow of the afternoon sun, saying little, but very friendly. Mrs. Forrester, on the sofa in the shadowy corner of the room, talked about Niel's plans and his journey.

"Is it true that Mary is going to marry Pucelik this fall?" he asked her. "Who will you get to help you?"

"No one, for the present. Ben will do all I can't do. Never mind us. We will pass a quiet winter, like an old country couple,—as we are!" she said lightly.

Niel knew that she faced the winter with terror, but he had never seen her more in command of herself,—or more the mistress of her own house than now, when she was preparing to become the servant of it. He had the feeling, which he never used to have, that her lightness cost her something.

"Don't forget us, but don't mope. Make lots of new friends. You'll never be twenty again. Take a chorus girl out to supper—a pretty one, mind! Don't bother about your allowance. If you got into a scrape, we could manage a little cheque to help you out, couldn't we, Mr. Forrester?"

The Captain puffed and looked amused. "I think we could, Niel, I think so. Don't get up, my boy. You must stay to dinner."

Niel said he couldn't. He hadn't finished packing, and he was leaving on the morning train.

"Then we must have a little something before you go." Captain Forrester rose heavily, with the aid of his cane, and went into the dining-room. He brought back the decanter and filled three glasses with ceremony. Lifting his glass, he paused, as always, and blinked.

"Happy days!"

"Happy days!" echoed Mrs. Forrester, with her loveliest smile, "and every success to Niel!"

Both the Captain and his wife came to the door with him, and stood there on the porch together, where he had so often seen them stand to speed the parting guest. He went down the hill touched and happy. As he passed over the bridge his spirits suddenly fell. Would that chilling doubt always lie in wait for him, down there in the mud, where he had thrown his roses one morning?

He burned to ask her one question, to get the truth out of her and set his mind at rest: What did she do with all her exquisiteness when she was with a man like Ellinger? Where did she put it away? And having put it away, how could she recover herself, and give one—give even him—the sense of tempered steel, a blade that could fence with anyone and never break?

PART TWO

PART TWO

I

IT WAS TWO YEARS before Niel Herbert came home again, and
when he came the first acquaintance he met was Ivy Peters. Ivy
got on the train at one of the little stations east of Sweet Water,
where he had been trying a case. As he strolled through the Pullman he noticed among the passengers a young man in a gray flannel
suit, with a silk shirt of one shade of blue and a necktie of another.
After regarding this urban figure from the rear for a few seconds,
Ivy glanced down at his own clothes with gloating satisfaction. It
was a hot day in June, but he wore the black felt hat and ready-
made coat of winter weight he had always affected as a boy. He
stepped forward, his hands thrust in his pockets.

"Hullo, Niel. Thought I couldn't be mistaken."

Niel looked up and saw the red, bee-stung face, with its two
permanent dimples, smiling down at him in contemptuous jocular-
ity.

"Hello, Ivy. I couldn't be mistaken in you, either."

"Coming home to go into business?"

Niel replied that he was coming only for the summer vacation.

"Oh, you're not through school yet? I suppose it takes longer to
make an architect than it does to make a shyster. Just as well; there's

not much building going on in Sweet Water these days. You'll find a good many changes."

"Won't you sit down?" Niel indicated the neighboring chair. "You are practising law?"

"Yes, along with a few other things. Have to keep more than one iron in the fire to make a living with us. I farm a little on the side. I rent that meadow-land on the Forrester place. I've drained the old marsh and put it into wheat. My brother John does the work, and I boss the job. It's quite profitable. I pay them a good rent, and they need it. I doubt if they could get along without. Their influential friends don't seem to help them out much. Remember all those chesty old boys the Captain used to drive about in his democrat wagon, and ship in barrels of Bourbon for? Good deal of bluff about all those old-timers. The panic put them out of the game. The Forresters have come down in the world like the rest. You remember how the old man used to put it over us kids and not let us carry a gun in there? I'm just mean enough to like to shoot along that creek a little better than anywhere else, now. There wasn't any harm in the old Captain, but he had the delusion of grandeur. He's happier now that he's like the rest of us and don't have to change his shirt every day." Ivy's unblinking greenish eyes rested upon Niel's haberdashery.

Niel, however, did not notice this. He knew that Ivy wanted him to show disappointment, and he was determined not to do so. He enquired about the Captain's health, pointedly keeping Mrs. Forrester's name out of the conversation.

"He's only about half there . . . seems contented enough. . . . She takes good care of him, I'll say that for her. . . . She seeks consolation, always did, you know . . . too much French brandy . . . but she never neglects him. I don't blame her. Real work comes hard on her."

Niel heard these remarks dully, through the buzz of an idea. He felt that Ivy had drained the marsh quite as much to spite him and Mrs. Forrester as to reclaim the land. Moreover, he seemed to know that until this moment Ivy himself had not realized how much that consideration weighed with him. He and Ivy had disliked each other from childhood, blindly, instinctively, recognizing each other through antipathy, as hostile insects do. By draining the marsh Ivy had obliterated a few acres of something he hated, though he could not name it, and had asserted his power over the people who had loved those unproductive meadows for their idleness and silvery beauty.

After Ivy had gone on into the smoker, Niel sat looking out at the windings of the Sweet Water and playing with his idea. The Old West had been settled by dreamers, great-hearted adventurers who were unpractical to the point of magnificence; a courteous brotherhood, strong in attack but weak in defense, who could conquer but could not hold. Now all the vast territory they had won was to be at the mercy of men like Ivy Peters, who had never dared anything, never risked anything. They would drink up the mirage, dispel the morning freshness, root out the great brooding spirit of freedom, the generous, easy life of the great land-holders. The space, the color, the princely carelessness of the pioneer they would destroy and cut up into profitable bits, as the match factory splinters the primeval forest. All the way from the Missouri to the mountains this generation of shrewd young men, trained to petty economies by hard times, would do exactly what Ivy Peters had done when he drained the Forrester marsh.

I I

THE NEXT AFTERNOON Niel found Captain Forrester in the bushy little plot he called his rose garden, seated in a stout hickory chair that could be left out in all weather, his two canes beside him. His attention was fixed upon a red block of Colorado sandstone, set on a granite boulder in the middle of the gravel space around which the roses grew. He showed Niel that this was a sun-dial, and explained it with great pride. Last summer, he said, he sat out here a great deal, with a square board mounted on a post, and marked the length of the shadows by his watch. His friend, Cyrus Dalzell, on one of his visits, took this board away, had the diagram exactly copied on sandstone, and sent it to him, with the column-like boulder that formed its base.

"I think it's likely Mr. Dalzell hunted around among the mountains a good many mornings before he found a natural formation like that," said the Captain. "A pillar, such as they had in Bible times. It's from the Garden of the Gods. Mr. Dalzell has his summer home up there."

The Captain sat with the soles of his boots together, his legs bowed out. Everything about him seemed to have grown heavier and weaker. His face was fatter and smoother; as if the features were running into each other, as when a wax face melts in the heat. An old Panama hat, burned yellow by the sun, shaded his eyes. His brown hands lay on his knees, the fingers well apart, nerveless. His moustache was the same straw color; Niel remarked to him that it had grown no grayer. The Captain touched his cheek with his palm. "Mrs. Forrester shaved me for a while. She did it very nicely, but I didn't like to have her do it. Now I use one of these safety razors. I can manage, if I take my time. The barber comes over once a week. Mrs. Forrester is expecting you, Niel. She's down in the grove. She goes down there to rest in the hammock."

Niel went round the house to the gate that gave into the grove. From the top of the hill he could see the hammock slung between two cottonwoods, in the low glade at the farther end, where he had fallen the time he broke his arm. The slender white figure was still, and as he hurried across the grass he saw that a white garden hat lay over her face. He approached quietly and was just wondering if she were asleep, when he heard a soft, delighted laugh, and with a quick movement she threw off the lace hat through which she had been watching him. He stepped forward and caught her suspended figure, hammock and all, in his arms. How light and alive she was! like a bird caught in a net. If only he could rescue her and carry her off like this,—off the earth of sad, inevitable periods, away from age, weariness, adverse fortune!

She showed no impatience to be released, but lay laughing up at him with that gleam of something elegantly wild, something fantastic and tantalizing,—seemingly so artless, really the most finished artifice! She put her hand under his chin as if he were still a boy.

"And how handsome he's grown! Isn't the old Judge proud of you! He called me up last night and began sputtering, 'It's only fair to warn you, Ma'm, that I've a very handsome boy over here.' As if I hadn't known you would be! And now you're a man, and have seen the world! Well, what have you found in it?"

"Nothing so nice as you, Mrs. Forrester."

"Nonsense! You have sweethearts?"

"Perhaps."

"Are they pretty?"

"Why they? Isn't one enough?"

"One is too many. I want you to have half a dozen,—and still save the best for us! One would take everything. If you had her, you would not have come home at all. I wonder if you know how we've looked for you?" She took his hand and turned a seal ring about on his little finger absently. "Every night for weeks, when the lights of the train came swinging in down below the meadows, I've said to myself, 'Niel is coming home; there's that to look forward to.' " She caught herself as she always did when she found that she was telling too much, and finished in a playful tone. "So, you see, you mean a great deal to all of us. Did you find Mr. Forrester?"

"Oh, yes! I had to stop and look at his sun-dial."

She raised herself on her elbow and lowered her voice. "Niel, can you understand it? He isn't childish, as some people say, but he will sit and watch that thing hour after hour. How can anybody like to see time visibly devoured? We are all used to seeing clocks go round, but why does he want to see that shadow creep on that stone? Has he changed much? No? I'm glad you feel so. Now tell me about the Adamses and what George is like."

Niel dropped on the turf and sat with his back against a tree trunk, answering her rapid questions and watching her while he talked. Of course, she was older. In the brilliant sun of the afternoon one saw that her skin was no longer like white lilacs,—it had the ivory tint of gardenias that have just begun to fade. The coil of blue-black hair seemed more than ever too heavy for her head. There were lines,—something strained about the corners of her mouth that used not to be there. But the astonishing thing was how these changes could vanish in a moment, be utterly wiped out in a flash of personality, and one forgot everything about her except herself.

"And tell me, Niel, do women really smoke after dinner now with the men, nice women? I shouldn't like it. It's all very well for actresses, but women can't be attractive if they do everything that men do."

"I think just now it's the fashion for women to make themselves comfortable, before anything else."

Mrs. Forrester glanced at him as if he had said something shocking. "Ah, that's just it! The two things don't go together. Athletics and going to college and smoking after dinner— Do you like it? Don't men like women to be different from themselves? They used to."

Niel laughed. Yes, that was certainly the idea of Mrs. Forrester's generation.

"Uncle Judge says you don't come to see him any more as you used to, Mrs. Forrester. He misses it."

"My dear boy, I haven't been over to the town for six weeks. I'm always too tired. We have no horse now, and when I do go I have to walk. That house! Nothing is ever done there unless I do it, and nothing ever moves unless I move it. That's why I come down here in the afternoon,—to get where I can't see the house. I can't keep it up as it should be kept, I'm not strong enough. Oh, yes, Ben helps me; he sweeps and beats the rugs and washes windows, but that doesn't get a house very far." Mrs. Forrester sat up suddenly and pinned on her white hat. "We went all the way to Chicago, Niel, to buy that walnut furniture, couldn't find anything at home big and heavy enough. If I'd known that one day I'd have to push it about, I would have been more easily satisfied!" She rose and shook out her rumpled skirts.

They started toward the house, going slowly up the long, grassy undulation between the trees.

"Don't you miss the marsh?" Niel asked suddenly.

She glanced away evasively. "Not much. I would never have time to go there, and we need the money it pays us. And you haven't time to play any more either, Niel. You must hurry and become a successful man. Your uncle is terribly involved. He has been so careless that he's not much better off than we are. Money is a very important thing. Realize that in the beginning; face it, and don't be ridiculous in the end, like so many of us." They stopped by the gate at the top of the hill and looked back at the green alleys and sharp shadows, at the quivering fans of light that seemed to push the trees farther apart and made Elysian fields underneath them. Mrs. Forrester put her white hand, with all its rings, on Niel's arm.

"Do you really find a kind of pleasure in coming back to us? That's very unusual, I think. At your age I wanted to be with the young and gay. It's nice for us, though." She looked at him with her rarest smile, one he had seldom seen on her face, but always remembered,—a smile without archness, without gaiety, full of affection and wistfully sad. And the same thing was in her voice when she spoke those quiet words,—the sudden quietness of deep feeling. She turned quickly away. They went through the gate and around the house to where the Captain sat watching the sunset glory on his roses. His wife touched his shoulder.

"Will you go in, now, Mr. Forrester, or shall I bring your coat?"

"I'll go in. Isn't Niel going to stay for dinner?"

"Not this time. He'll come soon, and we'll have a real dinner for him. Will you wait for Mr. Forrester, Niel? I must hurry in and start the fire."

Niel tarried behind and accompanied the Captain's slow progress toward the front of the house. He leaned upon two canes, lifting his feet slowly and putting them down firmly and carefully. He looked like an old tree walking.

Once up the steps and into the parlor, he sank into his big chair and panted heavily. The first whiff of a fresh cigar seemed to restore him. "Can I trouble you to mail some letters for me, Niel, as you go by the post-office?" He produced them from the breast pocket of his summer coat. "Let me see whether Mrs. Forrester has anything to go." Rising, the Captain went into the little hall. There, by the front door, on a table under the hat rack, was a scantily draped figure, an Arab or Egyptian slave girl, holding in her hands a large flat shell from the California coast. Niel remembered noticing that figure the first time he was ever in the house, when Dr. Dennison carried him out through this hallway with his arm in splints. In the days when the Forresters had servants and were sending over to the town several times a day, the letters for the post were always left in this shell. The Captain found one now, and handed it to Niel. It was addressed to Mr. Francis Bosworth Ellinger, Glenwood Springs, Colorado.

For some reason Niel felt embarrassed and tried to slip the letter quickly into his pocket. The Captain, his two canes in one hand, prevented him. He took the pale blue envelope again, and held it out at arm's length, regarding it.

"Mrs. Forrester is a fine penman; have you ever noticed? Always was. If she made me a list of articles to get at the store, I never had to hide it. It was like copper plate. That's exceptional in a woman, Niel."

Niel remembered her hand well enough, he had never seen another in the least like it; long, thin, angular letters, curiously delicate and curiously bold, looped and laced with strokes fine as a hair and perfectly distinct. Her script looked as if it had been done at a high pitch of speed, the pen driven by a perfectly confident dexterity.

"Oh, yes, Captain! I'm never able to take any letters for Mrs. Forrester without looking at them. No one could forget her writing."

"Yes. It's very exceptional." The Captain gave him the envelope, and with his canes went slowly toward his big chair.

Niel had often wondered just how much the Captain knew. Now, as he went down the hill, he felt sure that he knew everything; more than anyone else; all there was to know about Marian Forrester.

I I I

NIEL HAD PLANNED to do a great deal of reading in the Forresters' grove that summer, but he did not go over so often as
he had intended. The frequent appearance of Ivy Peters about the
place irritated him. Ivy visited his new wheat fields on the bottom
land very often; and he always took the old path, that led from what
was once the marsh, up the steep bank and through the grove. He
was likely to appear at any hour, his trousers stuffed into his top-
boots, tramping along between the rows of trees with an air of
proprietorship. He shut the gate behind the house with a slam and
went whistling through the yard. Often he stopped at the kitchen
door to call out some pleasantry to Mrs. Forrester. This annoyed
Niel, for at that hour of the morning, when she was doing her
housework, Mrs. Forrester was not dressed to receive her inferiors.
It was one thing to greet the president of the Colorado & Utah *en
déshabillé*, but it was another to chatter with a coarse-grained fellow
like Ivy Peters in her wrapper and slippers, her sleeves rolled up
and her throat bare to his cool, impudent eyes.

Sometimes Ivy strode through the rose plot where Captain Forrester was sitting in the sun,—went by without looking at him, as if
there were no one there. If he spoke to the Captain at all, he did so

as if he were addressing someone incapable of understanding anything. "Hullo, Captain, ain't afraid this sun will spoil your complexion?" or "Well, Captain, you'll have to get the prayer-meetings to
take up this rain question. The drought's damned bad for my
wheat."

One morning, as Niel was coming up through the grove, he
heard laughter by the gate, and there he saw Ivy, with his gun,
talking to Mrs. Forrester. She was bareheaded, her skirts blowing in
the wind, her arm through the handle of a big tin bucket that rested
on the fence beside her. Ivy stood with his hat on his head, but
there was in his attitude that unmistakable something which shows
that a man is trying to make himself agreeable to a woman. He was
telling her a funny story, probably an improper one, for it brought
out her naughtiest laugh, with something nervous and excited in it,
as if he were going too far. At the end of his story Ivy himself broke
into his farm-hand guffaw. Mrs. Forrester shook her finger at him
and, catching up her pail, ran back into the house. She bent a little
with its weight, but Ivy made no offer to carry it for her. He let her
trip away with it as if she were a kitchen maid, and that were her
business.

Niel emerged from the grove, and stopped where the Captain sat
in the garden. "Good-morning, Captain Forrester. Was that Ivy
Peters who just went through here? That fellow hasn't the manners
of a pig!" he blurted out.

The Captain pointed to Mrs. Forrester's empty chair. "Sit down,
Niel, sit down." He drew his handkerchief from his pocket and
began polishing his glasses. "No," he said quietly, "he ain't overly
polite."

More than if he had complained bitterly, that guarded admission
made one feel how much he had been hurt and offended by Ivy's
rudeness. There was something very sad in his voice, and helpless.
From his equals, respect had always come to him as his due; from
fellows like Ivy he had been able to command it,—to order them off
his place, or dismiss them from his employ.

Niel sat down and smoked a cigar with him. They had a long talk about the building of the Black Hills branch of the Burlington. In Boston last winter Niel had met an old mine-owner, who was living in Deadwood when the railroad first came in. When Niel asked him if he had known Daniel Forrester, the old gentleman said, "Forrester? Was he the one with the beautiful wife?"

"You must tell her," said the Captain, stroking the warm surface of his sun-dial. "Yes, indeed. You must tell Mrs. Forrester."

One night in the first week of July, a night of glorious moonlight, Niel found himself unable to read, or to stay indoors at all. He walked aimlessly down the wide, empty street, and crossed the first creek by the footbridge. The wide ripe fields, the whole country, seemed like a sleeping garden. One trod the dusty roads softly, not to disturb the deep slumber of the world.

In the Forrester lane the scent of sweet clover hung heavy. It had always grown tall and green here ever since Niel could remember; the Captain would never let it be cut until the weeds were mowed in the fall. The black, plume-like shadows of the poplars fell across the lane and over Ivy Peters' wheat fields. As he walked on, Niel saw a white figure standing on the bridge over the second creek, motionless in the clear moonlight. He hurried forward. Mrs. Forrester was looking down at the water where it flowed bright over the pebbles. He came up beside her. "The Captain is asleep?"

"Oh, yes, long ago! He sleeps well, thank heaven! After I tuck him in, I have nothing more to worry about."

While they were standing there, talking in low voices, they heard a heavy door slam on the hill. Mrs. Forrester started and looked back over her shoulder. A man emerged from the shadow of the house and came striding down the drive-way. Ivy Peters stepped upon the bridge.

"Good evening," he said to Mrs. Forrester, neither calling her by name nor removing his hat. "I see you have company. I've just been up looking at the old barn, to see if the stalls are fit to put horses in there tomorrow. I'm going to start cutting wheat in the morning, and we'll have to put the horses in your stable at noon. We'd lose time taking them back to town."

"Why, certainly. The horses can go in our barn. I'm sure Mr. Forrester would have no objection." She spoke as if he had asked her permission.

"Oh!" Ivy shrugged. "The men will begin down here at six o'clock. I won't get over till about ten, and I have to meet a client at my office at three. Maybe you could give me some lunch, to save time."

His impudence made her smile. "Very well, then; I invite you to lunch. We lunch at one."

"Thanks. It will help me out." As if he had forgotten himself, he lifted his hat, and went down the lane swinging it in his hand.

Niel stood looking after him. "Why do you allow him to speak to you like that, Mrs. Forrester? If you'll let me, I'll give him a beating and teach him how to speak to you."

"No, no, Niel! Remember, we have to get along with Ivy Peters, we simply have to!" There was a note of anxiety in her voice, and she caught his arm.

"You don't have to take anything from him, or to stand his bad manners. Anybody else would pay you as much for the land as he does."

"But he has a lease for five years, and he could make it very disagreeable for us, don't you see? Besides," she spoke hurriedly, "there's more than that. He's invested a little money for me in Wyoming, in land. He gets splendid land from the Indians some way, for next to nothing. Don't tell your uncle; I've no doubt it's crooked. But the Judge is like Mr. Forrester; his methods don't work nowadays. He will never get us out of debt, dear man! He can't get himself out. Ivy Peters is terribly smart, you know. He owns half the town already."

"Not quite," said Niel grimly. "He's got hold of a good deal of property. He'll take advantage of anybody's necessity. You know he's utterly unscrupulous, don't you? Why didn't you let Mr. Dalzell, or some of your other old friends, invest your money for you?"

"Oh, it was too little! Only a few hundred dollars I'd saved on the housekeeping. They would put it into something safe, at six per cent. I know you don't like Ivy,—and he knows it! He's always at his worst before you. He's not so bad as—as his face, for instance!" She laughed nervously. "He honestly wants to help us out of the hole we're in. Coming and going all the time, as he does, he sees everything, and I really think he hates to have me work so hard."

"Next time you have anything to invest, you let me take it to Mr. Dalzell and explain. I'll promise to do as well by you as Ivy Peters can."

Mrs. Forrester took his arm and drew him into the lane. "But my dear boy, you know nothing about these business schemes. You're not clever that way,—it's one of the things I love you for. I don't admire people who cheat Indians. Indeed I don't!" She shook her head vehemently.

"Mrs. Forrester, rascality isn't the only thing that succeeds in business."

"It succeeds faster than anything else, though," she murmured absently. They walked as far as the end of the lane and turned back again. Mrs. Forrester's hand tightened on his arm. She began speaking abruptly. "You see, two years, three years, more of this, and I could still go back to California—and live again. But after that . . . Perhaps people think I've settled down to grow old gracefully, but I've not. I feel such a power to live in me, Niel." Her slender fingers gripped his wrist. "It's grown by being held back. Last winter I was with the Dalzells at Glenwood Springs for three weeks (I owe *that* to Ivy Peters; he looked after things here, and his sister kept house for Mr. Forrester), and I was surprised at myself. I could dance all night and not feel tired. I could ride horseback all day and be ready for a dinner party in the evening. I had no clothes, of course; old evening dresses with yards and yards of satin and velvet in them, that Mrs. Dalzell's sewing woman made over. But I looked well enough! Yes, I did. I always know how I'm looking, and I looked well enough. The men thought so. I looked happier than any woman there. They were nearly all younger, much. But they seemed dull, bored to death. After a glass or two of champagne they went to sleep and had nothing to say! I always look better after the first glass,—it gives me a little color, it's the only thing that does. I accepted the Dalzell's invitation with a purpose; I wanted to see whether I had anything left worth saving. And I have, I tell you! You would hardly believe it, I could hardly believe it, but I still have!"

By this time they had reached the bridge, a bare white floor in the moonlight. Mrs. Forrester had been quickening her pace all the while. "So that's what I'm struggling for, to get out of this hole,"— she looked about as if she had fallen into a deep well,—"out of it! When I'm alone here for months together, I plan and plot. If it weren't for that—"

As Niel walked back to his room behind the law offices, he felt frightened for her. When women began to talk about still feeling young, didn't it mean that something had broken? Two or three years, she said. He shivered. Only yesterday old Dr. Dennison had proudly told him that Captain Forrester might live a dozen. "We are keeping his general health up remarkably, and he was originally a man of iron."

What hope was there for her? He could still feel her hand upon his arm, as she urged him faster and faster up the lane.

I V

THE WEATHER was dry and intensely hot for several weeks, and then, at the end of July, thunder-storms and torrential rains broke upon the Sweet Water valley. The river burst out of its banks, all the creeks were up, and the stubble of Ivy Peters' wheat fields lay under water. A wide lake and two rushing creeks now separated the Forresters from the town. Ben Keezer rode over to them every day to do the chores and to take them their mail. One evening Ben, with his slicker and leather mailbag, had just come out of the post-office and was preparing to mount his horse, when Niel Herbert stopped him to ask in a low voice whether he had got the Denver paper.

"Oh, yes. I always wait for the papers. She likes to have them to read of an evening. Guess it's pretty lonesome over there." He swung into his saddle and splashed off. Niel walked slowly around to the hotel for dinner. He had found something very disconcerting in the Denver paper: Frank Ellinger's picture on the society page, along with Constance Ogden's. They had been married yesterday at Colorado Springs, and were stopping at the Antlers.

After supper Niel put on his rubber coat and started for the

"*As Niel went through the sleeping town on his way to the livery barn, he saw the short, plump figure of Mrs. Beasley . . . waddling through the feathery asparagus bed behind the telephone office. She had already been next door to tell her neighbor Molly Tucker, the seamstress, about her exciting night.*"
—A Lost Lady

Forresters'. When he reached the first creek, he found that the footbridge had been washed out from the far bank and lay obliquely in the stream, battered at by the yellow current which might at any moment carry it away. One could not cross the ford without a horse. He looked irresolutely across the submerged bottom lands. The house was dark, no lights in the parlor windows. The rain was beginning to fall again. Perhaps she had rather be alone tonight. He would go over tomorrow.

He went back to the law office and tried to make himself comfortable, though the place was in distracting disorder. The continued rain had set one of the chimneys leaking, had brought down streams of soot and black water and flooded the stove and the Judge's once handsome Brussels carpet. The tinner had been there all afternoon, trying to find what was the matter with the flue, cutting a new sheet-iron drawer to fit under the stove-pipe. But at six o'clock he had gone away, leaving tools and sheets of metal lying about. The rooms were damp and cold. Niel put on a heavy sweater, since he could not have a fire, lit the big coal-oil lamp, and sat down with a book. When at last he looked at his watch, it was nearly midnight, and he had been reading three hours. He would have another pipe, and go to bed. He had scarcely lit it, when he heard quick, hurrying footsteps in the echoing corridor outside. He got to the door in an instant, was there to open it before Mrs. Forrester had time to knock. He caught her by the arm and pulled her in.

Everything but her wet, white face was hidden by a black rubber hat and a coat that was much too big for her. Streams of water trickled from the coat, and when she opened it he saw that she was drenched to the waist,—her black dress clung in a muddy pulp about her.

"Mrs. Forrester," he cried, "you can't have crossed the creek! It's up to a horse's belly in the ford."

"I came over the bridge, what's left of it. It shook under me, but

I'm not heavy." She threw off her hat and wiped the water from her face with her hands.

"Why didn't you ask Ben to bring you over on his horse? Here, please swallow this."

She pushed his hand aside. "Wait. Afterwards. Ben? I didn't think until after he was gone. It's the telephone I want, long distance. Get me Colorado Springs, the Antlers, quick!"

Then Niel noticed that she smelled strong of spirits; it steamed above the smell of rubber and creek mud and wet cloth. She snatched up the desk telephone, but he gently took it from her.

"I'll get them for you, but you're in no condition to talk now; you're out of breath. Do you really want to talk tonight? You know Mrs. Beasley will hear every word you say." Mrs. Beasley was the Sweet Water central, and an indefatigable reporter of everything that went over the wires.

Mrs. Forrester, sitting in his uncle's desk chair, tapped the carpet with the toe of her rubber boot. "Do hurry, please," she said in that polite, warning tone of which even Ivy Peters was afraid.

Niel aroused the sleepy central and put in the call. "She asks whom you wish to speak to?"

"Frank Ellinger. Say Judge Pommeroy's office wishes to speak to him."

Niel began soothing Mrs. Beasley at the other end. "No, not the management, Mrs. Beasley, one of the guests. Frank Ellinger," he spelled the name. "Yes. Judge Pommeroy's office wants to talk to him. I'll be right here. As soon as you can, please."

He put down the instrument. "I'd rather, you know, publish anything in the town paper than telephone it through Mrs. Beasley." Mrs. Forrester paid no heed to him, did not look at him, sat staring at the wall. "I can't see why you didn't call me up and ask me to bring a horse over for you, if you felt you must get to a long distance telephone tonight."

"Yes; I didn't think of it. I only knew I had to get over here, and I was afraid something might stop me." She was watching the telephone as if it were alive. Her eyes were shrunk to hard points. Her brows, drawn together in an acute angle, kept twitching in the frown which held them,—the singular frown of one overcome by alcohol or fatigue, who is holding on to consciousness by the strength of a single purpose. Her blue lips, the black shadows under her eyes, made her look as if some poison were at work in her body.

They waited and waited. Niel understood that she did not wish him to talk. Her mind was struggling with something, with every blink of her lashes she seemed to face it anew. Presently she rose as if she could bear the suspense no longer and went over to the window, leaned against it.

"Did you leave Captain Forrester alone?" Niel asked suddenly.

"Yes. Nothing will happen over there. Nothing ever *does* happen!" she answered wildly, wringing her hands.

The telephone buzzed. Mrs. Forrester darted toward the desk, but Niel lifted the instrument in his left hand and barred her way with his right. "Try to be calm, Mrs. Forrester. When I get Ellinger I will let you talk to him,—and central will hear every word you say, remember."

After some exchanges with the Colorado office, he pointed her to the chair. "Sit down and I'll give it to you. He is on the wire."

He did not dare to leave her alone, though it was awkward enough to be a listener. He walked to the window and stood with his back to the desk where she was sitting.

"Is that you, Frank? This is Marian. I won't keep you a moment. You were asleep? So early? That's not like you. You've reformed already, haven't you? That's what marriage does, they say. No, I wasn't altogether surprised. You might have taken me into your confidence, though. Haven't I deserved it?"

A long, listening pause. Niel stared stupidly at the dark window. He had steeled his nerves for wild reproaches. The voice he heard behind him was her most charming; playful, affectionate, intimate, with a thrill of pleasant excitement that warmed its slight formality and burned through the common-place words like the color in an opal. He simply held his breath while she fluttered on:

"Where shall you go for your honeymoon? Oh, I'm very sorry! So soon . . . You must take good care of her. Give her my love. . . . I should think California, at this time of the year, might be right . . ."

It went on like this for some minutes. The voice, it seemed to Niel, was that of a woman, young, beautiful, happy,—warm and at her ease, sitting in her own drawing-room and talking on a stormy night to a dear friend far away.

"Oh, unusually well, for me. Stop and see for yourself. You will be going to Omaha on business next week, before California. Oh, yes, you will! Stop off between trains. You know how welcome you are, always."

A long pause. An exclamation from Mrs. Forrester made Niel turn sharply round. Now it was coming! Her voice was darkening with every word. "I think I understand you. You are not speaking from your own room? What, from the office booth? Oh, then I understand you very well indeed!" Niel looked about in alarm. It was time to stop her, but how? The voice went on.

"Play safe! When have you ever played anything else? You know, Frank, the truth is that you're a coward; a great, hulking coward. Do you hear me? I want you to hear! . . . You've got a safe thing at last, I should think; safe and pasty! How much stock did you get with it? A big block, I hope! Now let me tell you the truth: I don't want you to come here! I never want to see you again while I live, and I forbid you to come and look at me when I'm dead. I don't want your hateful eyes to look at my dead face. Do you hear me? Why don't you answer me? Don't dare to hang up the receiver, you coward! Oh, you big . . . Frank, Frank, say something! Oh, he's shut me off, I can't hear him!"

She flung the receiver down, dropped her head on the desk, and broke into heavy, groaning sobs. Niel stood over her and waited with composure. For once he had been quick enough; he had saved her. The moment that quivering passion of hatred and wrong leaped into her voice, he had taken the big shears left by the tinner and cut the insulated wire behind the desk. Her reproaches had got no farther than this room.

When the sobs ceased he touched her shoulder. He shook her, but there was no response. She was asleep, sunk in a heavy stupor. Her hands and face were so cold that he thought there could not be a drop of warm blood left in her body. He carried her into his room, cut off her drenched clothing, wrapped her in his bathrobe and put her into his own bed. She was absolutely unconscious. He blew out the light, locked her in, and left the building, going as fast as he could to Judge Pommeroy's cottage. He roused his uncle and briefly explained the situation.

"Can you dress and go down to the office for the rest of the night, Uncle Judge? Some one must be with her. And I'll get over to the Captain at once; he certainly oughtn't to be left alone. If she could get across the bridge, I guess I can. By the way, she began talking wild, and I cut the telephone wire behind your desk. So keep an eye on it. It might make trouble on a stormy night like this. I'll get a livery hack and take Mrs. Forrester home in the morning, before the town is awake."

When daylight began to break Niel went into Captain Forrester's room and told him that his wife had been sent for in the night to answer a long distance telephone call, and that now he was going to bring her home.

The Captain lay propped up on three big pillows. Since his face had grown fat and relaxed, its ruggedness had changed to an almost Asiatic smoothness. He looked like a wise old Chinese mandarin as he lay listening to the young man's fantastic story with perfect composure, merely blinking and saying, "Thank you, Niel, thank you."

As Niel went through the sleeping town on his way to the livery barn, he saw the short, plump figure of Mrs. Beasley, like a boiled pudding sewed up in a blue kimono, waddling through the feathery asparagus bed behind the telephone office. She had already been next door to tell her neighbor Molly Tucker, the seamstress, the story of her exciting night.

V

$\int$ OON AFTERWARD, when Captain Forrester had another stroke, Mrs. Beasley and Molly Tucker and their friends were perfectly agreed that it was a judgment upon his wife. No judgment could have been crueler. Under the care of him, now that he was helpless, Mrs. Forrester quite went to pieces.

Even after their misfortunes had begun to come upon them, she had maintained her old reserve. She had asked nothing and accepted nothing. Her demeanor toward the townspeople was always the same; easy, cordial, and impersonal. Her own friends had moved away long ago,—all except Judge Pommeroy and Dr. Dennison. When any of the housewives from the town came to call, she met them in the parlor, chatted with them in the smiling, careless manner they could never break through, and they got no further. They still felt they must put on their best dress and carry a card-case when they went to the Forresters'.

But now that the Captain was helpless, everything changed. She could hold off the curious no longer. The townswomen brought soups and custards for the invalid. When they came to sit out the night with him, she turned the house over to them. She was worn

out; so exhausted that she was dull to what went on about her. The
Mrs. Beasleys and Molly Tuckers had their chance at last. They
went in and out of Mrs. Forrester's kitchen as familiarly as they did
out of one another's. They rummaged through the linen closet to
find more sheets, pried about in the attic and cellar. They went over
the house like ants, the house where they had never before got past
the parlor; and they found they had been fooled all these years.
There was nothing remarkable about the place at all! The kitchen
was inconvenient, the sink was smelly. The carpets were worn, the
curtains faded, the clumsy, old-fashioned furniture they wouldn't
have had for a gift, and the upstairs bedrooms were full of dust and
cobwebs.

Judge Pommeroy remarked to his nephew that he had never
seen these women look so wide-awake, so important and pleased
with themselves, as now when he encountered them bustling about
the Forrester place. The Captain's illness had the effect of a social
revival, like a new club or a church society. The creatures grew
bolder and bolder,—and Mrs. Forrester, apparently, had no power
of resistance. She drudged in the kitchen, slept, half-dressed, in one
of the chambers upstairs, kept herself going on black coffee and
brandy. All the bars were down. She had ceased to care about
anything.

As the women came and went through the lane, Niel sometimes
overheard snatches of their conversation.

"Why didn't she sell some of that silver? All those platters and
covered dishes stuck away with the tarnish of years on them!"

"I wouldn't mind having some of her linen. There's a chest full
of double damask upstairs, every tablecloth long enough to make
two. Did you ever see anything like the wine glasses! I'll bet there's
not as many in both saloons put together. If she has a sale after he's
gone, I'll buy a dozen champagne glasses; they're nice to serve
sherbet in."

"There are nine dozen glasses," said Molly Tucker, "counting them for beer and whiskey. If there is a sale, I've a mind to bid in a couple of them green ones, with long stems, for mantel ornaments. But she'll never sell 'em all, unless she can get the saloons to take 'em."

Ed Elliott's mother laughed. "She'll never sell 'em, as long as she's got anything to put in 'em."

"The cellar will go dry, some day."

"I guess there's always plenty that will get it for such as her. I never go there now that I don't smell it on her. I went over late the other night, and she was on her knees, washing up the kitchen floor. Her eyes were glassy. She kept washing the place around the ice-box over and over, till it made me nervous. I said, 'Mrs. Forrester, I think you've washed that place several times already.'"

"Was she confused?"

"Not a particle! She laughed and said she was often absent-minded."

Mrs. Elliott's companions laughed, too, and agreed that absent-minded was a good expression.

Niel repeated this conversation to his uncle. "Uncle," he declared, "I don't see how I can go back to Boston and leave the Forresters. I'd like to chuck school for a year, and see them through. I want to go over there and clear those gossips out. Could you stay at the hotel for a few weeks, and let me have Black Tom? With him to help me, I'd send every one of those women trotting down the lane."

It was arranged quietly, and at once. Tom was put in the kitchen, and Niel himself took charge of the nursing. He met the women with firmness: they were very kind, but now nothing was needed. The Doctor had said the house must be absolutely quiet and that the invalid must see no one.

Once the house was tranquil, Mrs. Forrester went to bed and slept for the better part of a week. The Captain himself improved. On his good days he could be put into a wheel-chair and rolled out into his garden to enjoy the September sunlight and the last of his briar roses.

"Thank you, Niel, thank you, Tom," he often said when they lifted him into his chair. "I value this quiet very highly." If a day came when they thought he ought not to go out, he was sad and disappointed.

"Better get him out, no matter what," said Mrs. Forrester. "He likes to look at his place. That, and his cigar, are the only pleasures he has left."

When she was rested and in command of herself again, she took her place in the kitchen, and Black Tom went back to the Judge.

At night, when he was alone, when Mrs. Forrester had gone to bed and the Captain was resting quietly, Niel found a kind of solemn happiness in his vigils. It had been hard to give up that year; most of his classmates were younger than he. It had cost him something, but now that he had taken the step, he was glad. As he put in the night hours, sitting first in one chair and then in another, reading, smoking, getting a lunch to keep himself awake, he had the satisfaction of those who keep faith. He liked being alone with the old things that had seemed so beautiful to him in his childhood. These were still the most comfortable chairs in the world, and he would never like any pictures so well as "William Tell's Chapel" and "The House of the Tragic Poet." No card-table was so good for solitaire as this old one with a stone top, mosaic in the pattern of a chess-board, which one of the Captain's friends had brought him from Naples. No other house could take the place of this one in his life.

He had time to think of many things; of himself and of his old friends here. He had noticed that often when Mrs. Forrester was about her work, the Captain would call to her, "Maidy, Maidy," and she would reply, "Yes, Mr. Forrester," from wherever she happened to be, but without coming to him,—as if she knew that when he called to her in that tone he was not asking for anything. He wanted to know if she were near, perhaps; or, perhaps, he merely liked to call her name and to hear her answer. The longer Niel was with Captain Forrester in those peaceful closing days of his life, the more he felt that the Captain knew his wife better even than she knew herself; and that, knowing her, he,—to use one of his own expressions,—valued her.

VI

CAPTAIN FORRESTER'S DEATH, which occurred early in December, was "telegraphic news," the only State news that the discouraged town of Sweet Water had furnished for a long while. Flowers and telegrams came from east and west, but it happened that none of the Captain's closest friends could come to his funeral. Mr. Dalzell was in California, the president of the Burlington railroad was traveling in Europe. The others were far away or in uncertain health. Doctor Dennison and Judge Pommeroy were the only two of his intimates among the pallbearers.

On the morning of the funeral, when the Captain was already in his coffin, and the undertaker was in the parlor setting up chairs, Niel heard a knocking at the kitchen door. There he found Adolph Blum, carrying a large white box.

"Niel," he said, "will you please give these to Mrs. Forrester, and tell her they are from Rhein and me, for the Captain?"

Adolph was in his old working clothes, the only clothes he had, probably, with a knitted comforter about his neck. Niel knew he wouldn't come to the funeral, so he said:

"Won't you come in and see him, 'Dolph? He looks just like himself."

Adolph hesitated, but he caught sight of the undertaker's man, through the parlor bay-window, and said, "No, thank you, Niel," thrust his red hands into his jacket pockets, and walked away.

Niel took the flowers out of the box, a great armful of yellow roses, which must have cost the price of many a dead rabbit. He carried them upstairs, where Mrs. Forrester was lying down.

"These are from the Blum boys," he said. "Adolph just brought them to the kitchen door."

Mrs. Forrester looked at them, then turned away her head on the pillow, her lips trembling. It was the only time that day he saw her pale composure break.

The funeral was large. Old settlers and farmer folk came from all over the county to follow the pioneer's body to the grave. As Niel and his uncle were driving back from the cemetery with Mrs. Forrester, she spoke for the first time since they had left the house. "Judge Pommeroy," she said quietly, "I think I will have Mr. Forrester's sun-dial taken over and put above his grave. I can have an inscription cut on the base. It seems more appropriate for him than any stone we could buy. And I will plant some of his own rose-bushes beside it."

When they got back to the house it was four o'clock, and she insisted upon making tea for them. "I would like it myself, and it is better to be doing something. Wait for me in the parlor. And, Niel, move the things back as we always have them."

The gray day was darkening, and as the three sat having their tea in the bay-window, swift squalls of snow were falling over the wide meadows between the hill and the town, and the creaking of the big cottonwoods about the house seemed to say that winter had come.

V I I

ONE MORNING in April Niel was alone in the law office. His uncle had been ill with rheumatic fever for a long while, and he had been attending to the routine of business.

The door opened, and a figure stood there, strange and yet familiar,—he had to think a moment before he realized that it was Orville Ogden, who used to come to Sweet Water so often, but who had not been seen there now for several years. He didn't look a day older; one eye was still direct and clear, the other clouded and oblique. He still wore a stiff imperial and twisted moustache, the gray color of old beeswax, and his thin hair was brushed heroically up over the bald spot.

"This is Judge Pommeroy's nephew, isn't it? I can't think of your name, my boy, but I remember you. Is the Judge out?"

"Please be seated, Mr. Ogden. My uncle is ill. He hasn't been at the office for several months. He's had really a very bad time of it. Is there anything I can do for you?"

"Oh, I'm sorry to hear that! I'm sorry." He spoke as if he were. "I guess all we fellows are getting older, whether we like it or not. It made a great difference when Daniel Forrester went." Mr. Ogden took off his overcoat, put his hat and gloves neatly on the desk, and then seemed somewhat at a loss. "What is your uncle's trouble?" he asked suddenly.

Niel told him. "I was to have gone back to school this winter, but uncle begged me to stay and look after things for him. There was no one here he wanted to entrust his business to."

"I see, I see," said Mr. Ogden thoughtfully. "Then you do attend to his business for the present?" He paused and reflected. "Yes, there was something that I wanted to take up with him. I am stopping off for a few hours only, between trains. I might speak to you about it, and you could consult your uncle and write me in Chicago. It's a confidential matter, and concerns another person."

Niel assured him of his discretion, but Mr. Ogden seemed to find the subject difficult to approach. He looked very grave and slowly lit a cigar.

"It is simply," he said at last, "a rather delicate suggestion I wish to make to your uncle about one of his clients. I have several friends in the Government at Washington just at present, friends who would go out of their way to serve me. I have been thinking that we might manage it to get a special increase of pension for Mrs. Forrester. I am due in Chicago this week, and after my business there is finished, I would be quite willing to go on to Washington to see what can be done; provided, of course, that no one, least of all your uncle's client, knows of my activity in the matter."

Niel flushed. "I'm sorry, Mr. Ogden," he brought out, "but Mrs. Forrester is no longer a client of my uncle's. After the Captain's death, she saw fit to take her business away from him."

Mr. Ogden's normal eye became as blank as the other.

"What's that? He isn't her lawyer? Why, for twenty years—"

"I know that, sir. She didn't treat him with much consideration. She transferred her business very abruptly."

"To whom, may I ask?"

"To a lawyer here in town; Ivy Peters."

"Peters? I never heard of him."

"No, you wouldn't have. He wasn't one of the people who went to the Forrester house in the old days. He's one of the younger generation, a few years older than I. He rented part of the Forresters' land for several years before the Captain's death,—was their tenant. That was how Mrs. Forrester came to know him. She thinks him a good business man."

Mr. Ogden frowned. "And is he?"

"Some people think so."

"Is he trustworthy?"

"Far from it. He takes the cases nobody else will take. He may treat Mrs. Forrester honestly. But if he does, it will not be from principle."

"This is very distressing news. Go on with your work, my boy. I must think this over." Mr. Ogden rose and walked about the room, his hands behind him. Niel turned to an unfinished letter on his desk, in order to leave his visitor the more free.

Mr. Ogden's position, he understood, was a difficult one. He had been devoted to Mrs. Forrester, and before Constance had made up her mind to marry Frank Ellinger, before the mother and daughter began to angle for him, Mr. Ogden had come to the Forresters' more frequently than any of their Denver friends. He hadn't been back, Niel believed, since that Christmas party when he and his family were there with Ellinger. Very soon afterward he must have seen what his women-folk were up to; and whether he approved or disapproved, he must have decided that there was nothing for him to do but to keep out. It hadn't been the Forresters' reversal of fortune that had kept him away. One could see that he was deeply troubled, that he had her heavily on his mind.

Niel had finished his letter and was beginning another, when Mr. Ogden stopped beside his desk, where he stood twisting his imperial tighter and tighter. "You say this young lawyer is unprincipled? Sometimes rascals have a soft spot, a sentiment, where women are concerned."

Niel stared. He immediately thought of Ivy's dimples.

"A soft spot? A sentiment? Mr. Ogden, why not go to his office? A glance would convince you."

"Oh, that's not necessary! I understand." He looked out of the window, from which he could just see the tree-tops of the Forrester grove, and murmured, "Poor lady! So misguided. She ought to have advice from some of Daniel's friends." He took out his watch and consulted it, turning something over in his mind. His train was due in an hour, he said. Nothing could be done at present. In a few moments he left the office.

Afterward, Niel felt sure that when Mr. Ogden stood there uncertainly, watch in hand, he was considering an interview with Mrs. Forrester. He had wanted to go to her, and had given it up. Was he afraid of his women-folk? Or was it another kind of cowardice, the fear of losing a pleasant memory, of finding her changed and marred, a dread of something that would throw a disenchanting light upon the past? Niel had heard his uncle say that Mr. Ogden admired pretty women, though he had married a homely one, and that in his deep, non-committal way he was very gallant. Perhaps, with a little encouragement, he would have gone to see Mrs. Forrester, and he might have helped her. The fact that he had done nothing to bring this about, made Niel realize how much his own feeling toward that lady had changed.

It was Mrs. Forrester herself who had changed. Since her husband's death she seemed to have become another woman. For years Niel and his uncle, the Dalzells and all her friends, had thought of the Captain as a drag upon his wife; a care that drained her and dimmed her and kept her from being all that she might be. But without him, she was like a ship without ballast, driven hither and thither by every wind. She was flighty and perverse. She seemed to have lost her faculty of discrimination; her power of easily and graciously keeping everyone in his proper place.

Ivy Peters had been in Wyoming at the time of Captain Forrester's illness and death,—called away by a telegram which announced that oil had been discovered near his land-holdings. He returned soon after the Captain's funeral, however, and was seen about the Forrester place more than ever. As there was nothing to be done on his fields in the winter, he had amused himself by pulling down the old barn after office hours. One was likely to come upon him, smoking his cigar on the front porch as if he owned the place. He often spent the evening there, playing cards with Mrs. Forrester or talking about his business projects. He had not made his fortune yet, but he was on the way to it. Occasionally he took a friend or two, some of the town boys, over to dine at Mrs. Forrester's. The boys' mothers and sweethearts were greatly scandalized. "Now she's after the young ones," said Ed Elliott's mother. "She's getting childish."

At last Niel had a plain talk with Mrs. Forrester. He told her that people were gossiping about Ivy's being there so much. He had heard comments even on the street.

"But I can't bother about their talk. They have always talked about me, always will. Mr. Peters is my lawyer and my tenant; I have to see him, and I'm certainly not going to his office. I can't sit in the house alone every evening and knit. If you came to see me any oftener than you do, that would make talk. You are still younger than Ivy,—and better-looking! Did that never occur to you?"

"I wish you wouldn't talk to me like that," he said coldly. "Mrs. Forrester, why don't you go away? to California, to people of your own kind. You know this town is no place for you."

"I mean to, just as soon as I can sell this place. It's all I have, and if I leave it to tenants it will run down, and I can't sell it to advantage. That's why Ivy is here so much, he's trying to make the place presentable; pulling down the old barn that had become an eyesore, putting new boards in the porch floor where the old ones had rotted. Next summer, I am going to paint the house. Unless I keep the place up, I can never get my price for it." She talked nervously, with exaggerated earnestness, as if she were trying to persuade herself.

"And what are you asking for it now, Mrs. Forrester?"

"Twenty thousand dollars."

"You'll never get it. At least, not until times have greatly changed."

"That's what your uncle said. He wouldn't attempt to sell it for more than twelve. That's why I had to put it into other hands. Times have changed, but he doesn't realize it. Mr. Forrester himself told me it would be worth that. Ivy says he can get me twenty thousand, or if not, he will take it off my hands as soon as his investments begin to bring in returns."

"And in the meantime, you are simply wasting your life here."

"Not altogether." She looked at him with pleading plausibility. "I am getting rested after a long strain. And while I wait, I'm finding new friends among the young men—those your age, and a little younger. I've wanted for a long while to do something for the boys in this town, but my hands were full. I hate to see them growing up like savages, when all they need is a civilized house to come to, and a woman to give them a few hints. They've never had a chance. You wouldn't be the boy you are if you'd never gone to Boston,—and you've always had older friends who'd seen better days. Suppose you had grown up like Ed Elliott and Joe Simpson?"

"I flatter myself I wouldn't be exactly like them, if I had! However, there is no use discussing it, if you've thought it over and made up your mind. I spoke of it because I thought you mightn't realize how it strikes the townspeople."

"I know!" She tossed her head. Her eyes glittered, but there was no mirth in them,—it was more like hysterical defiance. "I know; they call me the Merry Widow. I rather like it!"

Niel left the house without further argument, and though that was three weeks ago, he had not been back since. Mrs. Forrester had called to see his uncle in the meantime. The Judge was as courtly as ever in his manner toward her, but he was deeply hurt by her defection, and his cherishing care for her would never be revived. He had attended to all Captain Forrester's business for twenty years, and since the failure of the Denver bank had never deducted a penny for fees from the money entrusted to him. Mrs. Forrester had treated him very badly. She had given him no warning. One day Ivy Peters had come into the office with a written order from her, requesting that an accounting, and all funds and securities, be turned over to him. Since then she had never spoken of the matter to the Judge,—or to Niel, save in that conversation about the sale of the property.

VIII

ONE MORNING when a warm May wind was whirling the dust up the street, Mrs. Forrester came smiling into Judge Pommeroy's office, wearing a new spring bonnet, and a short black velvet cape, fastened at the neck with a bunch of violets. "Please be nice enough to notice my new clothes, Niel," she said coaxingly. "They are the first I've had in years and years."

He told her they were very pretty.

"And aren't you glad I have some at last?" she smiled enquiringly through her veil. "I feel as if you weren't going to be cross with me today, and would do what I ask you. It's nothing very troublesome. I want you to come to dinner Friday night. If you come, there will be eight of us, counting Annie Peters. They are all boys you know, and if you don't like them, you ought to! Yes, you ought to!" she nodded at him severely. "Since you mind what people say, Niel, aren't you afraid they'll be saying you're a snob, just because you've been to Boston and seen a little of the world? You mustn't be so stiff, so—so superior! It isn't becoming, at your age." She drew her brows down into a level frown so like his own that he laughed. He had almost forgotten her old talent for mimicry.

"What do you want me for? You used always to say it was no good asking people who didn't mix."

"You can mix well enough, if you take the trouble. And this time you will, for me. Won't you?"

When she was gone, Niel was angry with himself for having been persuaded.

On Friday evening he was the last guest to arrive. It was a warm night, after a hot day. The windows were open, and the perfume of the lilacs came into the dusky parlor where the boys were sitting about in chairs that seemed too big for them. A lamp was burning in the dining-room, and there Ivy Peters stood at the sideboard, mixing cocktails. His sister Annie was in the kitchen, helping the hostess. Mrs. Forrester came in for a moment to greet Niel, then excused herself and hurried back to Annie Peters. Through the open door he saw that the silver dishes had reappeared on the dinner table, and the candlesticks and flowers. The young men who sat about in the twilight would not know the difference, he thought, if she had furnished her table that morning, from the stock in Wernz's queensware store. Their conception of a really fine dinner service was one "hand painted" by a sister or sweetheart. Each boy sat with his legs crossed, one tan shoe swinging in the air and displaying a tan silk sock. They were talking about clothes; Joe Simpson, who had just inherited his father's clothing business, was eager to tell them what the summer styles would be.

Ivy Peters came in, shaking his drinks. "You fellows are like a bunch of girls,—always talking about what you are going to wear and how you can spend your money. Simpson wouldn't get rich very fast if you all wore your clothes as long as I do. When did I get this suit, Joe?"

"Oh, about the year I graduated from High School, I guess!"

They all laughed at Ivy. No matter what he did or said, they laughed,—in recognition of his general success.

Mrs. Forrester came back, fanning herself with a little sandalwood fan, and when she appeared the boys rose,—in alarm, one might have thought, from the suddenness of it. That much, at any rate, she had succeeded in teaching them.

"Are your cocktails ready, Ivy? You will have to wait for me a moment, while I put some powder on my nose. If I'd known how hot it would be tonight, I'm afraid I wouldn't have had a roast for you. I'm browner than the ducks. You can pour them though. I won't be long."

She disappeared into her own room, and the boys sat down with the same surprising promptness. Ivy Peters carried the tray about, and they held their glasses before them, waiting for Mrs. Forrester. When she came, she took Niel's arm and led him into the dining-room. "Did you notice," she whispered to him, "how they hold their glasses? What is it they do to a little glass to make it look so vulgar? Nobody could ever teach them to pick one up and drink out of it, not if there were tea in it!"

Aloud she said, "Niel, will you light the candles for me? And then take the head of the table, please. You can carve ducks?"

"Not so well as—as my uncle does," he murmured, carefully putting back a candle-shade.

"Nor as Mr. Forrester did? I don't ask that. Nobody can carve now as men used to. But you can get them apart, I suppose? The place at your right is for Annie Peters. She is bringing in the dinner for me. Be seated, gentlemen!" with a little mocking bow and a swinging of earrings.

While Niel was carving the ducks, Annie slipped into the chair beside him, her naturally red face glowing from the heat of the stove. She was several years younger than her brother, whom she obeyed unquestioningly in everything. She had an extremely bad complexion and pale yellow hair with white lights in it, exactly the color of molasses taffy that has been pulled until it glistens. During the dinner she did not once speak, except to say, "Thank you," or "No, thank you." Nobody but Mrs. Forrester talked much until the first helping of duck was consumed. The boys had not yet learned to do two things at once. They paused only to ask their hostess if she "would care for the jelly," or to answer her questions.

Niel studied Mrs. Forrester between the candles, as she nodded encouragingly to one and another, trying to "draw them out," laughing at Roy Jones' heavy jokes, or congratulating Joe Simpson upon his new dignity as a business man with a business of his own. The long earrings swung beside the thin cheeks that were none the better, he thought, for the rouge she had put on them when she went to her room just before dinner. It improved some women, but not her,—at least, not tonight, when her eyes were hollow with fatigue, and she looked pinched and worn as he had never seen her. He sighed as he thought how much work it meant to cook a dinner like this for eight people,—and a beefsteak with potatoes would have pleased them better! They didn't really like this kind of food at all. Why did she do it? How would she feel about it tonight, when she sank dead weary into bed, after these stupid boys had said good-night, and their yellow shoes had carried them down the hill?

She was not eating anything, she was using up all her vitality to electrify these heavy lads into speech. Niel felt that he must help her, or at least try to. He addressed them one after another with energy and determination; he tried baseball, politics, scandal, the corn crop. They answered him with monosyllables or exclamations. He soon realized that they didn't want his polite remarks; they wanted more duck, and to be let alone with it.

Dinner was soon over, at any rate. The hostess' attempts to prolong it were unavailing. The salad and frozen pudding were dispatched as promptly as the roast had been. The guests went into the parlor and lit cigars.

Mrs. Forrester had the old-fashioned notion that men should be alone after dinner. She did not join them for half an hour. Perhaps she had lain down upstairs, for she looked a little rested. The boys were talking now, discussing a camping trip Ed Elliott was going to take in the mountains. They were giving him advice about camp outfits, trout flies, mixtures to keep off mosquitoes.

"I'll tell you, boys," said Mrs. Forrester, when she had listened to them for a moment, "when I go back to California, I intend to have a summer cabin up in the Sierras, and I invite you, one and all, to visit me. You'll have to work for your keep, you understand; cut the firewood and bring the water and wash the pots and pans, and go out and catch fish for breakfast. Ivy can bring his gun and shoot game for us, and I'll bake bread in an iron pot, the old trappers' way, if I haven't forgotten how. Will you come?"

"You bet we will! You know those mountains by heart, I expect?" said Ed Elliott.

She smiled and shook her head. "It would take a life-time to do that, Ed, more than a life-time. The Sierras,—there's no end to them, and they're magnificent."

Niel turned to her. "Have you ever told the boys how it was you first met Captain Forrester in the mountains out there? If they haven't heard the story, I think they would like it."

"Really, would you? Well, once upon a time, when I was a very young girl, I was spending the summer at a camp in the mountains, with friends of my father's."

She began there, but that was not the beginning of the story; long ago Niel had heard from his uncle that the beginning was a scandal and a murder. When Marian Ormsby was nineteen, she was engaged to Ned Montgomery, a gaudy young millionaire of the Gold Coast. A few weeks before the date set for their marriage, Montgomery was shot and killed in the lobby of a San Francisco hotel by the husband of another woman. The subsequent trial involved a great deal of publicity, and Marian was hurried away from curious eyes and sent up into the mountains until the affair should blow over.

Tonight Mrs. Forrester began with "Once upon a time." Sitting at one end of the big sofa, her slippers on a foot-stool and her head in shadow, she stirred the air before her face with the sandalwood fan as she talked, the rings glittering on her white fingers. She told them how Captain Forrester, then a widower, had come up to the camp to visit her father's partner. She had noticed him very little,— she was off every day with the young men. One afternoon she had persuaded young Fred Harney, an intrepid mountain climber, to take her down the face of Eagle Cliff. They were almost down, and were creeping over a projecting ledge, when the rope broke, and they dropped to the bottom. Harney fell on the rocks and was killed instantly. The girl was caught in a pine tree, which arrested her fall. Both her legs were broken, and she lay in the canyon all night in the bitter cold, swept by the icy canyon draught. Nobody at the camp knew where to look for the two missing members of the party,— they had stolen off alone for their foolhardy adventure. Nobody worried, because Harney knew all the trails and could not get lost. In the morning, however, when they were still missing, search parties went out. It was Captain Forrester's party that found Marian, and got her out by the lower trail. The trail was so steep and narrow, the turns round the jutting ledges so sharp, that it was impossible to take her out on a litter. The men took turns carrying her, hugging the canyon walls with their shoulders as they crept along. With her broken legs hanging, she suffered terribly,—fainted again and again. But she noticed that she suffered less when Captain Forrester carried her, and that he took all the most dangerous places on the trail himself. "I could feel his heart pump and his muscles strain," she said, "when he balanced himself and me on the rocks. I knew that if we fell, we'd go together; he would never drop me."

They got back to camp, and everything possible was done for her, but by the time a surgeon could be got up from San Francisco, her fractures had begun to knit and had to be broken over again.

"It was Captain Forrester I wanted to hold my hand when the surgeon had to do things to me. You remember, Niel, he always boasted that I never screamed when they were carrying me up the trail. He stayed at the camp until I could begin to walk, holding to his arm. When he asked me to marry him, he didn't have to ask twice. Do you wonder?" She looked with a smile about the circle, and drew her finger-tips absently across her forehead as if to brush away something,—the past, or the present, who could tell?

The boys were genuinely moved. While she was answering their questions, Niel thought about the first time he ever heard her tell that story: Mr. Dalzell had stopped off with a party of friends from Chicago; Marshall Field and the president of the Union Pacific were among them, he remembered, and they were going through in Mr. Dalzell's private car to hunt in the Black Hills. She had, after all, not changed so much since then. Niel felt tonight that the right man could save her, even now. She was still her indomitable self, going through her old part,—but only the stage-hands were left to listen to her. All those who had shared in fine undertakings and bright occasions were gone.

I X

WITH THE SUMMER months Judge Pommeroy's health improved, and as soon as he was able to be back in his office, Niel began to plan to return to Boston. He would get there the first of August and would go to work with a tutor to make up for the months he had lost. It was a melancholy time for him. He was in a fever of impatience to be gone, and yet he felt that he was going away forever, and was making the final break with everything that had been dear to him in his boyhood. The people, the very country itself, were changing so fast that there would be nothing to come back to.

He had seen the end of an era, the sunset of the pioneer. He had come upon it when already its glory was nearly spent. So in the buffalo times a traveler used to come upon the embers of a hunter's fire on the prairie, after the hunter was up and gone; the coals would be trampled out, but the ground was warm, and the flattened grass where he had slept and where his pony had grazed, told the story.

This was the very end of the road-making West; the men who had put plains and mountains under the iron harness were old; some were poor, and even the successful ones were hunting for rest and a brief reprieve from death. It was already gone, that age; nothing

"She had always the power of suggesting things much lovelier than herself, as the perfume of a single flower may call up the whole sweetness of spring." —A Lost Lady

could ever bring it back. The taste and smell and song of it, the visions those men had seen in the air and followed,—these he had caught in a kind of afterglow in their own faces,—and this would always be his.

It was what he most held against Mrs. Forrester; that she was not willing to immolate herself, like the widow of all these great men, and die with the pioneer period to which she belonged; that she preferred life on any terms. In the end, Niel went away without bidding her good-bye. He went away with weary contempt for her in his heart.

It happened like this,—had scarcely the dignity of an episode. It was nothing, and yet it was everything. Going over to see her one summer evening, he stopped a moment by the dining-room window to look at the honeysuckle. The dining-room door was open into the kitchen, and there Mrs. Forrester stood at a table, making pastry. Ivy Peters came in at the kitchen door, walked up behind her, and unconcernedly put both arms around her, his hands meeting over her breast. She did not move, did not look up, but went on rolling out pastry.

Niel went down the hill. "For the last time," he said, as he crossed the bridge in the evening light, "for the last time." And it was even so; he never went up the poplar-bordered road again. He had given her a year of his life, and she had thrown it away. He had helped the Captain to die peacefully, he believed; and now it was the Captain who seemed the reality. All those years he had thought it was Mrs. Forrester who made that house so different from any other. But ever since the Captain's death it was a house where old friends, like his uncle, were betrayed and cast off, where common fellows behaved after their kind and knew a common woman when they saw her.

If he had not had the nature of a spaniel, he told himself, he would never have gone back after the first time. It took two doses to cure him. Well, he had had them! Nothing she could ever do would in the least matter to him again.

He had news of her now and then, as long as his uncle lived. *"Mrs. Forrester's name is everywhere coupled with Ivy Peters','"* the Judge wrote. *"She does not look happy, and I fear her health is failing, but she has put herself in such a position that her husband's friends cannot help her."*

And again: *"Of Mrs. Forrester, no news is good news. She is sadly broken."*

After his uncle's death, Niel heard that Ivy Peters had at last bought the Forrester place, and had brought a wife from Wyoming to live there. Mrs. Forrester had gone West,—people supposed to California.

It was years before Niel could think of her without chagrin. But eventually, after she had drifted out of his ken, when he did not know if Daniel Forrester's widow were living or dead, Daniel Forrester's wife returned to him, a bright, impersonal memory.

He came to be very glad that he had known her, and that she had had a hand in breaking him in to life. He has known pretty women and clever ones since then,—but never one like her, as she was in her best days. Her eyes, when they laughed for a moment into one's own, seemed to promise a wild delight that he has not found in life. "I know where it is," they seemed to say, "I could show you!" He would like to call up the shade of the young Mrs. Forrester, as the witch of Endor called up Samuel's, and challenge it, demand the secret of that ardor; ask her whether she had really found some ever-blooming, ever-burning, ever-piercing joy, or whether it was all fine play-acting. Probably she had found no more than another; but she had always the power of suggesting things much lovelier than herself, as the perfume of a single flower may call up the whole sweetness of spring.

Niel was destined to hear once again of his long-lost lady. One evening as he was going into the dining-room of a Chicago hotel, a broad-shouldered man with an open, sunbrowned face, approached him and introduced himself as one of the boys who had grown up in Sweet Water.

"I'm Ed Elliott, and I thought it must be you. Could we take a table together? I promised an old friend of yours to give you a message, if I ever ran across you. You remember Mrs. Forrester? Well, I saw her again, twelve years after she left Sweet Water,—down in Buenos Ayres." They sat down and ordered dinner.

"Yes, I was in South America on business. I'm a mining engineer, I spent some time in Buenos Ayres. One evening there was a banquet of some sort at one of the big hotels, and I happened to step out of the bar, just as a car drove up to the entrance where the guests were going in. I paid no attention until one of the ladies laughed. I recognized her by her laugh,—that hadn't changed a particle. She was all done up in furs, with a scarf over her head, but I saw her eyes, and then I was sure. I stepped up and spoke to her. She seemed glad to see me, made me go into the hotel, and talked to me until her husband came to drag her away to the dinner. Oh, yes, she was married again,—to a rich, cranky old Englishman; Henry Collins was his name. He was born down there, she told me, but she met him in California. She told me they lived on a big stock ranch and had come down in their car for this banquet. I made inquiries afterward and found the old fellow was quite a character; had been married twice before, once to a Brazilian woman. People said he was rich, but quarrelsome and rather stingy. She seemed to have everything, though. They traveled in a fine French car, and she had brought her maid along, and he had his valet. No, she hadn't changed as much as you'd think. She was a good deal made up, of course, like most of the women down there; plenty of powder, and a little red, too, I guess. Her hair was black, blacker than I remembered it; looked as if she dyed it. She invited me to visit them on their estate, and so did the old man, when he came to get her. She asked about everybody, and said, 'If you ever meet Niel Herbert, give him my love, and tell him I often think of him.' She said again, 'Tell him things have turned out well for me. Mr. Collins is the kindest of husbands.' I called at your office in New York on my way back from South America, but you were somewhere in Europe. It was remarkable, how she'd come up again. She seemed pretty well gone to pieces before she left Sweet Water."

"Do you suppose," said Niel, "that she could be living still? I'd almost make the trip to see her."

"No, she died about three years ago. I know that for certain. After she left Sweet Water, wherever she was, she always sent a cheque to the Grand Army Post every year to have flowers put on Captain Forrester's grave for Decoration Day. Three years ago the Post got a letter from the old Englishman, with a draft for the future care of Captain Forrester's grave, *'in memory of my late wife, Marian Forrester Collins.'* "

"So we may feel sure that she was well cared for, to the very end," said Niel. "Thank God for that!"

"I knew you'd feel that way," said Ed Elliott, as a warm wave of feeling passed over his face. "I did!"

SUGGESTIONS FOR
FURTHER READING

Biography

Bennett, Mildred R. *The World of Willa Cather*. Lincoln and London, Eng.: University of Nebraska Press, 1989. A study of Cather's Nebraska years, rich in anecdote, reminiscence, and information about the people, events, places, and cultural influences that shaped the novelist in her youth and early maturity.

Brown, E. K., and Leon Edel. *Willa Cather: A Critical Biography*. New York: Alfred A. Knopf, 1953. Written at the request of Cather's companion, Edith Lewis (and completed by Edel after Brown's unexpected death), this was the first biography, and it is still worth reading, especially for its illuminating critical perceptions. It seems somehow fitting that Edel (the great biographer of Cather's early idol, Henry James) should have had a hand in this beautifully written book.

Cather, Willa. *The Kingdom of Art: Willa Cather's First Principles and Critical Statements, 1893–1896*. Selected and edited with two essays and a commentary by Bernice Slote. Lincoln: University of Nebraska Press, 1966. A collection of the early journalism, well introduced and annotated.

——. *Willa Cather in Person: Interviews, Speeches, and Letters*. Selected and edited by L. Brent Bohlke. Lincoln: University of Nebraska Press, 1986. A fascinating collection, made even more valuable by the informed and informative background materials provided by the editor. Includes Cather's radio speech accepting the 1923 Pulitzer Prize for fiction (for *One of Ours*), as well as Louise Bogan's superb *New Yorker* profile (1931) of Cather, whom Bogan characterizes as "that rare accident of Nature, a perfectly natural person."

————. *The World and the Parish: Willa Cather's Articles and Reviews, 1893–1902.* 2 volumes. Edited by William M. Curtin. Lincoln: University of Nebraska Press, 1970. This indispensable collection, side by side with *The Kingdom of Art* (above), provides the material for many insights into Cather's life and mind, for in these early pieces she writes with abandon. The reclusive, correspondence-shredding author, who had perfected her famously "simple" style, was to come.

LEWIS, EDITH. *Willa Cather Living: A Personal Record.* New York: Alfred A Knopf, 1953. Reprinted, with a foreword by Marilyn Arnold, by Ohio University Press in 1989. A memoir by Cather's companion.

ROBINSON, PHYLLIS C. *Willa: The Life of Willa Cather.* Garden City, N.Y.: Doubleday, 1983. A straightforward, unpretentious, and deftly written chronicle.

SERGEANT, ELIZABETH SHEPLEY. *Willa Cather: A Memoir.* Philadelphia: J. B. Lippincott Co., 1953. Reprinted, with a foreword by Marilyn Arnold, by Ohio University Press in 1992. An evocative reminiscence by a close friend, full of acute observations and piquant anecdotes. Sergeant is affectionate and admiring; but she is also, on occasion, refreshingly frank about her friend's demanding and sometimes irascible nature.

Willa Cather: A Pictorial Memoir. Photographs by Lucia Woods and others; text by Bernice Slote. Lincoln: University of Nebraska Press, 1973. A handsome book, which juxtaposes excerpts from Cather's works with vintage photographs of the novelist and her family, friends, and colleagues, and original photographs by Woods of the places (Nebraska, Virginia, the Southwest, Quebec, New Brunswick) that Cather loved and immortalized in her novels and stories.

WOODRESS, JAMES. *Willa Cather: A Literary Life.* Lincoln: University of Nebraska Press, 1987. The definitive biography.

CRITICISM

ACOCELLA, JOAN. "Cather and the Academy," *The New Yorker,* volume 71, number 38 (November 27, 1995). A provocative essay that must have ruffled some feathers within the groves of academe.

AUCHINCLOSS, LOUIS. "Willa Cather," in *Pioneers & Caretakers: A Study of 9 American Women Novelists.* Minneapolis: University of Minnesota Press, 1965. This stimulating evaluation of Cather's works gives *O Pioneers!* a mixed grade, but allows that it is "the work of a major novelist who has at last discovered her form and her subject."

Critical Essays on Willa Cather. Edited by John J. Murphy. Boston: G. K. Hall & Co., 1984. This collection, which includes contemporary reviews as well as more recent academic studies, is especially valuable for reprinting two of the best essays ever written on Cather: Katherine Anne Porter's "Critical Reflections on Willa Cather" and Eudora Welty's "The House of Willa Cather."

GERBER, PHILIP. *Willa Cather.* Revised edition. New York: Twayne Publishers, 1995. An up-to-date and well-done critical and biographical study in the classic Twayne format, with helpful and interesting chapters addressing "The Question of Cather Biography" and "From Many Minds: Cather Scholarship."

LEE, HERMIONE. *Willa Cather: Double Lives.* New York: Pantheon Books, 1989. This superb study is refreshingly nuanced in its discussions of Cather's work.

O'BRIEN, SHARON. *Willa Cather: The Emerging Voice.* New York: Oxford University Press, 1987. An influential analysis of Cather's life and work up to the breakthrough of *O Pioneers!,* written out of O'Brien's conviction that Cather was a woman writer "whose apprenticeship was distinguished by her struggle to resolve the culturally imposed contradictions between femininity and creativity."

ROSOWSKI, SUSAN J. *The Voyage Perilous: Willa Cather's Romanticism.* Lincoln: University of Nebraska Press, 1986. An important work, which James Woodress has described as a "remarkably lucid, thoughtful, and convincing study of a subject that has been waiting for treatment."

Willa Cather. Edited with an introduction by Harold Bloom. New York: Chelsea House Publishers, 1985. The writers included here are Lionel Trilling, Alfred Kazin, E. K. Brown, David Daiches, Morton D. Zabel, Blanche H. Gelfant, Eudora Welty, and Dorothy Van Ghent, among others, and the collection is well worth seeking out. Of special interest to readers of the present volume will be John Hollander's introduction to *A Lost Lady* (originally written for a Limited Editions Club edition of the novel published in 1983), which he calls "one of the small triumphs of the American imagination."

Willa Cather and Her Critics. Edited by James Schroeter. Ithaca, N.Y.: Cornell University Press, 1967. A collection of reviews and essays by a wide range of admirers and detractors, among them H. L. Mencken, Edmund Wilson, Sinclair Lewis, Rebecca West, Lionel Trilling, Alfred Kazin, and Leon Edel.

CHECKLIST OF ILLUSTRATIONS

All of the illustrations in this edition are from the collections of the New York Public Library.

Cover and frontispiece: Original portrait photograph of Willa Cather, ca. 1917, photographer unknown.
Miriam and Ira D. Wallach Division of Art, Prints and Photographs

Page xiv: Portrait photograph of Willa Cather by Hollinger, 1915; used as the frontispiece to *The Song of the Lark* (Boston: Houghton Mifflin Company, 1937) (volume 2 of the Library Edition of *The Novels and Stories of Willa Cather*).
General Research Division

Page xvi: "Rich Farming Lands! On the Line of the Union Pacific Railroad!" Full-page advertisement bound in the back of Henry T. Williams' *The Pacific Tourist: Williams' Illustrated Trans-Continental Guide of Travel, from The Atlantic to the Pacific Ocean. . . . A Complete Traveler's Guide of The Union and Central Pacific Railroads, and All Points of Business or Pleasure Travel to California, Colorado, Nebraska, Wyoming . . .* [etc.] (New York: Henry T. Williams, Publishers, 1876).
General Research Division

Page xviii: "Crossing the Prairies," an illustration from *The Union Pacific Railroad: A Trip Across the North American Continent from Omaha to Ogden* (New York: Thomas Nelson & Sons [ca. 1870]).
General Research Division

Page xxi: Engraved cover of Lawrence D. Burch's *Nebraska As It Is: A Comprehensive Summary of the Resources, Advantages and Drawbacks of the Great Prairie State* (Chicago: C. S. Burch & Co., Publishers, 1878). *General Research Division*

Page xxvi: Willa Cather's poem "Recognition," inscribed by her on the front flyleaf of a copy of *April Twilights* (New York: Alfred A. Knopf, 1923). *Henry W. and Albert A. Berg Collection of English and American Literature*

Page xxviii: Photograph of Willa Cather and others at the dinner given in celebration of Mark Twain's seventieth birthday, held at Delmonico's in New York City, on the evening of December 5, 1905, from *Mark Twain's 70th Birthday: Souvenir of Its Celebration* (New York: Harper & Brothers, 1905). *Berg Collection*

Page xxxii: Typescript of Willa Cather's *My Mortal Enemy*, with the author's autograph revisions [1926]. *Manuscripts and Archives Division*

Page xxxvi: "Mormon Family, Great Salt Lake Valley," an albumen print on letterpress mount by A. J. Russell. Plate 48 in *The Great West Illustrated* (New York, 1869). *Wallach Division*

Page xxxix: Front cover of the August 1912 issue of *McClure's Magazine*, illustrated by Charles Dana Gibson, which featured Willa Cather's "The Bohemian Girl." *General Research Division*

Page xli: "No. 54. Front Street, North Platt[e] Station [Nebraska]," an albumen stereoscopic view on letterpress mount by A. J. Russell, from

the series *Union Pacific R.R. Stereoscopic Views. Across the Continent West from Omaha. No. 6 Bridges Series* (New York, ca. 1868–73).
Robert N. Dennis Collection of Stereoscopic Views, Wallach Division

Page xliii: Engraved portrait of Silas Garber, from *Portrait and Biographical Album of Johnson and Pawnee Counties, Nebraska, Containing Full Page Portraits and Biographical Sketches of Prominent and Representative Citizens of the County, Together with Portraits and Biographies of all the Governors of the State, and of the Presidents of the United States* (Chicago: Chapman Brothers, 1889).
General Research Division

Page xlvi: "On Elm Creek, Near Red Cloud, Webster County," an engraved illustration from Lawrence D. Burch's *Nebraska As It Is* (Chicago, 1878).
General Research Division

Page li: Portrait photograph of Willa Cather by Carl Van Vechten, taken in the office of her publisher, Alfred A. Knopf, on January 22, 1936.
Berg Collection

Page 2: "The Wind Mill at Laramie," an albumen print on letterpress mount by A. J. Russell. Plate 16 in *The Great West Illustrated* (New York, 1869).
Dennis Collection, Wallach Division

Page 36: "View of Plum Creek," an engraved illustration from Edwin A. Curley's *Nebraska, Its Advantages, Resources, and Drawbacks* (London: Sampson Low, Marston, Low & Searle, 1875).
General Research Division

Page 48: "Nebraska," an etching by Mahonri Young, 1922; signed and dated by the artist.
Wallach Division

Page 54: "Indian Summer," an original woodcut by J. J. Lankes, 1922; signed by the artist and presented by him to F. W. [Frank Weitenkampf, then curator of the Print Collection of The New York Public Library]. *Wallach Division*

Page 62: "No. 205. Ranch on the Plains," an albumen stereoscopic view on letterpress mount by A. J. Russell, from the series *Union Pacific R.R. Stereoscopic Views. Across the Continent West from Omaha. No. 6 Bridges Series* ([New York?: Union Pacific Railroad Company] [ca. 1868–73]). *Dennis Collection, Wallach Division*

Page 104: "Boone County, Nebraska.—Waterville, four miles north of the beautiful Pawnee reservation . . ." an engraved illustration from Lawrence D. Burch's *Nebraska As It Is* (Chicago, 1878). *General Research Division*

Page 135: "The Knoll," an original woodcut by J. J. Lankes [ca. 1920s]. *Wallach Division*

Page 155: An albumen stereoscopic view of a church in Pawnee City, Nebraska, by Howard Ellis, from the series *Pawnee City Views* (Pawnee City, Neb.: Howard Ellis, Artist and Photographer [ca. 1870]). *Dennis Collection, Wallach Division*

Page 182: "Manure Spreader Followed by Tractor Plowing Sod Near Omaha, Nebr.," an albumen stereoscopic view on letterpress mount published by the Keystone View Company (Meadville, Pa., New York, N.Y., [etc.]: Keystone View Company [ca. 1900]). *Dennis Collection, Wallach Division*

Page 183: "Handling Alfalfa Hay with Hay Loader on the Farm of W. J. Bryan, Lincoln, Nebr.," an albumen stereoscopic view on letterpress mount published by the Keystone View Company (Meadville, Pa., New York, N.Y., [etc.]: Keystone View Company [ca. 1900]). *Dennis Collection, Wallach Division*

Page 224: "No. 266. South from near Sherman Station [Wyoming]," an albumen stereoscopic view on letterpress mount by William Henry Jackson, from the series *Scenery of the Union Pacific Railroad* (Omaha: Wm. H. Jackson, Photographer [ca. 1870]).
Dennis Collection, Wallach Division

Page 248: "No. 224. T. C. Durant, Esq. & Heads of Depts. U.P.R.R.," an albumen stereoscopic view on letterpress mount by John Carbutt, from the series *Union Pacific Railroad, Excursion to the 100th Meridian, October 1866* (Chicago: J. Carbutt, under the auspices of the Union Pacific Railroad Company [1866]).
Dennis Collection, Wallach Division

Page 251: [The Forrester Place], an original woodcut by Bernhardt Kleboe, 1923; first published in *The Century Magazine* (May 1923), as the headpiece to the second installment of *A Lost Lady;* and also used on the dust jacket for the book edition of the novel, which was published on September 14, 1923.
Wallach Division

Page 284: "Mt. Olive Bridge," an original woodcut by J. J. Lankes, 1923; signed by the artist and presented by him to Frank Weitenkampf.
Wallach Division

Page 329: "The Village," an original woodcut by J. J. Lankes, 1923; first published in *The Century Magazine* (April 1923), as the frontispiece to the first installment of *A Lost Lady*.
Wallach Division

Page 358: [On the Forrester property], an original woodcut by Bernhardt Kleboe, 1923; first published in *The Century Magazine* (June 1923), as the headpiece to the third installment of *A Lost Lady*.
Wallach Division